Gods of Rain and Blood

Also by Donald Healey

The Road to Glorieta; a Confederate Army Marches through New Mexico

Boomers Away; Travels at the Edge of the Comfort Zone

Puffernut Flies South

The Bequest

Gods of Rain and Blood

Donald Healey

Granite Mountain Books, LLC
Prescott, AZ

Copyright © 2023 Donald Healey
Library of Congress Control Number: 2023919305

Published by: Granite Mountain Books, LLC
Prescott, AZ 86301

ISBN: 979-8-9890538-3-4

CONTENTS

NOTES

Cast of Characters – is available to read online or download as a PDF at the author's website, donaldhealey.com.

Chapter 1

The Wandering God

11 Bak'tun 14 K'atun 11 Tun 0 Uinal 18 K'in

(May 1, 1511)

Two boys trudged down a well-worn path and teetered on the edge of manhood. From time to time one or the other paused and glanced wistfully at a distant ridgeline. Viewed from where they walked, the arid jungle along its crest trembled with the apparent promise of a cooling breeze. The young men recognized the deceitful shimmers as tricks of the heat; nevertheless, the false illusion made their trek all the more oppressive. Each boy was burdened with a huge bundle of sticks. The sun beat down from a cloudless sky and the trail they followed through the scrub sweltered in a stifling stillness. Their bodies glistened with sweat and the heavier of the two huffed noticeably with each breath.

"Okib, I need to stop. Let's rest."

Okib looked back at his friend. No doubt about it, Naum was overweight.

"Not yet, the bee shrine is just a little farther. We'll stop there."

"Let's stop now, I'm hungry."

"That's just the problem, you eat too much. Besides, there's no shade here. We'll stop at the shrine and rest inside. Come on."

Naum looked sullen but followed his best friend down the trail. Truth be told, Okib was also tired, but he kept it to himself. For some reason that he could never quite explain, he always felt driven to outdo Naum. Whether they were collecting firewood, hunting birds, playing ball, or gambling with beans, he always had to win. He always had to be first. If easy-going Naum was aware that they competed, he never let on. And, for some reason, that made Okib only want to compete all the harder. The smaller boy hitched up his bundle of wood, squared his shoulders, and set off at an even faster pace.

Naum made a valiant effort to keep up and though still huffing and breathing heavily, he was right on Okib's heels when together they spied the shrine. The isolated stone building squatted like a hoary toad at the edge of the path. The ground around its walls formed a small island in the scrub, packed and flattened by countless generations of bare and sandal-shod feet. The building was a simple square with walls that flared slightly outward as they rose from the baked earth. Each wall was pierced by a short doorway and around the top of the small shrine ran a frieze of tiny columns. In a niche facing the path was a badly worn carving of the bee god, "Ah Muzencab."

His shrine was old and enigmatic. Built by dwarves in the time of magic, it was already a resting place for travelers long before the coming of the Lords of Itzá. In its youth, the building was brightly painted and if one looked closely, one could still make out the faded images of snakes, sun, rain, and maize that adorned its walls.

Gratefully, the boys cast aside their heavy bundles and ducked through the low doorway into the shadows and relative cool of the small interior.

"Just in time," said Naum. "How do you manage to walk so fast?"

"I'm not fast. You're just slow," laughed Okib.

"Maybe, but each time we collect wood, we have to go a little farther from the village. I'm not built for distance."

"I agree with that. Next time, let's try a different direction."

"Sure, but for now let's eat. I'm starved."

From pouches tied at their waists, the boys each pulled small gourd bowls and balls of half-cooked maize. Naum also produced a sweet potato. They broke the maize into their bowls and Okib added water from their drinking gourd. A quick stir dissolved the maize into nourishing liquor. With thirst and gusto they drank off the liquid and then used sweaty fingers to scrape up the tasty sediments. In short order, the maize was gone, the sweet potato divided and devoured, and Naum stared wistfully at his empty bowl.

"What's the matter," asked Okib, "didn't get enough?"

"I'm alright, I guess, but a bite or two more wouldn't have hurt. Collecting wood is hungry work."

"Right you are my friend, so have I got a surprise for you. In honor of Ah Muzencab and his commodious shrine ..." With a flourish and a mischievous grin; Okib pulled a leaf wrapped packet from his pouch and placed it before Naum. Curious and a bit wary, Naum undid the bundle. Hidden safely inside, sat two substantial chunks of honeycomb. Naum looked suspiciously at the gooey sweet and then at his grinning friend.

"Where did you get that?"

"I was tending the bees and no one else was around."

"You stole it! Your mother is going to punish you when she finds out."

Okib shrugged, "If she finds out. I'll eat your piece if you're scared."

Naum snatched up one of the combs. "I'll take my chances. Besides you're the one she'll take the stick to."

With that, Naum broke off a chunk and popped it into his mouth. Okib had just done the same when he happened to glance out a door. Up the trail a man was approaching.

"Naum; look someone's coming!"

Naum and Okib both stared intently. The trail was heavily used and it wasn't the least unusual to encounter other people from the village or even the occasional merchant from another village. The man who approached was clearly from farther afield.

In his youth the traveler may have stood tall and vigorous, but now he stooped and walked with a shuffle. On his back rode a large woven hamper; supported by a tumpline over his head. In his left hand, doing double duty as a walking-stick was a long flint-tipped spear.

The boys both knew that it was impolite to stare but as the stranger drew near they found it impossible to look away. The man was not black but his sunbaked skin was among the darkest they'd ever seen. His eyes were ringed with even darker circles and his lower lip protruded and hung down, weighted with a heavy jade pendant. His hair was braided with colored bands and then wound around behind his head in a sort of queue. Worn gauntlets of beaded jaguar pelt guarded his wrists and ankles, and the loincloth around his waist, dyed in yellows and reds, was hung with mysterious bulging pouches. The whole of the stranger was covered in a layer of fine gray dust that gave him an impression of immense age.

As the man drew abreast of the shrine Okib and Naum drew back into the shadows suddenly shy of this strange apparition.

"Ba'ax ka wa'alik? (Hello)," said the old man through the door. "How are you young gentlemen on this fine day?"

"Malob oqin" (Good afternoon) "Grandfather," they replied making the proper response.

"My journey has been long. Might I share your shade?"

Looking uneasily at each other the boys edged back. "Of course you are welcome grandfather," croaked Okib.

The old man set his hamper down next to the bundles of wood and spear first he clambered through a door. Once inside, he turned a couple of times like an old dog and finally made himself comfortable across from the boys.

"This is cozy," he said, "but I often wish the dwarves had built things a little larger." Grinning, the stranger gave them a wide lopsided smile that plainly highlighted his sole remaining tooth. Neither boy knew how to respond. Ignoring their obvious discomfort the old man continued on. "Traveling alone as I do, I look forward to passing the time with those I meet. You two are collecting wood. What village are you from?"

"K'optela Grandfather," said Naum.

"Ah, K'optela," sighed the dark man as if remembering a pleasant but long forgotten friendship. "Tell me about K'optela. How many live there these days and is old Hub-tun (Conch Stone) still nacon (war chief)? Water is precious. How are this year's crops? These are dangerous times. Does K'optela have enough holcánob (warriors) to defend it from bandits? They do; how many? And, who are your chilánob (priests)?" The questions went on and on. The boys began to fidget. They didn't want to be rude to an elder but they were anxious to be on their way. Also, the strangeness and intensity of their unexpected companion were a little frightening.

In mid-sentence, the old man suddenly stopped and pointed at the boys' hands. All four were sticky with honey and still held bits of comb.

"Boys, boys, you've let me ramble on, and here I see I've interrupted your devotions to Muzencab. Please excuse a garrulous old fool. Perhaps you would like to join me in prayer; the bee god always appreciates those who pay him heed."

So saying, he reached into one of his pouches and withdrew a small plate and three flat stones. He set the plate and stones in front of him and carefully adjusted their positions. When he was satisfied with their arrangement, he took incense from another pouch and placed a pinch on each stone. On the plate he prepared to kindle a flame.

"Grandfather, we really must go," said Okib

"We're expected with our wood," added Naum, "besides our devotions were already finished."

"Just so," said the dark man suddenly disinterested, "don't let me keep you."

With a distracted wave of his hand he sent the boys scuttling out a side door. Outside, Okib and Naum grabbed their bundles of wood and ran toward home as fast as their legs could carry them. Once well away from the bee god's shrine and with both of them wheezing and puffing, the boys slowed to a walk.

"You know who that was, don't you?" said Okib. "That was no man. That was Ekchuah, the merchant, the black war chief!"

"Do you really think so?" huffed Naum.

"I tell you, it was him! It was the Wandering God. Did you see that spear and his one tooth? We're lucky that we got away."

"I hope we didn't offend him by not joining his prayer. Do you think we should have offered him food?"

"How should I know?" said Okib "Let's just forget it and go home."

"Forget it? He might have cursed us! I think we should tell the chilánob."

"Are you crazy Naum? Do you feel cursed? I don't feel cursed. If you tell the priests, we'll only get in trouble. Besides, do you think I want na (mother) to find out about the honey?"

"Well, I guess we can keep it to ourselves, but I better not wake up tomorrow as a chic (coatimundi) or all covered with warts."

Okib smiled, "Come on then pick up your pace." He always liked it when Naum agreed.

Back at the bee shrine, the dark man finished burning his incense and emerged into the sun. Like Okib, he was also smiling. If there had been anyone to see him they might have noted that many of his years had fallen away and that he now stood rather proud and mostly erect. He no longer appeared as a decrepit withered old man leaning on his staff but rather as an elder only slightly past his prime, his flint lance suddenly more weapon than walking stick.

Ah-cambal smiled because yet again his Ekchuah disguise had served him well. His skin darkened with dye, his teeth blackened, a few props, and a little acting was all that he needed to move easily from place to place gathering valuable information. The ruse might not hold up under the scrutiny of a crowd of nobles or priests, but the spy was a cautious man. Ah-cambal avoided villages and towns and picked his encounters with great care. Lone wayfarers, pilgrims, lowly merchants, and boys collecting firewood were easily overawed and talkative in Ekchuah's presence. If they told others of their encounter with the Wandering God, well so be it. Ekchuah was the patron of wanderers and merchants. What was more natural than that he should appear to his chosen? Ah-cambal said a silent prayer, thanking the Wandering God once again for his continued protection, and promised that at dusk he would again burn copal in his honor.

The spy of course already knew that the nearby settlement was K'optela. For the past three days he'd stolen silently about its outskirts watching and observing; something that he'd done many times in the past. Information gleaned from the two youthful wood cutters was merely a finishing touch, a capstone that crowned his observations.

Ah-cambal prided himself on being thorough. K'optela was strong, its modest holcánob (militia) alert, and the town continued its allegiance and support of nearby Sotuta.

Two uinal (20 day months) had slipped away since Ah-cambal walked from his home on the Bay of Chectumal. The days had run swiftly and he'd seen and learned much. Wandering from place to place as Ekchuah or as an itinerant trader of sea shells and salt, he'd taken the measure of the fluid loyalties and conflicts that twisted and swirled around the borders of his brother's modest chiefdom.

From his seat at Ichpaatún, Ah-cambal's brother, Nachan Can, and his people acted as a conduit for trade goods passing to and from the busy river port of Lamanai and other communities to their south. Blessed with a rare and valuable commercial position, but bordered by powerful aggressive neighbors, Nachan Can, faced a constant struggle to keep Ichpaatún prosperous and secure.

K'optela and its surroundings were the last of the areas that Ah-cambal had set out to scrutinize. With the boys' information added to what he already knew, he was well satisfied that he understood the current political situation and was ready to report back to his brother.

More than at any previous time in Ah-cambal's memory, the glowing embers of many long-smoldering animosities were fanned and nurtured by the growing dryness and scarcity of the land. The constant bickering and intermittent warfare regularly interfered with Ichpaatún's trade and was a continual worry to Nachan Can and others not directly involved.

Travelers and traders regularly brought news from the rest of Ulumil cuz yetel ceh (The Land of the Turkey and the Deer / Yucatán) to the province of Chectumal, but as cacique (chief), Nachan Can couldn't trust the prosperity and security of his people solely to hearsay and rumor. Ah-cambal served as his brother's spy, his eyes and ears. The information that Ah-cambal gathered on his wanderings was firsthand. It was valuable information on which his brother could rely; information that Nachan Can used to hold his borders, and that provided forewarnings for the people of Chectumal before dangers or strife spilled across their land.

After the shade of the shrine, Ah-cambal squinted in the glare of the late afternoon sun. K'inich Ajaw (the sun-faced lord) was more than three quarters of the way through his daily journey, yet still he burned fiercely. Ah-cambal shouldered his woven hamper and headed in the same direction taken by Okib and Naum.

After a few hundred strides, he turned away from the wide dusty trail and struck out into the arid jungle. For a time his passage was slow and difficult. A profusion of life hindered his every step as he scrambled and pushed his way through the scrub and thorn. Lush when wet and blooming with orchids, bromeliads, and other exotic plants, the landscape was now well into a long dry season of drought. Everywhere life had taken on a harsher edge, jealously conserving and defending its moisture. Eventually, his feet began to trace a lesser path. The twisting ribbon was little more than a game trail but its way opened before him and his progress grew somewhat easier.

Until he reached his own lands, Ah-cambal planned to avoid other people and their possible questions. He would stick to the wilds.

As the day plodded steadily into dusk, he pushed harder toward the distant ridge. Except for a low range of karst hills that runs along the peninsula's northwest, Yucatán is a flat land with little that catches the eye. Ah-cambal loved the Puuc (hills). Their gradual crests rose like the tops of the mighty pyramids at Chichén Itza and Coba. When he stood on one of their summits the world spread out below him and stretched far into the distance. He felt he could almost touch the sky. Moreover, the soil, in the Puuc's valleys, was deep and fertile. The people who lived there grew vegetables, fruits, and herbs of many varieties. The hard won abundance was such that their crops provided not only for themselves but also usually fueled lively trade with surrounding communities.

The only drawback was the area's lack of water. Each time Ah-cambal passed through, the hills and valleys were a little dryer and the existence of their people a little more precarious. This season, the drought plaguing the land was making their subsistence even more uncertain. Life in the Puuc was gradually becoming untenable and even with its aguadas (seasonal ponds or small lakes) and the laborious construction of large numbers of chultunes (cisterns for the collection and storage of rainwater), people were slowly drifting away.

A long afternoon of constant climbing at last brought Ah-cambal to a suitable stopping place. Atop the ridge slowly returning to the earth reclined a small enclosure of ancient and weathered stone, an abandoned and forgotten watch post of once mighty Óoxmáal. Tired but satisfied with his day's work, he set down his hamper and spear, and turned to watch the drama playing out below.

As far as his eyes could see, mottled purple shadows crawled across the jungle. K'inich Ajaw had begun his descent into Metnal (Xibalba, the underworld) and soon the land would fall into darkness. In Metnal the sun faced lord would take on the form of Balam, the fearful jaguar god, and in that form do battle with the lords of night that he might prevail and again bring the day.

Ah-cambal made his promised devotion to Ekchuah, and for good measure also a small offering to the rain god Chaac. Afterwards, he ate a simple meal of dried meat and fruit, and settled with his back against the low wall to watch the dance of moon and stars across the sky. Sometime later, he awoke cold and a little stiff. The stars still wheeled overhead but something had changed. Something had disturbed his slumber.

Instantly alert, Ah-cambal stared intently into the darkness. Ix Chel (the moon goddess) no longer bathed the world with her radiance and the surrounding gloom was complete. He couldn't see anything or hear anything, but all his instincts screamed that he wasn't alone. An inch at a time he carefully reached for his spear and slowly drew it to him. As he watched and waited the silence grew oppressive. Small hairs stood up on his body and a prickly sensation tickled his neck and back. Without understanding its origin, he felt a primordial knot of fear form in his stomach. Ah-cambal frowned. As a well-seasoned traveler and veteran warrior he rarely encountered the emotions of fear and doubt.

The low chuff came from nearby, almost at hand. Then he saw the eyes, bright cold, and staring. Only yards away barely visible in the faint starlight stood Lord Balam. Jaguars were common enough but Ah-cambal needed only one glimpse to tell that the creature he faced was no ordinary animal. Lord Balam was huge and almost the color of the night itself. As the god stood motionless before him, Ah-cambal was overcome with a need to speak.

"Fearsome Lord, I am your servant," he said as he laid aside his spear.

If the god Balam had come to carry him away, Ah-cambal was prepared to go. His life had been a good one blessed with challenge and prosperity. The Jaguar Lord inched closer, ever staring but saying nothing.

"Why have you come, oh Lord?" asked Ah-cambal.

Surely, if Balam saw fit to forsake Metnal and stand before him, something momentous was at hand. The huge jaguar walked forward until the two were almost nose to nose. He sniffed at the man before him and another almost inaudible growl rumbled in his throat.

"You stand at the crossing of two paths," heard Ah-cambal. "One path leads to an uncertain future, the other to oblivion. You must choose."

"What paths my Lord, I see nothing?"

"You must choose."

When Ah-cambal awoke, he was alone. Lord Balam had defeated the lords of night and once again in the guise of K'inich Ajaw he was rising in the east. Above the ridge the sky lingered gossamer purple and a rare pre-summer chill pervaded the deep shadows of the small stone enclosure. Ah-cambal shivered and pulled tighter the edges of his well-worn travel cloak. For the first time in many uinal he felt the icy grip of advancing age. His hands were stiff and his knees creaked as he stood. In the cool before the new dawn he felt nearer to the shambling old man he so often portrayed.

He searched the ground, but not a broken twig or so much as a scuffed patch of earth betrayed the truth of the jaguar god's visit. Perhaps Lord Balam came to him in a dream. Ah-cambal wasn't sure, but he knew the visitation meant something important. Such an encounter, real or dream, was a powerful omen, a forceful portent discounted or ignored at one's peril.

Ah-cambal gathered dry sticks and twigs and built a small bright smokeless fire. Kneeling within its tiny circle of warmth and light, he unrolled a weathered but cunningly ornamented square of deer hide. Smoothing it onto the ground he then selected one of his many pouches. Inside rattled 260 reddish brown tzintè (coral tree) seeds. Ah-cambal lowered his head, chanted the proper devotions, and quickly scattered the kidney-shaped seeds onto the hide.

Casting the seeds was a divination, a cleromancy, that when performed correctly revealed the will of the gods. The 260 seeds reflected the 260 days of the sacred Tzolk'in, the great wheel of the moon calendar that connects the energy of heaven with the earth below. The seeds' apparently haphazard pattern was complex, but far from random. For someone like Ah-cambal who could read their secrets, the scattered tzintè seeds mirrored the actions of the gods. They answered questions. They foretold the future.

Stunned and uncertain, the spy stared at the swirled array. Three times he cast the seeds and three times they aligned themselves into an identical configuration. Each time, the story they told was the same; all the once great houses of Mayapán would bow before a strange people. The strangers would preach a new god and the virtue of a vahom-ché (an uplifted wood) of great power. Large deer would come into the land and the worship of the gods would cease! What could such a prophecy mean? The gods' message confused and dismayed Ah-cambal, but never in all his years had he seen the seeds deliver one with equal force.

The spy shouldered his few belongings. The gods had given him a message and it was time to return home and share what he'd learned.

The sacred Tzolk'in had turned and the day was 5 Kawak, the time of storm and change.

Chapter 2

The Viboras

The 2nd of May, Year of Our Lord 1511

Captain Valdivia was a tall self-assured man with a dignified patrician air. His carefully cropped beard framed a dark narrow face and his darker eyes moved constantly recording everything around him. Hands on his hips, he stood amidships and yelled orders to his helmsman. Aft of the captain, Andres de Cuellar put his shoulder to the tiller, the heavy beam swept a broad arc across her deck, and the *Viñas de la Barca* fell smoothly off the wind. More shouted orders and, shortly, running before a stiff breeze, the caravel sprinted away from the lush jungle draped coast of Darien and set out on the first leg of a hurried dash for the island of Hispaniola. Secured safely within his cabin, Captain Juan de Valdivia, the king's procurator and an emissary of Vasco Nuñez de Balboa, was transporting twenty thousand ducats of gold collected for his majesty Ferdinand of Spain. The captain also carried a petition for the Spanish governor in Santo Domingo and an account of an ongoing squabble for control of an isthmus that would someday be known as Panama.

Ten days out from Darien, revealed by the glow of a ruddy dawn, the *Viñas'* crew sighted turtles, a multitude large and small blanketing the sea. In the still of morning the salt air lay stagnant and heavy and in the distance the men thought they could make out low islands just south of Cuba. Everywhere around them floated turtles, so many turtles that the sea looked to be filled with wet bobbing rocks.

Far to the east, scudding black clouds churned across a blood red sky, dark silver edged lumps of coal that piled one atop another and threatened to overthrow the dawn. Overhead the ship's sails sagged, luffed, and then suddenly refilled with a sharp, teeth rattling, bang.

Bad winds coming, mused Valdivia.

A cautious sailor, he ordered his crew to make ready. As the men moved about squaring things away, the seas around *Viñas* grew agitated and dark waves began to splash against her hull.

Just before the unusual out of season storm fell upon them, the turtles disappeared.

Fierce gale force winds and driving horizontal rain, which seemed to grow out of nowhere, turned the world to darkness and raged unabated. Captain Valdivia took the only action open to him and ordered his caravel to run before the tempest. The wind howled from astern and, to make the *Viñas* easier to handle, the crew furled her lateen-rigged mizzen. The *Viñas de la Barca* was quick and lithe, but she was a small vessel and not originally designed for the open ocean. The addition of a bowsprit, and her square-rigged main and fore masts, helped keep her stable, but she still struggled against the wind, bucking and jerking in the high seas; not so much a thing of wood and iron, but a wild creature desperate to escape its tether.

Day and night her steersmen strained at the tiller and the *Viñas* plowed forward through angry mountainous swells, one after another. Wave after following wave swept the line of her deck. Thunder rang like hollow bells of a great cathedral, and forked lightning struck so close that the men squeezed their eyes shut in fear. The air stank of ozone, wet hair stood on end and with each howling gust of wind the *Viñas'* sails, lines, and yards became ever more entangled. Captain Valdivia raged back at the storm and drove his crew with a force of will that nearly matched the elements.

The caravel was built to draw just six feet of water, but after two days of unrelenting squall she wallowed low in the surging swell. Months in the warm Caribbean had taken their toll. Shipworms had bored her hull, and pin-sized holes gave once sturdy wood the porous texture of overripe cheese. Salt water sloshed in the *Viñas'* hold and to fight the leaks, the men not only worked her three pumps non-stop, they also struggled around the clock bailing with kettles and buckets.

Urged on by their captain, the determined crew of twenty-seven held their ground; but exhaustion hounded their efforts, and as hard as they worked the storm worked harder. No place on the little ship was dry and, despite tropical heat, the men shivered, worn out, chilled to the bone. Day and night the ship heaved and, though well experienced, several of the crew were sick.

Given temporary respite from the drudgery of the pumps, a tired sailor named, Gonzalo, huddled against a coil of rope under the protective awning of the quarterdeck. Wind and spray blew in through the few cannon ports, but with the hold awash and waves sluicing the deck his was as good a place as any. Unable to sleep from days of being wet, he drifted in and out of consciousness. During the moments of welcome oblivion his mind wandered back to his childhood and he dreamed of his older sister Consuela.

A warm summer breeze, and beautiful Consuela with her soft brown eyes and silken black hair, his small hand tucked into hers, leading little Gonzalo to their pond to learn to swim.

Wedged into a corner of the quarterdeck, the *Viñas'* cabin boy turned the ship's half hour-glass for the eighth time, and sang out the change of the watch.

"On deck, on deck, you dogs of the morning watch, it's your time. Shake a leg."

Gonzalo grunted, tried to stretch his aching muscles, and for the thousandth time cursed his sorry lot in life. Born in the port city of Palos de la Frontera, just beyond the splendor and power of Seville, Gonzalo Aroça was second son to a powerful father who lost his life fighting for the glory of Castile. Wealth and titles that his father's death left behind passed to his much older brother, Esteban. Because this was to be expected, Gonzalo's family selected for him a clerical career and resolved that he be educated as a priest. Shortly thereafter, his mother and Esteban had bundled him off to a monastic seminary in Valladolid.

At the monastery young Gonzalo quickly discovered himself ill-suited for a life of contemplation and prayer. Nevertheless, he worked diligently to meet the expectations of his mother and his brother. As time passed, he realized that all of his efforts had accomplished nothing. Each day became a joyless struggle between his family's plans for his future and visions of the life he would have chosen for himself. A year and a half after his arrival at the monastery, just after the closing benediction of lauds, he slipped quietly away leaving his kin's plans and intentions behind. Fleeing, he knew that he'd disgraced himself in his family's eyes. By that time their opinion no longer mattered.

Youth led to manhood and after years of knocking about Spain as an occasional soldier of fortune, Gonzalo made a decision to link his prospects to those of a well-known and ambitious adventurer, Alonso de Ojeda.

Flamboyant and short in stature, Ojeda had already made several voyages of exploration to the New World; he'd also become so popular at court that King Ferdinand granted him a twenty-square-mile estate on Hispaniola and named him governor over Nueva Andalusia, an area on the eastern coast of Darien. At the age of twenty-four Gonzalo leveraged the name of his estranged family and enlisted as an escudero, a gentleman volunteer, on Ojeda's next expedition.

Together with three hundred other adventurers Gonzalo, full of hopes and dreams, sailed out of the port of Cadiz. A salvo of cannons and a cavalcade of trumpets saluted the small fleet's departure and on shore, people gathered on nearby hills and cheered their fathers, sons, and brothers, uncles, cousins, and friends. As the boats sailed toward the open ocean on a voyage that promised unlimited possibilities, Gonzalo had prayed that God make him rich and influential.

That time, nearly two years before the storm, was the high point of the expedition. Everything that followed that hopeful departure had been fraught with frustration and failure. The three month crossing proved difficult, and the natives of Nueva Andalusia showed themselves to be both hostile and resourceful. Of the men who'd joined Ojeda, lured by visions of wealth and privilege, more than two hundred succumbed to poison arrows, sickness, and starvation. Plunder was elusive and where it existed, it was hard won. Making matters worse, another explorer, Diego de Nicuesa, royal mandate in hand, was contesting even what little they'd secured.

Sensing disaster, Ojeda abandoned most of his remaining men and returned to Spain. Many times since that day Gonzalo had heaped invective on the departed adventurer, cursing his weak leadership and false promises. On bad days, Gonzalo wished that he'd stayed in Palos and apprenticed himself to a carpenter. When an offer to join Valdivia on the *Viñas* and escape Darien presented itself, he'd jumped at the chance.

The soldier of questionable fortune shook his wet head, pulled himself up from his sodden bed of coiled rope, and struggled to his feet. Tired and groggy, he stepped from the shelter of the quarterdeck and staggered directly into the waiting arms of a surging wave. Before Gonzalo could steady himself, the wave swirled about his ankles, yanked his legs from under him and, arms flailing, threw him backward toward the deck. He never landed. With the deck rushing to meet him, a strong hand seized his belt, arrested his fall, and jerked him upright.

"None of that Jugador," shouted his rescuer, "I have need of you."

Gonzalo found himself staring into the bear-like face of, Juan Pintero. The two men first met while happily drinking and gambling away the night before they embarked from Spain. Introduced to Pintero by a game of liar's dice that emptied his purse and left him with a wary respect for the big man's cunning; Gonzalo nevertheless found himself drawn to Pintero's gregarious ursine charm. Gonzalo was a loner who kept to himself, but he also often felt alone. Something was missing from his life, and Pintero somehow wandered into that gap. The two would-be adventurers recognized in each other kindred spirits, and having cleaned Gonzalo out, the big boatswain promptly nicknamed the younger man, "Jugador," (Gambler) and took him under his wing. Ever since that night Pintero had proved himself a mentor and a fast friend.

"Thanks," groaned Gonzalo, "but it would have been kinder if you'd just let me slide overboard. I don't suppose you have a roast of mutton or a drought of wine tucked under that giant stocking cap of yours?"

Neither man had eaten a warm meal since they'd last scooped wooden bowls of thin broth from the communal cooking pot five days before. Pintero dug his meaty hand into his jacket pocket and handed Gonzalo a pair of soggy biscuits.

"Here, use your imagination, but follow me while you chew your 'mutton'. The rigging's fouled and Valdivia wants us aloft."

"Sweet Maria, in this?" moaned Gonzalo, "You can't be serious."

"We've got to take another reef in the main; if we don't, we're gonna lose it," growled the boatswain. "Come on; Andres and De Huelva are waiting for us up forward."

The *Viñas* jumped and shimmied, and great rolling curtains of rain still pounded across her deck, but as Gonzalo peered through the gloom, he realized with great relief that the storm was finally blowing itself out. The brilliant crackle of lightning had ceased, and along with it the hollow teeth grinding peals of thunder. The two men gripped the starboard gunwale and pulled themselves toward the shrouds. Their progress was slow, but soon Pintero hooked his arm through a ratline and pointed at the mainsail's spar.

"Look, we've got to clear that away."

High above, Gonzalo could see where their small topsail had torn loose and much of its rigging now lay entangled with lines from the main. Pintero leaned in to make himself heard.

"You're the wiry one Jugador; when you reach the spar, work your way out and try to untangle the block that's fouled the buntline. I'll tackle the lines wrapped around the halyards and Andres and De Huelva will deal with whatever's on their side."

Gonzalo looked at his large friend and smiled. No one else ever called him, Jugador, and somehow whenever the older man used the nickname it gave Gonzalo a sense of something shared. Pintero's gruff friendship was the closest thing to family he'd experienced since abandoning his home in Palos all those years ago. From his friend's craggy face, Gonzalo's gaze shifted to the wet flapping canvas, and he nodded grimly.

"Okay," shouted Pintero, "Let's get on with it."

The boatswain waved at the huddled forms of the two sailors, barely visible across the deck, and all four men pulled themselves into the shrouds and began to climb. The ratlines were wet and slippery and the men's fingers were cold and stiff. Hand over hand, one step at a time they pulled themselves aloft. Each gust of wind threatened to dislodge them and Gonzalo clung desperately to the ropes. If anyone but Pintero had asked him, he would have refused to climb. When they reached the spar, the boatswain cupped his hands around his mouth.

"There it sits," he yelled. "The faster we get done; the faster we get down."

Gonzalo began to inch his way toward the tangled buntline. At first as the *Viñas* shuddered and rolled and it was all he could do to hang onto his swaying perch, but then, as he clung to the spar; the rain continued to lessen, and the wind further eased its vicious attack. The ship abruptly discovered her stride and suddenly Gonzalo found that he could hold on and still manage to tug at the tangled lines.

Loosen some there, slide that through here, pull on that trailing line, and with a *whoosh* the heavy block that had fallen from above tumbled free. Triumphant, Gonzalo was about to cheer his success when, above the wind, he heard the agitated voices of Andres and De Huelva yelling and shouting. Back across the spar, past Pintero's shaggy head, both sailors were waving frantically and pointing at the sea.

The weather was clearing rapidly and everything below now seemed to shimmer; glints of brass and wet scrubbed wood, all set aglow by a soft light of early dawn. Not a ship's length in front of the *Viñas'* prow the water churned and swirled, a frothy expanse of phosphorescent white.

"Oh Christ! Hang on!" screamed Pintero.

Gonzalo recognized the turbulent swath for what it was, and a mind numbing rush of fear swallowed his friend's warning.

A last maniacal gust and the dying storm drove the *Viñas* onto the reef with the unchecked strength of an avalanche. Jagged claws of coral dug into her sides and the thick oaken timbers of her bottom ripped away. The little caravel screamed in her agony, came to a wrenching grinding halt, and, 1,300 leagues from home, ceased to be a ship.

At the same instant, her mainmast snapped with a booming *crack*, jerked forward, and flung Gonzalo and the other three men cart-wheeling into air. Gonzalo felt himself spin end over end and then with a force that knocked his breath away, he slammed into the sea.

For a fraction of a second a depression seemed to form at the spot where he landed; then the salty water came rushing back, grasping at his limbs, smothering his face, and pulling him down. Gonzalo spluttered and flailed as cold inky blackness surrounded him, pressed in upon him, trying to snuff out his life.

Up and down lost meaning. Water tried to force its way up his nose and his lungs screamed for air. His clothes fought his movements; dimly aware of what he was doing, he kicked off his boots, managed to unbuckle his belt, and shrugged out of his jacket. With frantic desperation and the last of his strength, Gonzalo pulled for what he thought was the surface. His consciousness drew to a flickering pinpoint, a tiny star in a faraway tunnel of darkness.

Then, as the star guttered and he felt himself drown, *Consuela reached down and grabbed his hand, beautiful Consuela with her soft brown eyes and silken black hair, his small hand tucked into hers.*

Gagging and retching, Gonzalo came to himself clinging to a floating chunk of the broken spar. He coughed, gasped, and shook. Consuela was gone; he was alive. Around him the restless sea rose and fell and, venting the last of its anger, roughly slapped him back and forth. The spar was his salvation and Gonzalo embraced it with the fervor of an ardent lover.

Awareness slowly battled its way through his confusion and little by little he took stock of his troubled surroundings. Nearby, lay the shattered ruin of the *Viñas de la Barca* caught on the shoals, its hull listing at a crazy angle. Pounded by the waves, she was still breaking up and even above the wind Gonzalo could hear the reports as her timbers shuddered and cracked. On her deck, obscured by the last of the rain, he could just make out the shadowy forms of Captain Valdivia and some others working wildly to clear away her long boat.

A dark blob floated closer at hand and caught his attention; Pintero's bobbing cap. With a sudden jolt of clarity Gonzalo remembered the other men with whom he'd been aloft. His own plight forgotten, he tried to pull himself higher out of the water and anxiously searched the sea. Except for the boatswain's cap and floating debris from the rigging, the ocean around the young escudero was empty. He reached for the cap and began to yell.

"Juan! Juan! Juan!"

Much later, miserable, exhausted, and delirious, Gonzalo still clutched the sodden wool cap and still hoarsely shouted his friend's name as the longboat drew alongside and several strong hands pulled him from the spar.

Captain Valdivia and sixteen more of the crew were aboard the longboat. The rest along with Juan Pintero, the *Viñas de la Barca*, and the king's twenty thousand gold ducats were all gone to a watery grave.

Chapter 3

Ichpaatún

11 Bak'tun 14 K'atun 11 Tun 1 Uinal 10 K'in

(May 13, 1511)

Nachan Can tried to smile. He was supposed to smile. It was an auspicious day and Ichpaatún was in a festive mood. As ruler of the small city-state a smile was expected of him, but each time that Nachan Can glanced at the puffed-up cluster of emissaries from Tzamá (Tulum, City of the Dawn) his satisfied smile withered and faded, unconsciously replaced by an aggravated frown which wrinkled the skin of his forehead, pressed the blood from his already thin lips, and made the tattoos on his face appear dark and sinister.

Pech'ob (Ticks), thought Nachan Can, *just like them to show up today.*

The ruler of Ichpaatún drank deeply from the frothy cup of b'alche that sat beside his bench. The intoxicating beverage, made from water, honey, and the bark of the balche tree relaxed him, but did little to allay his annoyance. If Yum Cimil, a god of death and human sacrifice, had suddenly appeared with all nine of his Bolontiku and, if the lesser gods had then dragged the emissaries of Tzamá writhing and screaming into their underworld realm, Nachan Can's smile might well have returned.

The complex relationship between Ichpaatún and Tzamá was rocky and one sided. Ichpaatún was a modest, but prosperous, commercial community that exploited the salt resources of the Bay of Chectumal and played the role of middle-man for the lucrative trade in cacao, jade, copper trinkets, flint, obsidian, and quetzal feathers that flowed from the river city of Lamanai located to the south and from the heart of old Petén. Tzamá, situated fifty leagues to the north, was large and powerful, a busy coastal seaport and trading center that augmented its own commercial success by exploiting Ichpaatún's.

Under thinly veiled threats of war and sudden destruction, Ah Tabai the ruler of Tzamá, who styled himself Yajawk'ak' (Lord of the Fire) demanded fealty and tribute from both Nachan Can and his people. Nachan Can loathed the arrangement. Ichpaatún did all the work, but with each turn of the ha'ab (365 day solar calendar) the ticks from Tzamá sucked a little harder.

Today should be a day of celebration, thought Nachan Can, still frowning.

From his seat atop Ichpaatún's modest temple pyramid, he enjoyed an unobstructed view across the small ceremonial plaza that spread out below. Preparations for the coming of age ceremony were already under way.

The low platform in the middle of the square had been carefully swept clean and then scattered with fresh leaves of the sihom (soap berry) tree. On one side of the platform stood a short line of three boys watched over by one of their fathers; on the other side waited four girls and an aged matron. A bench had been placed at each corner of the patio and on each bench sat another father. Chosen as chacs (helpers in religious rituals) to assist Ichpaatún's priest with the upcoming ceremony, the men had each fasted for three days and abstained from relations with their wives. Between them the four chacs held a sacred braided cord that encircled the patio, corralled their children, and kept the forces of evil at bay.

As behooved his position, Nachan Can had also abstained from relations with his wife. That was also part of his annoyance. At uaxaclahuntukal (38), his wife Ix Chan Ek (Lady Small Star) was still very beautiful and he'd been looking forward to taking her back into his bed. Now, instead of anticipating the pleasures of the post-ceremony feast and the charms of Chan Ek, he faced the prospect of endless wrangling with the accursed emissaries from Tzamá.

"Nachan Can, Sajal (lesser lord)."

Nachan Can turned to find his caluac (majordomo/steward) and confidant Itz'at (Learned Man) Acan kneeling at his shoulder.

"The delegation from Tzamá demands an immediate audience lord. Nacon (war chief) Gucumatz is particularly insistent".

"They can wait Acan!" snapped Nachan Can. "Tzamá is without respect and Gucumatz is Ah Tabai's snapping turtle! Today is a day of rebirth here in Ichpaatún. Today, my nephew, Tepeu, and two others become men and four girls become maidens. We will honor them as they deserve! Gucumatz can wait!"

Acan bowed still deeper before the displeasure of his lord. Nachan Can scowled at the emissaries. Insultingly, they were all staring back.

Guests should have brought gifts thought Nachan Can. *They should have made offerings for the wellbeing of our children about to become men and women. Instead, that strutting turkey Gucumatz comes dressed for war.*

The nacon from Tzamá was costumed to intimidate. At nearly six feet tall, Gucumatz was a giant, burly and broad-shouldered. His wide chest was protected by an ornate cuirass of heavily quilted cotton. A carefully embroidered loincloth, rich with beads and feathers, circled his waist. A small woven shield, reinforced with tanned and painted deer hide, hung from his left forearm. Against his well-muscled upper arms clattered the jawbones of defeated enemies, clacking bones that warned of the huge man's brutality and prowess in war. Gucumatz's shoulders were draped with the pelt of a large jaguar, the animal's rictus snarl only slightly more savage than the war chief's own. His head was crowned by a feather adorned wooden war helmet and in his right hand he casually gripped a heavy stone-headed war club.

At the ripe age of 58 Nachan Can looked at least half a k'atun younger, but his own days of swinging such a club were well past. Still, he wasn't impressed. Gucumatz was the implied threat. The real threat was Ah K'in Zac Nok (White Worm). The rotund Zac Nok was high priest of Tzamá and also a trusted and cunning advisor to Ah Tabai. His presence among the delegation meant that Ah Tabai was up to something.

"Acan," said Nachan Can in a milder tone, "go down there and once again tell Gucumatz and Ah K'in Zac Nok that Ichpaatún is honored to have them here and that I am personally honored that they've chosen to sanctify my nephew's coming of age with their presence. Also, remind them that since the ceremony is already underway tradition requires that I forego the extreme pleasure of their company until after it completes. Take Hoch Can (Digging Snake) with you."

Hoch Can, Nachan Can's son and war chief, who was also seated on the platform, stood and prepared to accompany Acan. Nachan Can turned to him.

"Hoch Can, lend your support to Itz'at Acan. Look resolute, but not threatening. Gucumatz is a hot-headed fool, so do nothing to provoke him. Acan knows what must be said and how to say it. Remain silent and follow his lead."

At barely eighteen years of age, Hoch Can was, untried as a warrior, and young to be appointed Nacon. Nachan Can had married late and his first wife was a sickly girl who in the ten years before she died never gave him an heir. On the other hand, Ix Chan Ek, his second wife, had quickly proved as fertile as she was beautiful and strong.

"I hear you father," answered Hoch Can. With a slight bow the young war chief turned away and followed the seneschal. The two men descended the pyramid's steep steps and Nachan Can nodded his approval as his son signaled to and was joined by two of his holcánob, both big men, barrel chested and broad in the shoulders.

Nachan Can watched intently as his heir and retainers reached the plaza. To his pleasure, the group from Tzamá stiffened at their approach.

Good, thought the sajal, *not as confident as you seem.*

Gucumatz drew himself up and bristled, but Acan, holding the short thick baton that was the symbol of his authority, ignored the nacon and addressed his remarks to White Worm. Nachan Can couldn't hear what his seneschal said, but he could easily see the emissaries' reactions. Zac Nok scowled his annoyance and Gucumatz's face turned dark red suffused with rage.

Worm said something back to Acan, and the nacon shouted at the seneschal with such force that Nachan Can could pick out certain obscenities. Hoch Can and his two warriors spread out slightly and stepped closer to Acan. Unfazed by the rude and threatening outburst, the wiry little steward grinned, made a deprecating gesture with his baton, and again spoke to Zac Nok. After a brief back and forth, Acan made a slight bow, Worm motioned angrily to Gucumatz, and, still scowling, the Tzamáns stamped away from the plaza. After the delegation's backs were turned, Itz'at Acan faced the pyramid, smiled at Nachan Can, and bowed deeply.

Nachan Can's own smile slipped back into place and a loud chuckle burst from his lips. His steward and his son had done well! No violence had ensued and Ah Tabai's people lost face. Thoroughly satisfied, the ruler of Ichpaatún reached for his cup of b'alche and turned back to his nephew's impending leap into manhood.

In the square in the center of the plaza, the ceremony of caput-sihil (rebirth) was proceeding oblivious to the dangerous game that had just played out at its edge. A stool had been placed in the center of the low platform and upon it sat the wizened form of Ah K'in (he of the sun/ high priest) May. The old priest was the brother of Nachan Can's mother. Fragile and at times easily tired, Ah K'in May no longer sat in on all of Ichpaatún's councils, but, favored in the eyes of the great god Itzamna, he still led the community's spiritual life.

A small brazier smoldered in front of the priest, and beside it were two bowls, one filled with ground maize, the other with incense. One by one the children stepped forward and Ah K'in May placed a pinch of the corn and a pinch of the copal into each of their hands and instructed them to toss it into the flames. Once the offerings were complete, the four chacs moved toward the center of the platform drawing in their braided rope as they went. Ah K'in May then took up the rope and the brazier and assigned one of the fathers to carry them beyond the confines of the village. He also admonished the man not to look behind him on his return. In this way any evil influences lingering about the square were exorcised. The chac set off running and Nachan Can again smiled.

With the purification of the patio complete, the three remaining chacs swept the platform clean of the sihom leaves that were previously scattered and replaced them with leaves of the copó tree. Mats were also laid down, and, in preparation for the next rites, Ah K'in May donned a tall feathered hat and a splendid tunic of gleaming blue-black feathers.

During the lull, Ak Uinic Ik (Dwarf-wind), Nachan Can's youngest sibling, approached the ruler's bench. At the age of uaclahuntukal (36), Dwarf-wind's appearance reflected his relatively short but dissolute life. His lips were wide and meaty, his face puffy, and his eyes, small, and close-set. Short in stature, there was a fleshiness to him that suggested more fat to come. In contrast, his hair was long, oiled, and carefully coiffed and his garments were crisp and exquisite.

"Brother," he whispered to Nachan Can, "Tzamá is a friend, an important ally. Do you really think it wise to antagonize Ah K'in Zac Nok and Nacon Gucumatz?"

Nachan Can's smile faded. Where he looked toward Tzamá with wary eyes, his brother, Dwarf-wind, looked northward with eyes clouded by avarice. For many turns of the ha'ab, his younger brother had worked diligently to ingratiate himself to Ah Tabai and his various ambassadors. Dwarf-wind's interests were his own, not those of Ichpaatún and his cupidity disgusted Nachan Can.

"A friend and ally who covets all that we possess," responded the ruler.

"Not true, not true" groveled Dwarf-wind. "I've consulted the heavens many times and there is no question that our prosperity depends upon the beneficence of Tzamá."

Although his studies and devotions were at best minimal, Dwarf-wind considered himself ah k'in (a priest). He also made much of his family's tenuous royal bloodline and because of it claimed to be a chilam, one who could reliably read the future. Nachan Can distrusted the honesty of his youngest brother's professed callings and also his motives. He was even less sanguine about his abilities of prognostication.

"Whether you consult the heavens, brother, or the dregs at the bottom of your b'alche cup," grumbled Nachan Can, "truth eludes you. Our prosperity depends not on Tzamá, but on luck, cunning, and the sweat of our brow."

"The Lord of the Fire values Ichpaatún," continued Dwarf-wind.

"The Lord of the Fire covets Ichpaatún," snapped Nachan Can.

"Brother, don't say such things," whined Dwarf-wind. "We must praise Yajawk'ak' and bow before him if we hope..."

"Enough!" growled Nachan Can. "If another man spoke thus...always the same song; no more of this! Our nephew is about to become a man. Honor him and keep your own counsel!"

Waved away in dismissal, Dwarf-wind gave his brother an unctuous bow and returned to his seat.

Down on the platform Tepeu knelt before Ah K'in May. The boy's head was covered with a square of white cloth, called suhuy nok, which his mother had woven for the purpose. Ah K'in May was resplendent in his tunic of midnight-blue feathers. Feathers of various other colors were worked into the garment as accents and other longer feathers dangled at the ends of cords, dancing at the slightest breeze. In his hand the old priest held a small bundle of decorated sticks, each hung with the rattle of a snake. After a long benediction, Ah K'in May dipped the bundle into a jar of virgin water, water that was collected from the hollows of trees or depressions in rocks of the forest and then infused with flowers and cacao. With great care and serenity he sprinkled Tepeu with the sacred liquid. When he finished, one of the chacs came forward with a bone and used it to further anoint the boy's face, hands, and feet. After this unction, Ah K'in May smiled and removed the cloth from Tepeu's head.

Other boys and girls followed in turn and then all were given flowers to smell and asked to draw in the smoke of a sacred pipe. Ah K'in May spoke a final prayer and only one rite remained.

Since the age of three, each child had worn a token of their innocence and chastity. For the boys, it was a small bead or plaquet fastened into the hair of their heads. For the girls it was a thin cord that looped about their waists and from which hung a small shell above their private parts. With great dignity, Ah K'in May produced a thin obsidian knife and cut away the counter braided into each boy's hair. Then, the mothers of the four girls came forward and removed the girdles from their daughters' waists.

The reborn young men and women left the platform, and family and well-wishers pressed eagerly forward. Nachan Can was well pleased. It had been a good ceremony; seven new adults added to his community. Food and drink were making their appearance and soon everyone would indulge in a long joyous celebration of eating, drinking, and merriment. With a resigned sigh, the ruler levered himself from his bench and signaled Learned Man Acan to join him. Bile gurgled in Nachan Can's stomach, the festival of em-ku would last until dawn, but it would be long over before he and Acan finished their disagreeable parlay with Gucumatz and White Worm.

"Come with us, Hoch Can," he called to his son. "You're both warrior and Nacon, but if you expect to rule in Ichpaatún after I'm gone you must also become a diplomat. Today, listen closely to Itz'at Acan and you'll learn how to speak volumes, but say little."

"How so father?" asked the young Nacon.

"Watch and see. Tzamá calls us vassals and demands much of us, but as I was forced to remind your uncle, Ah Tabai cares only for Ah Tabai. Gucumatz, or more probably the Worm, will bore us with protestations of Tzamá's love, but always remember that it's the strength of Ah Tabai's holcánob that binds us, not our friendship, nor his love. Although we're less powerful, the trick is to treat with Tzamá as equals. Deny Ah Tabai much of what he requires, yet always give him something that speaks of our goodwill and leaves enough doubt that he's reluctant to challenge us in open war."

Nachan Can had arranged for the negotiations to take place in a minor plaza, a small walled-in square situated just adjacent to the city's main gate; a small, crowded, walled-in plaza which he'd ordered hurriedly prepared for the occasion. When the emissaries from Tzamá arrived, the sajal welcomed them profusely, smiled in the face of their frowns and scowls of open disgust, and knew with satisfaction that his preparations were a success.

Seating mats had been placed on the stone floor and appropriately delectable bowls of food and drink placed near at hand, but not all the seating was equal. A newly constructed platform covered half of the diminutive plaza. The raised platform was only a hand's length in height, but as the Tzamáns trooped in, they found that it was already occupied by Nachan Can and his retainers. Seated on the mat covered stone, the emissaries would be forced to look up at their hosts. Zac Nok gave a wry smile, settled his fleshy bulk onto a mat, and nodded his acceptance and appreciation of the clever slight. Seeing his fellows sit, Gucumatz seethed visibly, but also took his place.

Small victories, thought Nachan Can, *small victories,* suppressing a smile.

After longwinded and meaningless pleasantries, the meeting proceeded much as Nachan Can expected. Zac Nok spoke at length about the magnificence of the Lord of the Fire, his many public works, his beneficence, and his deep concern for his children in Ichpaatún, then he presented Nachan Can with a long list of demands for additional tribute.

The lengthy list was written on a large sheet of amate bark which had been pounded with a beater, pressed, and then painted with a thin coat of lime plaster. Learned Man Acan accepted the sheet from Worm, gave it a perfunctory review, quickly passing it to his master. Nachan Can took the proffered list daintily as though he'd just discovered something distasteful along its edge.

He turned it around, looked at it briefly, and then handed it back to his steward.

"It is always our desire to assist and aid our brother the exalted Lord of the Fire, but these are complicated times in Ichpaatún. Perhaps, Acan, you can explain to our guests something of our present difficulties."

As he'd done earlier in the main plaza, Learned Man Acan bowed to Nachan Can and favored his sajal with a private smile. Then, despite having treated with the Tzamáns earlier, he once again greeted the emissaries at great length. He welcomed them as brothers, praising the friendship of each person in turn, the great priest Zac Nok, the powerful warrior Gucumatz, all the lesser emissaries, and most especially, the wisdom and generosity their magnificent Lord of the Fire. After weaving together one interminable and flowery welcome after another, the sinewy little seneschal launched almost gleefully into a tedious, rambling, rendition of facts and figures regarding the gathering of salt and Ichpaatún's ever fluctuating trade with old Petén.

Before the meeting, Nachan Can had ordered his servants to keep the emissaries well supplied with b'alche and as Acan's mind-numbing speech droned on and on, Gucumatz was soon in his cups. Eying his swaying companion and Learned Man with equal annoyance and hostility, Zac Nok abstained from his own drink and sullenly gritted his teeth. At length, Acan began to repeat things that he'd already discussed, and the Worm's tolerance, already grown thin, failed him completely.

"Enough!" he snapped at Nachan Can. "Your man has made his precious point. In the name of friendship, your true lord Yajawk'ak' asks Ichpaatún for a pittance and, for reasons which you claim are beyond your control, you're unable to comply!"

"Our utmost desire is to please Tzamá and our great lord," replied Nachan Can, "but, alas, as Itz'at Acan has so eloquently explained, these are trying times."

"Bah!" spit the bulky priest. "Our Lord of Fire asks little and you protest poverty, and offer nothing. We both know that there's a middle way."

Reacting more to Zac Nok's tone than his words, Gucumatz slammed down his b'alche cup. "Bah!" he slurred.

Nachan Can looked away amused. *Now we make some headway.*

While flames flickered in the small plaza's braziers and, out of the sight of man, K'inich Ajaw (the sun-faced lord) struggled with the lords of Metnal, Hoch Can watched closely as his father and Learned Man Acan grappled with Zac Nok, standing firm when they could, compromising when they felt they must, and bit by bit whittling away at Tzamá's list of demands.

Gucumatz was snoring, several of the other Tzamán emissaries were nodding, and Hoch Can's own eyelids had grown heavy, when Nachan Can abruptly announced, "It's settled then!"

Ichpaatún had agreed to send north two additional sea-going trade canoes laden with salt, cacao, and pumice. It was only an eighth of what Tzamá demanded, but Itz'at Acan had cleverly made Zac Nok a personal offer of several sacred stingray spines and a valuable eccentric flint which the steward claimed was chipped into the priest's own likeness. The Tzamán's eyes had gone wide with greed at the sight of the man shaped flint, and Nachan Can knew that his advisor had cinched the deal.

"Well, the goods you offer have some merit, I suppose what you offer may suffice for now," murmured the priest as Acan handed him the flint, "but when your fortunes improve..."

"When our fortunes improve of course we shall send more," replied Nachan Can, eager to be shed of the Tzamáns presence, "then we will certainly speak again. Now, let us all retire."

"You are wise," allowed Zac Nok, "but, before we go to our beds, there is another small matter which I almost forgot."

At the fat priest's words, the hairs on the back of Nachan Can's neck tingled and his satisfaction with the night's negotiations faded like drifting smoke in a breeze.

I've underestimated him, thought the sajal. *He's dangerous and my conceit has left me blind. Now, we learn the true reason for this visit.*

"Lord," began White Worm, looking directly at Hoch Can, "Yajawk'ak' is well aware that your first wife was barren, and it saddens him that you have but a single son and heir; it's such a pity that Hoch Can himself is already married and childless, and also that you have no daughters. As you know, the Lord of Fire has a marriageable son, young Yajawte' (Lord of the Tree)."

I'm grateful I have no daughters, thought Nachan Can. *The boy is an idiot. I've seen him standing slack jawed with drool dripping from his chin. The wife of such a lord will be cursed.*

"It's Yajawk'ak's fondest yearning," continued Zac Nok, "that our peoples unite and that our two lands become as one. Alas, since no woman in Ichpaatún is of equal rank with young Yajawte' marriage is out of the question."

"Your words are true; it's a cruel happenstance," responded the sajal, his every word slow and dripping with caution. He glanced over at Learned Man Acan, and his steward shrugged, equally confused and wary.

"Ah, but the brilliant Lord of Fire has a solution," announced Worm; a sly grin animating his jowly face. "He would open his home and also his great heart to the blood of your blood. Yajawk'ak' desires that your brothers, Ah-cambal and Dwarf-wind, your sister's son, Tepeu, who is today a man, and seven others whom you are to choose, return with us to learn our ways and be honored as guests in Tzamá."

"Hostages," breathed Acan.

Zac Nok glared at the seneschal, "Not hostages, as I said, Nachan Can, honored guests, merely an exchange to ensure the continued close ties between our peoples. And who can say, perhaps, after Hoch Can's time is past, one of these may come to rule in your stead and bind us even closer."

"Sajal, this must not be allowed," whispered Acan.

"Allowed! Watch your foolish tongue servant, lest I order it removed!" barked the sharp-eared Worm. "Yajawk'ak' commands that guests be sent and you will obey!"

Nachan Can jumped to his feet, his face suffused with anger, and pointed at Zac Nok. "You dare such arrogance! Tell your lord that we will send his canoes, but nothing more. Be gone Worm, and be grateful that I'm a man of patience."

"You forget your place," hissed the priest.

"My place!" shouted Nachan Can. "This is Ichpaatún! I rule here!" Then, turning to Acan, he ordered, "Have these ticks removed!"

Roused by the sudden commotion, Gucumatz struggled to his feet. He glared about, spotted two of Nachan Can's men laying hold of Zac Nok, and roared like an animal. With unfettered hatred in his eyes, he took a lurching step toward the sajal. The single step was as far as he got. Hoch Can jumped from his place and leapt between his father and the Nacon, swinging a large b'alche jug as he came. The heavy clay vessel caught the towering warrior on the temple, shattered, slashed his face, and left the giant reeling. Drenched in b'alche, his head and cheek covered in blood, Gucumatz staggered, groaned quietly, and then collapsed at Hoch Can's feet.

"Murder!" screamed Worm.

"Is he alive?" asked Nachan Can in a tone of deadly calm.

Acan bent over the big man and leaned close to his chest. "He lives lord, but he'll have a sore head and a foul temper when he awakes."

"Well then, we must see that he wakes somewhere else! Zac Nok, you and the others pick up this offal and go!"

Escorted by warriors of Ichpaatún's holcánob, and stumbling under the weight of their unconscious nacon, the Tzamáns made their way out of the small plaza and at the hour of Yahalcab (dawn) passed through the city gate.

Upset and angry, Nachan Can and his retinue trailed closely behind, one or two cursing the detested emissaries as they hurried away. As the first rays of K'inich Ajaw's new day pierced the eastern sky, Zac Nok abruptly whirled about and shook his fist at Ichpaatún's low walls.

"Nachan Can, he cried, "hear me well! Yajawk'ak' is your true lord, and he will not forget this day!" Then, the fat priest pivoted, and striding quickly for a man of his bulk, followed his party into the surrounding brush and disappeared.

"Well, Acan, what do you think?" sighed Ichpaatún's weary ruler.

The clever steward stared into Nachan Can's eyes and shrugged. "I fear it could have gone better, Sajal. The Lord of Fire is quick-tempered and vain, and as the Worm says, he will not forget."

Chapter 4

Adrift

The 16th of May, Year of Our Lord 1511

Gonzalo awoke to the shrill cries of an albatross. Far overhead, the raucous bird soared through shimmering thermals and traced lazy circles in a sky that had changed, almost impossibly, from angry black to crystalline blue. Farther above still, a re-emergent sun beat down, bright and strong. As though making up for lost time its angry rays heated the air and set the water a sparkle, dazzling and brilliant. The glare stung Gonzalo's eyes and his head felt like it might burst. All signs of the storm and its violent passage were long gone and the enveloping sea languished glassine and calm. Gonzalo heard someone cough, and for several moments the longboat spun slowly before his eyes.

"Well, well," sighed Captain Valdivia, "it's high time you joined the living." Gonzalo gazed stupidly at the captain and tried to sort out his surroundings.

"I'm not sure he's all here captain," quipped Geronimo. Fray Geronimo de Aguilar was a lanky, hawk-like, ascetic man, a Franciscan brother with a chip on his shoulder and a prickly demeanor. Originally from Ecija, Geronimo had arrived in Darien along with Valdivia. A latecomer to Nueva Andalusia and a companion to the king's procurator, he felt himself morally superior to the rugged adventurers who'd accompanied Ojeda and Diego de Nicuesa, and he treated them all accordingly.

"So Guerrero, are you with us or not?"

Gonzalo held his hand to his eyes and squinted. Shortly after they first met, the self-important Franciscan had taken to calling him "Guerrero." The word meant "soldier," but Geronimo used it as a sarcastic reference to Gonzalo's previous line of work, a jab intended to demean. The nickname stuck, others took it up, and Gonzalo had taken an immediate dislike to the mendicant brother.

"Ah, the good friar," croaked Gonzalo, "I see that our lord wasn't particularly selective about those of us he chose to save."

"Despite our sins, and your sins in particular, our lord Jesus Christ saw fit to save us all aboard this boat," snapped Geronimo.

"Perhaps you'd like to join me in a prayer of thanksgiving for your salvation?"

"I would," replied Gonzalo, "but alas I'm parched." His mouth felt like it had been scrubbed with sand and his shirt and breeches were stiff and scratchy with dried salt.

"Here, take this, but drink slowly."

Gonzalo looked around, and Hernando de Esquivel, the *Viñas'* steward, pressed a wooden cup into his hands. He thanked the balding Esquivel, grasped the small vessel, tilted it to his lips, and drained it in two gulps.

"Good," said Gonzalo smacking his parched lips and handing back the cup, "another!"

"That's your ration," grinned Geronimo, "be grateful to the Lord Our God that you received any. If you'd slept longer, you'd have missed even that."

Hernando handed back the cup. "Here, there are still a few drops."

Gonzalo took back the nearly empty cup and looked at Valdivia, "Captain?"

Valdivia shook his head. "It's not good Aroça. While you went for your swim, *Viñas* broke up fast. It was only by the grace of the virgin that any of us reached the longboat."

"We don't have any food," said Esquivel, "and only the friar here had the sense to grab a skin of water."

Geronimo deigned Gonzalo a smile. "The skin's half empty Guerrero. Soon we'll all be asking for more." Gonzalo upended the wooden cup and licked out the last two drops.

"I hoped for us to reach Cuba," said Valdivia, "but besides being without food and water, we're short of oars. Hernando tossed four into the boat, then that big oaf Vizcaino jumped in and smashed two beneath his boots."

Domingo Vizcaino, an ugly big-boned man with hair that grew thickly down his arms, grimaced and looked sheepish.

"We struggled for hours with the other two," continued the captain, "but it was useless. The wind and current drove us off our course. Cuba's lost to us; all we can do now is pray that God is merciful and that those same currents drive us to the island of Cozumel or onto the coast of Cabo Caloche (Yucatán)."

As the captain's words sunk in, Gonzalo looked about and felt his hopes sink, *from bad to worse.* The longboat was a double thwart boat with five rowing benches each intended to accommodate two oarsmen. With so many crammed aboard there was scarcely room to wiggle and a bare hand's-breadth of freeboard remained above the lapping water.

"How many?" asked Gonzalo?

"Nine of us lost including Andres de Cuellar," responded Valdivia, "but those of us that made it still nearly swamped the boat. When we picked you up, we were so near foundering and being lost, that not a man among us didn't commend himself to God."

"Some, I won't say who, uncharitably suggested leaving you to your fate," threw in Geronimo.

Gonzalo stared at those around him and realized that the Franciscan was probably telling the truth. The boat was badly overloaded and the men so tightly squeezed together that they lay heaped upon one another like bags of grain at a mill. It was clear that, while he'd lain blissfully unconscious, the sea had buffeted them mercilessly. Everyone looked frail and worn and one or two appeared worse.

Gonzalo hugged his knees; *no hope, no possibility of help*, he thought, *we've sailed off the edge of the world.*

On the second day after *Viñas* broke up, the ship's Portuguese carpenter, Alvaro Fernandez coughed twice, covered his chin with bloody spittle, and quietly died. Fernandez had been a squat muscular man with a wind burnt face, a hearty laugh, and a coarse bristle of wiry black hair that he kept cropped close to his head. He was still dressed in the worn and stained leather apron of his trade, a hammer tucked in his belt. Gonzalo always thought of Fernandez as a big man, but in death the powerful carpenter looked small and pitiful.

When the *Viñas* ran aground, Alvaro was thrown against his workbench and the blow crushed something inside of him. Angry and determined, he'd struggled his way into the longboat along with the scramble of others. His effort was futile; it was only because Fernandez was a stubborn man that he didn't accept that he was already dead. At sunset, Fray Geronimo spoke a few words and Gonzalo and Esquivel muscled the heavy carpenter over the side. The sea accepted him silently, closing over his body with only the smallest of murmurs.

Designed so that a mast could be stepped and a sail raised, the longboat was a versatile craft, but even if there'd been a wind, neither canvas nor rigging was aboard. For the next day and a half the men of the *Viñas de la Barca* tried to shelter themselves from the unrelenting tropical sun, alternating between restless sleep and fervent prayers for salvation. Late in the afternoon as the angry orange orb sank in the west and the day's heat crept from unbearable toward tolerable, Pedro de Urtubia, Valdivia's cabin boy struggled to his feet. An excitable gangly boy, all legs, elbows, and shins, Pedro pointed and gave a shout.

"Captain, there to port; I see something!"

"Where Pedro?" answered Valdivia. "What do you see?"

"There; there Captain less than a quarter league, something big." Everyone craned their necks toward where the cabin boy pointed. Something large and dark floated just visible on the surface and several sea birds wheeled above it.

"Vasco, Xavier; grab the oars," ordered Valdivia. "Let's see what Pedro's found."

The seamen, brothers from Cadiz, put the longboat's two remaining oars into the water and began to pull. At the tiller, Alonso Garcia Quintero, the *Viñas* pilot, swung the boat toward the bobbing mass. Fray Geronimo stood in the bow and shaded his eyes.

"The boy has sharp eyes captain," said the friar, "but it's only kelp."

By then, with Vasco and Xavier pulling strongly the longboat had edged among the floating green fronds. Valdivia turned and was about to cuff his cabin boy on the shoulder when Pedro pointed and shouted again.

"Crabs! Look crabs!"

They were tiny, only the size of a large thumbnail, but scores of them crawled over the raft of kelp.

"Quick boys," shouted Valdivia, "drag it aboard!"

For several minutes the water on both sides of the boat surged as men grabbed at the kelp and the tiny crabs. Stems and blade-like leaves filled the space around the sailors' feet and minute crustaceans scuttled about looking for places to hide. When the excitement died down, everyone dumped their catch into a metal helm belonging to Diego de Arana, the master-at-arms. Arana passed the helm to Esquivel, and the steward performed a quick count, a wide smile spreading across his face.

Hernando de Esquivel, a native of Badajoz, had been in charge of the *Viñas'* food stores, keeping her firewood dry, and trimming lamp wicks. He'd also been in charge of Pedro, the crew's only ship's boy.

"Fifty-five," he proclaimed, "That's three crabs each, and an extra for the captain, an extra for Pedro to keep his eyes sharp, and we'll draw lots for the other two. Good work De Urtubia!"

"Good work my ass," grumbled Andres Avellaneda, "look at the size of those crabs. I've got bigger lice on my crotch."

"No doubt," grunted Esquivel.

Andres Avellaneda was another volunteer adventurer, but unlike Gonzalo, he was heir to family titles, a respected hidalgo from Toledo with important connections at the royal court. He was also a vain and arrogant man with carefully arranged salt-and-pepper hair that showed more salt than pepper.

"Those damn things aren't worth a squirt of my piss."

"So, does that mean we'll be drawing lots for your share?" asked Valdivia in a quiet dangerous tone.

"No captain," answered Avellaneda, anger poorly hidden behind his dark eyes, "but it doesn't mean that I'll be kissing young Pedro's ass."

"What about the kelp?" asked Esquivel.

"We eat that too," replied the captain while still staring at the truculent hidalgo.

"Bah," said Avellaneda, "of that you can have my share."

The tiny crabs were soft, so Gonzalo ate his three, shells and all. When they were gone, he picked up a blade of the seaweed and began to chew. Geronimo de Aguilar, Captain Valdivia, and several others followed his example. Andres Avellaneda de Toledo sat sullenly and regarded them with ill-disguised contempt. Two days later, Esquivel upended the water skin and passed around the last precious cup.

On the morning of their ninth day adrift, the pilot huddled in the bow of the longboat along with an escudero, named Esteban Tavera de Alaniz, and three marineros, Cristobal Astudillo, Francisco Del Castillo, and Juan Velazquez.

"We're all agreed then?" asked Alaniz.

"Yes, yes," responded Velazquez, "for God's sake just do it!"

After checking with many sly looks to be sure that they were unobserved, the five men dipped the steward's discarded cup over the side and secretly began to drink sea water. The water was wet and cool as it passed their parched lips and at first the conspirators felt refreshed and even revived. Esteban Tavera used his body to hide their actions, while the pilot dipped the cup and the men drank again and again. The conspirators' relief was short lived. Salt quickly flowed throughout their dehydrated bodies sucking up moisture wherever it spread. Almost immediately their sated thirsts returned with a vengeance. One by one internal organs began to shut down. Near the hour of vespers Cristobal Astudillo, who was by then seated next to Gonzalo, became agitated and commenced to rave.

"We have to hurry, Aroça!" he yelled. "If we don't go now, he's going leave without us!"

"Who'll leave Cristobal?" asked the surprised escudero, "What are you talking about?"

"The King! The King!" screamed Astudillo.

Turning this way and that, he jumped up and stripped off his shirt, elbowed his way past Gonzalo, and lurched to the side of the longboat.

"What the Hell!" exclaimed Diego de Arana.

The master at arms grabbed for the crazed sailor as he stumbled past, but he wasn't quick enough to stop Cristobal's headlong plunge over the side. Before anyone else could react, Cristobal burst back to the surface and swam away from the longboat with wild powerful strokes.

Startled by the sudden commotion, Captain Valdivia roused the crew and shouted for them to give chase. In response, the exhausted Dorantes brothers wrestled their oars into the water. Because the oars were heavy and Vasco and Xavier both weak from exposure it took several minutes for them to overtake the delusional swimmer.

"Astudillo," shouted the captain, "Stop! I order you back!"

When Gonzalo and the master at arms reached out and tried to pull Cristobal aboard, he fought wildly, as if in the clutches of the devil himself, clawing, punching, and screaming obscenities. After Diego de Arana suffered deep scratches across his face, Captain Valdivia shook his head and ordered Gonzalo and the master at arms to let him go. Astudillo instantly turned and swam away. Sixteen pairs of eyes watched his splashing form as it dwindled in the distance.

On learning that Quintero and his companions drank from the sea, Captain Valdivia was livid.

"You stupid bastards," he fumed. The pilot and the other two men looked at him with uncomprehending eyes. "Jesus Christ! You know what happens. What were you thinking?"

Several hours later, Quintero slumped from his bench and his whole body began to shake grotesquely. Tangled amidst the other men's feet, the pilot flopped and trashed striking those near him and rocking the boat until Gonzalo and Geronimo were forced to hold him down and while Arana bound his arms and legs. Shortly afterwards, as the sun began to set, Francisco Del Castillo, and Juan Velazquez started to retch and couldn't stop. With no way to help them, their companions watched helplessly in the growing darkness as the two sailors retched themselves into unconsciousness.

When dawn broke, the three who drank seawater lay still and dead at Gonzalo's feet, each of their faces crusted in salty vomit. Fray Geronimo again opened his book of hours and read the office for the dead. After Gonzalo and Arana slipped three more corpses over the side, the longboat rode higher in the water.

The wind and currents determined the castaways' course, but Valdivia insisted that someone always man the tiller and keep a watch. By the time night fell on their twelfth day only Captain Valdivia, Gonzalo, and Aguilar remained alert.

"My friends," said the Franciscan, "I think we should prepare ourselves. Allow me to give you absolution."

"Make what preparations you like friar," said Gonzalo, "but make them for yourself."

"Don't be a simpleton" retorted Aguilar, "look about you. Our people are ill, and our sickness increases by the hour. Only more thirst and starvation lie ahead. Nothing can follow but death; soon we'll all succumb. Only a fool meets God unshriven and unrepentant."

"When and how I meet our lord is my concern," snapped Gonzalo. "Look to your own soul!"

Valdivia simply stared at the friar and waved him away as if shooing something distasteful. Geronimo opened his breviary and silently began to read. Later, Gonzalo dozed, and still later he awoke to a light tap on his shoulder. Valdivia hovered above him.

"Captain, what is it?"

"I need you to take over," replied the captain, his voice shaky and weak. "I fear the Franciscan may be right. I'm, I'm... I don't think I'll see the dawn."

Gonzalo helped the older man to lie down in the bottom of the boat, and like those about him, the captain lapsed into a fitful unconsciousness.

Gonzalo moved to the tiller and watched the stars wheel overhead. He felt worn and tired, but stronger than he had any right to expect. From his seat in the stern he could see the dark shadowed forms of his remaining companions slumped one atop another. Alone in the darkness he imagined himself upon a barge for the dead, a reluctant ferryman on an endless river Styx.

No that's not right, he thought, *this isn't the end. This isn't death.*

He didn't know the source of his confidence, but deep in his heart he knew that the book of his life still lay open. Sometime after midnight, he shook Valdivia to check if the procurator was dead. To Gonzalo's surprise the captain opened his eyes and sat upright.

"How are you captain?"

"Better," answered Valdivia, straightening his clothes. "I don't know why, but yes better; how about you?"

"I'm alright," said Gonzalo, "I drift in and out, but I'm alive."

"Well... why don't you get some sleep," said the captain. "I'll keep watch until morning."

"If it's all the same to you, I'd rather not," replied Gonzalo. "I'm afraid that if I close my eyes... well, I'd just rather not."

Valdivia nodded, "Then come sit with me and keep me company. These may be our final hours, best not to meet death alone." So saying, he took over the useless tiller and leaned back against the stern thwart. "Are you married Aroça?"

"No," replied Gonzalo. "I'm not opposed to it, but, well... it just never happened; how about you?"

"Nineteen years," sighed Valdivia. "Our marriage was arranged, but she's a good woman. We have two beautiful daughters." A shudder racked Valdivia and Gonzalo realized the older man was crying. "Yolanda and Innocencia, and I fear I shall never see them again," said the captain. "Do you have other family Aroça?"

Gonzalo thought for a moment of his beloved sister Consuela, dead in childbirth, his condescending older brother, and his overly pious mother. "No," he answered, "no family."

"That's a pity," said Valdivia, "every man should have a family."

For a long time the two men sat in silence. Far to the east, the sky took on a faint glimmer, the almost imperceptible herald of approaching dawn. To the west, the moon was setting. Gonzalo watched as cold and blue it sank toward the horizon. Something about its passing felt odd. The horizon seemed too close and the lower portion of the moon seemed covered as if by an eclipse. Yet the shadow was jagged. In a moment of clarity Gonzalo realized what it was. Land!

Chapter 5

Offerings of Blood

11 Bak'tun 14 K'atun 11 Tun 2 Uinal 2 K'in

(May 25, 1511)

K'inich Ajaw won his battle with the lords of night, emerged triumphant from red lak'in (East), and began a new ascendance. Once again, he brought light and warmth to the world. The Sun-faced Lord's return also brought a balmy morning breeze that whispered through the leaves of the sacred yaxché tree (ceiba) under which Ah-cambal slept. The breeze tickled his left ear and teased at the edges of the mantle in which he was wrapped. Deep in the embrace of a pleasant and reassuring dream, the middle-aged warrior tugged the mantle tighter and shifted his position. The dream was reluctant to let him go and he was reluctant to leave it, but the soft morning wind had done its work. Conceding a small defeat, Ah-cambal sat up, yawned expansively, and vigorously rubbed the sleep from his eyes. He was tired when he lay down, but he slept deeply and the comfortable yet unremembered dream left him feeling refreshed and renewed.

On each of the thirteen k'in (days) since Lord Balam's appearance, Ah-cambal had walked from dawn until dusk. Each morning he consulted his tzintè seeds, but they no longer told of strangers from the east, instead they spoke of mundane things, plantings, changes of the seasons, and the venerations expected by the gods. Sometimes he stopped and talked to people that he encountered, gathered local gossip, collected new information, or verified stories that he'd already heard. Other times, when the opportunity arose, Ah-cambal tarried to barter; no matter why he stopped, he soon picked up his trade basket and his spear and hurried on his way.

After nearly ka'a uinal (two 20 day months) away from home, his journey was drawing to a close. That knowledge and a slight tang of ocean carried on the breeze, lent urgency to his footsteps. With luck, few interruptions, and three more days of brisk travel, he would at last reach Ichpaatún.

Ah-cambal was energized by the prospect of his impending homecoming. He'd learned much on his rambles and suspected more; all of it was information that he was keen to share with his brother Nachan Can. He was also eager to meet with his uncle, May, and solicit the old priest's interpretation of the jaguar lord's visitation and the emphatic and repeated message of the seeds.

A search for knowledge drove Ah-cambal's reconnaissance and on that count he felt his efforts well rewarded. Unexpectedly, his trading had also proved profitable. Constant war between the Cocoms, Xius, and Chels had reduced trade in those provinces to a pitiful trickle, and everywhere that he'd wandered people were eager to bargain for his shells and salt. The guise of itinerant trader was a mummer's role and Ah-cambal's trade goods were props packed for show rather than commerce, but, his original intent notwithstanding, he'd quickly and gainfully disposed of everything that he carried. The trades were so successful that his practical side wished that he'd packed more. Instead of shells and salt his trade basket now rattled with the sound of valuable stone counters and cacao beans.

The yaxché tree, under which Ah-cambal passed the night, towered high overhead a true reflection of the great world tree and the surrounding cosmos. Many times over the years the warrior had camped beneath its welcome shade. Tall and straight, its trunk glowed white in the morning sun and its canopy stretched toward the bird of heaven. Massive roots in whose embrace Ah-cambal had slumbered anchored the ancient tree in the world of men and, unseen, they reached and twisted toward the water of the underworld and Metnal.

The yaxché was magnificent and sacred and Ah-cambal loved it well, but it was the cave that drew him back. The tree was one among many. The cave was unique.

At the bottom of a stone ledge, barely outside the ring of roots, there gaped a narrow opening, a grinning toothless mouth just wide enough to swallow a man whole if he was willing to wriggle like a snake. Ah-cambal discovered the dark portal as a young man and many times since he'd wormed his way across its shadowy threshold. Just beyond the entrance, the narrow hole abruptly widened into a spacious dry cave. Large clay jars littered the extensive low ceilinged chamber and in each jar rested the desiccated remains of corn, chili pepper, cacao, and other offerings. The cave also held small bowls of copal incense, grinding stones, decorated figurines, and scattered here and there the ancient bones of sacrificial victims; both animal and human. At the cavern's deepest extent, a wide passage plunged into darkness.

For generations, until the young Ah-cambal got down on his knees and peered inside, the cave laid forgotten and undisturbed. One peek at the dark interior told him the tale of a place long abandoned, but it also whispered to him of a great power that only slumbered. It was obvious to Ah-cambal that the cave was sacred, a once important site of ceremony and ritual. The opening was a portal to the underworld, the dwelling place of the rain god, the earth gods, the spirits of deceased ancestors, and evil gods of death and disease. Rivers were born inside sacred mountains and flowed to earth through caves. A cave was the source of the corn from which the first humans were created. Creation and death, good and evil all existed inside the cave. Ah-cambal had kept his discovery secret and over the years he'd returned again and again to commune privately with his gods.

Although he was lean and fit, age had increased Ah-cambal's girth, and with each visit the jaws of the cave's mouth seemed to draw a little tighter. Pushing his bundles before him, he squirmed and squeezed his way past the constriction. Once inside, he sat up and made himself comfortable near the entrance. Stray reflected shafts of morning light followed him inside and by their dim glow he laid out his own incense stone, kindled a tiny fire, and performed his morning devotion to Ekchuah. When his prayers were complete, he unrolled his weathered piece of deer hide, and cast his tzintè seeds.

The sense of wellbeing that pervaded Ah-cambal when he first awoke had deepened as he prayed to Ekchuah, but as he stared at the pattern of reddish brown kernels his contentment slipped suddenly away. The pattern troubled him deeply. On the sacred wheel of the Tzolk'in the day was 2 Ik, a day linked to breath, life, and violence. The tzintè seeds spoke only of violence. With a hopeful shrug, Ah-cambal scooped up his seeds and cast them again, but truth is truth. Just as they had when they warned of the strangers from lak'in, the 260 kidney-shaped kernels repeated their pattern. This time the message was again "violence." Unwilling to accept what he saw, he gathered the seeds and for a third time scattered them onto the hide. For a third time they screamed only of violence.

Nervous and badly shaken, Ah-cambal sat unmoving and pondered the message. As before when the seeds spoke of strangers, the reading was too clear and too forceful to be denied. In his experience such strong and unambiguous portents were unprecedented. Ah-cambal knew he was staring at truth and deep inside, in a place beyond logic, he knew what that truth was. Ah Puch, the skeletal lord of death, was abroad in the world. Regardless of what else came to pass, Ah-cambal knew that before the day was through he would stand before the god of protruding ribs and stare into his leering skull-like grin.

Slowly and deliberately he reached into one of his pouches and pulled out a small leaf of paper, a flat smooth rectangle pounded from the bark of the amate (fig) tree. Setting the piece of paper before him, he drew a small razor-sharp flint knife and in a deft movement slit the lobe of his right ear. Without flinching, he slit his other ear in the same manner. As blood began to flow from the small stinging cuts, he picked up the bark paper and one by one collected the crimson drops.

The gods can be petitioned, but before they grant their favors they require sacrifice. Sometimes they're satisfied with the fragrant smoke of copal, a scoop of maize, or a garland of flowers. Other times they demand blood. Ah-cambal's personal patrons were Ekchuah, the traveler's god, and Itzamna (Iguana House), the mighty god of learning who invented writing. For his blood offering, he turned to Hunab Ku, the creator of rivers, trees, and animals, Hunab Ku the faceless, the powerful and the incorporeal.

Once Ah-cambal staunched the last of his dripping blood, he laid the bark paper on his incense stone and lit it with a coal. Smoke rose slowly and his offering drifted upward, spread out like branches of the yaxché tree, and crept away across the ceiling of the cave. Ah-cambal moved to his knees and began to pray.

"Great Hunab Ku, a warrior kneels before you."

"Great Hunab Ku, a servant seeks your mercy."

"Great Hunab Ku, accept a warrior's poor offering."

"Great Hunab Ku, hear a servant's humble petition."

His words, forceful and clear, echoed off the walls of the cavern, disappeared into the dark, and returned to him as though a murmuring multitude had joined in his rhythmic chant.

"Great Hunab Ku, a warrior girds for battle.

"Great Hunab Ku, a servant fears this day.

"Great Hunab Ku, a warrior asks for your strength in the face of violence.

"Great Hunab Ku, a servant begs for your refuge in the face of evil.

On and on went the hypnotic supplication, praising the faceless lord's power and beneficence and petitioning his assistance; Ah-cambal swayed as he spoke, until the last of the blood-soaked bark turned to ash and the last of its sacred smoke faded and was swallowed by the darkness.

As the echoes of his chant died away, he sat back on his heels. The cave was a good place. He felt certain of that. He also felt certain that Hunab Ku had accepted his blood. The message of the seeds was unchanged and Ah Puch was still coming, but he would no longer face the encounter alone.

Outside the cave, Ah-cambal built another small fire over which he heated corn milk. Once the milk thickened to a sort of curd, he added ground pepper to give it spice and broke his fast. Afterwards, he quickly gathered his few possessions, erased the signs of his passing, and resumed his homeward journey.

Despite the warning of the seeds, K'inich Ajaw passed through the heavens and the day that unfolded was hushed and uneventful. Ah-cambal walked for hours without stopping, pausing only to drink water from a gourd slung by a cord across his shoulder. His large woven hamper hung from the tumpline about his head and the butt of his spear, held in his left hand, counted cadence to the rhythm of his footsteps. The only sounds were those of the breeze rustling through the trees, the humming of insects, and the rattle of the cacao beans in his basket.

Although not heavily settled, the land through which he walked was familiar. Ichpaatún was still leagues away, but the few people who lived in this land brought their harvests to the city's markets, came to its celebrations, and honored Ah-cambal's brother as their cacique (chief). Some of the scattered inhabitants lived in isolated huts others in patio groups where four or five humble structures clustered around a small courtyard. Built upon low earthen platforms, most of the huts were constructed of vine-lashed poles and thatch, their walls stuccoed with mud.

Some structures were houses or storage buildings; others were kitchens or small family shrines.

The single families and extended family groups who lived in this out-of-the-way region were farmers. A few were friends or acquaintances that Ah-cambal had visited in the past, but on this day he skirted their homes, avoided all contact, and pressed on toward Ichpaatún.

Much of Ulumil cuz yetel ceh (Yucatán) is a limestone plain covered by dry jungle, a land where rivers hide beneath the ground and where people are hard pressed to scrape an existence from its meager soil. The farmers grew crops of maize, beans, squash, and peppers on small plots called hun vinic (one man) and as Ah-cambal slipped past the widely spaced homesteads, he passed along the edge of one field after another. Some of the plots were recently planted, most lay fallow.

It's a hard life mused Ah-cambal.

With the end of each harvest, farmers must again clear land for the coming planting. They swing heavy stone axes and chop away at vines and saplings, a grasping green tangle that chokes every inch of their fields. Once that long and tedious job is complete, they set fire to the remaining brush and leave the ash to nourish the soil. Finally, they press their seeds into the earth and pray for rain. The arid jungle soil of Ulumil cuz yetel ceh was so poor that each plot could only be used once or twice before it needed to lie fallow for ten or more years until the woody growth returned.

Feeling glad that he didn't work the begrudging land; Ah-cambal hurried along and met no one. That was to his liking, but it also left him curious and more than a little uneasy. Whether clearing land, planting crops, or doing battle with ever encroaching weeds, a farmer's life is one of steady toil. Just the same, Ah-cambal saw no one and field after field that he passed was silent and empty. With each passing hour an unhealthy impression of silence and abandonment grew stronger and his thoughts grew more uneasy.

Something feels wrong. Why are the fields deserted? Where are the people? Why is everything so quiet? Where are the birds? This isn't right.

The breeze that blew so soft and cool with the dawn now gusted, hot and dry, a scratchy uncomfortable thing that set his skin a prickle and left him worried and edgy. The message of the seeds resonated in his skull and his long ground eating stride shortened. He moved from bush to tree. He gripped his spear with sweaty palms. Wary of every shadow, his eyes flitted back and forth and searched for unseen dangers.

At the boundary of yet another field, a bead of cold sweat rolled down his neck. Ah-cambal drew close at a spot where the intervening brush grew thickest. Careful not to make a sound, he stooped, and gazed from leafy concealment across the expanse of a recently planted field. The sight that spread before him made him feel ridiculous, but also much relieved. K'inich Ajaw shone down on the plot and, a few feet from where he crouched, a post carved into a crude likeness of the corn god, Yum Kax, smiled at him with benign goodwill. In the middle of the opening four adults and two children were hard at work, laughing and chatting. The two women, the younger carrying a babe, were pulling weeds with the help of a boy of perhaps thirteen tun (years) and a girl of perhaps seven. Two men, a father and a son, or a father and a son-in-law, were planting a late season crop. Each man carried a small sack on his shoulder and a pointed stick. One and then the other poked a shallow hole with his stick, dropped in a few seeds from his sack, and then covered the hole with the stick or his toe.

Ah-cambal watched the peaceful scene and felt his tensions slide away. Cursing himself for a skittish old fool, he stood up. He intended to hail the farmers and force his way through the screen of brush, but at that exact moment two men stepped from the foliage at the far end of the field. Ah-cambal froze and the malicious gusting breeze rattled the leaves above his head. Amid their rustle he seemed to hear the laughing tinkle of bells, tiny laughing bells, the heralds to Ah Puch's skeletal approach.

The two men carried bows, flint tipped arrows, and short spears with hard flint tipped points. Knives were stuck in their waistbands and they wore deer hide arm guards and half-greaves.

No farmers or hunters these, thought Ah-cambal, *warriors, but not any of Nachan Can's holcánob. Where are they from? Why are they here?*

Wild warlike tattoos covered both their faces. One man wore a dirty cuirass of thickly quilted cotton, the other a chest-plate of cured and hardened tapir hide. From where he crouched, Ah-cambal could just make out a faint design painted on the hide.

The chest-plate was worn and the glyph badly faded, so he shaded his eyes and squinted.

It looks like a rattlesnake; the sun symbol of Tzama'? No, that doesn't make sense. Warriors from Tzama' shouldn't be passing so close to Ichpaatún! Are they part of a diplomatic mission? Scouts? Spies?

From the startled reactions of the farmers, it was obvious that the two armed men were strangers to them also. The older farmer raised one hand in greeting and said something that Ah-cambal couldn't hear. The two newcomers hooted, an ugly guttural guffaw, and the man with the tapir hide chest-plate waved toward the jungle behind him. In response, six more men swaggered into the field. These six were also heavily armed and their bodies were painted in fearsome patterns of red and black. The last man was tugging a thick rope that, like a leash, was tied around the necks of two naked dejected looking men and three women.

Captives!

At the sight of the painted warriors and their miserable prisoners, the young farmer turned, waved wildly, and shrieked at his family.

"Run! Run now!"

Ah-cambal watched rooted by horror and surprise when, expressionless, the cotton clad warrior raised his bow and in one fluid movement notched and loosed an arrow. His bowstring sang gleefully of death, and his shaft flew straight and true to burst bloody and dripping through the young farmer's neck. With a wet cough, the young man staggered twice, half-turned, and sprawled onto the earth of his field.

The two homestead women cowered and screeched. Incited by their fear, five of the painted warriors shouted a harsh war cry and charged forward. The older farmer went mad with anger. He yelled his own battle cry, "Yum Kax! Yum Kax!" brandished his pitiful pointed stick, and ran recklessly to meet them.

Ah-cambal struggled with himself. He wanted to scream! He wanted to burst into the field, and rush to the farmers' aid.

These are my brother's people! These are my people! This is an act of war!

Before impulse thrust him into action, logic raised its ugly head and reason won out over instinct. The odds were too one-sided. He needed to do something, anything, but he knew with absolute certainty that charging from the brush would serve no purpose except to hasten his own death. Hot shame drowned Ah-cambal's rage. The farmers were lost. Nothing that he could do would change that.

Swinging his stick, the old farmer feinted to his left and skillfully parried the thrust of the nearest warrior's spear. His success was momentary. While he focused on the man to his front, another drove a spear deep into his side. With a startled gasp, the farmer groaned and sank to his knees. The red and black painted man who'd stabbed him braced a foot against the mortally wounded man's thigh. With vicious twist, he wrenched his spear loose and grinned as the farmer's savaged body collapsed.

Slumped on the ground, lost in fear and grief, the two women screamed out their anguish and pulled at their hair. The older women scraped ashes from the ground and rubbed them on her face. The other clutched her baby tightly to her breast and whimpered, a loud keening sound. The boy gripped a large stone in his fist and, in a short-lived act of defiance, jumped between the women and the oncoming warriors. The first of the strangers to reach him casually swung a heavy club and killed the boy as easily as one slaughters a trussed-up deer.

The little girl turned and fled, plunged through the dry wall of jungle at the field's edge, and passed only a spear's length from where Ah-cambal crouched unseen. With an angry shout the man with the bow loosed another shaft which chased after her but clattered harmlessly into the brush. Ah-cambal stayed where he was long enough to see the warrior wave at his companions. Then, as two of them started in his direction, he jumped to his feet, shouldered his basket, and ran.

The girl dashed through the undergrowth and darted away from the field in noisy panic. Ah-cambal ran silently behind her.

She's fast, he thought, *but not fast enough and too easy to follow.* After a few moments, he knew that the girl couldn't outrun her pursuers. *I couldn't save the others, but perhaps this one.*

There was only one thing to do. He tossed his basket of cacao beans and counters in the direction that he was running and stepped aside into a thicket. Then, he crouched. Ah-cambal was holcan, a warrior of some renown, and in his time nacon, but almost a k'atun (twenty years) had passed since his last battle and

the weight of his years weighed heavily. The men who were
following were holcánob in their prime.

"Great Hunab Ku," he prayed, "now is a warrior's time of need.
Remember his offering."

His knees felt watery and looking down he was chagrined to
see a slight tremor in his hands. Ah-cambal took a tighter grip on
his spear, shifted his position, and stilled the shake.

Not as old as that, he thought, as he took a deep breath and
settled in to wait.

With the pursuers sprinting close behind, the wait was short.
The two painted men burst out of the jungle, spotted Ah-cambal's
discarded basket, and came to a sudden halt. Certain that they
would hear the wild pounding of his heart, Ah-cambal crouched
as still as stone and held his breath. The two warriors looked
warily about, but despite the deep thud, thud, thud within his
chest, neither man spotted him hidden in the brush. Satisfied that
they were alone, they turned their backs and the shorter of the
two knelt to examine the basket.

It was the moment for which Ah-cambal waited and instantly
he vaulted from the thicket. Without compunction and with his
entire strength behind the blow, he rammed his short spear into
the larger man's back. The warrior screamed. His kneeling
companion turned and, with a look of shock, saw the gore covered
tip of Ah-cambal's spear jut from his friend's chest. Before the
man could react, or regain his feet, Ah-cambal drew his knife and
leapt. He slammed into the painted man and they both rolled
across the ground.

For a moment the surprise and suddenness of his attack gave
Ah-cambal the upper hand. He pinned the man beneath him and
grappled with him slowly forcing his blade toward the man's chest.
Then, his other hand slipped on the warrior's greasy paint. The
younger man rolled violently over and it was Ah-cambal who was
pinned. The smell of the man's sweat filled his nostrils. His
strength began to wane. The warrior grabbed Ah-cambal's knife
hand in both of his and twisted. Ah-cambal managed to hang onto
its handle, but the knife's razor sharp edge crept toward his face.
He was no longer a match for a warrior in his prime and the flint
point moved closer and closer.

Using the last of his strength, Ah-cambal heaved upwards
and, for the barest of instants, dislodged his opponent. At the

same moment his free hand flashed to his girdle, fingers fumbling. The young warrior roared, tightened his grip on Ah-cambal's knife hand, and pressed down. Ah-cambal grunted, strained, and jerked his free hand aloft. His fist clutched his small sacrificial blade. Screaming the name of the god, "Hunab Ku," he drove it into the younger man's flesh. Again and again the small blade rose and fell. Suddenly, the painted warrior went slack. Ah-cambal turned his other knife and shoved it into the man's chest. Heart-blood, thick and warm, flowed over his arm.

Groaning with the effort, he pushed the dead man off himself and staggered to his feet. The other man, still impaled with his spear, lay nearby gasping. A young man might have shouted and crowed, but Ah-cambal felt no need to revel in his victory. He mouthed a silent prayer of thanks to Hunab Ku, and then quickly and efficiently slit the gasping warrior's throat. The gods can always be petitioned, but sometimes they demand blood.

Working quickly, Ah-cambal wiped his knives on the man's girdle, retrieved and cleaned his spear, and walked briskly away. At a spot about a hundred strides from the bodies he once again concealed himself in the brush and settled down to wait.

Shadows lengthened and after a time, moving guardedly, another of the painted men stole into view. Pushing past foliage, he spotted the bloody corpses of his fellows and his eyes grew wide. For a moment he froze in disbelief, and then, abruptly, he dropped to a crouch and cast frightened glances at the surrounding jungle. Face contorted with fear, he turned in one direction and then another. Ah-cambal's discarded basket still lay close at hand and the painted man nudged it with his foot. The basket rocked from side to side and the beans and counters rattled. Cautiously the man stooped and peered inside. Ah-cambal could hear his surprised gasp as he recognized the contents. Still looking furtively about, the painted man scooped up the basket and, with many a backward glance, scuttled back the way he'd come.

Ah-cambal watched until he was out of sight and until he could no longer hear the sounds of his hurried flight. The strangers had taken valuable captives and they'd found a costly prize, but, unexpectedly, they'd also been bloodied by an unknown enemy. Ah-cambal felt certain that they would weigh their gains against the risk of any further pursuit and that their decision would be to his liking.

The loss of the cacao and counters in his basket was a disappointment, but when weighed against the day's possible outcomes he considered it a fair trade. His knees were stiff and creaked as he stood and stepped from concealment, and his ribs and knife hand were sore and painful.

But, I'm still alive, he thought, *and that's another fair trade.*

It was near dusk when he found the girl. Like a sad-eyed little sub (agouti) she'd gone to ground and wedged herself into a small crevice between two large rocks. Her dirt covered knees were drawn tight against her chest and her scratched arms wrapped about them as though trying to pull them even closer. She quivered and looked up at him with dark serious eyes. Ah-cambal bent down and smiled in what he hoped was a grandfatherly way.

"Hello there," he said. At first the girl said nothing and tried to squeeze herself further into her hole. "It's alright," he soothed. "You're safe now. No one will hurt you."

She eyed him suspiciously. "Are you one of the bad men?"

"No child, I'm not," he replied. "Give me your hand."

He held out his own and wiggled his fingers. For a moment the girl did nothing, but then Ah-cambal wiggled his fingers again.

"I'm a friend child. There's nothing to fear."

Slowly, cautiously, she extended her own small hand. Ah-cambal took it in his large rough one and gently helped her to her feet.

"There, isn't that better?" he said. The girl said nothing, but she smiled shyly. "Can you walk?" he asked.

"I can walk," she quietly replied.

"Good, then we must be going."

He again took her hand and began to lead her away. After a few steps the girl stopped in her tracks.

"Grandfather," she said, "where are we going?"

Ah-cambal looked down at his small charge and smiled. "Home child, we're going home."

Chapter 6

Bay of the Turtles

The 28th of May, Year of Our Lord 1511

"I see it too!" Captain Valdivia slapped Gonzalo on his shoulder. "I think it is land. God in heaven be praised! Quick, take a sounding. If there's a bottom, we're saved."

"Yes Captain."

With his fingers crossed for luck, Gonzalo tossed a weighted line over the longboat's side and held his breath as the lead descended. The line fed through his fingers. First one marker and then another disappeared into the inky water. Gonzalo counted as they slipped past.

"One braza (fathom), two brazas, three, four, five," suddenly, the line stopped sliding over his palm and Gonzalo stared at the last marker still in his hand. "It's six Captain! Only six fathoms. It is land! It's..."

Gonzalo tried to say more but tears choked off his words. Despite his earlier harsh exchange with Fray Geronimo, and the secret hope buried deep in his heart, he'd slowly allowed himself a brief vision of surrender, of giving over to death. To sight land and to know that it was within their reach felt like rising from the grave.

Valdivia went to his knees in the bottom of the boat and prayed. Gonzalo started to join him, but to his surprise found that he couldn't. His early brush with the priesthood had estranged him from God. When required, he still went through the motions of his faith. He said confession regularly, attended mass, and bowed his head when the Sacraments passed, but otherwise his beliefs were strained and shallow.

Let the captain pray, he thought. *God has never once given me encouragement, even in my darkest hours. I'm grateful for my salvation, but I'll not offer thanks to a god who needlessly kills good men like Juan Pintero and Alvaro Fernandez.*

Gonzalo wiped the tears from his eyes. "Captain, shouldn't we wake the others and try for the shore?"

Valdivia pulled himself back up onto his seat and cupped a hand to his ear. "Listen Aroça. What do you hear?"

"Nothing Captain, I..."

"Shush!"

Valdivia remained silent, so Gonzalo did the same. Far off, near the edges of his perception, something was pounding, a dull rhythmic sound, a continuous crashing rumble.

"Yes, I hear it. What is it?"

"It's breakers," said the captain. "It'd be a sorry thing to survive starvation and thirst, only to be dashed upon rocks in the dark."

"So what do we do?" asked Gonzalo.

"We stay at sea until daylight," answered Valdivia. "I think we're about a league away. Rouse Vasco and Xavier and we'll row parallel to the land until there's light enough to see."

Gonzalo squeezed past the considerable snoring bulk of Domingo Vizcaino. Then, he stretched his leg and stepped over the hidalgo, Andres Avellaneda, who was sprawled insensate in the bottom of the boat. Xavier Dorantes lay slumped on his bench, his thick arms resting on the gunwale, cradling his head. Gonzalo reached out and patted the seaman's back.

"Xavier, wake up."

The younger Dorantes brother stayed as he was and neither awoke nor moved. Gonzalo gave him a hearty shake.

"Xavier!"

In response, the seaman's arms slid from the gunwale. His head lolled to the side. Amid a rattle from the oar shipped at his side, he slipped off his bench and collapsed, wedged at Gonzalo's feet.

"Oh Jesus," grunted Valdivia, watching from the tiller. "Is he alive?"

Gonzalo bent over and felt for breath and then a pulse. He found neither. "He's gone Captain."

Valdivia groaned like a man in pain. On the other side of the bench the dead man's brother remained still and unmoving. Gonzalo grabbed his shoulders and gave him a hard shake.

"Vasco! Vasco for God's sake, wake up!"

When he released him, Vasco also sagged and fell forward.

"This is senseless!" yelled Gonzalo, looking at the sky. "What kind of a god are you?" Words spilled painfully from his heart. "These men were kind! They worked hard! They were honest! They believed in you!" He stood up and shook his fists at the heavens.

He'd railed at the Almighty in the past, but never before with such anger. "I'm through with you!" he shouted. "Do you hear me? Through! You're no god of mine! You don't deserve my devotion! You don't deserve anyone's devotion!"

Spent, Gonzalo fell to his knees, put his face in his hands, and again wept. The unexpected deaths of the Dorantes brothers also shocked and stunned Captain Valdivia, but he was equally appalled by Gonzalo's blasphemy.

"Aroça! You don't mean that! You're crazed. You don't know what you're saying. We can't know the mind of God! He chooses a path for each of us. Just because we can't understand his choice doesn't mean the choice is wrong. He's saved us. He's brought us to land! Fray Aguilar will say words over Vasco and Xavier, and we'll bury their bodies on dry land, but you, you must pray for God's forgiveness. And, when the time is right you must do penance!"

I've done my penance and I'll pray for nothing, thought Gonzalo as he straightened up. "Penance, yes Captain, but not now," he said. "What must we do for now?"

"Now, in spite of everything, you must row," answered Valdivia. "Rouse Domingo, at least we know he's still alive and can probably still pull a good oar."

Gonzalo shoved at the good natured cooper, and mid-snore the large man blinked and sat up.

"Gonzalo, where...what is it?" he asked, rubbing crust from his eyes. "It's still dark, why'd you wake me?"

"Xavier and Vasco are dead, Domingo. We've sighted land and you and I need to row."

The big man stared about shocked and bewildered.

"Land? Vasco and Xavier dead?"

"Yes," sighed Gonzalo, "both of them, but the rest of us are saved. Look!" and he pointed to the west.

During the next two hours, Captain Valdivia steered a course parallel to the shore while Gonzalo and Domingo pulled weakly at the oars. Inch by inch, refusing to be rushed, the morning sun crept slowly into the sky. The two rowers worked in silence, watching and waiting as the world around them shed its night colors of purple and black and cloaked itself in hopeful morning hues of pink and orange. Time moved at the pace of a snail, and the rhythmic rise and fall of the oars marked its passage. Gonzalo felt dizzy and tired.

I can see the land. I can't hear the breakers. I can see trees. Why doesn't the Captain turn?

The wait seemed endless, a repetitive limbo compassed by the arc of his dripping oar. With each passing minute Gonzalo's sense of anticipation stretched and grew, becoming first palpable and then almost intolerable. Just when he thought he could no longer stand it, Valdivia swung the tiller. Daylight burst full upon them and the longboat's prow pointed toward the distant coast.

Exhausted, but expectant and resolute, Gonzalo and Domingo dipped their oars again and yet again. The shore approached with agonizing slowness, first a league away, then a half a league, then less; all at once, they were rowing among gentle rolling breakers. At a shout from Valdivia, they gave a last determined pull. The boat slipped neatly across a shallow reef and floated into the calm turquoise waters of a wide sheltered bay.

Gonzalo saw a pair of large brightly colored sea turtles gliding beneath its surface. Overhead, the sky was an inverted bowl of burnished burning blue and before him stretched a beach, a quiet moon shaped crescent of white sand and crushed coral. Beyond the waterline, leafy palm trees waved backwards and forwards over an explosion of luxuriant jungle.

Gonzalo, Domingo, and Valdivia crawled through the boat shaking and waking the others. Of the seven, few of them were conscious, and after having gone six full days without water, and nine without food, only two among them were fit to stand. Nevertheless, Captain Valdivia was grateful and, raising his hands, gave thanks to God that no one else was lost. Prodded and shaken, almost all the men came to themselves, and as the bottom of the longboat scraped against the sand, they began to slip over the side and crawl through the warm shallow water.

The bodies of Xavier and Vasco were left behind in the boat, and Gonzalo along with Domingo and Valdivia, began to help the others drag themselves away from the lapping surf.

Of the ten men who survived the wreck of the *Viñas de la Barca,* and then their time at sea, Geronimo de Aguilar and the cabin boy, Pedro de Urtubia, were the only other two able to walk without help. Diego de Arana, the master-at-arms, draped an arm over Geronimo's shoulder and together they waded and stumbled ashore. Aguilar was dragging the other man away from the water when, without warning, Arana jerked backwards and shouted.

"Savages!"

Not thirty paces away a group of three women and several children stood stock still, slack jawed, and silent. They all appeared healthy and of good build, dark hair and dark eyes. The children were golden brown and naked as the day they were born. The women, also dark skinned, wore skirts, but were bare from the waist up, their torsos tattooed, except for their breasts. One woman carried a babe astride her hip, and the other three held large woven baskets.

For a moment, no one moved or spoke. The castaway Spaniards stared in curious disbelief and the women and children did the same. Neither party made a sound; then, Fray Geronimo beckoned, called to the natives, and broke the spell.

"Come, come, we mean you no harm. We wish your help. In the name of our Lord Jesus Christ and the Holy Virgin, I entreat you."

At the sound of the friar's voice, the women and children fluttered like a covey of flushed quail, dropped their baskets and other belongings, and, without uttering a word, fled into the underbrush.

"Stop them!" cried Valdivia. "Don't let them get away!"

His order went unheeded. Too weak to give chase, Gonzalo and the others collapsed and lay in the sand, simply grateful to be alive.

After a bit, Domingo hoisted up his considerable bulk and shuffled up the beach to investigate the baskets. One by one, smiling a wide lopsided grin, he carried them back to his companions. When the baskets proved to be overflowing with turtle eggs, Geronimo, who was on his knees praising God and all the blessed saints for their salvation, deemed them a miracle, a divine gift like manna to the Israelites. Domingo also proudly displayed a large stoppered gourd that one of the women had discarded. The jug was full of fresh clean water. Immediately its plug was pulled and the vessel passed from hand to hand. Each man felt that he could drain the gourd, but in turn each took only his share and then reluctantly handed it on. At the same time, the starving men attacked the baskets. They poked holes in the leathery shells and sucked the eggs with exclamations of thanks and delight. After the gourd was drained and the last egg emptied, the men felt somewhat revived and by ones and twos they dragged themselves into the shade of trees at the edge of the beach.

Gonzalo helped Rodrigo Sánchez de Segovia, an assistant to Valdivia who'd been in charge of keeping the expedition's accounts, to sit and then he sat down beside him. He braced his back against a palm trunk, stretched out his legs, let his mind go empty, and gazed back toward the water. The sand glowed painfully white in the glare of the morning sun and sparkles and shimmers danced across the clear water of the bay. Once or twice, he thought he saw the turtles poke their heads above the surface. The longboat, with its lifeless crew of two, bobbed and scraped against the shore. Frigate birds soared overhead and from behind him the jungle buzzed with the comings and goings of insects. His gaze returned to the Dorantes brothers, to all the world a pair of drunken sailors happily asleep at their watch.

There's beauty here, thought Gonzalo. *If we're all to die, this is as good a place as any. At least we're on dry land and our last meal wasn't kelp.*

After a moment Juan Suarez from the town of Zafra, the *Viñas'* last able seaman, flopped down next to him.

"Well Gonzalo, they say you landed in Darien with Ojeda, and they say you fought the savages, what are our chances?"

Gonzalo stared at the sailor, "I don't know Juan. These aren't the same people, but I can tell you if I ever see another poisoned arrow, it'll be too soon."

"Do you think they'll attack us?" asked Suarez wide eyed.

"How the hell should I know?" snapped Gonzalo. "I don't even know where we are?"

"It's has to be somewhere on the coast of Cabo Caloche (Yucatán)," threw in the exhausted Rodrigo. "I'm pretty sure we drifted past Isla de Cozumel, and I'd bet my purse this isn't Cuba."

"Oh Christ," moaned Suarez, "how will I ever get home to Zafra?"

"Zafra," laughed Gonzalo weakly, "I wouldn't worry about Zafra Juan, we'll be lucky if any of us lives out the week!"

"Enough of that Aroça," barked Captain Valdivia, who sat nearby listening, "The lord God saw fit to save our miserable lives and it's for a reason! I'm a procurator for his majesty King Ferdinand and although I may have lost my ship and his twenty thousand ducats in gold, I do not mean to lose this opportunity! We are going to survive! Another ship will come, and as soon as we are all fit, I mean to claim this land and all it contains in the name of our king!"

Gonzalo stared at the captain, incredulous, "What?"

"Here, here!" chimed in the master-at-arms. "Are we not Spaniards? You should be ashamed Aroça."

"I agree with the captain and Señor De Arana," threw in the hidalgo, Andres Avellaneda, who was now much recovered. "We've been saved because God wants us to prosper. He wants to give us this land and he wants us to bring his righteous word to its benighted people."

"His name be praised," whispered Fray Aguilar.

A twisted smile played across Gonzalo's face and he bit his tongue to hold back a caustic retort. He respected most of his companions, but at the moment he also thought of them as naïve fools. Latecomers to the New World, one and all, they weren't there when he'd landed with Ojeda and three hundred brothers-in-arms only to watch two hundred of them die penniless and suffering in the muck of Darien.

I'm a castaway among lunatics, only ten of us alive. All of us three-quarters starved and yet they rant about conquest and conversions. I think a week is about right.

The two years of Gonzalo's stint as an escudero weighed heavily on his mind. His hopes and dreams were reduced to rubble, and the future that stretched before him promised nothing but further hardship and uncertainty. Before he wrote down his name and agreed to come to the New World, his life was often fraught with trouble and difficulty; nevertheless, that old life now seemed infinitely preferable to the dangerous reality of his present situation.

Ojeda's expedition had sailed from Cadiz, but it was Seville with its enormous wealth and grinding poverty that Gonzalo thought of as home. Sitting in the sand, listening to the farfetched ramblings of his companions, he wrapped himself in a wistful longing. He missed Seville. He missed the opulently dressed nobles and the pícaros (vagabonds), the beggars and the prostitutes, the luxurious palaces and the squalor, the religious fervor and the open sensuality. He missed the muddy bustling city. He missed it all. The ground was solid beneath him, but

Gonzalo felt as though his world had crumbled away and a gigantic pit had opened beneath his feet. Dark, empty, and seductive, the pit beckoned.

Why did I ever leave Spain?

Just before he gave over fully to despair, a commotion drew him back from its brink. While the men had talked, Valdivia's cabin boy, Pedro, had wandered off by himself. Unexpectedly, he now ran back, and burst among the group, excited and breathless.

"Captain! Captain!"

"Yes boy, what is it?" answered Valdivia. "Spit it out."

"It's a village Captain, and there ain't nobody there!"

"A village Urtubia, where?" demanded the master-at-arms.

"Right here, close down the path," gushed the boy holding up a small fish, "and look, there's stuff to eat."

Everyone struggled to their feet and, finding the path, followed Pedro. For a hundred meters they shuffled and stumbled as he led them along a narrow track that wound through dry-leaf jungle and then skirted the edge of a small plant choked lagoon. Andres Avellaneda started to lag behind, when abruptly the way opened and, one by one, the men shambled into a wide patio of bare hard-packed earth. The edge of the lagoon bordered the open space on one side; on the other side stood several sturdy huts. They were oval in shape; made of spaced cane poles, lashed together with vines and plastered over with mud. The roofs were constructed of a heavy palm thatch and steeply pitched to throw off rain.

"Well done again Urtubia!" exclaimed Valdivia mussing the cabin boy's hair. "Well done indeed!"

Just as Pedro reported, the huts appeared unoccupied and their owners were nowhere to be seen. While everyone else stood about, nervous and unsure, Hernando de Esquivel, the *Viñas'* balding steward, entered the closest of the huts to reconnoiter. A moment later he emerged triumphant, holding aloft a small haunch of smoked venison.

"Look at this, boys!"

The sight of the meat produced a ragged cheer from the men and set off an excited search. The castaways rummaged through the compound, ransacked each of the dirt-floored huts in turn, and dragged all of the foodstuffs they laid hands on into the open.

They found six large clay jugs of fresh water, several baskets of dried fish, many ears of dried maize, beans, dried squash, more turtle eggs, and several plump fruits that resembled pebbly green pears. Behind one of the huts, Juan Suarez also discovered an undersized but fat dog, tied to a stake, another small leg of venison, and an enormous freshly gutted fish hanging from an eave.

There were also stacks of firewood and cook fires smoldering in two of the huts, but the castaways ignored them. The men were too tired and too hungry to cook. Instead they sat in the shade in front of the huts and without ceremony or conversation, devoured whatever foods could be eaten just as they were. The haunches of venison disappeared first and those were followed in short order by raw fish, turtle eggs, and the pebbly green pears. Bodies, worn, exhausted, and sated for the first time in days, most of the men lay down, and right where they were, drifted off to sleep.

The party's solitary military professional, Diego de Arana took it upon himself to stay awake and mount a guard. For a time Gonzalo and Hernando de Esquivel sat beside the master-at-arms and kept him company.

"Well 'Guerrero', what do you think of our chances now?" asked Arana.

Gonzalo winced at the jibe, but kept his answer noncommittal. "I feel better with my belly full."

"Me too," said Hernando, "I never knew water and raw fish could taste so good. Of course we can't eat like this at every meal, but if we're careful the food here should last us several days."

"What then?" asked Gonzalo. "We don't know the country. We don't have fishing tackle. We have a few weapons, but nothing that will serve us for hunting."

"You heard the captain and the hidalgo; God will provide!" asserted the master-at-arms. "This may have started as a disaster, but now it's our chance to go home rich!"

"Diego, you can't believe that!" answered Gonzalo. "Look at where we are. We're nearly destitute. We know nothing about this land, nothing about its people."

"That may well be," countered the master-at-arms, "but I, for one, am not ready to curl up and die. Just because that idiot Ojeda led you to ruin and let most of his other men starve and get slaughtered, doesn't mean we have to follow them into perdition. What's wrong with you Guerrero? Are you scared? I thought you were supposed to be a fighter."

"Yes," said Gonzalo, "I'm scared witless, and if you had any sense, you'd be scared too. There won't be any ship! Sun and thirst have addled your brains. Don't you understand? This is it!" Gonzalo waved his arms at the surrounding jungle. "If the natives don't kill us and if we don't die of starvation, this is it. None of us will ever see Spain again!"

"Do you hear that, Hernando?" snorted Arana. "Witless Guerrero plans to stay here!"

"Well, if he's not going back, do you think we should split his share?" laughed the steward.

Gonzalo dragged himself up and walked away. "You're both mad!"

The steward and the master-at-arms roared with laughter until Valdivia snapped at them.

"If you're going to guard do it silently and shut up so the rest of us can rest."

At dusk, Domingo Vizcaino carried hot coals and wood from one of the huts and built a large fire in the open patio. The evening wasn't cool, but just the same the castaways crowded around the blaze to be cheered by its warmth and light. Hernando Equivel filled an earthen pot with brackish water and dried beans and set it in the heart of the fire to boil. Juan Suarez, meanwhile, slaughtered the fat dog he'd found and, with minimal help from Rodrigo Sánchez, placed it on a spit to cook. Pedro poked squash into the embers at the edge of the fire to roast and the men settled down to wait.

After so many days without food their bodies had made short work of their previous meal, and more than a few stomachs growled as they watched Juan use a flat board to catch sizzling globs of fat as they dripped from the roasting dog.

The dog was still bloody when Hernando declared the beans soft enough to eat. Since no one cared to wait, Suarez declared that his contribution was also done and began to carve it into bite sized chunks. For a time silence reigned while the men again nourished their starved bodies. Some ate their portions with ravenous abandon; others, like Gonzalo, ate slowly and savored the flavors and textures of the food.

With the heat of the fire and a second good meal under their belts, most of the men recovered their spirits if not their strength. Gonzalo had just swallowed his last piece of squash and licked the last bit of grease from his fingers when Andres Avellaneda called for everyone's attention. Among the first to finish his meal, the hidalgo had disappeared into one of the huts while the others were still eating. He now stood before them holding a tiny wooden coffer, cunningly carved into the likeness of a frog.

"Look, here is the first of our treasure!"

So saying, he poured the contents of the box into his palm. Cupped in his hand were nine good sized pearls and a tiny golden bell no larger than an almond meat.

"Pearls and gold!" he crowed.

The other men crowded around the hidalgo and jostled one another to get a better look.

"Captain Valdivia, I salute you," said the pompous hidalgo. "You were right. We shall all return to Spain as rich men!"

The sight of the gold trinket, the handful of pearls, and Avellaneda's fanciful talk, overcame the men's exhaustion and launched them on another frenzied search of the huts. This time, everything was overturned and inspected. Baskets were emptied, mats were yanked up, and holes were dug. Their only finds were three small clay idols that Geronimo smashed, and one of wood that he threw into the fire. Their failure to find more plunder failed to dampen the Spaniards' hopes and soon they were squatted back around the fire passing around Avellaneda's tiny bell and talking as if it was already a homeward bound galleon full of gold. Gonzalo removed himself from the group. He hadn't joined in their hunt and he felt depressed and sick to his stomach.

Christ, he thought *here I am twenty-four and I'll probably never see twenty-five. No family, no money, and I'm marooned with inmates of an insane asylum.* He sat down away from the others and hugged his knees to his chest. *Maybe Juan was the lucky one, a gulp or two of warm sea water, and a quick end.*

Gonzalo let his head sag and held his face in his hands. After a time, someone moved near to him and he looked up to see Geronimo. The fire had died and in the gathering dark the friar's expression was impossible to read. Gesturing for permission, the Franciscan sat on the ground. For several minutes he remained very still, and then Gonzalo heard him speak.

"Aroça, is everything alright?"

"Yes, fine," lied Gonzalo. He felt Geronimo stare at him in the darkness.

"None of us are fine, Gonzalo, but we mustn't give in to despair. On the longboat I was ready to give up, but I was wrong. God has saved us for some purpose."

"And, what purpose is that; to build a ship from palm leaves and sea shells, fill it with stolen gold, and sail back to Spain?"

"Gonzalo, despite what you might think, I'm not a fool. I recognize our plight as well as you do. None of us may ever again see Spain, but I also know that in a mind filled with daydreams, there's a little less room for fear. The other men are scared too and their castle-in-the-sky visions of gold and pearls offer them more comfort than the bitter reality of your harsh truths. If the lie gives them hope, can it be that wrong?"

Gonzalo sat silently. He knew his own long-held daydreams quite well, but at this time and place they felt equally absurd. If he was sure of anything, it was that there was no place for a fool's fantasies in their present world.

"Very well," he finally sighed. "The others have their daydreams and I have my harsh truths. What of you?"

"Señor Avellaneda is a pretentious ass," replied the friar, "but he spoke truth when he said that God wants to bring the idolaters of this land into his fold. I find my hope in faith, not greed. I know our chances are slim, but I will put my trust in our Lord and do my best to spread his message of salvation."

"Whether a person wears blinders of gold or blinders of faith, they're still blind," grumbled Gonzalo. "If we're to survive, we need to see the world for what it is."

"Time enough for that tomorrow, Aroça; for now let's sleep with our bellies full and give thanks to God for our deliverance from the tempest."

With that, Geronimo levered himself up and walked away. Gonzalo looked at the sky and it was full of stars.

No one's home, he thought, *and nothing is preordained. Luck, good or bad, is just luck, and if I survive it'll be my own doing.*

His mood was still dark, but the thought that he was the author of his own destiny somehow lifted a cloud. To his slight surprise, Gonzalo realized that he was glad that he'd survived the storm, and also that he intended to live.

Geronimo is right, he thought, *time enough tomorrow.*

Gonzalo got up, and walked into one of the darkened huts. Inside, other men were already fast asleep and snoring. Lying down quietly, he stretched out on a mat of woven grass. Overhead, stars wheeled through the empty heavens.

Chapter 7

Xamanzamá

11 Bak'tun 14 K'atun 11 Tun 2 Uinal 5 K'in

(May 28, 1511)

Itzel (Rainbow) collapsed on the ground out of breath while the other women and children plopped down beside her.

"Did you see?" gasped Eme (Joy) as she settled her baby onto her lap, "the tall skinny one waved its arms, made signs, and then they all screeched! What were they? Do you think that they're gods?"

"I don't know what they are," huffed Itzel. "They look like men, but their faces... did you see their faces? They're so pale and they're all covered with hair!"

"I'm scared," said Eme. "Did you see the horrible way they limped and crawled from the sea and those awful voices? They're so ugly. Maybe they're demons who've escaped from Metnal."

Upon mention of Metnal two of the older children, who were listening, began to whimper.

"Hush," hissed Itzel, "you need to stay quiet."

"They look like monkeys. Maybe they serve the monkey gods Hun Chowen and Hun Batz," whispered Sacnite (White Flower). "What if the signs and screeching were a curse? What should we do? Do you think they followed us?"

"I don't think so, I think they stayed on the beach," said Itzel quietly, "but we should find Makiq and Ikan and tell them everything that's happened."

Sacnite's husband was far from home hunting for deer, but Itzel's husband, Makiq, and Eme's husband, Ikan, were pulling weeds in a field that was only a brisk walk away.

"Come, we should hurry."

It took time for Itzel and the others to locate Makiq and Ikan and still longer for them to convince the two laughing farmers that monkey demons had accosted their wives on the beach. When both men began to shuffle from side to side and snort and scratch, Itzel had enough.

"Makiq, I'm warning you, if you don't stop this instant, I'll take that digging stick away and give you a beating. The same goes for you Ikan."

"Oh calm down Chan Itzel (Little Rainbow)," said Makiq, "it's been a long morning, we're just having fun."

Itzel's scowl could have stopped the clouds in the sky. Faced with her plainly growing wrath, Makiq and Ikan quit imitating monkeys, stifled their skeptical sniggers, and reluctantly agreed to walk with her back to the bay.

Eme flatly refused to go. She sat on the ground with a pouty face and stated in a voice that brooked no argument that both she and Sacnite would stay right where they were.

"I saw those awful creatures once, and once is enough! You three go if you must, but the children stay here with Sacnite and me. See that you come back!"

By the time Itzel and the two men reached the beach K'inich Ajaw was high in the sky and the expanse of powdery white sand was deserted and silent.

"Well," said Makiq, "it looks like the same beach to me, lots of sand, no monkey gods."

For a moment Itzel stared at the sand mystified and wondered if she and the other women had imagined the hairy strangers. Broad smiles were beginning to spread across the two men's faces when she spotted the longboat.

"Look," she whispered, jabbing her finger toward the water, "there!"

Inch by inch, the afternoon ebb tide was tugging the Spaniard's longboat away from the shore and out of the bay. The heavy boat was unlike any craft that either of the farmers had ever seen. With each gentle swell it rolled from side to side and, still slumped at their posts, the mute Dorantes brothers swayed in rhythm to its motion.

"Is that them?" asked Ikan. "Are those the monkey gods? What are they doing?"

"I thought there were more," said Makiq.

"I don't know," replied, Itzel. "Maybe those two are leaving, but... there were more."

"Then where are they?" demanded Makiq."

"I don't know. I don't know. I don't know," growled Itzel. "How should I know where?" Then she saw the baskets. "There," she whispered, "our baskets."

Glancing furtively about, the three crossed the beach. The abandoned baskets rested on the sand surrounded by a discarded carpet of empty turtle eggs. "You see," she said, "the others were here. They ate all the eggs we collected!"

Ikan picked up the empty water jug and shook it. "They also drank your water."

Makiq stared at the sand. A maze of footprints led up the beach to the palms at the edge of the jungle and from there the footprints wandered off to the right.

"Look," he said, "they went toward our homes."

"I think you're right," answered Ikan starting to move up the beach, "their tracks lead toward the path. We should follow them."

"No, wait," said Itzel, "I don't think we should go by the path. We should circle around away from the lagoon where the jungle is thicker and we can stay hidden."

"My wife is right," said Makiq. "We should go silently and see but not be seen."

Several minutes later Ikan knelt, held still, and quietly parted the leaves in front of him. What he saw took his breath away. As preposterous as their story had sounded, his wife and the others had spoken the truth.

"See," he whispered to Makiq. "It's as they said!"

Some of the monkey gods were slumbering next to a large fire that they'd built in the middle of the homestead's plaza. Three were sitting nearby gesturing and speaking in a guttural tongue. Judging from the sounds of snoring, still others were asleep inside huts.

"Great Chac," murmured Makiq, "they've burnt our firewood and ransacked our homes."

"Look at the bones!" hissed Itzel. "They've eaten the dog, the venison, and even the fish you caught this morning."

"Metnal take them," swore Ikan under his breath. "They've eaten everything. Why would they do such a thing?"

Makiq was a cautious farmer and as such he carefully memorized the sacred Tzolk'in, reading its turns and counting its days so that he knew the auspicious signs under which to sow his seeds, the proper occasions to make his offerings, and best time to bring in the harvest.

"Today is 5 Chik'chan," he whispered to Itzel and Ikan. "It's a day of ill omens, a day that belongs to the sky serpent! People born under its sign are paupers, ragged beggars, wanderers with no home of their own. They live always on handouts and theft, depending solely on what they can take from others. In this they imitate the snake that goes about homeless and naked, exposed to the sun and wind, living today in one hole and tomorrow another. Perhaps these strangers are evil servants of the snake."

"Good or ill, whatever they are, the coming of these creatures must be an important omen," said Itzel. "We must collect Eme, Sacnite, and the children and go to Xamanzamá so that we can tell the Batab Kinich (Ruler Eye of the Sun) what we've seen."

The two men nodded agreement, Ikan quietly let the branches slip back into place, and without another sound the three watchers slipped away.

Much later, Ac Yanto, the self-styled Batab Kinich, shifted uncomfortably on his woven mat and grunted his disgust.

"All lies, I don't believe a word of it!"

As befitted his station, the batab (minor ruler) of Xamanzamá (North of Tzamá) was seated with his back to the brilliant frescos which adorned the whitewashed front wall of his large and commodious house. The thatch of its ample roof extended out over his head and shielded the whole of the patio from K'inich Ajaw's hot breath. Seated in a loose semi-circle in front of him were his Ah Cuchcab (council of minor nobles and priests).

"Why would gods appear before a bunch of peasants? More likely those diggers drank themselves into a stupor and imagined the whole thing. Hairy monkey gods eating their food, it's absurd!"

Xamanzamá's high priest, Ah K'in Cutz (Wild Turkey), leaned forward.

"I won't deny that their story is fanciful, but I don't think that we should dismiss it outright. I know this farmer, Makiq. I've spoken to him several times when he sought my advice about planting and other spiritual matters. He always struck me as sober and level-headed; frankly I don't think he's imaginative enough to have made this up."

Ac Yanto hated to be contradicted. *Cutz is too presumptuous, too full of himself. He should use my title when we're in council. He thinks himself powerful and dangerous, but I'm dangerous too. His day will come.* The Batab's face betrayed none of these thoughts.

"Perhaps, perhaps," he mused. "What council does the ah k'in offer?"

Several of the Ah Cuchcab had been whispering and before the priest could respond, the oldest of the group spoke up.

"Lord, if there is any truth to the peasants' wild tale shouldn't we send a messenger to Tzamá to inform Yajawk'ak' (Lord of the Fire)."

Ac Yanto was instantly livid. As batab he ruled supreme over the social, religious, and military life of Xamanzamá, but it was Ah Kumix Uinic the previous ruler of Tzamá and the father of the current Halach Uinic (Great Man) who had appointed him to his position. In truth, his main responsibility was to make sure that his people paid the regular tributes that Tzamá demanded. Mention of his sovereign always made Ac Yanto feel smaller and less important.

"I am ruler here!" he bellowed. "Do you think we are such children that we must go running to Ah Tabai whenever we see a shadow?"

The suggestion withered in the face of the batab's anger. The council remained silent, squirmed uneasily, and one or two edged away from the old man who'd spoken.

"Have the Nacon assemble his warriors!" shouted Ac Yanto. "And, send for my chair and carriers. We shall all go to these so called monkey gods and see for ourselves."

"Lord, do you think that is wise?" said Ah K'in Cutz in an insinuating tone.

The Ah Cuchcab all looked shocked and Ac Yanto spluttered, "What do you mean priest?"

"Why Great Lord, until we know more," said Ah K'in Cutz, "perhaps it would be better that we proceed with caution. Send the Nacon, your two lesser chilánes (priests), and a large force of holcánob, but don't accompany them yourself."

"And why should I remain behind ah k'in?" snapped the petulant batab.

Ah K'in Cutz regarded the ruler. *Once this man was someone to respect, a powerful warrior; now he's all flab. Rich food and sycophants have made him fat and stupid.*

Speaking softly, the priest continued, "Think of it Lord, the farmers describe these strangers as servants of the monkey gods and old legends speak of Kukulkán returning from the east. If these creatures are indeed gods or even some kind of divine messengers, they may well present a great danger. Until their motives are clear I counsel you not to risk your illustrious self in their presence. On the other hand, if the tale proves false is it not better to have others rush out and look the fool?"

Ac Yanto stared at the sly priest. *Damn you Wild Turkey*, he thought. *Why must you always be cunning and right?*

Gesturing toward the others, he spoke in a voice that was much calmer than he felt.

"Ah K'in Cutz's council is wise. Send only for the Nacon. The rest of you leave. The ah k'in and I will tell the Nacon what must be done."

Chapter 8

A Savage Host

The 29th of May, Year of Our Lord 1511

Gonzalo opened his eyes to a bright morning sun whose strong slanted rays streamed through the open door of the hut in which he'd slept. Before true wakefulness returned, he rolled up onto an elbow and was shocked to discover himself lying on a well-worn mat of woven reeds. His blurry sleep encrusted vision slowly revealed a thatched roof above him, mud plastered walls, bodies of other men sprawled on a hard-packed earth floor, and a strange disarray of scattered belongings. None of what he saw made any sense. Still fatigued from his ordeal and groggy from sleep, he could conjure no recollection of how he might have come to such an unlikely place.

Confusion and then alarm lay siege to his exhausted sleep muddled mind and for a tottering moment he felt himself balance on a knife edge of panic. Tightness constricted the back of his throat.

What Hell is this?

Then, someone outside stirred and one of the nearby sleepers coughed. The mundane sounds washed away his unreasoning fear and memories flooded in to take its place.

The storm, the longboat, Juan Pintero, so many companions dead; we were shipwrecked.

Gonzalo groaned and crawled to his feet. His muscles were sore and stiff and protested at the movement; otherwise he found that his legs and hands were steady. As he took stock of himself he was surprised to realize that his aches were minor and, that for the first time since the *Viñas* floundered, a sleep had left him somewhat refreshed.

Shipwrecked and tired, he thought, *but I'm alive and my body is whole. That's as good a beginning as any.*

Buoyed by sudden and unwarranted optimism, he walked to the door and stepped out into the sunlight.

Someone had stirred the night's fire back to life, adding fresh wood, and a lazy ribbon of light, blue-grey, smoke drifted slowly upward through still morning air. A multitude of birds chattered excitedly in the trees and young Pedro de Urtubia squatted at the fire's edge intent upon three large squash and several small ears of maize that he was roasting on the coals. A few paces away, Captain Valdivia stood in quiet conversation with Diego de Arana. Gonzalo noted that the captain and the master-at-arms both looked much recovered and, although somewhat haggard, they appeared very near to their old selves. Across the patio, Fray Geronimo knelt, his back toward the others, lost in prayer.

"Captain, Diego," hailed Gonzalo. The two men acknowledged him with distracted nods.

"Aroça," replied the master-at-arms, then the two returned to talking.

"Hola Gonzalo," greeted Pedro looking up with a broad smile. "Breakfast's almost ready. There's water in the jug by your feet."

"Thanks," said Gonzalo as he bent to retrieve the stoppered gourd. He took a long swig and then stretched. "Is everyone else still asleep?"

"Yep, but I've been up since the sun rose," answered Pedro. "I tried to go back to sleep, but, well, I was too excited. Last night by the fire, you heard Señor Avellaneda. He said that we'll all go home rich. I know things are tough, but I can't get that out of my head. Do you think we'll find anymore gold today, or pearls?"

At Pedro's words, Gonzalo flinched inside. If anything, he felt more annoyed with Avellaneda's folly than he had the night before, but he couldn't find it in his heart to ridicule the cabin boy's fantasy.

"I don't know Pedro," he responded without conviction, "none of us can know what a new day may bring, but I'm sure that if any of us find a treasure, it'll be you."

For his restraint and deceit, Gonzalo was rewarded with another wide grin. "I can't wait until everyone's up," gushed Pedro.

"Well, I wouldn't hold your hopes too high," replied Gonzalo. "There's a lot of work to be done before the captain lets anyone wander off to hunt for gold."

Captain Valdivia and the master-at-arms continued their private conversation and Pedro questioned Gonzalo about his time in Darien and elaborated on his dreams of wealth; meanwhile by ones and twos, the remaining castaways crawled from their chosen beds and drifted over to the fire. As each of the men approached, Gonzalo eyed them over with curiosity and appraised their condition. Everyone looked tired and thoroughly worn, but he was pleased to observe that like the captain and the master-at-arms several also appeared much improved.

If strength returns to us all, we may have a chance.

When all ten of the remaining Spaniards were assembled, Geronimo, who'd by then finished his morning devotions, once again led them in prayers of thanksgiving for their salvation. When he concluded, Captain Valdivia addressed the group.

"Men because of our grievous losses, I've appointed Señor Arana my second in command. From now on you must obey him just as you would me. The two of us have discussed our situation at length and this is what we've decided. Our first challenge in this new land is to recover our health and as today is the Sabbath, we'll honor it as God intended and spend most of it in rest and contemplation. That's not to say that any of us can remain completely idle. If we're to thrive in this place, there's much work to be done and many small tasks that we must accomplish while we rebuild our strength."

Gonzalo threw Pedro a knowing look, and then the master-at-arms spoke.

"As the Captain says, we'll rest today, but first we must look to our immediate welfare. Food and security are our pressing concerns. Since Hernando is already our steward, he's to be in charge of all our foodstuffs." Then, he addressed the steward directly. "Hernando, after we eat what Pedro's cooking, I want you to take Rodrigo and Señor Avellaneda and go over this village once again from top to bottom. Leave no corner unsearched, no rock unturned. Collect every bit of food that you can find and anything else that you feel might contribute to our welfare. Once you're finished, the captain and I want you to make a plan to ration the food and then let us know exactly how long it will last."

"We'll do our best," replied Hernando.

"Good, good," said Diego. "We must all do our best."

Returning his gaze to the other men, he continued. "As for security, we'll set watches and each of us will take a turn. During the day, one of us will guard the path that leads from the beach and at night one of us must stay awake while the others sleep."

The master-at-arms then turned to Juan Suarez. "Suarez, how do you feel this morning?"

"Right enough sir," answered the able seaman.

"Very well then, you'll take the first watch on the path. Go there now. Take a position somewhere within earshot. I'll have Pedro bring you some food and either the captain or I will relieve you around midday."

"Aye sir," responded Juan. Then he rose from where he sat and headed for the path. As he neared the edge of the clearing, he paused and turned back to the master-at-arms. "Sir, I'm unarmed."

Valdivia and Arana exchanged a look and then the captain unsheathed his long dagger and flipped it to the seaman.

"Here, take my dirk."

"Thank you Captain," said Juan as he deftly caught the weapon and thrust it into his belt.

He then saluted and walked briskly down the path. When he was gone, Valdivia faced to the others.

"There's another duty we must perform today. We need to see to our fallen comrades and to the safety of our boat. After we eat, the two strongest of us, Señor Arana and I have agreed that's Gonzalo and Domingo, must return to the beach with Fray Aguilar and see that the Dorantes brothers are properly buried and the longboat secure."

A short time later, after the last of Pedro's maize and squash were eaten, Gonzalo gathered together Geronimo and the burly cooper. They found two flat pieces of wood that could serve for shovels, and the three of them set out for the beach and their gloomy task. A short distance from the huts, they encountered a bored Juan Suarez, seated on the trunk of a fallen palm, whittling on a stick with the captain's dagger.

"Where you off to?" asked the sailor who hadn't heard the captain's final orders.

"We're going to do for Xavier and Vasco," said Domingo, "give the boys a Christian burial."

"Well, do a good job of it," said Suarez. "Them was good shipmates and they deserved better'n they got."

"We'll commend them into God's hands," said Geronimo, "where the worth of all men is known."

"Aye, friar, God will know their worth," responded Suarez, "but when you say words over 'em, see you say 'em good." Then, the seaman crossed himself and returned to his whittling.

"Don't be afeared," said Domingo, "Fray Aguilar here will see that the boys get their due."

Gonzalo and Geronimo chimed agreement and the three of them continued down the path. A short walk later, they stepped out onto the white crescent of sand that rimmed the bay of turtles.

"We should bury them above the water line," said Geronimo. "They'll be safe from a high tide, but the sand there should still be loose enough for easy digging."

While Gonzalo and Geronimo discussed the merits of location and the transitory nature of life, Domingo, a practical man, scanned the beach.

His simple statement, "They're not here," jerked his companions back from their reverie.

"Oh Hell," swore Gonzalo drawing a stern look from the Franciscan. "They're gone! The longboat's gone! It must have pulled the cursed anchor stone."

"You know Gonzalo," said the big cooper, "we was all pretty stove up. Maybe the stone never got set."

Gonzalo heard the truth in the cooper's words. "You're probably right," he sighed.

"So what do we do now?" asked Geronimo. "Should we go back and tell the captain?"

"Not yet, no not yet," answered Gonzalo. "First we search. Let's walk out onto that point to our left. Maybe the boat went aground somewhere close by and we'll be able to spot it."

From the jutting point, they had clear views of the bay and also of a league of beach in both directions; nothing but sand, palms, sea, and jungle scrub; no longboat, no Dorantes brothers.

"Well," said Gonzalo after they'd all strained their eyes to no avail, "I guess they're really gone."

"It's a crying shame," said Domingo. "We should have done better by Xavier and Vasco."

"Yes, but they were sailors," offered Geronimo. "God has chosen to consign their bodies to the deep. It's fitting. Kneel with me here, both of you, and I'll read the office. God will gather their souls wherever they may have wandered."

The three men knelt on the rocky point, the friar read from his breviary, and afterwards he led Domingo and Gonzalo in personal prayer for their lost friends.

Gonzalo, who felt true affection for the Dorantes brothers, tried to remain solemn and attentive, but his mind kept returning to the disappearance of the longboat. Friends or not, the loss of the Dorantes was a spiritual injury, the loss of the boat was a serious practical matter. The rope on board, the few tools, and the longboat itself all might have contributed to the castaways' survival and possibly even to a future rescue. Without their boat they were tied to the unexplored land until another could be constructed. By the time Geronimo finished his prayers, Gonzalo felt agitated and anxious to return to the village.

"We need to get back," he told his companions. "We've done all we can for Xavier and Vasco. Now, the important thing is that we let the captain and Señor Arana know that our boat's gone."

Geronimo and Domingo agreed and the three trudged slowly back from the rocky point and up the beach toward the path. Just as they were about to step into the screen of foliage, a distant lilting sound wafted into Domingo's ears. He grabbed at his friends.

"Wait! Do you hear that?"

Gonzalo and Geronimo paused and as the three listened, the lilting sound was joined by the faraway thudding of a repeated percussive beat.

"What can it be?" asked Geronimo.

"Why, it sounds like music," said Domingo with growing wonder.

Gonzalo took several steps back toward the water and looked up the beach in the direction from which the sounds seemed to come. What he saw sent his mind reeling and made his knees go watery.

"Oh sweet mother of God!" he gasped.

By then, he'd been joined by Geronimo and Domingo who also looked up the beach and were equally stunned.

"More savages," breathed the cooper, "and this time it looks like all of 'em."

What they beheld in the far distance was a huge procession. An apparent leader was carried on the backs of other natives and he was accompanied by a mass of people. Some walked before him playing on reed flutes, others beat drums and chanted. The immediate impression was of a great host on the march.

"God, oh God, they'll be here in minutes," mumbled Gonzalo. "We've got to warn the others."

The three Spaniards turned and fled up the path. Pausing only to collect a surprised Juan Suarez as they ran past, they burst excitedly into the open patio before the huts.

"Captain," shouted Gonzalo, "savages!"

"There's at least a hundred," spluttered Geronimo. "They're nearly on our heels."

"You're sure?" demanded Diego de Arana.

"Of course we're sure!" yelled Gonzalo.

"We saw 'em," said Domingo with a wild look in his eye, "and they're coming."

"Captain?" asked Diego

Juan de Valdivia stared into the wide anxious eyes of his recently appointed second-in-command and then looked at the worn and haggard faces of his other men. Even if they were better armed, a fight was out of the question. The ordeal in the longboat had seen to that.

Can't fight, he thought, *can't run either. We know nothing of the land fifty paces beyond these huts and the men are exhausted. Hell, Rodrigo can hardly stand.*

"We go to meet them," declared the Captain. "There's no other choice. Destitute though we are, we're still Spaniards! We're emissaries of the king and we shall treat with these natives as such. Come, come everyone; we must face them with courage."

"Remember that we're Christians," cried Geronimo holding up his cross. "God will sustain us." Gonzalo wasn't so sure.

"Alright then," said Diego buckling on his cuirass, "You heard our captain. Let's show these savages what it means to be men."

With the helmeted master-at-arms in the lead, the castaways reluctantly retraced their footsteps back to the beach. By the time they walked out onto the sand, the natives were almost upon them. Captain Valdivia stepped to the front with Diego by his side. Both officials stood grim faced; white knuckled hands clutched the hilts of their swords. The other men clustered closely behind. Andres Avellaneda pulled his own sword from its scabbard, while Juan Suarez and one or two others drew their knives.

In any situation that called for bloodshed, the Spaniards' few weapons would have been poor. In the face of the horde arrayed before them they were inadequate to the point of farce. Gonzalo, himself unarmed, stared incredulously at his companions and struggled to suppress a hysterical giggle.

Up close, the natives were impressive, far more impressive and formidable looking than any he'd encountered in Darien. Headdresses of many feathers adorned some of those in the lead. Others were draped in brightly feathered cloaks of red and green. Almost all were heavily tattooed, painted with fierce designs, and ornamented with many piercings. Several musicians played the reed flutes and drums that had first signaled their approach and, in the van, two natives, painted in red and black, carried heavily smoking censers that were sculpted with faces of a demon. In all there were nearly fifty serious looking warriors armed with clubs, arrows, and other evil looking weapons.

Whether the warriors were large or not, to Gonzalo they appeared forbidding and lethal. Remembering all of his fallen comrades in Darien and their many grisly deaths, he shivered with apprehension.

So, this is how it ends, he thought.

Then, he glanced over at Pedro who stood at his left. The cabin boy was also quaking with fear so Gonzalo, exuding a confidence he didn't feel, stifled his own anxiety and laid a reassuring hand on the young sailor's shoulder. Andres Avellaneda stood on Gonzalo's right and the hidalgo's legs were stained wet with urine.

At a signal from the Nacon of Xamanzamá, who was being carried, the music came to an abrupt stop and the whole procession shuddered to a halt. The bearers lowered the nacon's platform to the ground and in the ensuing silence Ch'o Ho'ol (Rat Skull) stepped forward. The war chief was a big man, thick through the chest, shoulders, and his skin was smooth and dark. His nipples were pierced from side to side and threaded with intricately worked pieces of shell. Strange designs covered his torso and his shoulders were draped with the skin of some savage beast whose wicked claws hung menacingly over his biceps. A leather shield was strapped to his left forearm and in his right hand he held a short flattened club, its edges lined with glittering blades of obsidian. Wrinkles at the corners of his unsmiling eyes hinted at age and experience.

While Gonzalo watched in worried fascination and wondered what would come next, Captain Valdivia and the master-at-arms courageously walked forward to meet the impressive warrior's advance.

"I am Juan de Valdivia," declared the captain in a strong ringing voice. "I am the Governor General of this expedition, procurator and servant of his majesty King Ferdinand, the high and mighty ruler of Castile and León."

Rat Skull, the Nacon of Xamanzamá, stared at the captain in puzzled silence and then turned to the two chilánes who'd accompanied him.

"Well, priests? Ac Yanto and Ah K'in Cutz sent you along for a purpose. What manner of beings are these? The digging peasants declared them servants of the monkey gods, Hun Chowen and Hun Batz. What say you?"

The two lesser holy men stammered. "Great Nacon, their appearance is strange. How are we to know?"

"Idiots!" growled the warrior, and then he turned and addressed the Spaniards in the same language, a tongue that sounded every bit as harsh to the castaways as it was unintelligible.

When his pronouncement elicited reciprocal looks of confusion, the nacon pointed first at the captain and then at the master-at-arms. Then, he swept his open hand outwards toward the ocean.

"I think he asks if we come from the east," whispered Geronimo who stood behind De Arana, his wooden cross clutched tightly to his breast.

"Yes, from the east," answered Valdivia looking directly at the savage. "We're emissaries of your great father, your king who lives with the rising sun." Then he too pointed to the company of Spaniards and out to sea.

Rat Skull made another guttural response and took another step closer.

"Take care," urged one of the chilánes. "They could be more than they appear."

Cocking his head inquisitively to one side, the warrior gingerly stretched out his hand and ran his fingers across Diego's metal cuirass.

"It's a shell," exclaimed Rat Skull, "but neither of copper nor gold!"

The natives behind him reacted with a startled murmur. Next, the Nacon of Xamanzamá reached up and felt the edge of the master-at-arms' helm.

"Quick, give him your helmet," hissed Valdivia.

At his captain's order, Diego removed his helmet and held it out to the chief. "This is a gift for you, a gift from His Majesty King Ferdinand."

"And from the Holy Father in Rome," blurted Geronimo.

The nacon didn't understand the strangers' words, but he understood their intent. Accepting the metal helmet, he examined it closely, and then with a sly look of pleasure, he removed his own headdress of feathers and placed the helm onto his head. After adjusting the headpiece, he turned and faced his followers who responded with a hearty cheer and beat weapons against their shields.

Holding out his hand, Valdivia immediately tried to further assure the natives of the castaways' good intentions with a second offering.

"Here, these gifts are also for you."

Rat Skull held out his own hand and the captain passed him six shiny brass buttons that Andres Avellaneda had earlier reluctantly plucked from his waistcoat. The Nacon rolled the buttons in his hand and gave an ugly smile that never reached his eyes. Next, he spoke loudly to the two feather-cloaked priests who stood close behind him.

"If these hairy creatures are indeed messengers of the gods, the gods have chosen poorly. If they're men, then it is they who've chosen poorly."

The Spaniards were ignorant of his words, but they produced a twittering of unpleasant laughter from the crowd. Still smiling, the Nacon pointed at the captain and then to the rest of the Spaniards. Next, with emphatic signs he communicated his desire to leave and also that he wanted the castaways to accompany him.

"We're grateful for your offer," responded Captain Valdivia holding up his palms, "but we must remain here, close to this bay."

The war chief understood that he was being refused and gesticulated toward the Spaniards in such a threatening manner that both Valdivia and Arana drew their swords. At the sight of their bare weapons, Rat Skull shouted once and his warriors rushed forward.

In their weakened condition it was useless to think that any of the castaways could defend themselves. Nevertheless, Andres Avellaneda and Juan Suarez thrashed about as warriors tried to lay hands on them. The two Spaniards yelled. They struck at those nearest. Incited by their example, Domingo Vizcaino tackled the first savage to reach him and threw the man to the ground.

"Don't fight!" cried Valdivia. "Don't fight!"

Hernando de Esquivel turned and tried to flee. Geronimo waved his cross in the warriors' faces and called upon God to smite them.

The Spaniards' resistance was as futile as it was short-lived. None of them were injured by the natives, but in a matter of moments all were relieved of their weapons and swiftly and efficiently restrained. Gonzalo allowed his hands to be trussed behind him without a struggle.

So be it, he thought. *Captive is better than dead, and I'll not die on this accursed beach.*

Once the Spaniards' hands were all bound, one of the warriors tied a long length of rope about the captain's neck. Next he secured the rope around the master-at-arms' neck and so on until all the men were linked together with Gonzalo at the end of the line. When the warrior was satisfied with his work, he shouted to his nacon. Rat Skull then came forward and again stood face to face with Captain Valdivia and the master-at-arms. For several minutes he spoke to them in a stern and earnest manner, gesturing often and pointing at them and away from the beach. With a final dour exclamation, he then turned and strode back to his seat.

At his signal, the bearers again hoisted him back to their shoulders; drummers started to pound their instruments, flutes took up the cadence, and the whole procession began to retrace its path up the beach. As they were led away, Captain Valdivia shouted encouragement to his fellows.

"Take heart men, but don't resist. I don't believe they mean to kill us. We're still alive and as long as we stay alive, there's always hope."

Amen! thought Gonzalo.

In their weakened condition, the march from the beach tested each of the Spaniards' resolve. The natives chattered among themselves, but they paid little attention to their strange captives except to urge them onward with guttural exclamations and occasionally shove them when they lagged.

After shuffling and stumbling for what felt like miles, Valdivia's weakened assistant, Rodrigo, caught his food on a root and sprawled full length onto the ground; as he fell, he also dragged down Andres Avellaneda and Fray Geronimo who were roped on either side.

Exhausted and spent, the unfortunate Rodrigo lay still and unconscious while shallow breaths wheezed in and out of his heaving lungs. Geronimo crawled over to his insensate companion, shook Rodrigo gently, and the other Spaniards crowded around until their guards yanked them back.

As was proper, the captives trailed behind the Nacon of Xamanzamá, but when the scrawny one with hair the color of a chac ib can (red bean snake) collapsed it caused a commotion and he waved his hand for everyone to stop.

These are not gods or even the messengers of gods, thought Rat Skull for the hoo kal (100th) time. "Cut him loose," he called.

"Should I kill him?" asked the practical warrior that he'd addressed.

"No," answered the nacon. "Just cut him loose and have someone carry him."

Gonzalo and the other Spaniards watched in confusion and mounting dismay as the chief of the natives yelled to one of his minions and a heavily muscled warrior leaned over Rodrigo. When the native brandished a knife of coal black stone, they thought Rodrigo lost; then, to their enormous relief, the husky warrior sliced free the rope from about Rodrigo's neck and with a grunt hoisted the unconscious assistant onto his shoulders.

Weak, thought the nacon. *These strangers are bizarre enough to be from Metnal, but they're far too weak to be other than they appear.*

Rat Skull again waved his hand, the flutes and drums took up their rhythmic pulse, and the procession resumed.

"You see," said Captain Valdivia, addressing his master-at-arms in a lowered voice, "they mean to keep us alive."

"For now Captain," grunted Diego, "the day's not over."

They'd walked and stumbled perhaps another half hour or more when Gonzalo detected an elusive hint of wood smoke.

"Do you smell it Pedro? I think it's smoke," he asked the cabin boy who was roped immediately to his front.

At first the scent, floating on the breeze, was faint in their nostrils, barely existent, but as they continued the smell grew stronger.

"Pedro," he whispered. "It must be cook fires. We must be coming to their village."

A short time later, the procession began to pass by a series of huts. At first Gonzalo thought that they'd entered a village, but as they shuffled past one hut after another he began to comprehend that they were walking past outlying huts that ringed a still larger settlement. With each hut they passed, more and more people began to shadow their footsteps.

"God, Gonzalo," cried Pedro, "there's so many of them! What are we going to do?"

The cabin boy's outburst was loud with fright. Before Gonzalo could respond, Juan Suarez, who was also roped to Pedro, turned and hissed.

"Shut up you little fool! Your voice carries. Don't draw attention to us!"

By then the procession was surrounded by a crowd of curious savages, all babbling excitedly in their strange tongue. A few of the bolder ones tried to touch the Spaniards, but these were shooed away by their captors. Young boys, naked and yelling, ran ahead shouting that their nacon had returned and that he'd captured the monkey gods! The crowd grew to a throng and everywhere about the castaways swirled a scene of great commotion.

Men, women, and children pressed forward, everyone pushing and shoving to catch a glimpse of the captives. Most of the men were girded with loin cloths. Some of the women were unclothed from the waist up. Others wore a sort of underskirt and a modest loose fitting garment that fastened below their armpits and concealed their breasts. Many of the natives wore sandals of woven fiber, but most walked barefoot. Countless wild and fearsome tattoos decorated their exposed flesh. Naked children shoved and squeezed between legs. Shouts and laughter mixed with the shrill sounds of the procession's flutes and the resumed loud pounding of its drums. Everything surrounding the Spaniards turned to chaos, an alien blur of motion, color, and clamor.

With his head spinning, dazed by the strangeness, Gonzalo was thankful when, near dusk, the rope was at last removed from about his neck and he was thrust behind his fellows into the darkened interior of a small hut.

Outside, the cacophony of noise continued, but thickly plastered walls muted the sounds, and a mat that was hung over the door by their captors shut out the disorienting swirl of exotic sights. Gratefully, the men slumped to the floor.

"How's Rodrigo?" asked Valdivia.

Gonzalo, who was closest, helped the captain's assistant to sit up and then looked into his face.

"Well Sánchez, are you alive?"

Rodrigo squinted through groggy eyes, "Yes, I think so, but I feel like I've been run down by an ox cart. Where are we?"

"Safe for the moment, I think," answered the captain. "We've been taken to the savages' village."

The inside of the hut was bare, but a brief inspection turned up two large jugs of water that were passed greedily from hand to hand. When the first jug was drained, Diego de Arana took the second and set it aside.

"We're all thirsty," he said, "but we don't know when, or if, we'll get more, so we'd better stretch it out."

"What now?" demanded Andres Avellaneda. "What do we do next?"

"Well," answered Valdivia, "we can't fight, and I doubt that we can escape. Does anyone have any suggestions?"

As the castaways looked from one to another and the silence grew, Gonzalo responded, "What else can we do? We wait."

"We pray!" added Geronimo.

Some undetermined time after the Spaniards were thrust into their hut, the savages began to dance and make a great revelry, although for the captives there was neither pleasure nor revels. All night long, especially after midnight, their ears were assaulted by the shouts of hundreds of voices, loud bells, flutes, tambourines, and other instruments; a mighty crashing sound that rolled on and on without end. None of the Spaniards easily found their sleep.

Chapter 9

Za'azil

11 Bak'tun 14 K'atun 11 Tun 2 Uinal 6 K'in

(May 29, 1511)

Za'azil lay naked on her bed, a low platform made of small rods covered with woven reed mats and a thick mantle of quilted cotton. As the chosen nacon (war chief) of Ichpaatún, tradition required that her husband, Hoch Can, abstain from all relations with Za'azil, but the morning was hot, they were both young, and the house was quiet and empty. They'd rushed their lovemaking, lest someone arrive and they be discovered, yet despite the hurried pace, they were both sated.

Hurried or deliberate, thought Za'azil, *our love is always good.*

The pleasure they found in each other's bodies blazed clear and unquenchable, a flame that burst to life the first time that they'd made love and which had burned brightly ever since.

That wasn't the problem. Hoch Can was heir to Ichpaatún and he needed an heir of his own. Their problem was that no matter how keenly the fires of their desire burned, or how frequently they fanned them, Za'azil didn't conceive.

The day was hot and, despite the thick thatch which formed its roof, the heat crept into the back rooms of their house. Sweat glistened on her smooth belly. She felt languid, reluctant to stir. Across the room, Hoch Can wrapped a hand-broad strip of cloth between his legs and then about his waist. One end he left to hang in front, the other behind.

Za'azil loved Hoch Can and was a dutiful wife, so she'd embroidered his loincloth embellishing it with elaborate patterns worked from bright feathers and colorful beads. As she watched Hoch Can dress, she felt a surge of pleasure. Some of it was pride, taken in her own careful handiwork, but that accounted for only a small part of her satisfaction, a tiny pleasure which quickly paled in comparison to the soaring delight that she felt when she gazed upon her lean and handsome husband.

The three tun (years) which had flown past since her wedding day, when old Ah K'in May had given her to Hoch Can, were the best of her life. She and Hoch Can played together when they were children; they passed into adulthood in the same ceremony of caput-sihil (rebirth), and as their bodies blossomed they began to share shy smiles and stolen glances that had nothing to do with childhood.

When Nachan Can and Ix Chan Ek began to search for a suitable wife for their son, Za'azil had hardly dared to hope that she might be chosen. Her father was a humble although well-respected trader of salt, but there we're other girls with more prominent families and better claims to high rank and nobility. The okinal (afternoon) when she heard that Nachan Can had sent Itz'at Acan to negotiate with her father and settle upon a dowry, she'd hugged herself with joy and burned several precious blue-painted cakes of pom in fervent thanks to Ixchel.

Her mother made her wedding garments and on the day of the marriage she'd been feted by family and friends. As had been arranged, that night, following the banquet, she was given to Hoch Can. It was as they lay together for the first time that Za'azil learned that Hoch Can's mother, Ix Chan Ek, had favored another and that she had also not been Nachan Can's first choice. Her new husband had caressed her and told her how he'd begged his father and pleaded with his mother and how faced with his earnest desire and his repeated pronouncements of love their objections had slowly melted away.

Please Ixchel, she silently prayed. *Let this be the time, give us our own child.*

Larger polities boasted both a hereditary war chief and a second nacon who served a fixed but temporary term. Ichpaatún, being of modest size and means, made do with temporary war chiefs. Every three tun (years) the city's leader and his advisors selected a different warrior to hold the position. Some talented men served more than once and in the time since Hoch Can's father, Nachan Can, came to rule, Hoch Can's Uncle, Ah-cambal, had been chosen to lead Ichpaatún's warriors three different times. At the recent festival of Pacum-chac it had been Za'azil's husband Hoch Can himself who'd been unexpectedly selected.

The people of Ichpaatún had lifted him to their shoulders and with great pomp they'd carried him to their temple platform. There, they seated him, burned incense about him as though he were a god, and for five days ate and drank to their young nacon.

All the while the men of the city performed the Holcan-okot, the great dance of the warriors.

Za'azil had been excited by the ceremony and by the immense honor of Hoch Can's appointment, but she'd also been terrified. The position of nacon carried both privilege and responsibility. During the three years of his tenure Ichpaatún would provide for all of Hoch Can's wants bringing him iguanas, fish, and all else he needed, but in return, in addition to leading the city's holcánob (warriors) in time of war, he was expected to hold himself pure and maintain a distance from the city's daily life. This meant that he was to abstain from other meats. He was to mingle but little with the townsfolk. The vessels and household articles for his use were to be kept apart. He was only supposed to be waited on by men and, the part that had terrified Za'azil, he was forbidden to hold congress with all women, herself included.

Three years without knowing her beloved husband, three more years in which she couldn't bring forth a child. The burden of it had seemed more than she ever could bear, but Hoch Can had held his position for less than a uinal (20 days) before he crept back into her bed. If she conceived while he was nacon a great scandal would follow, but, scandal or not, it would be worth it.

Wagging tongues of Ichpaatún already gossiped that she was barren. Others implied that Hoch Can was less than a man. The weight of the whispers followed them about like unseen and malevolent spirits, leaving them both ill at ease, and adding a hint of wanton desperation to their secret lovemaking. The return of Hoch Can's uncle, Ah-cambal, had thrown salt on the wound.

"Must you go?" she asked, already knowing the answer.

Hoch Can took in the sensuous lines of his beautiful wife, noted the beads of sweat on her ripe body, and experienced a renewed stirring of desire. Reluctantly, he pushed the feeling aside.

"It's a council of war," he sighed, "and I am nacon."

The ejection of the emissaries from Tzamá, following the coming of age ceremony of Hoch Can's cousin, Tepeu, had left Nachan Can and his councilors troubled and anxious. Reflecting their ruler's mood, the whole of Ichpaatún had slowly become nervous and wary. The arrival of Ah-cambal four days ago with stories of Tzamán slavers and bloody slaughter had thrown the already edgy city into turmoil. There was great fear of an imminent attack, and time and again, Za'azil was left alone as Hoch Can was repeatedly called to council.

That wasn't the salt. The salt was the xchúupal (girl). When Ah-cambal had come rushing through the city gate, the same gate that witnessed the departure of Gucumatz and White Worm, he hadn't been alone. To the surprise of the holcánob on guard and to the considerable astonishment of many who saw him, the elder warrior carried, draped across his shoulder, the body of a sleeping child. Word spread quickly of his return and, even before Ah-cambal reached his home, he was summoned before Nachan Can.

After giving his wayward spy a warm embrace, the first words from the sajal's mouth had been, "So brother, you leave with shells and salt of considerable value, yet you return with nothing but a small girl. Perhaps your skills as a trader are in decline."

The girl, who was by then awake, clutched Ah-cambal's leg and stared wide-eyed at Nachan Can and his retainers.

"Sajal," said Ah-cambal, meeting his brother's gaze, "we have much to discuss, but I think it better that we speak in private."

Nachan Can nodded his approval and then gestured to those about him.

"Learned Man, you stay. The rest of you go."

When the three men and the child were alone, Ah-cambal poured out his tale. Sometime later the sajal called for his son to join them.

As Hoch Can stepped into the shade of his father's porch, Ah-cambal grasped his shoulders and then gave him a hearty hug.

"Nephew, it does my old heart good to see you so well and strong."

"Welcome home uncle!" exclaimed Hoch Can. There was much love between the two men and their faces both reflected their joy.

"Hoch Can," said Ah-cambal. "I have someone very special I want you to meet." Then, indicating the girl still holding tightly onto his leg, he said, "This is Óolal (Happiness)."

Hoch Can felt confused. "Óolal, you say uncle, but why is she with you?"

"It's a long story nephew, one which I've already told to your father and Itz'at Acan, but it's a story that you must know also. So, sit here beside me and you shall hear it."

Hoch Can and the others seated themselves, the girl crawled into Ah-cambal's lap, and the old warrior again recounted his tale. When he finished, the young nacon felt stunned.

"Father," he said, "surely this means that Tzamá intends war. We must make plans."

"Perhaps, war is coming; perhaps not," Nachan Can answered calmly. "We'll discuss the possibilities and make preparations, when and as we must. But, that's not why I called for you. We need to speak of another matter."

"What then?" asked Hoch Can.

"Óolal," responded Ah-cambal. "She is under my protection nephew, but she is a child and I am an old bachelor. The Tzamáns have made her an orphan and, as one of your father's people, she deserves better. Your father, Itz'at Acan, and I have discussed what is to be done with her, and it is our wish that you to take her into your household."

"Uncle," said Hoch Can, "Za'azil and I have no need of another servant. We are well taken care of. Besides, this girl is too young to do any useful work."

"Nephew, you misunderstand me," answered Ah-cambal. "It is true that Óolal is of low birth, but she is brave and intelligent and her family honored your father as their cacique (chief). We want you and Za'azil to take her into your home not as a servant, but as a daughter."

Hoch Can stared at the three older men, at a loss for words. As the silence grew awkward, Nachan Can spoke.

"You are without child my son."

His father's voice was kindly, but the young nacon of Ichpaatún felt as though he'd been cursed at and punched in the stomach.

Three nights had passed since Óolal had come into Za'azil's home. *My daughter*, she thought, once again trying the words, trying to decide how they felt. Even as she and Hoch Can were making love the child had played just outside the house.

"Hoch Can my husband, Ah-cambal spoke to me this morning and he councils that we should send our new daughter to Ah K'in May for instruction."

"Damn Ah-cambal!" shouted Hoch Can slamming his hand against the wall and kicking a bowl at his feet. "She's not our daughter!" and then he took a step forward and raised his fist as if to strike her.

"You would beat me?" Za'azil asked, more in wonder than fear.

With her words, the anger inside Hoch Can blew out like a doused candle and she read the well of sadness in the wrinkles at the corner of his eyes.

"My beloved," she said and then she took him into her arms and held him tightly.

"She's not our daughter," he repeated quietly, then, he gently pushed her away. "I must go," he whispered and hurried from the room.

Alone, Za'azil slumped to the floor and hugged her knees. Silent sobs rocked her and the well of tears that had built inside her chest broke through and ran down her face. Outside, Happiness, the child with the ironic name, played silently drawing animals in the dirt.

Chapter 10

A Gift from the Gods

11 Bak'tun 14 K'atun 11 Tun 2 Uinal 7 K'in

(May 30, 1511)

Under Ac Yanto's shrewd and self-serving rule Xamanzamá had grown quickly in both power and wealth, but under the equally selfish thumb of nearby Tzamá the city had, of late, fallen upon harder times. For several uinal before Makiq and the other peasants brought their news of monkey gods cavorting on his beaches Ac Yanto had found himself faced with one trying problem after another.

As excited word of Rat Skull's return leapt through Xamanzamá, embellished by wilder and ever wilder descriptions of the war chief's prisoners, the story jumped quickly from mouth to mouth like tongues of wildfire through dry summer brush. Ac Yanto's high priest Ah K'in Cutz (Wild Turkey) mused that the nacon's capture of the strangers couldn't have come at a more opportune time.

Rains had failed to come and last season's harvest in Xamanzamá was disastrously poor. It was the poorest yield in even the memory of the withered crone Ix B'akab', the oldest person in the city. Nevertheless Lord Ah Tabai, the fierce and jealous overlord of nearby Tzamá, had taxed Xamanzamá more heavily than usual. This season was again dry and, what crops there were, were still many uinal from maturity, yet due to Tzamá's greed the floors tiles of Xamanzamá's granaries were already visible beneath withered ears of maize. Ah K'in Cutz, Ac Yanto, and the city's other nobles hoarded food and the shadowed specter of the god Zaccimi (White Death) risen from Metnal, and wielding hunger like a cudgel, stalked among those less fortunate.

Xamanzamá was as coiled and tense as high priest, Ah K'in Cutz, had ever seen it.

This is good, he thought. *Rat Skull's return will distract our people from their bellies. Let them believe that our nacon has triumphed over the very gods! Whatever the truth of his victory, it will give the peasants a reason for optimism. Better still, it gives them an excuse to celebrate, and celebrating they'll forget their hunger. How can I use this to my advantage?*

All Rat Skull's return gave to Xamanzamá's ruler, Ac Yanto, was a splitting headache, one that whacked away at the back of his head like a tiny dwarf with a blunted war club. All night long while his subjects sang and danced, the Batab Kinich sat in tedious council with Ah K'in Cutz, whom he loathed, and his other advisors. None of them had visited the prisoners. Until they reached a consensus it didn't seem prudent.

Rat Skull was adamant that, despite their bizarre appearance, the creatures that he'd captured were mere men, nothing more. The two lesser chilánes (priests), old Kish (Stingray Spine) and Thup Paal (Last Child), who'd accompanied the war chief, were wary, less sanguine, and, to Ac Yanto's mind, far more annoying. They argued for continued caution, all the while blabbering about the monkey gods, Hun Chowen and Hun Batz, and the widely prophesized return of Kukulkán.

Saying much and contributing nothing, Ac Yanto's other councilors bickered among themselves, prattled on and on, and once again whispered of Lord Ah Tabai and the wisdom of sending a messenger to Tzamá to inform the Lord of Fire.

Chattering chic'ob (pisotes), thought Ac Yanto, *if only Ah Puch (the skeletal lord of death) would play for them on his tiny bells. And, that damnable priest, Wild Turkey, as usual he just sits there smiling and says nothing.*

Disgusted, the ruler of Xamanzamá lurched to his feet and hurled down his nearly empty b'alche cup. The delicate clay vessel, that he'd raised once too often that night, shattered with a crash, startling those nearest, and dousing several of the Ah Cuchcab (councilors) with shards of pottery and the sticky dregs of his drink.

"Enough! Enough you worms! Damn you all. You go round and round like old women and still you go nowhere! Rat Skull, you say these strangers are men, men like any others. What makes you sure of this? How can you know? Maybe they've tricked you?"

"Great Lord, you are most wise," clucked Kish, the elder of the two chilánes. "Messengers from Metnal would be both clever and devious. It is likely as you say that Rat Skull has been deceived!"

A Gift from the Gods   93

"Lord," answered the nacon, glaring at the old priest, "one of them had urine running down his leg. On the way back from the bay another tripped and fainted. And if that's not evidence enough, guards outside the hut heard one of them shit. God's don't shit! I say that they're men."

"I agree with the nacon," thrust in Wild Turkey, speaking for the first time. "They are men."

"Ah, at last, the great ah k'in finally graces us with his opinion," quipped Ac Yanto.

"Only a reflection of your own greatness, oh Batab Kinich," oozed the high priest.

Ac Yanto gritted his teeth and with an unusual display of restraint managed to hold his temper in check.

"So then, they're men! What do you recommend my most trusted of advisors?"

Ah K'in Cutz gazed about the patio in front of the ruler's house and fixed each of the Ah Cuchcab in turn with his stare.

"In this time of hunger, the strangers are a gift from the gods! Sacrifice them!"

"No!" shouted several of the Ah Cuchcab at once.

"And why not?" demanded Wild Turkey. "Their arrival is auspicious! If this year's crops are to thrive, and our people are to return to prosperity, the gods require blood. At the very least, a sacrifice will draw our peasants' attention away from their empty bellies. I know this! You know this! We all know this! Without these strangers we must go far afield to wage war and take captives or else we must sacrifice from among our own. Are these true options? If the gods have seen fit to present us with these outlandish creatures, must we not show proper respect for their gift?"

Cutz believed profoundly in the power of his gods; he was also, at all times, a shrewd and cynical schemer. An elaborate blood offering might appease the heavens, but he weighed of equal importance the likelihood that it could distract the attention of Xamanzamá's populace from their otherwise growing misery.

"We mustn't be rash," urged one of the younger councilors. "Surely there are risks. What of reprisals?"

"Risks," hissed Ah K'in Cutz with a hard look that made the young man's pod shrivel, "there are no risks. These are mortal men and the gods will be well pleased to receive them as offerings.

As for reprisals, what people are these strangers from? What city? Where is their village? Who is their cacique (chief)? No, they are alone I tell you; when they're gone none will know or care!"

"But what of Yajawk'ak' (Lord of the Fire)?" demanded one of the lesser nobles. "If these strangers are indeed a gift from the gods, surely they must belong to the Halach Uinic (Great Man) of Tzamá?" Several other nobles mumbled and nodded their agreement.

"Lord Ah Tabai does not know of these monkey men," answered Wild Turkey in a hushed voice. "And, there is no immediate reason that he should."

The dwarf with the blunted war club was still busy at work, but Ac Yanto thought that perhaps, just perhaps, his headache was about to go away.

Chapter 11

Requerimiento

11 Bak'tun 14 K'atun 11 Tun 2 Uinal 7 K'in

(May 30, 1511)

Consuela waved a delicate gloved hand toward the sumptuously laden table. "Sit down little brother," she smiled. Savory aromas tickled Gonzalo's nose and bowls and platters of every description steamed enticingly before his hungry eyes. The table was thick and heavy, made of polished oak, and already seated around it were a beautiful dark-haired, dark-eyed, woman, a young dark-haired boy and an older dark-haired girl. "But sister, who are these people?" asked Gonzalo. "Your wife and children of course," answered Consuela, still smiling. Gonzalo felt befuddled and disoriented. He was sure that he knew neither the woman nor the children. Nevertheless, his older sister's words rang of irrefutable truth. Feeling a sudden and inexplicable joy, he reached out and drew back a high-backed leather-seated chair.

Abruptly, before he could take his proper place at the head of the table, the room began to shudder and then violently to quake. Dust rose in tiny wisps from the chamber's thick walls and blocks of stone began to crack and drop from its vaulted ceiling. Gonzalo fell to his knees in terror and threw his hands over his head. Swirling clouds of powdered mortar filled the air. As he watched terrified and cowering, shrouded in the flying dust, Consuela, the woman, the children, and the food laden table all dissolved. As inconsequential as a morning mist before a hot afternoon sun, they wavered and then, without another sound, vanished into the cloud of rubble.

Gonzalo woke gasping, drenched in sweat; above him hovered the bulk of Juan Suarez. The hearty sailor had him gripped tightly by the shoulders and was shaking him back and forth.

"Guerrero, Gonzalo, wake up! Something's afoot outside."

"Enough, enough," grunted Gonzalo, "I'm awake. Get off me."

When Juan released him and leaned back on his heels, the tired escudero sat up dazed. For a few moments he sifted through feelings while vestiges of his dream unraveled and drifted away.

"What's going on?" he mumbled thickly.

"Can't say," answered the seaman, but something's up and the captain wants you awake."

Seated on the dirt floor where he'd slept, Gonzalo gazed about the small room. The hut's interior was still shrouded in darkness, but light leaked in here and there telling him the sun was up.

And so, at least I live to see another dawn.

His other companions were huddled against the wall farthest from the door, and Valdivia motioned him over.

"It's the chanting Aroça," said the captain.

Gonzalo listened. "I don't hear any..."

"That's just it," interrupted Diego de Arana, "it's stopped."

"It went on all night," volunteered Pedro. "Then, just before Juan woke you, exactly as Señor De Arana said, it just died away."

"We don't know if it means anything Aroça," said Valdivia, "but it's best we all be ready and on our guard with our wits about us."

No sooner did the captain finish speaking, than the mat covering the hut's door was flung roughly aside. Unhindered, abrupt sunlight flooded into the small space and eyes now grown accustomed to the semi-darkness proved suddenly useless.

Gonzalo, who threw a hand in front of his face, was among the first to recover. Still shading his eyes, he made out a hulking form silhouetted in the doorway. As the Spaniards blinked furiously, and before any of them could move, the form stepped into the room and resolved itself into the large scowling warrior who'd carried the insensate Rodrigo the day before.

Captain Valdivia and his master at arms each struggled to their feet while the native stepped forward and gestured toward them both. The gestures were followed by a rapid burst of the savage's unintelligible language and then, while Valdivia tried to explain that they didn't understand, the warrior moved back to the entrance and waved to someone waiting outside.

Almost immediately, three modestly clothed women stepped into the gloom. Each of them carried a large flat tray woven from palm leaves and, like the table in Gonzalo's dream, each tray was piled high with food. Without meeting the gaze of any of the captives, the native women placed the trays on the floor and shyly retreated back out of the hut's door. As they stepped outside, the three were replaced by a burly bowlegged man of middling height who lugged with him two large clay jugs which sloshed with the sound of water. This man set down his load beside the women's trays and then, with his eyes also downcast, beat his own hasty exit.

With a hard-faced look, the large warrior gestured at the food and water.

"We thank you for..." said Captain Valdivia, but, even as he started to speak, the savage gruffly cut him off with another rush of his perplexing tongue.

"O'och, hantik! (food, eat)," he grunted.

Then, with a final emphatic gesture at the castaways, he too spun about and ducked out of the hut. Behind him, the thick door mat dropped heavily back into place and the room again plunged into shadows.

"So what do you make of all that?" asked De Arana, looking at the captain.

"I don't know Diego," replied Valdivia, "but we have to accept it as a good thing. At least for now they don't mean to starve us."

"If we take this food and drink as anything; we must take it as a sign from God," spoke up Geronimo. "Captain, God wants us to lead these people into his glory. Even though they don't know of Jesus, the Blessed Virgin, or even any of the saints, God has softened their hearts toward us. It's obvious that he's done this thing so that we might grow strong and teach them to praise his name."

Gonzalo stared at Geronimo. *The man never ceases to amaze me,* he thought, *we're castaways, prisoners of savages, I can't remember the last time I slept in a real bed, and the good friar sees a few fish, some vegetables, and two jugs of water as a sign from God!*

To Gonzalo's immediate chagrin the friar wasn't alone in his conviction. Andres Avellaneda de Salamanca also saw the hand of divine providence in the food lying at their feet.

"The Franciscan's right!" he gushed. "God intends to give us glory and riches!"

Digging into his pocket he pulled out the pitiful trinkets he'd discovered the night before and again held them before him.

"He's shown us that there are riches in this land. All that's needed is for us to show the savages that we're their betters, bring them into God's arms, and this land is ours!"

Geronimo amazed Gonzalo, but Andres Avellaneda frightened him. *The man's insane!*

"I'm not sure about signs from Our Lord," said Captain Valdivia cautiously, "but I agree with Fray Aguilar. We must try to bring Our Lord's holy word to these idolaters. I also agree with Señor Avellaneda that we must show these heathen that we're their natural superiors. That much at least is our duty to God and to our king. I say that we use some of this water to clean ourselves and then straighten our clothes, each man as best he can. When next the savages come, we must treat with them not as their prisoners, but as their guests, as Spaniards, and as men to be reckoned with!"

Unexpectedly, Domingo, the big cooper spoke up. "Captain, begging your pardon sir, but might we not eat first?"

"Our large friend shows uncommon wisdom," threw in Juan Suarez.

"Yes, yes, Vizcaino's quite right," chuckled Valdivia. "First we eat."

"No!" interjected Geronimo. "First we pray." So saying, the Franciscan moved to his knees. One by one, the other castaways also knelt.

Mercifully, to Gonzalo's mind, Geronimo's prayers of thanksgiving were brief and Hernando, the steward, soon apportioned and handed out the food. The three trays yielded up a good quantity of cooked fish, boiled roots, fruits, and round flat cakes of maize. As the men filled their bellies and slaked their thirsts, they began to feel marginally optimistic about their situation. Such good treatment seemed to bode well and each of Spaniards from Captain Valdivia to Pedro, the cabin boy, lost some degree of their fear and felt to some extent safer.

Following their meal, as Captain Valdivia suggested, the Spaniards cleaned themselves and as much as possible and made ready. Then, having done all they could to prepare themselves, they sat down to await their captors' pleasure.

The wait was short. Gonzalo was just beginning to feel restless when the mat covering their door was again flung aside and a red-painted savage beckoned them forth. Waiting outside, Gonzalo and the others discovered the tattooed chief from their capture on the beach. The big man's head was capped by Diego's helm and his shoulders were again draped with his fierce cape of fur and claws. With his eyes focused on the Spaniards like those of a hawk on an unsuspecting covey of quail, the imposing savage stood apparently at ease, armed as though for war and attended by an entourage of other warriors.

Rat Skull kept his expression blank and he watched intently as the hairy strangers emerged from their hut. As each one of them stepped forth, he examined the captive closely from head to toe. Like most of Xamanzamá, the nacon hadn't slept, but as the night of celebration had worn on disquiet had found a foothold and grown insidiously in his breast. He'd begun to question himself and wonder about the things he'd told the Batab Kinich and Ah K'in Cutz. In council he'd insisted that his bizarre prisoners were mere men, but in the dark of night, with "Monkey Gods" on every tongue, and the captives no longer bound before him, he'd begun to doubt.

What if I'm wrong? he'd thought. And, amid the sounds of revelry, he'd remembered the insinuating words of the elder chilán, "Messengers from Metnal are clever and devious. It's likely that Rat Skull has been deceived!"

Could Kish have been right? Could I have been deceived?

That idea had worried the nacon, prevented him from taking pleasure in the revels, and had kept him on edge throughout the night. But, now as he watched his captives huddle before him in the bright sun, his tension slid away and the poisonous thought vanished like ahau can (rattlesnake) into his hole.

I was right, he thought, *men, just men.*

With the Spaniards gathered, standing shoulder to shoulder outside the hut, the tattooed chief's warriors closed in around them. The armed savages numbered less than those on the beach, but they looked fearsome and their robust strength was evident. Despite their short stature, to the worn castaways, the painted men, armed with war clubs and axes, still appeared as giants.

As the natives approached, Gonzalo's heart started to beat faster and an icy tingle of fear and apprehension ran up his spine. For three shaky breaths, he wrestled against a sudden and futile urge to flee. But then, to his great surprise and his extreme relief, the savages didn't lay hold of him, nor did they bind anyone. Instead, the natives took up positions which surrounded the castaways and emphasized their status as prisoners, yet somehow maintained a respectful distance.

Once his warriors arranged themselves, Rat Skull pointed and curtly addressed the tall prisoner with the narrow hairy face, the one who seemed to be their leader.

"Ko'oten, beya' (You come, this way)."

Then the nacon turned and took a couple of steps. Sensing no movement behind him, Rat Skull paused, turned back annoyed, and with impatient signs indicated that the captives should follow.

Men, he thought, *and stupid men at that.*

The chief's words meant nothing to the Spaniards, but his command was clear.

"Alright," said Valdivia acknowledging to himself that any resistance might jeopardize their position, "this savage wants us to go with him, and so go we must. Stand tall men, and walk with pride. Remember we're Christians, emissaries of God and of his majesty King Ferdinand."

At a sedate pace, their fierce captor led Gonzalo and the others deeper into the village. Almost immediately, the previous night's commotion and clamor reasserted itself everywhere around them. Men, women, and children shouted and yelled and a swarm of natives suddenly appeared as if sprouting from the earth. The throng pressed in on all sides and strident calls from conch shell trumpets assaulted the Spaniard's ears. At the same time the piping of clay flutes, reed pipes, and deer-bone whistles accompanied and competed with a growing roar of unintelligible voices. The result was a wild din that rose and fell and turned the morning into what Gonzalo could only imagine was a perfect copy of ancient Babel. Many of the natives appeared intoxicated and dissolute from a night of drinking and, as the dense crowd trailed along and jostled for position the castaways found themselves grateful for their surrounding cordon of warriors.

As the procession inched forward, Pedro and Rodrigo shuffled along at Gonzalo's side.

"Where do you think they'll take us?" asked the boy.

"No idea," answered Gonzalo. "Guessing won't change anything, so I suppose we'll know when we get there."

"I think it's somewhere important," mused Valdivia's assistant with a serious look on his face.

"What makes you say that?" asked Gonzalo. "Maybe they're just leading us to another better guarded hut."

"Look at your feet," answered Rodrigo. "I think we're on some kind of a road."

Gonzalo glanced down. He hadn't noticed the transition, but somewhere, as they'd walked, the trail they followed among the huts, had changed from a simple dirt track to a slightly raised pathway, one that was paved over smoothly with a stucco of white limestone.

Looking past the heads of those who walked in front of him, Pedro's eyes followed the band of white as it stretched out into the distance. Then he pointed.

"What's that?" Two hundred meters away the clustered huts, which had steadily grown larger and better-built, suddenly stopped and the white road ended just as abruptly terminating against three wide steep stone steps that appeared to lead to a raised platform.

"I'm not sure," answered Gonzalo, "but it looks like some sort of plaza."

As the castaways drew near to the platform, two pairs of painted and tattooed natives appeared at the top of the stairs; each pair strained under the weight of a large circular stone basin. Dark grey clouds rose from the basins and even at a distance the smoke carried to Gonzalo's nostrils a pungent aroma of earth, wood, and musk. With great care, the bearers placed the smoldering censers at the top of the steps, one to each side so that their columns of aromatic incense formed a sort of entrance. Then, as the warrior with Diego's helm climbed up to the platform, the men who'd carried the basins prostrated themselves before him. Warily, the Spaniards followed their captor up the steps.

In Darien, campaigning with Ojeda, Gonzalo had marched through native villages, one after another. All were meager affairs with poor houses constructed of sticks, mud, and grasses. Already, the tightly thatched and well plastered huts of this land upon which he'd been cast had impressed him, but the sights that now spread before him as he stepped out onto the platform beggared anything Nueva Andalusia had as yet offered.

"Holy Mother of God," whispered Hernando de Esquivel, and Geronimo crossed himself. Gonzalo could scarcely believe his eyes.

The plaza into which they were being led was rectangular in shape. It was tightly paved with smooth stone and it stretched for nearly one hundred meters on a side. That in itself was remarkable, but lining the spacious plaza's edges, raised on slightly higher platforms were five striking buildings constructed of skillfully worked stone. The structures were modest in size, but nonetheless they were the most impressive buildings the castaways had encountered since leaving Spain. The dressed stones of each building were covered in smooth stucco and their surfaces painted in garish hues of red, orange, and yellow. Elaborate murals covered their walls and the largest of the five buildings was fronted with a wide colonnaded portico. The sight was so singular and so unexpected that Valdivia and his men stood rooted in place, speechless until their escort again ushered them forward.

Noisy people lined the plaza and clouds of incense drifted in the air. When the trailing crowd flowed in behind, the sound swelled as though leading to some pre-planned crescendo. Long thin Trumpets of hollow wood, rattles, and small bells of shell and clay intensified the already exotic music of conches, flutes, and pipes. Drums covered with animal skin lent a regular cadence to the cacophony and below it all rumbled deep mournful bass notes of a great horizontal drum fashioned from the hollowed trunk of a once massive tree.

Amidst the seeming turmoil, their guards herded the Spaniards across the middle of the plaza until they halted and stood before another short series of steps that led up to the largest of the five buildings.

The elder chilán, Kish (Stingray Spine) briefly surveyed the plaza and then stepped back into the shadows of the corridor.

"All is in readiness my lord."

Ac Yanto acknowledged the lesser priest with a dismissive grunt. Then, he stood up, threw a fleeting look at the retainers and advisors gathered about him, and paced out into the sunlight. At the Batab Kinich's appearance a sudden hush fell over the crowd and as was proper, according to their rank, the people began to either bow or prostrate themselves.

Ac Yanto, with Ah K'in Cutz a pace behind him, looked out over the square. The only heads not bowed were those of Rat Skull's ten captives. At first glance, a slight shiver crawled across the batab's shoulders.

Just as Rat Skull described them, he thought. *The prisoners are singularly odd, hairy, monkey-like, and strangely attired.*

Then, as his eyes remained fixed on the creatures, the batab began to see what Rat Skull had seen. The captives' appearance was peculiar and their dress outlandish, but if one scrutinized them closely, it was plain they were men.

Satisfied, Ac Yanto looked beyond the prisoners and took in the mass of bowed heads that filled the plaza. The sight gave him a sly thrill of pleasure. The square was full to bursting and in the excitement of the "monkey gods'" capture, his people, as Ah K'in Cutz had predicted, seemed to have forgotten Xamanzamá's nearly empty storerooms.

This morning will grant me many days of peace, thought the batab, and then he seated himself on a thick stone bench that faced the plaza. Ah K'in Cutz stepped forward and stood at his left shoulder

"Well Cutz," said Ac Yanto partially turning to his loathsome, but useful advisor, "it would seem that for once our zealous nacon was right. Send your acolytes down and see if they can discover what Rat Skull's brought to us."

"I will send them at once, my great lord," answered the high priest, but in such a tone that bile rose in Ac Yanto's stomach.

His arrogance grows, thought the batab while Cutz leaned back and whispered to Kish.

Watching the elder chilán and his younger companion make their way to the plaza floor to question the prisoners, Ah K'in Cutz was nearly beside himself with delight.

Rat Skull's captives are men, but I'll sacrifice them as demigods, he thought, *as messengers of Metnal. The ceremony will be talked about and remembered for a baktún (144,000 days). My star will eclipse Ac Yanto's and that flabby fool will be forgotten.*

Then, it was time to put aside his daydreams of power and wealth. The high priest of Xamanzamá watched closely as Kish approached the strangers and then addressed them in a loud voice that to Ah K'in Cutz sounded as though it was tinged with a hint of fear.

"Tu'ux a kah? (Where is your village?)" The monkey men chattered among themselves and stared at Kish, but answered him with gibberish.

"Tu nail? (Your house?)," added the younger chilán, but again neither priest could understand the strangers' harsh responses.

"Biix naach? (How far?)," tried Kish with no better result.

Rat Skull, who still stood next to his charges, glared at the two ineffectual priests. Then, he turned to the tall narrow faced prisoner that he'd decided was cacique (chief) and asked the question foremost in his soldier's mind.

"Hai p'eel holcánob? (How many warriors?)"

The well-ordered aspect of the plaza, its startling buildings, and everything the scene implied astonished the Spaniards. That surprise was quickly eclipsed by the appearance of Ac Yanto and his retinue. All of the natives began to bow and grovel, and at the same time the chief's entrance reduced the crowd's noise to a kind of low musical chattering. Combined with the strangeness of the place and heady smell of smoking censers, the effect was one of an intense otherworldliness which left Gonzalo and his companions off balance and confused.

From the moment the occupants of the colonnaded building appeared, it was obvious to the castaways that the people emerging from it were local nobility. The robust, although slightly soft looking middle-aged man at their center was the most elaborately garbed savage they'd yet encountered. His hair grew long like a woman's, but it was ringed on the top into a sort of tonsure so that it grew short on the crown and long below. All of it was oiled and the long part was braided, adorned with shells and colored cloth, and then tightly wrapped behind his head. Like most of the natives that the Spaniards had already seen, a narrow strip of cloth served the man as breeches. And, like the warrior who'd captured them, a large square mantle draped over his shoulders, and leggings of tanned painted leather wound about his calves. There, the similarity of the man's garments ended. Every square inch of his colorful clothing shimmered with cunningly worked feathers, shells, and bright stones. His face and chest were richly tattooed and as he sat before the Spaniards on a bench of stone, they could see that although unarmed, he carried some sort of a rattle in one hand and what could only be a scepter in his other.

The other savages who accompanied this personage, while less elaborately attired, were nevertheless more richly dressed than the other people gathered in the plaza. One man in particular drew Gonzalo's interest. The native stood just behind the seated figure and he was attired in a cape made entirely of scarlet and yellow bird feathers. He was of medium height, lean and well-muscled, and, although he found it difficult to gauge, Gonzalo judged the native's age to be near his own. A handsome face and the feathered miter-like hat that adorned the man's head were what caught Gonzalo's attention, but it was the eyes like chips of cold flint that held it.

Captain Valdivia was the first of the castaways to speak.

"We've been mistaken," he whispered to his companions. "This savage who took us prisoner is someone of consequence, but he doesn't rule here. Look at how his head hangs bowed; it's that savage on the bench who's their chief."

While the captain was speaking, two of the natives made their way down the steps to stand in front of the Spaniards. Gonzalo wasn't sure, because they were differently attired, but he thought that he recognized them from the party who'd seized him on the beach.

The older of the pair addressed the castaways in his mysterious idiom. Although his voice was loud, the sounds that came out of his mouth were unintelligible to the Spaniards.

"He has to be greeting us, or perhaps asking who we are," said Diego de Arana.

"I agree," answered Valdivia, then he spoke to the savages.

"I am Captain Juan de Valdivia, Procurator for his Christian Majesty King Ferdinand, Governor General of this expedition and of these lands."

He punctuated his words by pointing to himself and then spreading his arms in an expansive gesture that started toward the east and then swept around to take in all his surroundings. This statement and action garnered looks of confusion from the two natives and then the younger one spoke.

"Perhaps we should try Latin," said Geronimo.

When Valdivia nodded his agreement, the friar faced the younger man and tried the captain's statement in that language.

Again, the castaways' words were received with perplexed expressions and bewilderment.

Diego de Arana then tried some rough French he'd acquired while soldiering. Consternation again resulted, followed by another unintelligible outburst from their large captor.

"Mierda," cursed Valdivia. "We have to make these savages understand us."

"Captain," spoke up Andres Avellaneda, "I agree that we must make ourselves understood, but such an undertaking may take days. In the meantime, must we not fulfill our obligation to our sovereigns and assert their authority. Not considering what these savages may or may not understand, you must read them the king's requerimiento (proclamation)."

Valdivia regarded the escudero from Salamanca coolly. Ferdinand II of Aragon and his daughter Queen Joanna of Castile wished to solidify their authority over the newly discovered Americas and to that end they'd tasked members of the Council of Castile to create a document legitimizing their claim. At a final audience with Ferdinand, just before his expedition's departure, the monarch had presented Captain Valdivia with a first draft. The document, which he'd accepted from the king's own hand, declared that God had made Saint Peter and, through him, his papal successors rulers of the entire world and further that Pope Alexander had granted the Americas to the Spanish Crown. When the puzzled captain asked what he should do with the draft, Ferdinand responded briskly.

"Why you must read it sir! As soon you disembark upon the New World and encounter natives. You must read them our Requerimiento so that they will understand that they are our subjects and vassals of Spain, and that we require their unconditional obedience."

Andres Avellaneda de Salamanca also attended in the audience chamber on that day and now the pompous escudero was reminding Valdivia of their king's instructions.

Valdivia stood silent for a moment. *Avellaneda has the temerity to remind me of my obligations to the crown... But, maybe, just maybe, what he suggests isn't without some small merit. If we can't communicate with these savages, perhaps we can impress them.*

"Rodrigo, give me the papers that you saved."

Valdivia's assistant stepped over next to the captain, reached into an inside pocket of his waistcoat, withdrew a thick packet of oiled leather, and then handed it to the captain.

When the *Viñas de la Barca* sank, there'd been a mad scramble for the long boat; nevertheless, Rodrigo Sánchez de Segovia, thinking of his duty, had grabbed the ship's manifest and other documents that he deemed essential, stuffed them into a water resistant pouch, and shoved the pouch into his pocket. Other than the castaways themselves, the small cache of papers was nearly all of their ill-fated ship that remained.

Captain Valdivia opened the packet's flap and extracted a single folded sheet of parchment.

"Men," he said. "Señor Avellaneda is right. We must meet our obligation to our king. I'm going to read his Requerimiento to those heathen at the top of the steps."

"Captain, to what possible end?" asked Gonzalo. "The natives won't understand a single word."

"As I said," retorted Valdivia, annoyed to be questioned, "to fulfill our duty to our sovereigns, but also Aroça to put on a show for these savages. It's vital that we hold their attention until we can turn this situation to our advantage. Diego, you and Rodrigo stand here at my side; Andres, you and Juan Suarez, at my side also. The rest of you go to your knees, and you friar, lead them in silent prayer. We will show these heathen that we're both proud Spaniards and good Christians."

"God be praised," said Geronimo, holding before him his large wooden cross and sinking to the ground.

One by one, Hernando, Domingo, and Pedro also sank to their knees and steepled their hands in supplication. Gonzalo was last to join them. When he also raised his clasped hands, Captain Valdivia began to read.

"I am Captain Juan de Valdivia, servant of the high and mighty kings of Castile and Léon, the conquerors of the barbarian peoples."

Valdivia's voice rang strong and clear across the plaza, his enunciation as sharp as Toledo steel and at his first words both Diego de Arana and Andres Avellaneda felt their chests swell with pride.

This is my doing thought the haughty Avellaneda. *When we return to Spain, Ferdinand will hear that it was only at my urging that the procurator carried his words to the savages.*

"And, being their messenger and captain," continued Valdivia, "I notify and inform you, that God, our Lord, One and Eternal, created the heaven and the earth…"

When the captain reached a passage, where he told the savages that they must convert to Christianity and subject themselves to Spain's will or, "I shall enter with power among you, and I shall make war on you on all sides," Gonzalo raised his head and looked about the plaza.

Surreal shapes and colors jammed his vision. Scented smoke filled the air and half a thousand sets of jet black unreadable eyes bored in upon him and his pathetic group of companions. Slowly, shaking his head, Gonzalo lowered his clasped hands.

Chapter 12

A Strange and Evil Land

11 Bak'tun 14 K'atun 11 Tun 2 Uinal 7 K'in

(May 30, 1511)

Ah K'in Cutz locked his sharp eyes on one of the captives. Sometime during the previous night's council, Rat Skull had mentioned that one of them had fainted, a skinny creature with his hair the color of chac ib can (red bean snake). Now, that same strange looking captive was removing something from under his clothing. Ignoring the ruler, Ah K'in Cutz moved rudely past Ac Yanto and stood at the top of the stairs to get a better view. When the tall captive pulled a white leaf from the object, unfolded it, and began to speak, Cutz gaped in surprise.

As high priest of Xamanzamá, Ah K'in Cutz was literate. He even possessed óox hu'unob (three books) objects of almost incalculable sacred value. Although he couldn't see the white leaf clearly, he felt absolutely certain that their captive was reading. In that moment he immediately knew two things. First, that the man who was reading must be of noble birth as no one else would be capable of such a thing. The second was that he, Ah K'in Cutz, must possess the white leaf and the packet it came from.

"What's happening, Cutz?" demanded Ac Yanto irritably. "What's he saying?"

"I have no idea about his words," replied the high priest, "but what's happening is most interesting. The man is reading."

"He's reading, are you sure?"

"He reads lord, from the white leaf he holds in his hands, and you realize of course that means he is ah chibal (elite class). And, if he is ah chibal, it is likely that one or more of those standing with him are also ah chibal."

"You're sure? The white leaf looks too thin to be a book."

"Nevertheless, my lord, I'm sure it is. This is a most auspicious turn of events."

"How so Cutz?" asked the batab.

"Because ah chibal are important and of greater value than holcánob (warriors), merchants, or peasants, my lord," answered the priest. "When we sacrifice these captives our offering will find that much greater favor with the gods."

"What of the others, the ones who're kneeling before me?" asked the batab.

"Those, we keep," answered Cutz. "They beg for their lives, so they have less courage than those who stand defiant before you. They are ok'ob (lice) and the gods would look upon them with distain."

Ac Yanto frowned, puzzled. "But, what do we do with them?"

"Nothing, great lord. This is another gods-given opportunity. We hold them as prisoners. If a bird whispers in Ah Tabai's ears and the Lord of the Fire demands to know why he wasn't presented with the strangers, we tell him that we sacrificed a few peasants to appease our own people, but that we saved the ah chibal (elite class) for him. It may not even be a complete lie. I suspect that the kneeling one who holds up the hudzit te (wooden stick) is chilán (a priest). If word of the monkey men never reaches Ah Tabai, we sacrifice the chilán and the others on a more auspicious day. A few of your Ah Cuchcab (council of minor nobles and priests) may suspect, but it is only you and I that will know the truth."

Ac Yanto stared at Cutz. *Impressive*, he thought, *but too devious to keep around much longer. Who knows, maybe the Yajawk'ak' will learn the reality of this day and then it will turn out that only Cutz knew the truth.*

Smiling, he turned to the priest. "The tall bearded man's sounds begin to annoy me. See to it."

"I hear your command," answered Ah K'in Cutz. Then, he turned back to the plaza and yelled to Rat Skull.

"Enough of this! Nacon, the Batab Kinich orders you to prepare his captives."

At the high priest's shout a great roar went up from the assembled crowd and Rat Skull's warriors lunged forward and restrained their hairy faced prisoners. To a man, with the exception of the one who might be ah k'in (a priest), the captives struggled, but as the crowd shouted encouragement to Rat Skull and his warriors, the monkey men were quickly overcome. The kneeling captives were just as quickly bound, while the others were restrained.

"Kish, have the chacs (helpers in religious rituals) bring the tall monkey with the narrow face to the stone," ordered Ah K'in Cutz as he descended the steps.

Kish bowed to the high priest and beckoned to the four chacs, well-muscled but older men, who immediately laid hold of the captive who'd been speaking and dragged him toward the stairway of another building.

Near the foot of its stairs, a circle of cut and fitted stone created a low round platform. In the middle of the platform rose a larger stone, a wide flat pedestal, four or five palms in height, and decorated with many carvings. While the captive struggled, Kish and Thup Paal, the fleshy younger priest, anointed the stone with a sort of blue paint, a color sacred to the gods.

Ah K'in Cutz stopped briefly to pick up the white leaf the tall man had dropped, and to relieve the strange red haired captive of the packet from which it came. He wanted badly to examine the objects, but instead he stuffed them into a fold in his girdle, and stepped up onto the pedestal supporting the anointed stone.

For a moment, he stood in silence looking out over the sea of expectant faces. The act he was about to perform was one of great solemnity and, despite the high priest's calculating and cynical attitude toward the politics which surrounded it, Ah K'in Cutz viewed the act itself with utmost gravity. He took his office seriously.

When he acted as ah k'in, he touched the power within himself and, at those times, he knew beyond a shadow of a doubt that he was more than just a mortal. At those times, he became semi-divine, an intermediary between the people of Xamanzamá and the thirteen heavens, the abode of the sacred gods and of the deified ancestors.

Failed harvests were the cause of Xamanzamá's empty granaries, and the failed harvests were the result of a god's displeasure. The dzonot (natural limestone sinkhole, cenote) behind the plaza's main building still provided the town's people with fresh water for drinking, but carrying the precious liquid to their far flung plots of maize, beans, and squash required tedious backbreaking work and without rain Xamanzamá's hun vinic (fields) were dry.

There were many gods in the heavens and in Metnal, but it was Chac, the rain god who needed to be appeased. Ah K'in Cutz knew every detail of the ceremony that he was about to perform and he knew that he would conduct it with skill and grace. Still, the gods must be petitioned with humility.

In silence, he made his own appeal. *Noble and terrible Itzamna (Iguana House), I call upon you and your wife Ix Chel (Moon Goddess), heed this plea of your lowly servant, your people of Xamanzamá are in need. Hear me oh, great ones and soften the heart of your son Chaac so that he looks with favor on the sacrifice I make to him this day.*

Then, Ah K'in Cutz began to chant, "Chaaac! Chaaac! Chaaac! ..."

As the great rain god's name echoed around the plaza, another great visceral bellow erupted from the crowd.

Head bowed, Gonzalo rocked back and forth, buffeted by the crescendo of noise. Instinctively, he tried to cover his ears, but a rope passed around his upper arms and cinched tight thwarted his movement. All around him the thunder of voices rolled on. When his guards had leapt forward and grabbed at him, he'd jumped to his feet and tried to throw them off. He'd thrashed about with all his strength, but like the other Spaniards he'd been quickly subdued. Once trussed tight, along with Geronimo, Hernando, Domingo, and Pedro, he'd been forced back to his knees.

Why, he thought, *did I ever follow Ojeda to this strange and evil land?*

Even when he'd still had his faith, Gonzalo was never a man who found it easy to call upon God and ask for his help. Now, with Geronimo praying loudly, his other companions all shouting, and the plaza awash with savage cries, he found it impossible.

From where he knelt, a wide corridor had been left open through the press of bodies and at its end Captain Valdivia, struggled against the four savages who held him.

Near the captain, the striking savage with the eyes of cold flint stood on a low platform, stock still, staring at the sky, and chanting. In front of him rose a thigh-high altar of stone that two of the natives had just painted blue. As Gonzalo watched, the flint-eyed savage, who he realized must be a priest of the demon, removed his feathered cape and motioned at two men standing just behind him.

At his signal, the men both used their open palms to beat a tattoo upon a large tortoise shell from which the flesh had been removed. With each strike a deep mournful sound rolled out across the plaza and as the sad echo reverberated off the stone, the crowd fell silent.

Immediately, the pair of natives who'd tried to question the Spaniards also laid hold of Valdivia and stripped the captain of his waistcoat and shirt. When he was bare-chested, with equal efficiency, the younger of the two smeared him with blue paint just as he'd done with the altar.

Once the whole of his torso was stained with indigo, the men holding Valdivia swiftly lifted him and laid him on his back across the stone. The four then took hold of his arms and legs, and spread him out.

The captain was a brave man, but every man's bravery has its limits. With dawning awareness of what was to come, he began to scream.

"God help me! Christ have mercy!"

The other castaways took up their captain's cries and horror contorted Gonzalo's face as the impure priest, chanted loudly in a harsh singsong and brandished a jet black knife of glittering obsidian. Oblivious to Valdivia's terrified screams, the savage skillfully inserted his blade between the captain's ribs on his left side and opened his chest below the nipple.

Pedro, kneeling beside Gonzalo, gasped and fainted. The crowd shrieked. And then, like a ravenous beast, the smiling priest plunged his hand into the raw opening and tore out Juan de Valdivia's living heart.

Gonzalo reeled as if he'd been punched in the stomach and the air sucked from his lungs. The strong coppery odor of blood filled the plaza and carried on it a sharp tang of stark terror to his nostrils.

As a soldier, Gonzalo was no stranger to death. He'd seen companions die at the hands of savages in Darien and he'd seen men die badly in battle in Spain, but he'd never witnessed an end as unspeakable as the one he'd just beheld.

Even in death the desecration continued. While Valdivia's body was tossed casually aside, the unholy priest placed the captain's heart on a plate. Then without another look at the corpse, he carried the heart up two steps, laid it before a large pottery idol with goggle-like eyes, and began to anoint the demon's countenance with blood.

As red rivulets of the captain's life dripped slowly from the abomination's face and pooled around its feet, Gonzalo thought not of the stern strong willed officer who'd commanded their ill-fated enterprise, but of a sensitive man who believed he was dying, hanging onto a tiller, and crying for a good woman and two beautiful daughters. That endless night in the longboat, death had seemed so close at hand, but no one can predict the future.

Events take their own course, he thought, *and no matter how strongly a man swims against the current, he's still swept along. We work, we eat, we sleep, we make love, and then when fate decides, we die. Perhaps, I shall die soon. Juan loved his daughters... What were their names? I should remember.*

A new commotion in the space near the idolaters' altar yanked Gonzalo back from his reflection. The crowd had shifted position. The focus of their attention was now a half-dozen tall decorated posts set into the paving stones of the plaza.

As Gonzalo watched, amid wild cheers and shouting, Diego de Arana, Andres Avellaneda, Rodrigo Sánchez, and Juan Suarez were dragged over to the posts.

"What are they doing to them?" cried Hernando at Gonzalo's elbow.

"We must pray," responded Geronimo, "only God can help us now!"

"But, what are they doing? What's to become of us?" whined the steward.

"We're in God's hands," answered the Franciscan.

"We're in the pit of Hell," growled Domingo Vizcaino.

"But, God cares what becomes of us, doesn't he?" pleaded Pedro, somewhat recovered from his faint.

"Of course he does," answered Geronimo. "He watches over us all."

"Look!" shouted Hernando.

Across the square, the savages were stripping their companions of their clothing. When the four Spaniards stood completely naked before their captors, the same heathen who'd painted Valdivia began to dose them with blue. Diego de Arana and Juan Suarez stood stoically while they were anointed, but when the savage reached Andres Avellaneda, the escudero began to scream and didn't stop. When his turn came, Rodrigo Sánchez collapsed and had to be dragged back to his feet.

Naked and blue, the castaways were then surrounded by a noisy crowd of warriors, all of them armed with bows and arrows. Tall pointed hats of straw were placed on the heads of the four unfortunates and then, in time to a thunderous beat of drums, the warriors began to push and pull them in a sort of solemn shuffling dance in, out, and around the poles. Gonzalo and the others watched in wretched disbelief as, one by one, the warriors hoisted their companions up and bound each of the four men to a post.

"Oh God, oh God, they're going to burn them!" yelled Domingo.

The unfolding horror of the moment was too much for Pedro and Hernando de Esquivel and one and then the other succumbed to the utter hopelessness of their situation. Faced with the awful anticipation of what must surely come next, tears flowed freely down the young cabin boy's cheeks and the balding steward began to sob uncontrollably.

"Bastards! Filth eating heathens! Sons of whores!" shouted Domingo.

While Geronimo prayed, Pablo sniffled, and Hernando wailed, the normally sweet tempered cooper spewed an unending litany of obscenities. Gonzalo, alone of the five, knelt silently, eyes fixed on his trussed shipmates; he was almost unable to bear what he was seeing, yet unable to look away.

Rodrigo was the last to be bound to a post and, once he was secure, the warriors ended their dance and made room in front of the captives. Smoldering pots of incense were carried forward and placed beside each post, and then the unclean priest who'd savaged Valdivia advanced and stood before Diego de Arana.

In one hand the priest held a stone knife, smaller than the one he'd used to open the captain's chest. With the other he gripped the base of a painted stone bowl.

The master at arms stared into the cold flint eyes of the tattooed savage who stood before him.

"I'm Diego de Arana," he bellowed, "son of Xavier Bartolome de Arana, a servant of Christ and their Holy Catholic Majesties

Ferdinand of Aragon and Queen Joanna of Castile. I defy you and all of your heathen gods!"

At his outburst the priest stepped close, and returned the Spaniard's stare. Diego spit in the native's face. Without bothering to wipe the spittle from his cheek, the idolatrous pagan reached out, grabbed hold of the master at arms' genitals, and sliced them several times with his knife. Diego screamed in pain and surprise. While the crowd echoed his howls, the unclean priest collected his running blood into his stone bowl.

When the flow of blood slowed, the savage moved to stand in front of Andres Avellaneda. The escudero, who'd stopped screaming, whimpered, and Gonzalo could see that he'd fouled himself. When the priest pierced Avellaneda's penis and scrotum, Gonzalo again wished he could cover his ears. Once, Rodrigo and Juan had also been defiled, the savage again returned to the idol of the demon and again anointed it with Spanish blood. Then, as the impure deity dripped gore, the priest again raised his voice.

"Chaaac! Chaaac! Chaaac! ..."

With his chant echoing through the square, the warriors resumed their dance. Again, they wound in and out among the decorated posts, passing in front of and around the four blue-painted and bleeding captives. Faster and faster they whirled, drums feeding their frenzy.

Gracefully and without warning, one of the warriors lifted up his bow. In a single swift motion, he drew its string taut and loosed a shaft. One second, Diego de Arana was alive, the next, an arrow was buried deep into his heart.

Gonzalo watched in utter despair as three other warriors loosed arrows, ending the lives of Andres, Rodrigo, and Juan.

After the first four warriors, all four of the captives were dead, but, to their living companions' horror, the dance continued until each man's chest grew into a gruesome hedgehog of feathered shafts.

When savages next came and laid hold of him, Gonzalo felt as if he wandered through fog. His hands, bound behind him, had grown fat and numb. Overcoming wave after wave of nausea, he allowed himself to be dragged to his feet. Although the world wavered around him, he decided that if this was the end, that he would not meet it on his knees.

It's strange to see my own death as finally inevitable.

Gonzalo knew that all men must eventually die, but no matter how many times he'd said the words, he'd never really accepted them. With his future finally stolen away, he saw his past with more clarity than ever before. There were many regrets, many choices that he wished he'd made, and others that he wished he hadn't.

Chapter 13

Ah Tabai

11 Bak'tun 14 K'atun 11 Tun 3 Uinal 10 K'in

(June 22, 1511)

"No!" railed Gucumatz. "I want that hunpedzkin (poisonous lizard) dead now! There's a place of honor for Hoch Can's miserable head at the top of my tzompantli (skull rack) and Buluc Chabtan (war god who receives human sacrifices) awaits his due!"

Ah Tabai, Lord of the Fire, ruler of Tzamá, stared at his war chief and frowned slightly.

"When the time is right my old friend, not a moment before. Hoch Can's life is yours, I promise you that, but not now, not today. I have spoken. This discussion is at an end!"

"I hear you Yajawk'ak' and I obey great lord."

Although the nacon's voice was low, Ah Tabai could sense the yelling and suppressed anger that seethed just beneath his words.

Even in his rage, he bends to my will, mused the Lord of Fire. *Gucumatz is truly a warrior of incalculable value. My control over him is so complete, it's as though he is an extension of my arm and it is my hand alone that wields his mighty war club.*

Catukal kin (22 days) had passed since Gucumatz and Ah Tabai's other emissaries returned from Ichpaatún, yet despite the passage of time, half of the big man's face was still swollen, mottled an angry purple, the color of faded squid ink tinged with unhealthy shades of yellow. The large jug that Ichpaatún's young nacon, Hoch Can, smashed against Gucumatz's head had also cut a jagged gash across his forehead and cheek, an ugly wound which was slowly knitting into an equally ugly scar.

Ah Tabai knew intimately his muscular war chief's demeanor and knew well that the volatile giant would never forgive such an outrage.

On walking unsteadily back through Tzamá's gates, the injured nacon's first act had been to call upon his lord, and request that he turn out all of the city's holcánob (warriors), rally its vassal towns, and straight away march them against

Ichpaatún. For a brief moment, Ah Tabai had even entertained the notion.

After all, he'd thought, *an assault on one of my envoys is no different than a direct insult to my own person.*

Subsequent to an equally short contemplation, Ah Tabai had shrewdly refused.

Injured pride is never a sensible reason for unplanned or precipitous action. That's how disasters are made and the Lord of Fire does not make disasters.

Since Ah Tabai's refusal to immediately take up arms, Gucumatz had made himself annoying and tedious and sullenly refused to discuss anything but his revenge. Normally, such self-centered one-mindedness from a retainer would have enraged Ah Tabai and rapidly led the retainer to a quick and unpleasant end. Gucumatz was a special case. The nacon was loud, at times foolish, quick to anger, and a debaucher. Nevertheless, when it came to projecting Tzamá's power, the war chief was without peer. Gucumatz was at best a mediocre tactician, but he was fierce and incredibly brutal in battle. When the madness of combat took him, he became the earthly manifestation of his patron Buluc Chabtan (god of war and violence). When he was sober, no warrior could stand before his might.

On one occasion, enemy forces had even offered surrender to Tzamá's holcánob simply because they heard that Gucumatz stood at its head. Best of all, from the Lord of Fire's view, the large warrior was trustworthy, malleable, and unerringly loyal.

"You are of course wise brother, but we mustn't delay too long. Nachan Can grows arrogant and this slight to Gucumatz and to your own authority must be answered."

Ah Tabai looked to his right where Zac Nok sat eating put (papaya). The fruit was slightly overripe and its juice dribbled over Worm's fleshy chin.

Ah Tabai felt vaguely repelled. Zac Nok and Ah Tabai were both true sons of Tzamá's old ruler, Ah Kumix Uinic, but coming from different mothers they bore no resemblance to one another. Where White Worm was fat and somewhat slovenly, the Lord of Fire was thin, sharp featured, and fastidious. Ah Tabai often felt slightly embarrassed by his half-brother's appearance, but just as often, he was more than willing to overlook Zac Nok's shortcomings because of his exceptional mind.

Worm was brilliant. At times Ah Tabai even wondered if perhaps his own intelligence paled next to that of his rotund half-brother. Despite the fact that he was Lord of Fire and Zac Nok was only Tzamá's high priest, their long relationship went beyond simple respect.

Just as three strong rocks were used to support the flat stones upon which pom (copal incense) was offered to the gods, Ah Tabai, Zac Nok, and Gucumatz were a tripod that supported the greatness of Tzamá. An auspicious triumvirate which coalesced soon after old Ah Kumix Uinic's death and that had single-mindedly returned the city-state to a position of power and respect which it had not enjoyed since the days of their storied ancestors.

"I agree," answered Ah Tabai. "Our friend Gucumatz here deserves his revenge, and Ichpaatún must be punished, but this issue now goes far beyond what can be addressed by a one-time raid and the sacrifice of a hot-headed young nacon and a few captured holcánob. As you say brother, Nachan Can has grown arrogant. Ichpaatún continues to profess its fealty, but with each turn of the ha'ab (vague year 18 months of 20 days followed by an intercalary month of five days) they grow more conceited and send us less tribute. Their promised trade canoes arrived ho'olyak (yesterday), but all three of us know that what they sent is a pittance. I am Lord of Fire, yet Nachan Can haggles with me as if we were merchants bargaining over the price of salt."

The drought which was causing such problems for Xamanzamá, its neighbor just up the coast, was a lesser difficulty in Tzamá. When it became obvious that poor crop yields were going to be a problem, Ah Tabai had simply demanded an increase in tribute from all of his vassal villages and towns. With Gucumatz and his unstoppable holcánob backing his demands, goods continued to flow into Tzamá and hardship was a problem for others. With one exception, Ichpaatún far to the south was mostly unaffected by the drought, yet they sent no more than they had before.

"They're chattering tuch'ob (spider monkeys), we should destroy them all," growled Gucumatz.

"Exactly my point," said Ah Tabai. "They are our inferiors. They withhold their wealth and it is time we took it from them. Shall I leave a cacique like Nachan Can to rule on my border? Shall I leave his warriors to grow fat at home and raise insolent children while my other vassals march behind Gucumatz at my command? This is not a time for half measures!"

"I agree," responded White Worm. "Nachan Can's refusal to send us his brothers, Ah-cambal and Dwarf-wind, his nephew, Tepeu, and the others is also a slight that we cannot accept. Ichpaatún must be brought under your heel, but we must not let passion rule our actions."

"Again, exactly my point," said Ah Tabai. "It is time that Nachan Can and his entire line are brought to an end and that Ichpaatún and its wealth come under our direct rule, but we must proceed wisely and with caution. In battle, Nachan Can is able to field less than half the warriors that Gucumatz commands, but why meet them at all? If we can use stealth and guile to achieve our ends and not risk our holcánob at all, is that not much better?"

"As always brother," answered Zac Nok, "you are not an ordinary man, you speak with wisdom beyond your years."

Ah Tabai smiled. "I'm glad you agree brother, but if we are to permanently breach Ichpaatún's walls we will need to put our heads together. As a war chief, Hoch Can is young and untried, but Nachan Can and his damnable brother Ah-cambal are another tale. If we are to hand them defeat when they least suspect it, we will need a plan that is as devious as it is shrewd."

"I'll still have Hoch Can's tz'is aw't (f**k ass) head!" growled Gucumatz.

"Of course you will," responded Ah Tabai, "but you will take it when Nachan Can is unsuspecting and the gods favor our actions. For now, rest my friend, continue to heal, and think upon how we can best bring your revenge to fruition."

"As you wish, Yajawk'ak'"

The three men were seated on mats on the porch in front of the two chambered temple dedicated to Chak Ek' (the planet Venus) that squatted atop Tzamá's great pyramid.

Emelkín u Ockín (sunset), just before the sun-faced lord began his descent into Metnal, was Ah Tabai's favorite time of day and he often enjoyed it by taking his evening meal atop the pyramid, surrounded by his retainers and family. From where he sat, he could gaze out over his walled city, its surrounding communities, and even up the coast. On clear days he could see the smoke from the cook fires of distant Xamanzamá. Everything his eyes beheld, and even things beyond, all of it was under his thrall. The Lord of Fire took pleasure in the view. With Zac Nok and Gucumatz at his side he had struggled many tun (years) to make the view a reality, many of them exceedingly bloody, but now, now he was the undisputed ruler of the Ekab. When K'inich Ajaw rose in the east, all of the land his eyes first met belonged to Ah Tabai.

Soon, reflected the Lord of Fire, *all of Ulumil cuz yetel ceh will be mine.*

Zac Nok was about to speak when his niece came running up and threw her arms around Ah Tabai. Like her brother, Yajawte', Ix Moson-cuc (Lady Whirling Squirrel) was slow of mind; nevertheless, she was Ah Tabai's favorite.

"Uts taat (good father), she gushed, "can I have one of the monkey men?"

"What monkey men, chan xchúupal (little girl)?" laughed her father.

"The messengers from Hun Chowen and Hun Batz (monkey gods)," answered Whirling Squirrel. "They say that they are covered with hair and that they only speak the monkey language."

"Who says this?" coaxed Ah Tabai.

"Everyone father, porters from Xamanzamá brought the news. They say that Ac Yanto sacrificed one who was tall and who screeched and also four others that were his servants."

Ah Tabai looked at his brother who shrugged, then motioned to Gucumatz.

"Find out what Whirling Squirrel's prattling about."

"I'll find out Lord," said the warrior as he set down his b'alche, wiped his lips and levered himself to his feet.

"Father, will Gucumatz bring me a monkey man?" giggled Whirling Squirrel.

"Perhaps little daughter," answered Ah Tabai hugging her, but not now, for now, go play with your sister." Whirling Squirrel smiled vacantly and danced happily away.

By the time Ah Tabai and Zac Nok had eaten most of their bil (hairless dog raised for food) Gucumatz returned.

"Well?" asked the Lord of Fire.

"Most interesting Lord; it seems that a uinal (20 days) ago, that puffed up hoh (crow) Ac Yanto, captured ten strangers on his beach. If rumors can be believed the strangers were bearded, covered with hair, and spoke in a language of Metnal (the underworld). The common people believe them to be messengers from the monkey gods. Ah K'in Cutz placed one on the stone and gave his heart to Chac. Four more were tied to the post and also given to the rain god. The merchant from Xamanzamá who I questioned assured me that Ac Yanto still holds the other five. Since it will be some time before the merchant has the use of his right hand, I am sure that he believes what he told me is the truth."

"Does Ac Yanto still call himself Batab Kinich (Eye of the Sun)?" asked Ah Tabai.

"He does my Lord," answered Gucumatz.

Ah Tabai seethed, "First I have to deal with deceit from Ichpaatún, and now that snake Ac Yanto slithers behind my back. If Xamanzamá captured strangers, I should have been informed. Anything that washes up from the sea is mine!"

"Shall I drag Ac Yanto before you Lord," asked Gucumatz, an evil smile lighting his hard face.

"No need to be hasty, our large friend," threw in Zac Nok. "Just as your revenge upon Ichpaatún should wait for its proper time, so Ac Yanto can also wait."

When the old ruler of Xamanzamá died, many years before, it was without a proper heir. His two brothers were dead and he had outlived his two eldest sons. There was a third son, Cutz, but he was a boy, a mere scribe. Ah Tabai's father, Ah Kumix Uinic, had marched his warriors north and promptly installed his trusted nacon, Ac Yanto, as the city's ruler. Ac Yanto had once been as formidable as Gucumatz.

Now, he is flabby and duplicitous, thought Ah Tabai, *and through his carelessness Cutz is Xamanzamá's ah k'in* (high priest).

"So what do you make of this, brother?" asked Ah Tabai.

"I don't know," answered Worm, "but Ac Yanto is an ah çay (an ant) whose time is past. He is of little consequence."

"Still, I am the Lord of Fire; I will summon him here, see him on his knees, and demand an explanation."

"A good plan, brother," said Worm, "but when you do, I suggest that you also send for Ah K'in Cutz, and see him also on his knees. These rumors stink of his hand. And, speaking of plans,

I have a thought about Ichpaatún and its hot-headed young nacon."

The Lord of Fire looked at his half-brother and smiled, he had expected no less.

Chapter 14

The Place of Ajtzak

11 Bak'tun 14 K'atun 11 Tun 3 Uinal 13 K'in

(June 25, 1511)

When out spying for his elder brother, or merely wandering from place to place for his own solitary pleasure, Ah-cambal spent much of his time away from Ichpaatún. During those extended periods when he, of necessity, remained at home, he found it expedient to stay in the hut set aside for unmarried men.

Elders always tell younger men that since their tun (years) give them superior experience of life, whatever they say should be received with confidence. And, also that if the listening young men follow their sage wisdom they will surely gain greater respect in their own lives.

So much was respect given to older men that, except at festivals, marriages, and in other cases of obligation, youths didn't mingle with their elders. Young men also visited little among the married people. Consequently it was the custom in Ichpaatún, as well as all of the other towns of Ulumil cuz yetel ceh, to maintain for them a large building, whitewashed and open on all sides. This was a private space, where the young men could keep to themselves, play ball, games of chance, and otherwise find amusement. Here also, they nearly always slept, all together, until they were married.

Ah-cambal's presence in the house was a perpetual, although unintentional, discomfort to its other occupants, young men who inevitably felt the need to be on their best behavior in his company.

It was sufficiently awkward that Ah-cambal was their elder. More than that though, he was a highly respected elder, an almost legendary figure and brother of their sajal. He was a warrior of wide repute, a quasi holy man, and a man of an age to be taatich (grandfather) many times over.

The distress was particularly acute for his nephew, Tepeu, who had only recently come to the men's house. Still trying to find his own place in the house's hierarchy, he was greatly embarrassed by his uncle's eccentric choice of lodgings. For his part, Ah-cambal went about his days oblivious to the younger men's discomfort.

He was among Ichpaatún's elite and possessed a substantial house of his own, but he was also a man of few wants. He cared little about either possessions or what roof sheltered his sleep. During those times when he'd served as the city's nacon, because it was expected, he occupied his own house and accepted the retainers his brother provided. He viewed both the house and the servants as encumbrances, unwanted additional burdens that duty forced him to shoulder.

The simple asceticism of the men's hut suited him better. Nachan Can supplied for all his other wants, and the constant hustle and bustle amid the exuberance of youth kept Ah-cambal's own age from stalking him too closely.

He awoke to find his own elder uncle, Ah K'in May, prodding him with a walking stick.

"Get up! K'inich Ajaw has again defeated the lords of night and it's high time we were on our way!"

"Uncle!" said Ah-cambal, rubbing sleep from his eyes. "Stop poking me! What are you talking about?"

The old priest paused in mid prod, and stared off myopically for a moment as if pondering the question.

"I want you to walk with me nephew. It is a beautiful day for walking and we can talk. Also, there's something you must see."

"Very well Uncle," said Ah-cambal climbing to his feet and rolling his sleeping mat. "Where are we going?"

Ah K'in May was his long-departed mother's elder brother and May had always considered it his duty to see that Ah-cambal and his brothers were properly educated. With the exception of Dwarf-wind, Ah K'in May was largely responsible for the men they'd become and Ah-cambal loved the old man.

"Where we're going is my secret," winked May, "but it is a secret that will soon be revealed."

"Is it far Uncle?" asked Ah-cambal.

"Not far my sister's son, but you should bring a walking stick," answered Ah K'in May.

Ah-cambal adjusted his girdle and picked up his staff that was leaning against a pole. "Oh, and perhaps a gourd of water," added the old man. When Ah-cambal returned with two gourds of water, his uncle eyed them.

"And, perhaps something for each of us to eat, we may be wi'hi (hungry) by chumuc kin (midday)."

After Ah-cambal wrapped some muxubbak'ob (tamales) and xi'im (corn) in banana leaves and stuffed those into a string sack, the two set out.

At first they walked south to the Bay of Chectumal, then Ah K'in May drew Ah-cambal northward, skirting its shore.

The bay's tide runs high, and next to where they walked, half a league of ocean bottom was exposed. In the distance, among the uncovered seaweed and mud, people from Ichpaatún were hard at work catching fish in the tide pools.

At an age of more than can k'atun (4 times 20 years) Ah K'in May, ancient and bent, was nearly the oldest person in Ichpaatún. On this morning, he seemed almost spry and Ah-cambal was surprised by his steady pace.

"So nephew," May said conversationally, "where is my grandson Digging Snake? It's been many yahalcab (sunrises) since he visited with me. Grown men should visit their grandfathers more often. I look forward to his company and to the pots of b'alche he brings to share."

"Hoch Can is away on our sajal's business, uncle," answered Ah-cambal.

"Sajal's business," grunted May petulantly. "I remember when you and your brother Nachan Can spent all your days sucking on your mother's teats and then couldn't hold your piss. You don't visit me often enough either."

"I'm sorry," said Ah-cambal. "I'll try to do better and I'm sure that Digging Snake will see you as soon as he returns."

"Well, where is he?" asked May.

"Remember, uncle, Digging Snake is nacon."

"Hoch Can is nacon," repeated May as if testing the thought. "Is he old enough? Of course he is... So much time has passed."

"Raiders have pillaged along our borders and he's out with several of his holcánob to track them," said Ah-cambal.

"Now I recall," said the old man. "Your brother told me of this. You speak of Ah Tabai. I knew his father, Ah Kumix Uinic, an ugly flat-faced toad. He also was an ambitious man, but not nearly as ambitious, I think, as this son. Does the Lord of Tzamá continue to press us?"

"He does uncle. His raids are small and infrequent, but they sow fear and uncertainty among the distant homesteads. At the same time, Ah Tabai continues to send us emissaries who profess friendship, commiserate with us, and deny all involvement. Of course, they lie."

"It is good that Hoch Can tries to suppress Tzamá's incursions," responded Ah K'in May, "but it is probable that such attacks are mere distraction. Raids are fit work for a vicious animal, like Ah Tabai's dog, Gucumatz, but a few slaves taken, some crops stolen, and a farm or two burnt is too crude a result to be the end of the Lord of Fire's plans."

"Nachan Can and I also think this, uncle. Ah Tabai has most of the Ekab under his thumb, but he wants us all. Ichpaatún's tribute no longer satisfies him. The eggs of the turtle are no longer enough and he dreams of the turtle itself."

"The Ekab are one people," replied the old priest. It is good that there should be one ruler of all Ekab, but Ah Tabai is not he; such a ruler must be one who wins and binds the loyalties of all. Many years have passed since I sat in every council and advised you and Nachan Can on such matters, but heed my words. The line of the lords of Tzamá is devious and the blood of treachery and deceit runs deep within the veins of Ah Tabai and White Worm. You and your brother must be vigilant."

"We make what preparations we can, uncle," said Ah-cambal. "Holcánob guard our walls at all hours and on nearby paths we've set barricades of xul'ob (stakes with fire hardened tips), trees, and stones, watched over by ah hulob (archers), but as long as Tzamá's true intention remains hidden, there is little that we can do except watch and wait."

"It is well you prepare," said May, "but remember that uolpoch (a very poisonous snake) who drops from the thatch of the roof is more to be feared than ahau can (rattlesnake) who slithers boldly across your threshold."

By hatzcab kin (midday), keeping to the coast, the two men had walked a respectable distance from Ichpaatún. As they crossed a blunt rocky headland, Ah K'in May touched Ah-cambal's wrist and pointed toward the dry jungle.

"Now, we must go inland."

Ah-cambal was more than a little curious about his uncle's mysterious destination, but he knew that any questions he asked the old man about his secret would be deftly deflected until May was good and ready to reveal it.

After walking through thick underbrush for perhaps hoo bak (5x 400) paces, along no apparent path, Ah K'in May stopped and looked carefully about.

"New plants grow," he mumbled, "old trees fall, and my memory is not what it used to be."

"What is it, uncle?" asked Ah-cambal. "Are you lost?"

"No my sister's son," answered May, "but I am old, and things change."

Then, without another word, he stamped his walking stick on the ground, turned abruptly, and led Ah-cambal back the way they came. As he walked, May swung his staff back and forth swatting at the vegetation. After a short distance, his efforts were rewarded with a loud clack and he stooped and tugged at a lush vine. Once he pushed the tangle of leaves aside, Ah-cambal was staring at a large roundish stone. All detail was now weathered beyond recognition, but once someone had carved the rock's surface with elaborate designs.

"Good," huffed May.

Again without a word of explanation, he turned in a new direction and plunged back into reluctantly yielding brush. Ah-cambal was starting to question May's reason, when suddenly a dense patch of jungle parted and he found himself standing on the lip of a tiny dzonot (natural limestone sinkhole). He was confounded by what he saw. With the many pairs of sandals that he'd worn out wandering to and fro, Ah-cambal thought that he knew all of the dzonotob near Ichpaatún. But, this small dzonot was one that he'd never seen. He'd never even heard anyone speak of it.

The small sinkhole spanned a distance slightly less than the height of three tall men. Trailing ferns and vines covered its perpendicular sides and, motionless, clear dark water glistened at its bottom.

Across from Ah-cambal a steep set of shallow weathered steps were carved into the limestone, steps that dropped down and twisted around, curving to disappear at some unseen destination directly beneath his feet.

Ah K'in May gripped Ah-cambal's arm firmly with his long spindly fingers and led him around the sinkhole's edge to the top of the steps. On the other side of the dzonot, just below where they had stood, a natural weathering in the limestone had been enlarged by the hand of man into a deep low ceilinged niche.

"Uncle," said Ah-cambal in surprise, "what place is this?"

"As I said, my sister's son, I'm an old man; this place is a legacy that today I must pass on to you. Come."

And, with that, he began to feel his way down the worn steps. When they entered the niche, Ah K'in May motioned to Ah-cambal that he should sit. The back of the space was shrouded in shadow, but Ah-cambal could make out a low bench of stone and upon the bench two large clay figurines. As his eyes adjusted to the dim light, he could see that one figure was that of a woman. She was barefoot. Her hands were unbound. She was bare breasted, and a rope dangled from about her neck. The floor around the bench was littered with the remains of many offerings, and when Ah-cambal peered closely, he saw that there were also human skulls set into small recesses in the wall behind her. He looked at his uncle with wonder.

"This place is holy to Ixtab (Rope Woman)," said May.

Ah-cambal stared at the female figure. If a person ended their own life by hanging, it was the goddess Ixtab who accompanied and guided their soul. Such a suicide was an honorable death, so Ixtab would lead the departed beneath the spreading branches of the sacred ceiba tree, there to be joined by the souls of warriors who died in battle, sacrificial victims, and others beloved of the gods. Nothing in that place would give pain. There would be an abundance of food and delicious drink and they would be able to rest in peace forever.

"Uncle," said Ah-cambal in shock, "I think there are still many turns of the Tzolk'in before you. Surely, you don't mean to end your life!"

Ah K'in May laughed. "Sister's son, have no fear on that account. I wait for the next turn of the sacred wheel as eagerly as you."

"Then why are we here, uncle?"

"We are here to honor Ixtab, nephew, but more importantly, we are here to honor her ancient companion."

Like the sinkholes around Ichpaatún, Ah-cambal was familiar with the faces of the gods, but just as the small dzonot was a mystery to him, so was the countenance of the other clay figurine. Ah K'in May saw his confusion.

"It is Ajtzak," he said, "one of the thirteen creators. Remember your lessons; it was he who constructed the second humans from wood."

Ah-cambal knew of the god; Ajtzak was one of the old ones. His deeds were remembered, but few still prayed to him and fewer still made offerings.

"Uncle, I'm confused, what is this shrine?"

"As I told you nephew, this is a place sacred to Ixtab," said May, "but while that is true, and it is true that she came here long ago, long before my time, it is also true that she is a latecomer and a guest. The Lord Ajtzak arrived here first and it is he to whom this shrine is consecrated. Many k'atun ago, before you were born, my own uncle, Can-yah-ual-kak (Vigorous Enemy of Fire), brought me here even as I've brought you. He wasn't as old as I am, but he was dying. Long ago this place was forgotten and he believed that he was the only one who knew of its existence. All gods deserve reverence and he feared that if he died without sharing his secret that no one would be left to honor Ajtzak. He passed that responsibility to me and throughout my life I have come here again and again to make offerings and keep the gods company."

"But why haven't you told anyone else about Ajtzak?" asked Ah-cambal, thinking of the sacred cave that he himself had discovered and chosen to keep secret.

"Ajtzak tasks were complete and he was already ancient when the first true men stepped forth upon the earth," answered Ah K'in May. "Before the first turn of the great wheel he'd already laid aside his burdens. He's a great god and if he wanted many to know of his shrine, they would. I believe that like any other old man he enjoys company and wishes to be remembered. However, also like an old man, I believe that he enjoys his solitude and quiet. I've often thought of sharing the secret of this place, but then I think of the noise and confusion of many people petitioning Ajtzak, vying to make offerings, and I hold my tongue."

"Then why bring me here now, uncle? You're not dying. Why am I here?"

"You, my sister's son, have grown and aged into a man who truly respects the gods. I'm proud of you and I would have brought you here eventually so that you could keep Ajtzak and Ixtab company after I'm gone, but today we're here because my mind is troubled."

"Tell me, uncle, what is it that worries you?"

"The prophecy of the seeds," answered the old man. "After you told me of their message, I too cast my tzintè seeds and, as yours did with you, my seeds told me of strangers who would enter into our land and of a world where we would no longer worship our gods. Like you, I am troubled. I have thought and thought upon this matter and prayed to Itzamna, but insight eludes me."

"I too have prayed and pondered," said Ah-cambal. "The message of the seeds is too powerful to be ignored so I watch for strangers, yet without understanding I feel my efforts are wasted."

"While the true meaning of the prophecy remains hidden from us," responded May, "We both know that something is coming. The future is clouded and Tzamá is at our gates. Your vigilance is well warranted. Bringing you here to Ajtzak is my own provision against times of uncertainty. Until the gods make themselves clear, all we can do is take sensible precautions and remain watchful. For now, Ajtzak and Ixtab await our devotion. Will you see to the fire?"

While Ah-cambal kindled a small flame and Ah K'in May placed chunks of aromatic incense before their altar, the likenesses of the gods watched with unseeing eyes. The sacred Tzolk'in had turned and the day was 7 B'en, a time of impending possibility.

Chapter 15

First Blood

11 Bak'tun 14 K'atun 11 Tun 3 Uinal 13 K'in

(June 25, 1511)

Hoch Can waited alongside Yaotl (Warrior) and Teyacapan (First Born). As was proper, he held his body still and quiet; nevertheless, inside the young nacon restlessness and apprehension churned and struggled against his outward calm. Some distance ahead, at the edge of a small cleared garden plot, their companion, Chicahua (Strong), engaged in earnest conversation with a young farmer. Hoch Can longed to hear what the stranger said, but he also worried that if he approached with Yaotl and Teyacapan, the farmer would become frightened and, in his fright, flee.

In the time since daybreak the four warriors had passed two looted homesteads. At each place, they had shouted, loud and long, that they were there to help and that they were friends from Ichpaatún. Both of the ransacked homesteads were silent and deserted. No one answered. The farmer talking with Chicahua was the first person they had encountered the entire day.

As Hoch Can watched, the young farmer began to nod emphatically and point toward the north. Chicahua appeared to become agitated, and then he gave a joyful leap and ran back.

"The farmer says that Tzamáns passed his field this same okinal (afternoon). He says that he hid when they approached, but that he could see that they were carrying bundles and leading two women as captives. The tracks Teyacapan has been following belong to the muan'ob (evil death birds) from Tzamá. If we're lucky we'll catch them before dusk."

"At last," breathed Yaotl

"Now," said Hoch Can, his eyes blazing, "the kitam'ob (wild pigs) will get what they deserve. The gods put that farmer in our path and when we return to Ichpaatún I will make a sacrifice of thanksgiving to Yum Kaax (god of the woods and the hunt)."

The young war chief's blood was up and it was difficult for him to contain his excitement.

Soon, he thought, *I'll prove myself as nacon. Everyone will hear of my deeds and they will know that I am more than just Nachan Can's son.*

Before the hunters had set out from Ichpaatún, his father had taken Hoch Can aside and suggested that there was no reason that he should endanger himself.

"Your holcánob are seasoned warriors," he had said. "Let Yaotl or Chicahua lead the pursuit of Ah Tabai's dogs. No one will think less of you."

Hoch Can was furious. "You think me a coward or that I lack ability?"

"It's not that," replied Nachan Can evenly. "I don't question your courage or your skill. I worry that the raiders from Tzamá will be from among Gucumatz' best, warriors who both know and who enjoy killing. You are my only son and I treasure you."

"Father," Hoch Can answered, "either I am nacon or I am not. I must go!"

In the end Nachan Can had relented and, amid a shower of Za'azil's tears, Hoch Can had proudly led his small band of holcánob out through the city's gate.

Now, their prey was nearly at hand and the young nacon's heart pounded.

"Teyacapan," he said in a voice that he noted belatedly was loud and brusque, "take the lead! Hurry! Don't lose their trail!"

Immediately, the four warriors began to jog, hastening at their top speed to take advantage of the remains of K'inich Ajaw's day. They drank from their gourds as they ran, but they did not pause to eat or even to rest. Half a uinal (10 days) had come and gone since they left Ichpaatún and although they had seen many signs of the raiders' passage, this was as close as they had yet come to overtaking them.

K'inich Ajaw descended into Metnal and Ix Chel had taken his place in the heavens long before Teyacapan stopped, turned his face, and signaled with his hand.

"Look!"

Not far ahead, flickering light of a small fire shown through the brush.

"They're ours!" said Hoch Can in a low voice. "They're settling in for the night. We can take them."

"Not now, my nacon," said Yaotl, the oldest of the group. "They have made camp, there is no need for us to hurry. They won't go anywhere before dawn. We should wait and cut their throats while they sleep."

Hoch Can had never killed and he wanted his first combat to be honorable and glorious, but he heard the experience and wisdom in Yaotl's words.

"Very well, we will proceed with caution and wait for them to fall asleep."

Led by their young nacon, the three holcánob from Ichpaatún crept forward in silence. At the end of what seemed an eternity they found themselves looking out through a screen of dry brush at a small open space in front of a rocky outcrop. In the center of the space, seated by the light of the fire were five men. Nearest to Hoch Can was a hard-looking tattooed warrior armored in a filthy cuirass of quilted cotton. On the opposite side of the fire, another large man, with an ugly scar across his face and only one eye, wore a tapir hide chest-plate painted with the faded and chipped image of a rattlesnake. Two of the other men were on the near side of the fire and the third squatted on his haunches next to the warrior with the chest-plate.

Behind the five, away from the fire, Hoch Can could just make out two bound figures huddled together against the rock.

Hoch Can, Chicahua, Yaotl, and Teyacapan crouched in the shadows and waited for the Tzamáns to fall asleep. After a time, the enemies let their fire die low and began to lie down upon the ground. One by one, they shut their eyes until only the warrior with the quilted cuirass remained. Seemingly on guard, he sat close to the fire and stared into its glowing embers. Just when Hoch Can thought he could endure the wait no longer, the man's head nodded and slowly settled onto his chest.

"Now!" whispered the young nacon. "I'll make an end to that one. Chicahua, you take the one with the chest-plate. Yaotl, and Teyacapan..."

"We already know what we need to do," interrupted Yaotl. "None of the Tzamáns leave here alive."

The four readied their knives and other weapons and began to edge slowly toward the sleeping group.

Hoch Can was only two paces away from the man who had been on guard when the warrior abruptly turned his head. For a moment the two locked eyes and then the Tzamán gave a great shout and sprang to his feet. In an instant the others were also on their feet and the advantage of surprise was gone.

Yaotl screamed, "Ichpaatún! Ichpaatún!" and charged. He swung his heavy war club as he attacked and one enemy's head collapsed in a spray of gore.

Shouts and pandemonium erupted. Shocked by the sudden death and the tumult, Hoch Can froze. Before he could react the warrior with the cuirass snatched up a spear, swung it like a staff and smashed it into his right knee. The leg collapsed.

Hoch Can hit the ground hard. His eyes wide with horror, he watched the big Tzamán expertly flip the spear around for a killing blow. In slow motion the warrior's muscled arm raised and tensed, ready to plunge the weapon's ugly point into Hoch Can's heart. The young nacon tried to scrabble backwards.

As the black glistening blade plunged downward, Yaotl's stone-headed club slammed into the warrior's stomach. The Tzamán doubled with a grunt of expelled air. Hoch Can rolled and felt a line of fire race across his side as the deflected spear scrapped across his ribs and buried itself deep into the ground.

The raider gasped for breath and tried to retrieve his weapon, but Yaotl's club came down again. This time the vicious blow shattered the man's neck and he crumpled, a lifeless bag of meat.

Hoch Can struggled to his feet. Of the four remaining enemy two lay dead near the fire and one was nowhere to be seen. Only the scarred one-eyed warrior still stood. Armed with a knife and a club edged with obsidian blades, he balanced on the balls of his feet, feinting first to one side and then to the other. Blood dripped from his left shoulder.

Chicahua, similarly armed, crouched warily before him with a shallow oozing wound across his middle. Both men panted heavily. Their weapons were chipped, the edges tinged with red. As they began to circle one another, Hoch Can, thought he saw an opening. Yelling his name, "Hoch Can!" he leapt boldly across the remains of the fire.

His attention momentarily diverted, the one-eyed warrior whirled to meet the sudden new challenge. Just as suddenly, Chicahua lunged forward and plunged his knife deep into the man's back. With a wet cough the Tzamán sunk to his knees and pitched forward onto the rocky dirt.

Hoch Can stood shaking in shock and disbelief. Only a few heartbeats before he had stared into his enemy's living eyes. Now, four of the raiders were dead. He heard a wet "thwack" and turned to see Yaotl systematically crushing their skulls. Then, his eyes fell upon Teyacapan.

His friend was sprawled on his back. Blood drenched his stomach and the splintered shaft of an arrow jutted from the middle of his chest. Suddenly, Hoch Can's legs no longer supported him and the young nacon sank to the ground.

"My fault," he moaned, "All mine!"

Chapter 16

Ah K'in

11 Bak'tun 14 K'atun 11 Tun 4 Uinal 7 K'in

(July 9, 1511)

Thup Paal (Last Child) had served as an apprentice and acolyte for an entire turn of the ha'ab (a year). Everyone else considered him a holy man, but it didn't make any difference. A harsh whispered command from Xamanzamá's high priest still made his lungs contract and his hands quiver and sweat.

Day in and day out, Thup Paal strived his very best to please Ah K'in Cutz, but, regardless of how well he thought he accomplished any task, his best never seemed to satisfy the taciturn priest. As was proper in a relationship between ah k'in and acolyte, Cutz gave him instruction in the ways of the gods, but to Thup Paal's unending dismay the lessons that he received were at best sporadic and divulged little.

Each time that Thup Paal felt sure that Cutz was about to induct him into an important mystery, the ah k'in would change the conversation and reveal nothing. Shared knowledge took the form of precious droplets jealously doled out one by one.

Most of the time, Ah K'in Cutz treated Thup Paal like a no-status servant. He ordered him about with contempt, cruelly criticized his every action, or more commonly simply ignored him.

Although Xamanzamá's ruler, Ac Yanto, was his own mother's suku'un (elder brother), Thup Paal scarcely knew his uncle. Ac Yanto had many sisters and Thup Paal's mother had three older sons. When one day the Batab Kinich had drunkenly deigned to notice him and had loudly announced, to one and all, that his "favorite" nephew would be apprenticed to the ah k'in, Thup Paal was ecstatic.

Pudgy, of only average intelligence, and lacking in athletic prowess, he had resigned himself to life as nothing higher than a common scribe. His unexpected appointment felt like a miracle. Even a lesser chilán was a personage of great respect and, with Kish already aged, Thup Paal had dared to think that one day he might even stand as ah k'in.

His optimism had proved as short lived as it was unexpected, and promptly faded into nothingness after only his first meeting with his new master. For reasons that Thup Paal couldn't fathom, Ah K'in Cutz took an instant dislike to his new chilán.

Over time, a certainty had grown in Thup Paal that the high priest in fact loathed him. The priest's apparent hate worried and confused the new chilán. He had no idea what action he could possibly have performed to earn the man's enmity.

From time to time, his uncle secretly called Thup Paal into his lordly presence and questioned him in detail about the ah k'in's activities. On more than one of these occasions, Thup Paal attempted to broach the subject of his supposed mentor's enmity.

The result was always the same; his uncle merely accorded him an annoyed look and waved the matter away. While the Ac Yanto took a keen and abiding interest in everyone with whom Ah K'in Cutz met, and demanded to hear meticulous repetitions of every word the priest uttered, he appeared completely unconcerned that the ah k'in detested his nephew.

Thup Paal, walked through his life perplexed. He cherished his status as chilán, and he enjoyed the unprecedented opportunities to sit with his illustrious uncle, but on many days he wished that Ac Yanto had just left him alone to become a lowly scribe.

"Well," demanded Ah K'in Cutz when the pestle Thup Paal was using made a loud scraping sound. "Is the pigment ready?"

"No, Ah K'in," he cringed, "not yet, but soon."

Cutz glared at the dim-witted chilán who had just interrupted his concentration.

All I ask of the fool is to heat some clay and chohbil (indigo) leaves with copal and then grind them into powder and even that he can't do in silence.

Annoyed, Cutz' dropped his angry stare to the wrinkled white leaf held in his hands. The leaf also offended him. With a grimace, he released it, let it flutter to the ground, and kicked it away with his big toe. Thup Paal instantly stopped his grinding and hurried over, stooping to pick it up.

"Leave it!" snapped Cutz. The lesser chilán cowered away and edged back to his pestle.

At first, the white leaf had ensnared Ah K'in Cutz' imagination. Now it disgusted him. Two full uinal (40 days) had passed since he sacrificed the hairy-faced strangers. Immediately after the ceremony, suffused with excitement, he had brusquely excused himself from Ac Yanto and hurried to his private alcove within the temple. Once alone, with his heart pounding, he'd spread out the thin white sheet from which the tall ah chibal had seemed to read. One by one, he had then pulled six other similar sheets from within what had proven to be an animal hide packet. Those other sheets he had also laid out before himself onto a stone bench.

The leaves were remarkable. They were smooth, white, pliable, and incredibly thin. The pages of his own óox hu'unob (three books) were made from the inner bark of the o amate (fig tree). The fiber was beaten into a pulp that was then pressed into sheets and folded into panels. Once dry, the fibrous panels were painted with a thin coat of lime plaster. The strangers' sheets were much, much, finer. Cutz thought that perhaps they were made from some type of bleached skin or possibly the bark of an unknown tree, but try as he might, he couldn't fully visualize the process which had created them. And the writing, the writing was unlike any that Ah K'in Cutz had ever seen! There were no symbols, no images of the gods, no color; nothing but row upon row of tiny black squiggles! The squiggles looked like the tracks that large sinik'ob (ants) might have made if they had stumbled drunkenly across the white leaves after wandering through a scribe's pot of black ink.

Kin (day) after kin, Cutz had studied the scrawls. In the beginning, he felt certain that the leaves would soon reveal powerful and amazing secrets, but, as more and more time slipped by, he had come to doubt that he would ever decipher them. Eventually, he began to doubt that the squiggles were writing at all.

I was sure that the ah chibal read, he thought, *but there's no knowledge in these leaves. They're nothing, elaborate props in a pageant acted out by fools. I've wasted my time.*

Several kin'ob (days) after the sacrifice Cutz had taken one of the leaves to the hut where the remaining captives were held and had ordered the holcánob on guard to drag out the one who he suspected might be chilán (a priest).

Fearing death, the man had wailed and groveled, acts that Cutz had found both degrading and distasteful, but then, when he yanked the hairy creature to his feet, handed him the leaf, and pointed to the prisoner's mouth, something remarkable had happened. The captive had stared at the leaf. Then, he made fawning gestures, began to move his finger along the ant tracks, and as his finger moved, he had chattered on and on in his false tongue. At the time, Ah K'in Cutz was greatly impressed and truly believed that the man was reading.

How could I not have seen? thought Cutz. *All of it was performance, merchants or even slaves from some far off province trying to make themselves appear as something more than they are.*

On the other side of the narrow chamber, the statue of the god, still encrusted with the strangers' blood, stared sightlessly at him with its strange goggle-encircled eyes. The god was Chaac, a deity who gave life and sustenance, but he was also the great lord of water, and as such, he was feared for his ability to call down hail, thunder, and lightning. All of the paintings and sculptures of Chaac that Ah K'in Cutz had ever seen depicted him with a human body covered with snake-like scales, a long nose, small fangs, a shell in his ear, and un-ringed eyes.

The idol standing before him was unquestionably Chaac, but he was also unquestionably very different. The image of the god had come to Xamanzamá from the distant north, long before Cutz was even born. The figure's eyes stared out through goggles. He wore an elaborate headdress, carried an axe and a shield, and his fangs were those of a jaguar.

The very first time Cutz laid eyes on the idol he felt a strong attraction to the strange incarnation of Chaac. Somehow, the old idol struck him as more martial and more powerful than the deity's usual form.

Xipil (Noble of the Fire), the priest who preceded Cutz as ah k'in of Xamanzamá, had told him that in the north Lord Chaac was called by another name, "Tláloc." A name that meant, he who is the embodiment of the earth. His predecessor had also carefully explained to Cutz about the rites and rituals the jaguar incarnation expected. Following these dictates, Ah K'in Cutz had ordered that the sacrificed strangers be buried in the earth. He had refreshed the blue paint covering their foreheads, sown seeds into their faces, and, before covering them with dirt, had placed a digging stick for planting into each offering's right hand.

Just as Cutz had predicted to Ac Yanto, the sacrifice of the "monkey gods" and their unusual burial, had captured the imagination of Xamanzamá's common people. For a time, they forgot their failed crops, their nearly empty cooking pots, and their hungry bellies. But, just as Ah K'in Cutz had come to doubt the strangers' "writing," the commoners were beginning to doubt the efficacy of his ceremony.

If their ruler Ac Yanto was truly the divine Batab Kinich (Eye of the Sun) and if their high priest, Ah K'in Cutz, truly curried favor with the gods, why had Chaac not heeded their petition? Where was the rain? Why did their crops continue to wither?

Ah K'in Cutz walked over and ran his hand across the god's bloody face.

"Have I offended you Lord? Were the strangers an unworthy sacrifice?"

He pondered the matter. *If the strangers were not ah chibal'ob as I proclaimed, perhaps Chaac found them an affront.*

For a moment he considered another sacrifice and briefly indulged the fantasy of Ac Yanto stretched across the stone, struggling as Cutz raised his knife. The pleasant vision didn't last. Another secret that his predecessor had revealed to him was that the goggled-eyed Chaac had a predilection for the blood of innocents.

Perhaps, he thought, *that is why Lord Chaac has rejected their blood and my petition. Maybe, if I sacrifice a child.* Then, he thought, *to what end? Lord Chaac has already made his decision.*

"Ah K'in?"

Cutz glanced up to see Kish standing at a respectful distance.

"What is it old friend?" asked Cutz. The elder chilán stared pointedly at Thup Paal still grinding away with his pestle.

"Thup Paal," growled Cutz, "get out!"

The chilán laid aside his work, and began to straighten the tools and ingredients that he had set out.

"Ah Puch take you!" cursed Cutz. "I said get out! Leave us now!"

The mere sight of the chubby lackwit was a constant insult to the ah k'in. Even though his own father had once ruled in Xamanzamá, Cutz, like Thup Paal, had formerly been a mere scribe, a ruler's third son with few prospects. Then one by one his brothers and uncles had died. With each death he'd seen himself edge closer and closer to power. Finally, a time came when he took for granted that on his father's death Xamanzamá would pass into his hands.

All of that surety ended abruptly on the day when old Ah Kumix Uinic marched in from Tzamá at the head of his warriors and installed his own nacon, Ac Yanto, as ruler. When Cutz complained that it was his birthright to be cacique, Ah Kumix Uinic had publicly struck him in the face for his impudence. In jest, Ac Yanto had later appointed Cutz as Xamanzamá's fourth chilán, never for an instant considering the possibility that disease, accidents, and old age would, someday make the bitter young man ah k'in.

Thup Paal was a slap in the face; Ac Yanto's way of reminding Cutz that no matter how high he had risen, he was still stood no closer to true power than he had been when he was himself a lowly scribe.

Thup Paal is a worthless relative sent to mock me and spy on me, thought Cutz for the thousandth time.

The fact that Ac Yanto also secretly closeted with his oafish nephew on a regular basis was like a thorn stuck into the ah k'in's side. Thup Paal fears were warranted. Cutz hated him.

Kish watched in silence as the younger man hurriedly set aside his work, hung his head, and shuffled outside.

"A small delegation arrived from Tzamá, Ah K'in"

Kish, the elder of Xamanzamá's two chiláanes, was an old friend of Cutz' father, and also Ah K'in Cutz' most valued ally. Ac Yanto and the members of his council, who were often clam-mouthed and circumspect in Cutz' company, offhandedly ignored the old priest and in so doing often carelessly spilled their secrets in his presence. Unnoticed, Kish quietly and dutifully collected the scattered secrets and brought them all to Cutz.

"Tell me" said Cutz.

"Three lesser Ah Cuchcab, Ah K'in," said Kish. "They insolently demanded to see the Batab Kinich, then delivered a message from the Halach Uinic (Great Man) of Tzamá, and immediately left."

"And?" asked Cutz. "What message did the Lord of the Fire send to our illustrious ruler?"

"Rumors are spreading in Tzamá and talk of the sacrificed monkey gods has reached the ears of Yajawk'ak'. He demands that Ac Yanto present himself and explain the truth of the matter."

Well, well, mused Cutz. *Maybe some good will come from the strangers after all. Even if the rains don't arrive, if Ac Yanto is forced to grovel before Ah Tabai the sacrifice wasn't a total loss.*

"And, how did our Batab Kinich react to Tzamá's demand."

"He blustered loudly," answered Kish, "and talked of the demands of his position and of his many reasons for delay."

"And?" asked Cutz

"The Tzamáns left with Ac Yanto's word to Ah Tabai that he could not come at once, but that he would make the journey soon. I think the summons shook him."

Then, Kish looked uncomfortable. "There is more Ah K'in."

"Well, what is it? Spit it out."

"The Lord of Fire also demands your presence."

"Metnal!" cursed Cutz. "That will be White Worm's doing."

The ah k'in of Xamanzamá and the ah k'in of Tzamá knew each other well. Many times they had sat together and had taken each other's measure. With their first meeting, each recognized in the other a kindred spirit. As a result, the two high priests held a deep and abiding mutual distrust.

For an instant Cutz felt a singular and unexpected moment of anxiety, then he thought better of the summons.

"It is just as well," he told Kish. "I have nothing to fear, and it is not in our best interest to leave the Lord of Fire to speak only with Ac Yanto. Thank you, old friend. You have done well. I promise to act suitably surprised when the 'great' Batab Kinich tells me that I must accompany him to Tzamá."

"Blessings on you Ah K'in," said the elder chilán. "Xamanzamá is rightfully yours. Someday all our máako'ob (people) will bow before you."

Cutz nodded an acknowledgement and gave a slight bow as the old man withdrew.

Ac Yanto will try to avoid Ah Tabai's wrath, he thought. *He'll blame me for our silence. The batab's a fool. I'll present Ah Tabai with the remaining strangers and portray the others' sacrifice as a gift to the gods in the Lord of Fire's honor. Ah Tabai is vain. He'll be flattered.*

The sacred Tzolk'in had turned and the day was 8 Manik', the time of opportunity. Ah K'in Cutz picked up the white leaf that he had dropped and then gathered the other sheets from which the false ah chibal'ob had pretended to read. Working carefully, he tore the leaves into narrow strips, then, he stepped across the alcove and stood before Tláloc. Slowly, piece by piece he fed the strips into the smoldering brazier at the god's feet. As the last scrap turned black and curled and its grey smoke rose before the unfathomable goggled-eyes, a hard smile crept across the ah k'in's cold but handsome face.

Chapter 17

Captives of Xamanzamá

The 12th of July, Year of Our Lord 1511

According to the tally of days that Fray Geronimo struggled valiantly to maintain, it was a Saturday. He also believed that it was the feast day of the martyrs Nabor and Felix.

These two canonized unfortunates were Roman soldiers who came to an untimely end when Emperor Diocletian decreed that their Christian-thinking heads be hastily separated from their otherwise Roman bodies.

Although there would be no feast, and his stomach growled at the mere thought, Gonzalo commiserated with the martyrs. Lately, his world had grown overfull with untimely endings and he found the saints' day particularly fitting.

"It was only by the grace of God that none of us were sacrificed to the demon along with the captain. It was God's holy hand that held us safe!"

The moment the remaining Spaniards were shoved back into the rude hut where their captivity began, Fray Geronimo had loudly asserted that they owed their deliverance to God. The hut had since become their only home, and continuing through each and every one of the forty-three days since their companions' murders, Fray Geronimo had repeated, again and again, his unwavering contention that their salvation from death could be nothing other than another work of divine intervention.

"Our Lord God stood beside the five of us on that day!"

Gonzalo was hungry, dirty, and exhausted, a state that was fast becoming the only condition that the young escudero could remember. He was also surly. On top of his execrable situation, he had listened to the Franciscan make his dogged assertion once too often.

"The only god that I, or that any of us, saw watching over us that day," declared Gonzalo with distain, "was the one made of clay who dripped with Juan and Diego's blood."

"Guererro, once again your words stink of blasphemy!" snapped Geronimo. "That foul idol was an outrage, an incarnation of the demon. It was an abomination before God! I know you feel anger, that you grieve, and I know that our future looks bleak. Even so, many people with far greater tribulations find their world tolerable. Don't allow your anger to become a sin that stains and blackens your soul."

Gonzalo's tired head whirled like a stirred pot. "Far greater tribulations," he cackled. "I saw how you cried out when that unclean priest pulled you from the hut to read Captain Valdivia's letters! You're just as frightened as the rest of us! You saw what they did with his heart. They put it on a God damned platter!"

"There may be blasphemy in his words, Geronimo," butted in Hernando de Esquivel, "but Gonzalo also speaks truth. How can our God not have abandoned us? They're cannibals; I think the accursed savages feasted on our friends."

Geronimo didn't respond. Instead, as he was often wont to do, he turned his back on his companions and began to pray aloud.

"O Lord my God, my light, life of my soul, holy guide, consolidation of my grief, why O Lord, dost thou command of me tasks that I cannot perform? Lord, dost thou not know the measure of my cup, the extent of my limbs, and the worth of my abilities? Lord, dost thou perchance fail me in my labors..."

As the Franciscan's supplication droned on, Gonzalo, Hernando, Domingo, and Pedro looked at one another in surprise. Each of them in turned had despaired of their situation, but Geronimo's quiet prayer was the first time that any of them suspected that the friar himself entertained a possibility that they were forsaken.

Pedro, who even in the depths of their adversity had remained mostly ebullient, appeared suddenly shaken.

"Do you think that they'll fatten us and eat us too?"

Despite affection for the lad, Gonzalo could not control himself and again burst into exhausted laughter.

"Fatten? Look at us boy, we're all starving."

"Do you think that we're going to die?" whimpered Pedro.

Gonzalo looked into the young cabin boy's frightened eyes and felt shame for his laughter.

"You and I both want to live, Pedro, but what we want matters not. Everyone dies, Captain Valdivia, you, me, all of us. That's just the way it is. We all die. I will die. You will die. Geronimo, Domingo here, Hernando, everybody you have ever met will die. Death is the only universal truth, Pedro. All that matters is whether we face it as men."

"But, is there nothing we can do?" moaned Pedro.

If nothing else, we can hope, thought Gonzalo, *it's not much but our survival demands it.*

"We all die, Pedro" he said earnestly. "But, beyond that, there are no rules in anyone's life. Nothing is preordained. Words written in the Bible or spoken by priests, law and tradition, all of these are mere cow shit if you have strength and if you truly believe in yourself. Nothing outside of a man binds him to a particular destiny." Gonzalo patted the boy's shoulder. "Have courage, Pedro. While we live, our hope also lives."

Geronimo turned abruptly back to face his companions. "Guererro, you lead the boy to perdition. We are all children of God, would you have this child stand before Our Lord unrepentant?"

The five survivors were on edge. Their squabbles, sometimes whispered and other times shouted, were familiar and often repeated. The days which crept by since the sacrifice of their companions had presented the remaining castaways with a litany of hardship. Near constant fear grated their nerves to rawness and whittled away at their courage.

The large trays of food presented to them on their first morning of captivity had been replaced by a single shared bowl of cold maize gruel. The gruel was thin and there was never enough to fill their empty and cramping stomachs. Their water jug was also often empty and, despite their fervent pleas to have it refilled, they frequently thirsted for hours on end.

Each morning, they were ordered from their hut and, from the crack of dawn until the hot sun fully set, they were forced to labor without respite. They carried heavy logs, and baskets and blocks of sharp-edged stone. They scrabbled and coughed in dusty pits digging with sticks and their hands. Any work that was onerous, dangerous or degrading, they found themselves compelled to endure. Their hands bled, and their clothes were reduced to tatters. At night, bone tired and soul weary, the five huddled together like dogs seeking the comfort and warmth of another body.

A guard always stood outside their hut or escorted them when they were taken to work. Their principal jailer was the same hulking warrior who had slung poor dead Rodrigo across his shoulders and lugged him during their trek from the beach. The sour-faced savage spoke little and he smiled even less.

At first, Gonzalo attempted to communicate and tried to learn the idolater's name, but he quickly gave up when his efforts yielded harsh and painful rebuffs.

The warrior's true name was Tun Ch'ajom (Stone Scatterer) but because he chose not to reveal it and because he was endowed with bulging muscles and long, dark, meticulously oiled, hair, Pedro decided to call him Sansón (Sampson). The other castaways thought the name as fitting as any.

The native carried a stout quirt-like rod and for the slightest reason, a hesitation, an attempt to ask a question, or a stumble, he used it to raise welts across a Spaniard's back or face.

While such punishments were frequent, sudden, and brutal, Gonzalo suspected that Sansón applied his beatings with a profound and callous indifference. The large savage did not appear to go out of his way to abuse his charges. Nevertheless, over time the Spaniards came to view him as a stupid devil, remorseless and unfeeling. For while the large warrior took no particular pleasure in the castaways' discomfort, neither did he seem to care if they were abused by others who did.

Constant privation and toil took a heavy toll on the five, but without the tormenting they might have endured it. It was the relentless torment that rendered their condition unbearable. While Sansón ignored their actions, others, who among those native folk were very lazy and cruel, often kicked, struck, and beat the castaways. The attacks and mistreatments came at all hours. Sometimes the Spaniards were set upon while they strained under heavy loads. Other times they were ill-used while being led from one labor to another or eating their one meal. From time to time, they were even pulled from their hard dirt bed in the middle of the night.

Rowdy youths were the worst. Not content with merely shouting abuse and striking them frequently, they menaced the castaways. They held knives or arrows over their hearts and through pantomime indicated their desire to kill them as they had their companions. At times, they held one or another of the captives down and for amusement, pulled hairs from the Spaniard's beard.

After their second beard-pulling incident, Gonzalo found a seashell that he secretly sharpened against a stone and then used it to crop his own beard as close to his face as he could manage. Pedro, who was still young, needed no such a remedy, but Hernando and Geronimo soon borrowed the shell and followed Gonzalo's example.

Despite the many exhortations of his companions Domingo stubbornly refused. The big cooper was inordinately proud of his bushy facial hair and as he put it, "Damn them! No godless savage will make me cut it!"

The first view of the castaways with their crudely trimmed whiskers produced peals of laughter from Sansón and their other guards. Immediately thereafter, the captives' tormentors' focused their attention onto poor Domingo. Because of his unusual height and girth, Domingo had already received more than his share of their vicious ministrations, but from that day on, things grew much worse for the good-natured cooper. Four days after the "feast" day of Nabor and Felix, events came to a sudden head.

The five Spaniards were hard at work in a quarry carrying rough blocks of undressed limestone. Domingo, covered in white dust, stooped to lift another large chunk when two laughing young warriors approached. One of them, well-muscled and heavily tattooed, raised a foot and gave the off-balanced cooper a powerful shove that sent him sprawling onto the ground. The two savages roared with malicious delight. Domingo knew from past experience not to react and so he lay where he fell.

Still laughing, the warrior who shoved him bent over Domingo and plucked several hairs from the cooper's beard. When the big castaway winced, the savage laughed even louder and motioned to his friend. The second warrior also tugged out several hairs and was delighted with Domingo's pained reaction. Drawn by the two instigators' laughter, other savages gathered and soon the big man was surrounded by a half dozen grinning tormentors. As the group swelled and grew more boisterous, the savages no longer contented themselves with a few hairs and they began to tear at the unfortunate Spaniard's beard in earnest.

Domingo started to struggle, but the crowd held him down. Blood dribbled from his cheeks. Pain clouded his eyes. Still, it went on. A native knelt on his chest, took a firm grip on a large tuft, and as he tugged, a place deep inside the good-natured giant snapped. Domingo bellowed like an enraged bull, heaved upwards, and scattered those holding him. Roaring, he raised his ham-like fists and lashed out in a maddened frenzy.

Under the vigilant and unfeeling eyes of Sansón, and fearful of also bringing torment upon themselves, Gonzalo and Domingo's other companions had watched in silence and dismay as the savages set upon their friend.

Surging back after his outburst, the savages again overpowered Domingo and threw him to the ground. Their torment was now fueled by their anger. They beat him, stripped him naked, and tore at the last of his beard.

When in pain, he cried out, "Help me! For God's sake, help me!" Gonzalo could restrain himself no longer. He screamed and charged forward in fear and horror as one of the natives plunged an arrow into the big cooper's arm and then again into his thigh. Gonzalo leapt on the nearest of the idolaters, threw an arm about the man's neck and began to pound at his kidneys with his free fist.

Almost instantly a fierce blow to the head struck him from behind. Stunned, Gonzalo released his grip and staggered drunkenly. As he stumbled, the world began to recede. A vortex of darkness opened in front of him and, without another sound, he pitched forward into its inky gloom.

"Here, drink this."

Gonzalo's eyelids felt as though they were sewn together with rough jute twine. His seemingly futile effort to drag them apart took on Herculean proportions, and then, unexpectedly, light flooded in. The hot brightness stung his eyes and washed out his vision. For a single blurry moment Geronimo, larger than life, floated in front of him. The friar squeezed a scrap of wet cloth and water dribbled across Gonzalo's lips; then, his impossibly heavy eyelids fluttered and the hungry darkness swallowed him again.

The next time that he managed to open his eyes, they stayed open. Gonzalo's head ached furiously, but his thoughts were surprisingly clear. Everything about him was cloaked in deep shadow. Now, however, the dense gloom was a comfort, the natural darkness of night.

He lay still breathing evenly. The dirt floor of the hut was cool beneath his body and he could just make out the thatch of the roof above.

"Look," whispered Pedro's voice. "His eyes are open."

Stiffly, Gonzalo turned his head toward the sound, "Pedro?"

"Thank God," said Hernando "We thought both of you would die."

"Both?" croaked Gonzalo.

Then, Geronimo was back at his side, supporting his shoulders and helping him to drink.

"That devil, Sansón, hit you with his club. You've been unconscious for a day and a half."

Gonzalo coughed several times while the friar steadied him.

"Drink slowly; our jug is nearly empty. I'm sorry; we don't have any food."

Slowly, wincing, Gonzalo managed to sit up. "Hernando, you said 'both' is it Domingo? Is he dead?"

"Not yet, but I fear it won't be long."

The balding steward nodded toward the far wall, and Gonzalo suddenly realized that the large form of his friend was stretched out in the darkness.

"It's the heat and the filth," offered Geronimo. "His wounds have mortified. Now he burns with fever. There's nothing that we can do for him except pray that Our Lord cradles his soul and holds him to his bosom."

As though in response to the Franciscan's words, Domingo moaned. His hands began to open and close as though he struggled to clutch onto his fleeing life. A moment later his feeble movements turned to jerky spasms. Then, with a final rattling breath, he was gone.

"Thus is the land to which our sins have consigned us," sighed Geronimo.

The death of yet another Christian left the remaining four Spaniards perplexed and melancholy. Pedro began to cry softly.

How strange life is that I would find myself in such a place, thought Gonzalo. *This cannot go on.*

He turned to the others. "When we came ashore, we were ten, now we are four. I told Pedro here, that all men make their own destiny. It is time that we make ours. If we stay here in this place, our only future is to join poor Domingo and the captain. We have to escape."

"Escape, escape to where?" demanded Hernando. "This whole land is accursed."

"We don't know that," answered Gonzalo. "All we know is that this is a place of death. What lies out there in the jungle can certainly be no worse than what we face if we remain." To his surprise, Geronimo agreed.

"Guererro is wrong about who controls our destiny, but he is right that we must escape. While Our Lord God justly lays upon each of us the burdens of our lives, he expects each and every man to bear his own cross. To simply sit here and wait for our lives to end is an affront to his glory."

"But how," complained Hernando, "how can we possibly escape? We're weak. Sansón or another of the idolaters is always on guard. We know nothing of the country beyond this village and the beach."

"I don't know how," answered Gonzalo, "but I know that we must."

"Pray with me," said Geronimo. "Trust in God."

Chapter 18

Heat and Comfort

11 Bak'tun 14 K'atun 11 Tun 6 Uinal 14 K'in

(August 25, 1511)

K'inich Ajaw, the sun-faced lord, had moved far to boox chik'in (black west), but the Plaza of the Bees, tightly enclosed by residences and ceremonial buildings, still sweltered from the glory and intensity of his passing. Seated in the hot shade beneath an overhanging roof of thatched palm at the front of Ah Muzencab's (bee god's) temple, Nachan Can, his son, and his two brothers, argued and sweated.

From time to time an infrequent breeze off the Bay of Chectumal managed to find its way into the open expanse of stone. The four men greedily welcomed each of the gentle puffs, but rather than bringing them expected relief, one after another, the soft breezes simply evaporated into the plaza's oven of radiated heat.

Nachan Can finished speaking and wiped his brow. In the silence that followed, Dwarf-wind struggled clumsily to his feet and stood fuming above him. As was customary for the ruler-of-Ichpaatún's youngest brother, he was oiled and perfumed. As was also usual, he was dressed in finery excessive for commonplace day to day affairs, especially so for a casual meeting with relatives on such a warm day. What was not customary was the fierce glare in his beady eyes and the hard angry set of his wide fleshy lips.

"I will have this!" growled Dwarf-wind. "You are Sajal and even though you are my brother, I have always bowed before you. This time, I will not bow. I will have what is mine. That which was offered, was offered to me and not to you! Sajal, or not, the choice is mine, not yours. You are not the only one of us here with a claim to royal blood, or even the only one here who knows what is good for Ichpaatún. I will accept the Lord of Fire's proposal!"

Nachan Can listened to his brother in stony silence.

"Father you cannot! Surely you will not allow this?" stormed Hoch Can.

"Hold your tongue, Boy!" snapped Dwarf-wind. "You have no say here!"

"He is our nephew, and he is nacon," chided Ah-cambal.

Dwarf-wind glared at his other older brother. "You stay out of this too."

"Father," continued Hoch Can earnestly, "how can you even consider such a thing? Teyacapan has not yet finished his journey to the underworld and yet we speak of marriages and alliances with his murderers!"

"Hoch Can," hissed Dwarf-wind, "you repeat lies as easily as a common fishmonger repeats gossip. Tzamán merchants, who only left from me at chumuc k'in (midday) again brought condolences and renewed assurances from our Lord of the Fire that he works tirelessly beside us to bring this disagreeable banditry to an end."

"Disagreeable banditry!" choked Hoch Can spluttering with fury. "Teyacapan wasn't killed by some bandit. He was killed by one of Gucumatz's warriors. Ah Tabai wages war against us!"

"Brother," said Dwarf-wind, "our nacon may be my nephew, and he may be your son, but one small and costly victory against bandits does not make him wise. Hoch Can raises his voice in anger when he should listen to his elders. He is young and foolish and his words go too far. Tzamá is our most valued trading partner. Despite what any of you may think, I know the Lord of the Fire to be our steadfast friend. Tzamá's offer is a wondrous opportunity!"

"Uncle," spat Hoch Can through clenched teeth. He was about to say more, but his father, Nachan Can, cut him off.

"Hoch Can, my son, I don't agree with much of what your uncle, Dwarf-wind, says, but this day is hot and I agree with him that your words have likewise become heated. You allow your anger to overshadow your reason. Leave us until you cool down and find your senses."

Hoch Can stared at his father. For a few blinks he sat in silent disbelief. Then, Ah-cambal laid a friendly hand on his shoulder and broke the spell. Without another word, Hoch Can shook off his uncle's hand, jumped to his feet and, stalked away.

Za'azil laughed with pleasure as her new daughter, Óolal, squealed in mock terror and edged away from a tiny crab. The minuscule creature, disgusted that it had been plucked from its comfortable watery home in the bay, waved its insignificant claws in proud defiance at its retreating foe. Then, it scuttled under a leaf.

"Do you think the xib babaal (monster) is gone?" giggled Za'azil. "Perhaps we should shout for Ah-cambal to come with his spear."

"We don't need to call for Grandfather," said Óolal frowning and putting her small closed fists on her hips. "It is only a bau (crab) and I'm very much bigger."

If he heard that anyone else had called him "Grandfather," Ah-cambal would have bristled, but Za'azil knew that from Óolal he accepted the label with a secret satisfaction.

"You are indeed much bigger, Chan (little) Óolal, and very brave," said Za'azil as her adopted daughter's serious expression and valiant stance clouded her eyes with tears of laughter.

The two sat in comparative comfort, shaded by the large yaxché whose canopy spread over the front of their home, sheltering it during the hottest parts of K'inich Ajaw's day. Since, their patio was located outside of Ichpaatún's enclosed stone plazas, breezes off the bay also brought greater respite from the heat.

Za'azil and Óolal had spent a productive morning splashing through the bay's many tide pools, catching scores of finger-sized fish. Now, a carpet of the tiny silver ocean-dwellers spread out before them on woven mats where, unprotected by the overhanging yaxché, the sun and heat would quickly dry them for storage and later use.

Za'azil was content with her life. Ahau Chamahez (God of medicine and good health) smiled upon her and her family. Hoch Can loved her madly and the child, Óolal, brought a joy to her that had before been missing. Still, Za'azil was not completely at ease. Day in and day out, she worried about her husband.

The fact that their love-making had failed to produce a child and the attendant rumors of impotency weighed heavily on Hoch Can's mind. After his father and uncle demanded that he adopt Óolal, the innuendos had increased. Za'azil loved her new daughter, but forcing her upon Hoch Can had been like adding manatí oil to a smoldering fire. He was never mean or cruel to the child, but neither did he happily accept her into his home. Instead, he ignored her presence and treated her as though she did not exist. For many days he had silently raged, refused to speak to Óolal, and, even with Za'azil, he had grown withdrawn and sullen.

Then the chance had arrived to lead his band of holcánob against the marauding Tzamáns. Despite Za'azil's heartfelt pleas, her husband had grasped for the opportunity like a drowning man clawing for a floating log. It was an opening, a possibility to prove his prowess, and his manhood.

Since his return, things had grown even worse. To Hoch Can's dismay at his inability to sire a child, had been added a crushing guilt brought on by the belief that the blood of Teyacapan's death lay snuggly cupped in his hands.

The moment Za'azil spied her husband, she knew that he was more upset and disturbed than when he left her in the morning to speak with his father and uncles. Hoch Can walked with his handsome head bent low and his muscular shoulders slumped as though crushed under a heavy burden. Without acknowledging Za'azil, seated at the foot of the yaxché, and without even a look about himself, he disappeared into the interior of their dwelling.

"Óolal," asked Za'azil, "can you do something for me?"

"Of course, Mother," was her grave reply. "As I said, I am big."

"Well then my big girl," smiled Za'azil, "take this basket, fill it with driest of the fish and carry them to my own mother."

As befitted a salt trader and his wife, the home of Za'azil's parents was on the far side of the small city, much nearer to the bay. It would take Óolal some time to reach their patio. There was nowhere in Ichpaatún where a child was unsafe, and Za'azil wanted time to speak with Hoch Can alone. Also, she was sure that her mother would dote on her adopted daughter which would give her even longer to be in private with her husband.

After helping Óolal select which fish to put in her basket, Za'azil shooed her on her way and went into their home. She discovered Hoch Can in the near stifling darkness of their sleeping chamber. He was seated on the low bed of rods, reed mats, and quilted cotton. His back was propped against the outer wall, his head was in his hands, and beads of sweat lined his brow.

"What is it my sweet husband? What has happened?" asked Za'azil in a low soothing voice.

Hoch Can looked up at her through eyes that were damp with tears and ringed in red.

"One of my best friends is dead through my own incompetence and now my uncle, Dwarf-wind, is to marry the daughter of one of his Tzamán murderers."

The news that Dwarf-wind was to wed a Tzamán shocked Za'azil, but she chose to ignore the revelation and focus on the core of her husband's pain.

"Hoch Can," she whispered, "Teyacapan died a warrior's death. It was a death he would have wanted. That is not your fault."

"My father told me to let Yaotl or Chicahua lead the pursuit of the Tzamáns. If I had listened to him, Teyacapan would still be alive."

"You can't know that," said Za'azil.

"I'm inexperienced. I made too many mistakes," groaned Hoch Can. "I let my foolish pride blind me. Yaotl and Chicahua are tested holcánob. Neither of them would have made my errors."

"Husband," said Za'azil, raising his face so that their eyes met, "when the skeletal lord, Ah Puch, is abroad in the world he cares nothing for anyone's experience. When a man is chosen, the skill and ability of his nacon mean nothing. Each man's time is measured by the gods as they see fit. You say that you were blinded by your pride, but it is blind pride to say that Teyacapan's life was yours to save or to lose."

"I led. I am nacon. It was my plan," sighed Hoch Can

Za'azil lowered herself onto the quilted mat beside her husband. "We are young my beloved. There will be many other plans, and other men that you love will die. That is the way of the world. Someday, you will rule here in Ichpaatún and Teyacapan will be but one of many that you have lost. To be a ruler is a difficult calling, but that is your path. That is what the gods have placed before you!"

Hoch Can looked away, surprised at the intensity and determination of her speech. When their eyes again met, Za'azil placed her right hand onto his damp thigh. She understood Hoch Can and knew that his pain dwelt deep within his heart, buried in a place that her words would not reach. Determined to ease his hurt, she placed her left hand on his other leg. Despite the room's heat, she felt his skin prickle as though chilled. Slowly, she began to slide her hands up and down his legs. At first, she though that Hoch Can might thrust her away, but then she touched his manhood, through the cloth of his suyen (sarong-like garment) heard him groan, and felt his member stiffen. Za'azil gripped his shoulders and pulled Hoch Can away from the wall. Then, she pushed him back onto the sleeping mat. Moving deftly she bent over him, removed the suyen, and grasped his erection. Gradually, in smooth even strokes, she began to move her hand up and down the shaft, meanwhile her other hand played lightly across his chest and groin. At first, Hoch Can lay completely still with his eyes closed, but as the pressure and rhythm of her attentions increased his body began to tense and move in concert. Then, his eyes opened and, to her joy, Za'azil saw them filled with yearning rather than pain. Sitting up, Hoch Can gently removed her huipil and pic (loose outer garment and underskirt) and pressed his naked body tightly against hers. He kissed her neck, stroked her back, and cupped her breasts into his strong hands. Za'azil squeezed his member tightly and returned his kisses. His hands teased at her nipples, lightly pinching and tugging. Then Hoch Can lowered his head, took a nipple into his mouth, moved a hand between her legs, and she heard herself moan. As he continued to suckle at her breasts and stroke her womanhood, she became wet and gave herself over to desire. For a time they writhed together, their sweat-slick bodies intertwined. Then as their hunger for each other reached a crescendo, Hoch Can raised her to her knees and moved behind her. Za'azil felt the hot tip of his member press against the soft lips of her sex. Then, he was inside her, the two of them joined. Hands gripping her hips, he moved forcefully in and out and she pushed back eager to meet his thrusts.

After release, the two of them lay contentedly next to one another. Hoch Can took Za'azil's chin into his hand and stared into her eyes.

"Beloved," he whispered, "you are like the smoking star and the flowers of the fields. I desire you even to the heavens."

Za'azil gazed back into Hoch Can's eyes and felt a tear slide down her cheek.

As the shadows of the afternoon grew and the glory of K'inich Ajaw's passing faded, the cooling breezes finally overcame the heat trapped within the Plaza of the Bees. Nachan Can and Ah-cambal, still seated under the thatch of the bee god's temple, watched their brother, Dwarf-wind, walk away. His weak chin was held high, his flabby shoulders were pulled back, and there was an air of victory in his step.

"You've been unusually silent," said Nachan Can. "Do you believe I made the wrong decision?"

"I believe that you have reluctantly made the only decision that you can, my Sajal," answered Ah-cambal seriously. "There is no question; Hoch Can, is right. The raiders that plagued us were from Tzamá and certainly the Lord of Fire knew, and approved, of their actions. On the other hand, Gucumatz is a formidable warrior who we have offended and his holcánob is much larger than our own. We cannot afford open war with Tzamá."

"You and I both know that Ah Tabai's offer to wed one of his daughters to Dwarf-wind is not what it appears," answered Nachan Can, "but at least accepting it removes our growing conflict from the point of a spear and gives us time to look for a political solution."

"Our sibling, Dwarf-wind, is a foolish t'u'ul (rabbit)," responded Ah-cambal, "a t'u'ul who, blinded by his ambition, charges heedlessly into the Lord of Fire's snare. But you, my older brother, you are the Lord of Ichpaatún and I think not such an easy catch. Agreeing to accept the offer, you have given us time and with enough time, and enough care, anything is possible."

Nachan Can smiled at his brother. "I think I shall go and make an offering of pom (copal incense) to Itzamna. Will you join me?"

"You are wise, Brother," said Ah-cambal standing up, "and I will come. If ever there was a season when it was prudent to petition the favor of our gods' I think that we have stumbled into it."

Chapter 19

Gods Drink Blood

11 Bak'tun 14 K'atun 11 Tun 6 Uinal 17 K'in

(August 28, 1511)

Hook al (one hundred) small clay braziers smoldered on the narrow knee-high steps of Tzamá's great temple and their drifting smoke filled the night air with the musky smells of burning pom and aromatic wood. The Lord of Fire had sent forth criers and, as ordered, his subjects had gathered. Now, stretching out from the pyramid's base a restless carpet of humanity filled Tzamá's walled inner city to bursting.

A royal bloodletting was a sacred occasion of the greatest solemnity and to honor it, women brewers filled yet another ornate earthen chicha jar to within a narrow finger's width of its massive rim. Even empty, profuse relief decorations and an odd shape rendered the heavy vessel ponderous and unwieldy. Full to its brim with a fermented mix of nixtamal (corn boiled with lime), honey, and water, an old man grunted quietly and staggered under its bulk.

Just as the scrawny slave cautiously shifted his weight and began to pour, Gucumatz, oblivious to the elderly man's struggle, laughed at some nearby jest and carelessly swung aside his already half-full cup.

The slave shuddered and blanched. He tried desperately, but the viscous flow could not be stopped. Sweet sticky corn liquor splashed against the volatile nacon's elaborate jaguar-skin leggings and splattered down over his fine tapir-hide sandals. Gucumatz whirled, his eyes blazed, and his scarred face contorted with erupting anger.

"You careless pek xe (dog vomit)!" he roared.

The old man tried to shy away, but the broad-shouldered warrior grabbed him by his bird-like neck and shoved him violently to the ground. As the drudge fell, the cumbersome chichi jar slipped, once and for all, from his clawing grasp and cracked open. The rest of its valuable contents sloshed wildly about and gushed out onto the dressed stone around him.

"You'll suffer for that!" hissed the nacon.

"Great Lord," whimpered the slave, crawling to his knees in the middle of the puddle. "I...I, forgive me."

"Your worthless life is forfeit," growled the nacon, drawing his glittering flint knife.

"Ko'oh (dear) Gucumatz," came a sarcastic yet soothing voice from his side, "remember what great things we are about this aak'ab (night). Do not sully yourself or spoil the gods' favor for the sake of this xet' (lump).

Entranced by the silky voice, Gucumatz turned to stare into the dark bottomless eyes of Ix Co-tancas-ek (Lady Mad Seizure Star) Ah Tabai's eldest daughter. Slowly, he sheathed his knife. Behind his back, the unctuous slave quivered and crawled away with as much stealth as he could manage.

Earlier, Gucumatz ate several of the hallucinogenic mushrooms that White Worm had proffered and now, unexpectedly, he discovered that he suddenly felt noble and quite magnanimous.

The old slave and the chicha are of no consequence, he thought. *They don't even deserve my attention.*

The depths of Mad Seizure Star's eyes sparkled and twirled like the heavens spinning far away above Gucumatz' head.

"You are right, most hats'uts (beautiful) tonight is a night of import, truly a night for greater things."

When K'inich Ajaw descended into Metnal and the brilliance of his day faded, the cloth of the sky had turned slowly from a warm bird's egg blue into a heavy shimmering veil of the deepest purple. Amid the growing darkness, like tiny mice creeping from their nests, the lesser lights of other gods had emerged to shine forth. First one dim sparkle had appeared, and then another, and then another. Each new glimmer bursting into the darkness until the wash of their tiny flickering lights, just beyond Gucumatz' reach, became so bright and so close as to be almost as white as the loose cotton mantle which hung so seductively from the delicate curves of Mad Seizure Star's shoulders.

Even under the influence of Worm's mushrooms, such splendor might normally have been wasted on the Nacon of Tzamá, but tonight was a special night. Tonight the war chief paid unusual attention to their grandeur.

To those priests who could read their signs, the lights of the gods revealed powerful portents and omens. If an ah k'in was clever, the lights told him when to plant, when to harvest, and, to Gucumatz's mind most importantly, when to go to war.

In Tzamá no one was cleverer than White Worm and the nacon knew well that Worm and his assistants had spent many sleepless nights studying the heavens. According to the lights of the gods, Hun Ahau (Chak Ek' - the planet Venus) would soon look favorably upon their endeavors against Ichpaatún.

For Gucumatz the day could not arrive too soon. The scar that the poisonous lizard, Hoch Can, had placed on his face had knitted, and the fierce black and yellow-tinged bruising had faded. Gucumatz' wounded pride remained. Stoked by it, his anger, always just below the surface, still burned brightly.

When had he received word that Max-cal (Monkey Throat) and Koh-tun (Stone Mask), two of his best warriors, had been set upon and slain by a war party led by Ichpaatún's young nacon, his rage was ferocious. He had once again ranted, bellowed, and insisted that Ah Tabai allow him to call out Tzamá's holcánob and march them against the southern upstarts.

Just as he had responded to Gucumatz' previous demands, the Lord of Fire had flatly refused. At first Tzamá's burly nacon sulked and fumed, but later, when he again listened to Zac Nok's plan for revenge, he banked his hate, and reluctantly agreed to delay his vengeance.

Gucumatz was a blunt instrument, but, intoxicated or sober, he was rarely a fool. He had lost count of the number of battles that he had won against Tzamá's enemies, but deep inside he knew that just as many were avoided by Ah Tabai's deft diplomacy. What is more, despite his own renown in combat, he also knew that many of his greatest victories were the result of White Worm's guile and scheming rather than his own prowess with a war club.

I must keep my wits, he thought, looking ruefully down at his splattered leggings. *Tonight is about the Worm's guile, about petitioning the good will of the gods, and,* glancing at the statuesque woman standing at his side, *about Mad Seizure Star.*

Like Ah Tabai's idiot son, Yajawte', and his slow-minded daughter, Whirling Squirrel, his elder daughter, Mad Seizure Star, was touched by the gods. But, where the gods' influence had left the two younger children feeble minded, it had left Mad Seizure Star calculating, cruel, barren, and oversexed.

To Gucumatz way of thinking, she was the perfect companion, and, since Ah Tabai did not seem to mind, he took her to his bed as often as the opportunity arose.

Musicians tested their instruments. Jesters and dwarves cavorted about him. And, through a mushroom-induced nimbus of rainbow colors, Mad Seizure Star seemed to float at the nacon's side.

White Worm is indeed formidable, mused Gucumatz. *His plan to offer her in marriage to Nachan Can's fawning brother, Dwarf-wind, is a deceit worthy of the Hero Twins, Hunapu and Xbalanque. As Worm predicted, that idiot, Dwarf-wind, pissed himself with glee. Ichpaatún's message accepting the betrothal came so quickly that their messenger collapsed from exhaustion.*

Gucumatz again stared at Mad Seizure Star and as he remembered the curves of her voluptuous body and the feel of her firm nipples against his rough hands, a great roar of laughter burst from his belly.

Those pleasures are mine, he thought, *pleasures that Dwarf-wind will crave but never know.*

"Hush you much (toad)," snapped Mad Seizure Star, pointing past his shoulder. "It begins!"

Such a multitude of people were gathered, that from where Gucumatz stood and swayed near its summit, it seemed to him as though Tzamá's great pyramid, which rose from their midst, rested upon the undulating mottled back of some great and godly creature. Clutched in the creature's thousand fluttering hands a quivering field of torches spread out before him and echoed the flickering god-lights from the heavens. Reluctantly, Gucumatz pulled his gaze away from the hypnotic ripples of flame and shadow and turned to follow Mad Seizure Star's gesture.

Outlined against the darkness by the ruddy glow of smoking braziers, the two chambered temple of Venus rose before him. As Gucumatz waited, a sudden prodigious beating of drums shattered the stillness. Then, heralded by a flurry of conch shell trumpets, Tzamá's Lord of the Fire stepped slowly and regally from one the temple's three doorways.

Ah Tabai's head was adorned with an elaborate headdress from which grinned the oiled shrunken head of a human victim.

Jade ornaments embellished his person and jaguar-skin sandals covered his feet. The rest of his raiment was his finest and fiercest armor as though arrayed for a coming battle. As he cleared the door's lintel, he thrust aloft a great flaming brand. Behind him, in the opening, two of Worm's acolytes also clutched blazing torches which lit their ruler from behind, cast his long shadow down the pyramid's steps, and made him grow larger than life. At his appearance, the sea of people rumbled, and to Gucumatz it sounded as if something in the belly of the great many-headed beast had growled in anticipation.

The Nacon stared at the glowing form of Ah Tabai who, with his arms upraised, stood still and god-like before the gathered masses of Tzamá. As always, the Halach Uinic (Great Man) was impressive and Gucumatz nodded his spinning head in appreciation. Not only was his old friend the political leader of Tzamá, he was, even before Worm, the city-state's spiritual leader, and that was another role that Ah Tabai played with an adept flair which befitted his cleverness.

The gods crave blood, thought Gucumatz, *and this night Ah Tabai will offer them his own, but he is also shrewd enough to offer the people the thing that they crave most, spectacle.*

At that moment, the conches resonated for a second time, drums again splintered the night with a sound of huum chaak (thunder) and White Worm emerged from the temple's far right-hand door. Shambling, glaze-eyed, beside him shuffled Ah Tabai's first wife, Ix Cucul-patz-kin (Lady Sunstroke). The pair was also backlit by acolytes holding torches, and like the Lord of the Fire, Worm pushed aloft a flaming brand.

The priest's fleshy face was painted with sacred patterns in red and black and he was costumed nearly as magnificently as Ah Tabai. On his head perched a large stuffed moo (scarlet macaw) its wings outstretched. Over his considerable bulk draped an ostentatious cape made of tightly woven, but freely hanging, hemp strings. Upon the swaying strings were sewn a flock of small stuffed birds with brilliant feathers, and each time that Zac Nok moved, their wings and crests reflected a shimmering rainbow of color. Gucumatz saw the cape as a thing almost alive, dancing with scarlets, yellows, greens, and flickering hints of purple.

For several slow heartbeats the storied war chief lost himself into the garment's shifting glamour. Then, abruptly, a great roar rolled up from the masses below and yanked his narrowed attention back to the unfolding ceremony.

The people had recognized the symbolism of Worm's attire. Taken together, the macaw and the torch represented drought. Although, the lack of rainfall that plagued Tzamá's corner of The Land of the Turkey and the Deer was scarcely felt by the likes of Ah Tabai, Gucumatz, and the other social elite, who lived within the defensive walls of Tzamá's ceremonial center, it was a heavy curse upon the backs of the city's ordinary subjects.

In return for his vassals' adoration, fealty, and tribute it was the Lord of the Fire's role to ensure the fertility of the earth and guarantee the abundance of their crops. In this time of failing crops and hunger Ah K'in Zac Nok's macaw costume and the presence of Lady Sunstroke surely meant that, as a supreme gesture of their deep concern, both the lord of Tzamá and his adored first wife would offer royal blood to alleviate the suffering of their unfortunate people.

As the noise from the crowd rose and fell, the Lord of Fire seated himself on a raised stone dais in full view of all those who waited expectantly below. Lady Sunstroke, wearing an elegantly patterned white cotton robe and a headdress of quetzal-feathers, knelt at her husband's feet. Gucumatz watched intently as she reached forward and loosened the cloth that girdled Ah Tabai's loins.

Lady Sunstroke was Mad Seizure Star's mother, and although she was not as young nor as alluring, Gucumatz often imagined what it would be like to take them together into his bed. As the garment fell away and she began to stroke Ah Tabai's manhood, Gucumatz felt his own shaft stiffen. Then, just as quickly, he remembered what was to come next and his lust and envy wilted.

The Lord of Fire rose majestically from his dais and again faced the mass of people waiting below. They could see that his member was erect and hard, and they rewarded him with undulating cheers.

As the sudden clamor rose in volume, White Worm stepped forward, and just as swiftly the voices dwindled into eerie silence. In his outstretched hands the high priest supported a small but exquisite tray. Carved from the finest jade into the form of a coiled serpent, it reflected the flickering flames of nearby torches and glowed with an eerie green light, as if twitching and alive.

Bowing slightly, Worm offered the tray first to Ah Tabai and then to Lady Sunstroke. From its smooth surface, each of them picked up a single stingray spine, long pointed and bleached white by the sun. Zac Nok then produced three small reed stalks which he set beside Ah Tabai and also a knotted length of hemp twine that he placed beside Lady Sunstroke. Four lesser chilánes came forward in pairs bearing two woven baskets. One basket they put on the floor at the Lord of Fire's feet, the other they set in front of Lady Sunstroke's knees.

Even as Ah K'in Cutz had done at Xamanzamá before he plunged his hand into Captain Valdivia's bloody chest, White Worm began to chant the sacred name of the rain god.

"Chaaac! Chaaac! Chaaac! ..."

His strong deep voice resonated from the hollows of the Venus Temple and rolled down the steps of the pyramid to where it was echoed by the waiting crowd. The deep hollow rhythm of a tunkul set a measured cadence and upon each beat the name of the rain god reverberated through the darkness.

The Lord of Fire grasped his stiff penis with his left hand and Gucumatz flinched involuntarily as, stone-faced, his friend used his other hand to shove the stingray spine, from side to side, through his member. When Ah Tabai withdrew the spine, his blood dripped freely into the basket at his feet where absorbent strips of pounded bark paper waited to receive it. With an unreadable expression, the Lord of Fire inserted one of the reed stalks through the hole that he'd made and, without pause, again shoved the stingray spine through his penis. By the time that he had inserted the third reed into place, Ah Tabai's jaw was clenched and his face was drenched in sweat. With great care, the ruler of Tzamá turned slowly, gestured with the bloody spine, and nodded to Lady Sunstroke.

A high keening rose from the crowd, and Worm's acolytes held their torches above her head. Bathed in their ruddy light, Lady Sunstroke stuck out her tongue, pinched it between two fingers, and then thrust her own stingray spine through it crosswise. Whimpering quietly, she removed the spine and threaded one end of Worm's hemp cord through the hole.

Gucumatz watched, fascinated, as Lady Sunstroke shuddered and began to draw the cord slowly through her tongue. Beside him, he heard Mad Seizure Star quietly chant the name of the rain god.

Throughout Lady Sunstroke's pain, the tunkul kept up its mournful cadence and the name of Chac murmured and echoed again and again from a thousand hopeful lips. When the last of the knotted cord completed its bloody passage and fell into the basket before her, Lady Sunstroke appeared dazed and almost insensate to her surroundings.

At a signal from White Worm, half a dozen slaves muscled a large smoldering brazier to the top of the pyramid's steps, and two lesser chilánes then lifted her up and assisted her to stand next to it.

When they released her, Lady Sunstroke slumped and once more sank to her knees. With an inscrutable glance at his half-brother, Ah Tabai walked cautiously to his lady's side and stood there rigid, but splendid and unsupported.

White Worm combined the contents of the two collection baskets into one and he now held it aloft before the gathered populace.

"You!" he bellowed, "You have offended our great god Chac! Because of your shameful offenses he has withheld from you the blessings of his life-giving rain! Behold! Although you are unworthy, for your sake the Lord of the Fire and Lady Sunstroke have shed their royal blood. To complete their sacrifice, I now offer their wondrous gift to Great Chac that he may find it pleasing and so bring an end your self-inflicted suffering!"

With a flourish, White Worm tossed the blood soaked cord and strips of bark paper onto the brazier. Almost instantly a dense twisting column of whitish smoke surged upward and reached toward the heavens.

As a wild beating of drums and a shrill chorus of flutes and ocarinas greeted the sacred smoke's appearance; near pandemonium gripped the ecstatic crowd seething at the base of the pyramid. Drowning all, renewed chants of "Chaaac! Chaaac! Chaaac! ..." again saturated the night.

Gucumatz smiled a wide smile and ogled Ah Tabai and Zac Nok with mushroom-fueled awe and respect.

With those two at my side, I am truly invincible, he thought. *This sacrifice will be etched into stone and painted by scribes into their books. Lord Chac will certainly hear their petition and, rain or* no rain, it will be many uinal before dirt-eating peasants again dare to bring their snivels before the Lord of Fire.

Then, through the cloud of his intoxication he remembered that the night held a deeper more sinister meaning and his smile grew even wider.

Worm's cunning knows no bounds and my vengeance will soon be at hand!

The secret was known only to the three of them: White Worm, Gucumatz, and Ah Tabai. Everyone else accepted the royal blood-letting as solely an offering to appease the rain god Chac and end the onerous drought, but many gods drink blood.

Closeted away and unbeknownst to all but his two co-conspirators, White Worm had painstakingly prepared each of the pounded sheets of fig bark that would be used to soak up the blood of Ah Tabai and his lady. On each scrap, he had carefully scribed the name glyph for their hated neighbor to the south. Later, when droplets of blood splattered down on the sheets, each tiny glyph had become a cry for war against Ichpaatún!

Tzamá's chants and the smoke of their ruler's blood sacrifice carried the people's supplication to Chac, but hidden within the vapors another appeal also rose, a darker appeal meant to attract the attention of darker gods.

Suddenly, Lady Sunstroke jerked erect and pointed upward into the smoke. Swaying, she shuddered and screamed.

"The vision snake, he comes!"

Gucumatz also let out a slight gasp; in that instant he too saw the hallucinatory serpent. Its scales were pale gold, glazed, and shining and it twisted and undulated, wrapping itself around the column of sacred smoke. His jaw hung slack with wonder; as he stared, transfixed, the head of the serpent shimmered, lost its reptilian shape and took on the aspect of a fierce warrior with a thick black line that ran around his eyes and down his cheek.

Mad Seizure Star and others next to Gucumatz still chanted the name of Chac, but despite their chorus the warlord knew beyond any shadow of doubt that he stared into the face of another god, a vengeful god of war and violence.

"Buluc Chabtan," he breathed. Then he filled his lungs and shouted the name, "Buluc Chabtan!" *The gods have heard. Ichpaatún will fall!*

Again and again Gucumatz roared the name of his patron god. "Buluc Chabtan! Buluc Chabtan! Buluc Chabtan! ..."

Warriors who stood near at hand heard their nacon's shouts and also took up the chant.

"Buluc Chabtan! Buluc Chabtan!"

One voice at a time the god of war's name replaced that of Chac, until finally only the one remained and all of Tzamá thundered.

"Buluc Chabtan! Buluc Chabtan! Buluc Chabtan! ..."

The sacred Tzolk'in had turned and the day was 5 Wo Chikchan, the time of the snake.

Chapter 20

Runner

The 2nd of September, Year of Our Lord 1511

"And, I tell you that we must!" chided Gonzalo. "Are you content to be a slave here until the day you die?"

"Better the purgatory I know," snapped Hernando, "than the unknowable Hell that awaits you and your folly!"

"Be reasonable Hernando," urged Geronimo. "We've been over this a hundred times. It's our duty to ourselves, to our king, and to God Almighty to escape from these heathens."

"To what purpose?" retorted the balding steward. "This is a land of nothing save blood-thirsty heathens! Do you expect to find the Holy Father and all his cardinals waiting for us beyond the next stand of trees?"

"Of course not," soothed the friar, "but we may find other natives who are more amenable to the words of Our Lord."

"Or, other savages that are even worse than these!" groaned Hernando. "We're alive! Why do you two want to cast our lives away?"

"What lives?" grumbled Gonzalo. "Is this your idea of a life?"

"What say you, Pedro?" demanded the steward. "You were only a cabin boy aboard the *Viñas*, but in this place your word weighs as much as any of ours."

"I... I'm not sure, Nando. Don't like it here, but," with a sideways glance at Gonzalo, "I'm afraid of what lies beyond," answered Pedro.

"There you have it!" declared Hernando. "It's two against two. We stay."

Gonzalo turned and spat into the corner. Each night when the four Spaniards were returned to their hut, always weary and exhausted, their arguments rekindled and burned along familiar paths. For differing reasons, Gonzalo and Geronimo were both convinced that the castaways' only viable future lay in escape. Hernando was equally convinced that any attempt at flight was sheer madness, a madness that would assuredly lead to disaster. All three men courted Pedro de Urtubia, but the gangly cabin boy remained unconvinced one way or the other.

Gonzalo's and Geronimo's arguments were emotional. Those of the steward were self-centered and laden with fear. Normally, Pedro would quickly have sided with Gonzalo, but over the course of the month and a half since the demise of Domingo Vizcaino, the lot of the four survivors had marginally improved.

Following the grisly death of their good natured friend, the brutal and rowdy youths who so plagued their day to day existence appeared to lose interest in their vicious games. Slowly, the unprovoked torments grew less and less frequent and then, one day, they ceased altogether. Gonzalo and the others had no idea whether someone ordered that they be left alone or whether their tormentors simply lost interest in captives that were no longer exotic. Whatever the reason for the unexpected change, the four survivors were grateful and Geronimo had demanded they join in prayers of thanksgiving. Just the same, the four remained watchful and wary and the three older men continued to judiciously crop their beards using Gonzalo's sharpened shell.

Backbreaking labor still filled their days, but, without the constant torment, their existence had become almost bearable. Also, after Domingo died, the castaways' shared daily ration of maize porridge remained unchanged and their water jug was filled no less often. Since the cooper had been a large man, the four survivors suddenly found themselves with more to eat and drink. Their stomachs were still never full, but they were less empty than before and they all thirsted less often. These changes somewhat bettered the Spaniards' fortunes, but not everything improved.

Over the same period their hard-hearted jailer, Sansón, with his protruding muscles and his long oiled hair, had grown ever more callous and spiteful. To account for the change, Gonzalo surmised that as the excitement and notoriety surrounding their imprisonment had diminished into drudgery and routine, what the large savage once conceived a prestigious post now weighed heavily on him as a lowly and onerous duty.

Regardless of whether Gonzalo's hypothesis was correct, Sansón's actions fit the supposition. His stout quirt-like rod was ever in his hand and the beatings he applied with it were now more frequent and more severe.

Three grisly and terrifying months had passed since Gonzalo waded ashore and, while Hernando de Esquivel seemed willing to accept their condition, Gonzalo felt ready to pound his two fists into the ground and scream his lungs out at the heavens. The despair that he experienced his first day on the beach and again in the plaza as his companions were sacrificed was gone. In its place, his determination to survive and to regain control of his life had grown and hardened into a tightly twisted knot. Every fiber of his being screamed for freedom. In his heart, he knew that Hernando de Esquivel's arguments held truth, but not since all those many years ago when his family sent him away to the monastery to be educated had the young escudero felt so desperate and completely ensnared.

The next morning, when Sansón ordered the Spaniards from their hut to return to their Sisyphus-like labors Gonzalo's heart pounded and sweat beaded onto his brow. Although he was unaware of the reason for his anxiety, somewhere at its core, his body knew that he'd reached a dangerous decision.

Once the four castaways were standing outside, Sansón gestured for them to pick up large woven-reed burden-baskets. Together with another guard, a wiry mole-faced native with large wooden hoops in his ears, he then marched the captives in a direction that Gonzalo knew would eventually lead them to a dusty limestone quarry and another day as beasts of burden. The captives were herded only three hundred meters when Gonzalo drew closer and spoke quietly to Geronimo who walked just before him.

"Hssst... Geronimo, be ready; I'm going to run."

"What are you talking about? What do you mean, 'run'?"

"I mean run," whispered Gonzalo. "I can't continue as I am and still call myself a man."

"Don't be a fool!" argued the Franciscan. "We all need to escape, but this isn't the time."

"If not now, when?" shot back Gonzalo. "You know as well as I do that Nando and Pedro may never be ready!"

At that point, the mole-faced warrior, who was bringing up the rear, became annoyed with his prisoners incomprehensible chatter. He yelled at them an equally unintelligible curse, and hurled a smooth walnut-sized stone which struck Geronimo soundly in the thigh. When the friar yelped with pain and bent to rub his leg, Gonzalo leaned closer.

"It's now, I'm going now," he hissed.

"Then, go with God, Aroça," whispered the Franciscan.

To Gonzalo's utter amazement, Geronimo flung himself onto the ground, and began to howl in Latin at the top of his lungs. He thrashed wildly about, and threw handfuls of dirt and grass into the air. In an instant, Sansón was towering over him, prodding the writhing Spaniard with his quirt. Hernando and Pedro shouted and tried to move in closer. The mole-faced savage kicked at Geronimo's flailing legs.

Gonzalo watched his two friends and his two keepers crowd around the flopping figure and suddenly he understood the cause of the friar's seizure. Without a sound, he carefully edged a single step backward, then another. His basket slipped to the ground. Then, he ran.

Away from the path, he stumbled over roots and uneven ground. He ran with reckless abandon forcing his way through a maze of dense dry growth that impeded him at every step. Brush slapped at his face and arms and tore at his ragged clothing, but each bush, vine, and tree that he passed provided more cover and more protection. His bare feet were hardened and callused from months of toil, still sharp stones and thorns tried to slow his progress.

Behind him, he heard Sansón bellow with rage and someone set out in pursuit. He didn't worry about where he was headed. He didn't spare a backward glance. He just ran.

I need to vanish into this jungle, disappear, become like one of its illusive creatures.

The landscape was alien and meaningless and he ignored it completely. One tree flashed past, another, and then another. He ducked under raking bushes. He bulled his way through clutching vines. He splashed across marshy stands of reeds. His world narrowed until it was limited to the pumping of his two lean sinewy legs, the pounding of his heart, and the air that rushed into and out from his lungs.

Gonzalo knew how to run. He had spent much of his life running. When after running from the monastery, he presented himself as a fifteen year-old "soldier of fortune" to Ferdinand's forces, about to march on Milan, he was laughingly commissioned as a messenger. For nearly a year, he did nothing but run. Later, as he aged, he ran shouting into battles. On occasion, he ran screaming away from them. He had run after laughing women through fields bright with flowers. He had run down dark cobbled alleys pursued by the angry shouts of a jealous husband. Now, he again ran. He ignored the heaviness in his limbs, the aching rise and fall of his chest, and strained to feel nothing.

After a time, he realized that he no longer heard the sounds of pursuit. He didn't slacken his headlong rush, but slowly Gonzalo began to take stock of his surroundings. The sun was on his left, which meant that he was running south. He also realized that he could hear the ocean. That was also on his left, and he began to angle in that direction.

If I can just reach the shore and get out of this damn tangle, I'll have a fighting chance. Once I get onto open sand, I can run faster.

Maybe an hour later, maybe only minutes, Gonzalo burst through a screen of swaying scrub and discovered himself standing on a beach. For a moment he paused. The sky was a hazy blue with a few wispy clouds that moved leisurely from east to west. To both his right and to his left a wide swath of impossibly-white, seaweed-littered, jungle-edged sand curved gently away until it was lost into distant mist-shrouded horizons.

Gonzalo bent over, put his hands on his knees, and gasped. His breath came in ragged gulps and his heart raced. Every moment that he stood there wheezing, he felt exposed, but there was little that he could do except wait. After a bit the pounding in his temples thankfully slowed and his panting subsided.

Taking a deep breath of salty air, he straightened. Then, he turned to his right, put one foot in front of another, and slowly began to trot. His mad dash had left him worn and his legs were sore, but he drove himself to keep a steady pace.

Just as the ache in his legs and a mounting pressure in his chest again demanded that he pause to rest, a wild and startled screeching of shore birds caused him to look back over his shoulder.

Mierda! Mother of God!

His mole-faced jailer was charging from the jungle onto the sand. With a shout of triumph, the savage turned and tore in his direction. Gonzalo looked away and tried desperately to redouble his pace.

The young escudero's body knew how to run, but it was hungry, thirsty, and exhausted from months of abuse. Little by little Gonzalo's pursuer chipped away at his lead. Gonzalo raced on without looking back, but even so, he could sense the savage getting closer and closer. He had just decided that his only chance of escape was a mad dive back into the jungle, when sudden emphatic shouts from Mole-face brought his head up.

Not thirty paces ahead, two armed savages emerged from the greenery carrying the corpse of a small deer. For a single instant everyone froze. Gonzalo stared wide-eyed into the hunters' surprised tattooed faces and they stared back. Mole-face yelled, and the savage carrying the deer cast it aside.

Pedro, Hernando, and Geronimo all cowered away from the door to their hut as an enraged and yelling Sansón heaved Gonzalo through the opening. His limp body sprawled onto the dirt at their feet and for the second time in as many months, the escudero lay before them cut, bruised, and unconscious.

"Oh Aroça, what have they done to you," whispered Geronimo.

"They've done less than I told you they would," said Hernando. "At least he still breathes."

Pedro knelt by his battered friend and then looked up at his two other companions. "I'm still afraid to escape, Nando," he confessed, "but I'm also afraid to stay here any longer. We can't go on like this. Gonzalo was right to run and ... once he recovers, we all have to run."

"Bah," retorted Hernando, "look at the shape he's in. He's half dead. Do you want Sansón to pound you like that?"

"Don't frighten Pedro," chided Geronimo. "Gonzalo was rash to run, but he might not have been caught. If we plan carefully and we pray, then, when the proper time comes, The Lord will watch over our flight. With God and luck on our side, we'll succeed."

"Luck! Guererro is lucky," snorted Hernando. "He's lucky he only got a beating. And, you're lucky your antics didn't earn you the same. If any of us runs off again, we may all end up with our balls on a platter; shot full of arrows like: Diego, poor Señor Avellaneda, and the others. Is that what you want?"

"I ... I want to go back home," whispered Pedro.

"Well, lad, this Hell is all the home we have now or are ever likely to have, so forget your notions of escape."

At the steward's harsh words, Pedro's eyes filled with tears and he quietly began to sob.

"Hush," soothed Geronimo, "don't listen to Hernando. This isn't a place of punishment or purification to which we've been consigned. We're not waiting for our transgressions to be burnt away and our souls to be saved. Our friends who were sacrificed all died in God's grace and friendship. The four of us still live. We are prisoners it's true, but nothing more. When one is cast into a cell, and life and faith remain, there is always hope for escape. Now, help me with Gonzalo and once we've eased his discomfort as best we can, we'll again pray for our own deliverance."

Chapter 21

Batab Kinich

11 Bak'tun 14 K'atun 11 Tun 7 Uinal 10 K'in

(September 10, 1511)

A fat salty globule of sweat dribbled off Ac Yanto's brow and slipped wetly down the side of his nose. From there, it slid into the corner of his left eye, blurred his vision, and stung.

"Metnal take this insufferable heat!" grumbled The Batab Kinich as he wiped it away.

He then twisted around to glare menacingly at the two slaves who were fanning him and holding a palm frond above his head. Both men turned a shade lighter and trembled.

Ah K'in Cutz glanced up from his work and regarded Xamanzamá's lord and master with only slightly guarded contempt.

The fat chic (pisote) styles himself 'The Eye of the Sun' yet he curses the glory of K'inich Ajaw's hot breath.

"If I am to succeed, great batab, I must work here where the light is best."

Ac Yanto scowled detesting the high priest. "Very well Cutz, but hurry it along, there are many more pressing matters that require my attention."

"The work of ruling is indeed demanding," coughed Ah K'in Cutz in a manner that insinuated that it was not. "I will do my best."

In point of fact, only one thing demanded Ac Yanto's attention, but it was a matter that the ruler of Xamanzamá wished that he could push far from his mind. More than three uinal (60 days) had come and gone since Ah Tabai's first summons had arrived. A summons which demanded that Ac Yanto present himself in Tzamá and explain, in person, to the Halach Uinic (Great Man) everything concerning the sacrifice of the "monkey gods." Ac Yanto had hoped that if he equivocated, flattered, and delayed that eventually Ah Tabai would lose interest and drop the matter entirely. Exasperatingly for the batab, that had not happened, instead four subsequent delegations from Tzamá had also presented themselves to repeat their Lord of Fire's demand, each one more strident than the last. Like Ah Tabai's first deputation, the initial three groups had consisted of a few lesser ah chibal.

Little better than merchants really, Ac Yanto had fumed, and, despite their vigorous protests, the batab had simply brushed them off, and offered nothing beyond feigned sincerity and vague excuses.

"Although it is my great and urgent desire to honor our exalted Lord of Fire's invitation, alas, difficult and delicate affairs here in Xamanzamá require me to await a more opportune time. Please convey to Lord Ah Tabai my deep disappointment, my unbounded respect, and assure the Halach Uinic that I will visit him just as soon as conditions here improve."

Annoyed but otherwise impotent, the messengers from Tzamá were forced to depart with nothing to show for their efforts other than the ruler of Xamanzamá's nebulous assurances.

The final delegation, that had only just departed, was a different animal entirely, and, to Ac Yanto's mind, a particularly nasty animal at that. Instead of another simpering group of Ah Tabai's toadies, Cheb, one of Gucumatz's burly battle-scared lieutenants, had marched into Xamanzamá at dawn accompanied by a heavily armed party of unsmiling holcánob. The impertinent warrior had assured Ac Yanto, in no uncertain terms, that the Lord of Fire's patience had run out. And, that if the batab did not present himself to his "master" before the end of the current uinal, the next visit he received would be a considerably less cordial one from Nacon Gucumatz himself. His ultimatum delivered, Cheb and his party had rudely turned their backs on Ac Yanto and, without another word, swaggered arrogantly away.

The batab was furious and he railed to one and all at their ill-mannered conceit. At the same time, however, he had also accepted that his excuses were at an end and that he now had no choice but to travel to Tzamá and face Ah Tabai's displeasure.

That was when the day suddenly turned insufferably hot and Ac Yanto began to sweat. It was likewise when he remembered that the whole sordid mess could probably be laid at Ah K'in Cutz's feet. Stomping away from his commodious house, trailing his retinue behind, he set off to have words with the aggravating priest.

When he found Cutz, the unpredictable chilán was on his knees in a sunny open spot outside the colonnaded entrance of Xamanzamá's largest building. The Tzamán delegation had upset Ac Yanto and he had planned to slake his agitation and anger by publically berating the ah k'in; however, when he looked down at what the man was doing, he changed his mind. Before him lay a distraction that temporarily pushed the Tzamáns from his thoughts and deflected his intention.

A woven reed mat was spread out on the stones and Cutz and his two assistants Kish and, *that young fool*, Thup Paal were kneeling beside it. Rat Skull, and several other curious onlookers were hovering nearby. Cutz and dried-up old Kish both looked cool and oblivious to the day's heat, but Thup Paal was sweating heavily.

Stretched out on the mat, between the three men, lay the unconscious body of Paklah-sus (Slapped Sand). Slapped Sand was a man in his prime, of middling height, strongly built, and deeply weathered by the sun. Rat Skull valued him as a reliable and fierce member of his holcánob, but of greater importance to Ac Yanto's way of thinking, Slapped Sand was an ah men pakbal (master mason) of considerable skill, a true artisan, responsible for many works and architectural embellishments in Xamanzamá, all of which glorified Ac Yanto.

Uaxac kin (8 days) earlier, Slapped Sand had been hard at work, standing upon a hastily assembled wooden scaffold, when suddenly the entire structure fell to pieces. With a low rumble from the collapsing scaffold and a loud screech of surprise from the master mason, Slapped Sand teetered, fell the height of two tall men, and sprawled heavily onto the unyielding pavement below. As he lay there stunned, two large baskets of dressed stone, which had also been upon the scaffold, clattered down violently around his head.

Ac Yanto had heard about the accident when it occurred, but had quickly dismissed it from his mind. If some annoyed god or other had orchestrated Slapped Sand's accident, it appeared that at least Ahau Chamahez (god of medicine and good health) had remained by his side. The mason was a bit confused and disoriented, but no bones were broken and other than a pounding headache, a few scrapes, and several bruises he appeared none the worse for his experience.

The next day, however, it began to appear as if Ahau Chamahez may also have abandoned him. Slapped Sand complained of nausea, a ringing in the ears, and a taste of dung in his mouth. His headache grew much worse and, with each passing day, his condition deteriorated. His confusion became profound. His speech slurred. He drifted in and out of consciousness and on the sixth day after his fall Slapped Sand repeatedly convulsed.

According to what the batab had heard, when Ah K'in Cutz examined him on the following morning the mason was unresponsive, his right eye nearly all pupil, and a small amount of clear fluid was draining from his nose and also his right ear.

Now, in the time since Ac Yanto and his retinue first came upon Cutz and the unfortunate mason, K'inich Ajaw had moved from directly over head to the batab's left shoulder. The spectacle that at first captured his attention was proceeding slowly and thoughts of the Lord of Fire were creeping back.

"Well," he demanded, again feeling annoyed. "How much longer must I stand here?"

Ah K'in Cutz purred without looking up. "I'm sure the gods look more favorably upon my actions because of your illustrious presence oh great one, but if you wish to leave, I will do my best to carry on without your added support."

"Paklah-sus is a valued subject," balked Ac Yanto. "I will stay."

What he thought was, *Wild Turkey grows more arrogant and insulting by the day. It may be that his usefulness is at an end and an accident of his own will soon be in order.*

The ruler of Xamanzamá would have preferred to shout something insulting at his high priest and then stalk away, but the truth was that even though Ac Yanto was hot, uncomfortable, and annoyed, he still wished to remain.

In his younger days as a warrior, and nacon, the batab had seen war clubs smash open many a man's head; he even smashed several open himself. He also witnessed the skulls of dead sacrificial victims split and their gooey contents removed. Something that he had never seen, however, was someone attempt to open the skull of a living person without ushering that person onto his journey to the underworld.

Ac Yanto cared little whether Slapped Sand lived or died, but what Cutz was doing to him held a gruesome fascination for the sweating ruler.

If that damnable priest would only hurry it along, it's still a distraction that takes my mind away from Ah Tabai.

Ah K'in Cutz was also fascinated by his own actions and he cared not a bit whether his titular lord stayed or left. When he first examined Slapped Sand, Cutz had recognized immediately that the luckless stone mason was suffering from damage to his ts'o'om (brain), and while he had never before encountered a still living person with just such an injury, he had heard it described.

Cutz' predecessor, Xipil (Noble of the Fire), had long ago lectured that a blow to the head that made little or no mark could sometimes leave a man's skull intact but damage the matter inside and cause it to swell. Xipil had gone on to explain that, encased within the skull with no means to expand, the swelling inevitably led to a variety of afflictions and eventual death.

When young Cutz questioned his teacher about treatments the old ah k'in at first answered that such cases were hopeless. After a moment of reflection, however, he described a risky procedure wherein a hole was opened in the victim's skull to drain off accumulated fluids.

Cutz had instantly envisioned himself petitioning the help of the gods and heroically performing just such a procedure. Now, many years later, his offerings had been made and Slapped Sand was stretched out before him lying on his stomach.

While a queasy looking Thup Paal held the unconscious mason's head still, Ah K'in Cutz had used a sharp knife to cut a palm sized circle into the man's scalp and then scrape it away. Once Kish cauterized the wound with hot coals and sopped up the blood that spilled with pieces of pounded bark, Cutz had then scraped inside the hole until all that remained was the white of Slapped Sand's exposed skull. After that, he began to use a coarse stone pestle to grind away the bone. The rod-shaped pestle was roughly a hand in length and slightly bigger around than Cutz's thumb. The ah k'in held it between his flattened palms, pressed it against the mason's skull and spun it rapidly to abrade away the surface.

The work was slow and tedious, so Cutz allowed Kish to spell him from time to time, but, unlike Ac Yanto, neither the priest's excitement nor his interest flagged.

While Slapped Sand's shallow breath wheezed in and out, and Thup Paal continued to sweat and rigidly hold his head, Ah K'in Cutz and Kish took turns spinning the pestle. Little by little the bone dwindled thinner and thinner until during one of Kish's efforts a single drop of moisture oozed up into the depression.

"Stop!" shouted Cutz who then motioned the older man aside.

Looking closely, he could see that the bone in the hollow that they had ground had grown as thin as a flower petal. Taking up a tiny flint blade, he worked carefully around the edges of the plug. The moment the thin scrap of bone was free, a quantity of clear, slightly thick, fluid ran from hole. Ac Yanto and Rat Skull both leaned in for a closer look and Cutz could smell the batab's hot breath. Within the hole they could all see the pinkish wrinkled surface of Slapped Sand's brain.

"Is that it?" asked Ac Yanto, feeling vaguely disappointed that the final moment was not more spectacular. "Is that all there is?"

"It is as you see," responded Ah K'in Cutz. "The pressure is relieved."

"But will he live?" questioned Rat Skull.

"As with all things," replied Cutz, "his life is in the hands of the gods. Slapped Sand may die immediately, he may die after a short time, or, if he is extremely fortunate, he may live a long and full life."

If he dies, thought Cutz, *that will be Metnal's doing and the mason will soon be forgotten, but if he lives... if he lives it will be the name of Ah K'in Cutz that everyone remembers.*

"What happens next?" demanded Ac Yanto.

"We bind the wound, Uncle," piped Thup Paal, "then we move him back to his home, and we wait."

"Bah," grunted Ac Yanto casting his nephew a dirty look. "I've wasted enough time here. Cutz, when you finish, attend me at my patio."

"As you wish, oh great one," sighed Cutz.

"And be prompt," snapped the batab, his thoughts returning to the summons. Then, he motioned to those attending him and stomped away.

Later that okaank'iin (evening) long after Slapped Sand had died, an event that Ah K'in Cutz was always reasonably sure would happen sooner rather than later, the priest went to speak with Ac Yanto.

During the afternoon Kish had busily and diligently collected details about the Tzamán emissaries' meeting with the batab. These he had duly reported to Ah K'in Cutz who, upon hearing them, regarded Ac Yanto's agitation as yet another example of the man's weakness. To remind the batab that he, Cutz, was an ah k'in, sacred to the gods, and not at his low-born ruler's beck and call, Cutz had kept him waiting.

"A pregnant aak (tortoise) is faster! Where have you been?" snarled Ac Yanto.

The ruler was seated on a mat in his accustomed place at the back of a narrow stone patio that paved the space in front of his large house. Cutz saw that a b'alche cup and a jug sat at the batab's side and, even though K'inich Ajaw had begun his descent into Metnal and darkness had supplanted the light of his day, three sycophantic members of Ac Yanto's Ah Cuchcab still attended their ruler eager to curry his favor. Although the evening was yet warm, servants had set a small fire which cast flickering shadows across the broad planes of Ac Yanto's face

"Alas, despite our efforts, Paklah-sus has begun his journey to the underworld," responded the ah k'in with a feigned hint of sadness.

Ha, just as I expected, thought the batab. *And, yet again, Cutz presumes and addresses me as an equal in public.*

"Perhaps your ministrations hurried him on his way."

"Great one," said Cutz with a weary long-suffering sigh, "the gods determine the outcome of all things. If I had saved the mason it would only have been because it was the gods' intent. Such was not their wish."

"I'm beginning to question your ability to interpret our gods' intent," grunted Ac Yanto getting to the matter that was foremost on his mind. "When the strangers were found on the beach, you proclaimed them a gift from the gods. Is that not so?"

"And, so they were and so they are, great one," answered Cutz, glancing at the three Ah Cuchcab. "But perhaps if we are to discuss the will of the gods it is better that you and I do it in private as befits our status."

When opportunities to rebuke Ah K'in Cutz presented themselves, Ac Yanto preferred to do it in public with as large an audience as possible, but on the other hand he trusted his Ah Cuchcab no more than he would trust a nest of spiders in his bed.

If they stay, he thought, *every word that I utter will soon be whispered into the Lord of Fire's ear.*

Turning to the three councilors, he gestured in dismissal. "Leave us."

"As you wish great Batab," they chorused, then, with slight looks of dissatisfaction or disappointment on their faces the men stood and straightened their garments.

"May Itzamna and Ix Chel always guide you and watch over you," said one.

Grovelers, thought Ac Yanto as he nodded an indifferent acknowledgement. When, for a second time he brusquely waved them away, the three Ah Cuchcab bowed and slunk off.

"You urged that we sacrifice the strangers, Cutz!" blustered Ac Yanto as soon as his councilors were out of earshot. "You claimed that Lord Chaac would find them a fit offering and that the Lord of Fire could be appeased! You said there were no risks, and yet the Lord of Tzamá grows threatening and still no rains have come!"

"These are small things," said the Ah K'in. "Calm yourself."

"Calm myself! How dare you, you impudent lout!" hissed Ac Yanto, scowling. "I am Batab Kinich! And, displeasures of the rain god and the Lord of Tzamá are not small matters easily dismissed!"

"And I am ah k'in here," said Cutz glaring back. "And these displeasures you fear are easily dismissed."

"I fear nothing," growled Ac Yanto with growing menace in his voice.

"Tell me then, Lord of Xamanzamá," asked Cutz in a smug tone. "If the rain god was so displeased by our sacrifice, is the drought that he inflicts upon us any worse now than it was before?"

"It is the same," admitted Ac Yanto grudgingly, "but without the rains it looks to the people as though we are out of favor with the gods and their restlessness grows. Curse you Cutz! This is your fault! What do you have to say for yourself?"

"Why should I say anything?" snapped the ah k'in. "Our people were already upset and they already questioned your favor with the gods. The sacrifice I performed gave you more than three uinal (60 days) of calm. What have you done with those days?"

Ac Yanto felt ready to explode at the chilán's temerity. The ways of the warrior die hard and, flabby or not, violence seethed just below his tattooed exterior. Reflexively his hand went to his waist searching for the ghost of his killing knife that was no longer there. When the batab's fingers closed on air, he suddenly remembered his thoughts on the day of the sacrifice.

I wasn't thinking of Lord Chaac, nor of the drought, nor of rain. I was thinking of how well the 'monkey gods' messengers' had distracted the people and how their sacrifice would give me many days of peace. Could that damnable Cutz be right? Could the gods have heard me, and granted me what I truly wished? Have I squandered their gift?

For a moment the Lord of Xamanzamá sat in silence while he mastered his anger, then he grumbled.

"I have done what there is to be done. The granaries are nearly empty and the rains have not come." *But, if the drought continues much longer,* he thought, *the people may turn against me.*

Cutz watched silently as Ac Yanto filled his b'alche cup from the jug at his side and took a long deep swallow, another, and then another. When the cup was empty, the batab wiped his hand across his mouth and glared bitterly at the younger man.

"Your foolish sacrifice of the strangers failed, Cutz! It failed miserably! Since you were unable to gain the attention, much less the beneficence, of our Great Lord Chaac, I will now end this drought myself! I will offer the rain god my own blood, the sacred blood of Xamanzamá's Batab Kinich!"

Cutz stared at the ruler dumbfounded.

Is it possible that Ac Yanto doesn't know?

Kish's excited whisperers had carried word of the royal bloodletting in Tzamá to Cutz seven days ago, and the ah k'in found it almost inconceivable that the batab's own spies had failed to bring him similar accounts.

"A generous offer, great one," he said slowly, "but if stories are to be believed, an unnecessary one."

"Stories? What stories, Cutz? What are you gibbering about?" demanded Ac Yanto, his anger again ignited. "Why would an offering of my blood be unnecessary?"

"Your few drops are unnecessary, great one, because our illustrious Lord of Fire and his obedient wife, Lady Sunstroke, have already offered up a river."

Ac Yanto, who had just refilled his cup and was in the midst of another deep guzzle, spluttered and coughed.

"What lie is this?" he growled.

"There is no lie," said Cutz, "only a truth unheard. Twelve days past, Ah Tabai gathered the people of Tzamá and made personal sacrifice to Lord Chaac to end the drought. A multitude witnessed his offerings and shortly all in Xamanzamá will have heard their tales. What you or I do now is of little consequence as soon all eyes will be focused upon the Halach Uinic and all expectations settled upon his shoulders."

Now it was Ac Yanto's turn to be dumbfounded. *How is it that Cutz knows of this sacrifice and I do not? Someone will pay for my ignorance!*

The batab's head spun, both from the b'alche and from the ah k'in's surprising revelation.

"If what you say is true and if the Lord of Fire has sacrificed his own blood..."

"Oh, I can assure you that it is most certainly true," butted in Cutz, enjoying the ruler's confusion.

"If he knows," said Ac Yanto registering still greater bewilderment, "that the gods turned their faces away from your offering of the hairy strangers and that the strangers are of little or no value, why does Ah Tabai still demand our presence and an explanation?"

"Why does Ah Tabai do anything?" retorted Cutz. "He wishes to remind us that we are his vassals and that the feet of his holcánob are upon our necks. When we go to Tzamá, he will expect us to grovel, and of course we shall, but I think there is another reason behind his summons."

"And, what reason is that?" sneered Ac Yanto.

"The Lord of Fire, Gucumatz, and the Worm are readying themselves for war. And, when Tzamá goes to war, they will expect that you and I and all of Xamanzamá to stand at their side."

"War? What war?"

The batab reached for the b'alche jug, but then thought better if it and set it back. *Perhaps the drink has gone to my head. Is Cutz really talking about war?*

"There was more to the Lord of Fire's sacrifice," answered the ah k'in. Then he related to Ac Yanto all the details of the Tzamán bloodletting that Kish's whisperers had collected.

By the time Cutz was finished, a chill was slipping down the batab's neck.

"Truly," he asked in slightly drunken awe, "Ah Tabai summoned Buluc Chabtan?"

"So people who were there claim," responded Cutz cautiously.

When he was nacon of Tzamá, Ac Yanto had respected the strength and wisdom of Ah Tabai's father, Ah Kumix Uinic. Later, after the father had appointed Ac Yanto batab of Xamanzamá and passed away, he had held a diminished respect for the ruler's son. What Cutz was telling him changed that.

Is it possible? Could Buluc Chabtan really have answered Ah Tabai's call?

Inside Ac Yanto there still lived a warrior and a leader of warriors and the thought that the god of war and violence would appear to Ah Tabai made his blood race.

Perhaps Ah Tabai truly is the Lord of Fire. With Buluc Chabtan and Gucumatz at his side in battle, he would be unbeatable.

"This changes everything," slurred the batab. "In the morning we must make preparations to go to Tzamá."

"I agree, nodded Cutz. "It is time that we visit the Halach Uinic, but not everything has changed. Ah Tabai is still Ah Tabai, and the Lord of Fire will still expect us to kneel before him and present him with the remaining 'messengers of the monkey gods'."

"So we give them to Ah Tabai, so what?" grunted Ac Yanto.

"One does not give broken gifts to the Lord of Fire," purred the ah k'in. "A change is required. The strangers are guarded by Tun Ch'ajom (Stone Scatterer). He allowed one of them to die, and he almost beat a second to death when that one tried to escape. He should be replaced."

Ac Yanto's meeting with Cutz had not gone as he expected. Somehow it felt like the damnable priest had gotten the better of him. The batab's head was beginning to ache and he felt petulant.

"As you say, we will take the hairy strangers to Tzamá. But, their condition is of no import, healthy or half-dead Ah Tabai will see that they are of no value. Tun Ch'ajom stays!"

Chapter 22

A Banquet for the Gods

11 Bak'tun 14 K'atun 11 Tun 7 Uinal 13 K'in

(September 13, 1511)

"It's just not fair!"

"Oh please, Okib, not again," groaned Naum.

"Well, it's not," snapped the smaller boy. "More wood! More wood! We've collected firewood for days. It's nothing but firewood."

"You should be proud. It's an important job," said Naum. "The ceremony begins saamal hatskab k'iin (tomorrow morning) and you know that every stick that we bring back will get used."

"I know, I know," whined Okib. "The wood we've gathered will all go up in smoke, but why us?"

"Because we were chosen," responded Naum quietly. "It's an honor that the chilánob (priests) asked us."

"They told us you mean," said Okib peevishly. "Some honor, we've been through the em-ku (coming of age rite) we're men now. Yet here we are still scrabbling through the brush and thorns loaded down with bundles of sticks. Why couldn't the priests have asked us to walk the old sacbe (white road) and collect flowers, fragrant leaves, and virgin water, anything but firewood?"

"It's an important job," repeated Naum.

"You sound like an old t'uut' (parrot)," grumbled Okib. "I want to hunt turkey. I want to be holcán (a warrior) but what do we do? We're men, but what's changed? We now sleep in the young men's house, but how do we spend our days? Just like before, that's how! We spend our days collecting firewood. Only now, it's not just wood for our mothers, it's wood for the whole village!"

"I'll tell you what," said Naum, when their path through the dry jungle brought them under the shade of an overhanging tree, "It's too hot for complaining. What do you say we throw down these bundles and rest a while?"

Okib looked at his larger companion and noted the sheen of sweat beading his round open face.

Collecting wood with Naum isn't really that bad, there's no better company, and at least no one looks over our shoulders and criticizes our every move.

With that thought, the smaller boy smiled, tossed aside his gathered wood, and plopped down with his back propped against the trunk.

"This spot is as good as any." With secret pleasure he noted that Naum's bundle was smaller than his own. "Hey Naum," he needled. "How come you eat more, but I'm always the one who works harder?"

The two friends were as close as brothers and such taunts were common fare.

"You eat less because you're the size of a runt rock-lizard," answered Naum, growling with put-on animosity, "and as for working harder, this day is long from over."

"Uts (okay) it's a challenge!" crowed Okib. "Take a drink, stop your unseemly sweating, and then we'll see who can bring in the most wood!"

A wide grin stretched across Naum's face and he reached for the water gourd that Okib offered. "You're on," he said, "but be prepared to lose."

"Lose, not even with one arm tied behind me! Come on then, let the contest begin!" crowed Okib as he sprang back to his feet.

"Not just yet," protested Naum, wiping his brow. "Slow down; remember, sweat, tired."

"Well, alright," grumped Okib nearly quivering to be off, "but don't sit there too long."

Naum chuckled inside at his friend's sudden about face. *One moment it's, "Why us?" the next it's, Okib, cacique of the firewood collectors! A bit of a challenge and suddenly his onerous chore is a pleasurable afternoon.*

Naum did not have a single sly or manipulative bone in his body, but he was also not one to pass up an opportunity to loaf. He was sweaty and tired and he knew well his best friend's fervid competitive nature. He also knew that, given a slight shove, Okib would collect so much firewood during the remainder of the day that he himself could slack off and take it easy. That was just fine with Naum.

Much later, after their final loads of wood were collected and stacked, and after K'inich Ajaw had left the sky to begin his nightly subterranean journey to the west, the two young men lay in their k'aanob (hammocks). Both were tired from their labors, but for a time they chattered quietly, too worked up to sleep.

As dictated by the great wheel of the moon calendar the chilánob of K'optela regularly conducted rituals and offerings to honor the gods, secure their goodwill, and to reinforce the crucial connection between the energy of heaven and the earth beneath their feet. Such rites occurred almost daily in the boys' village, some quiet and modest, others noisy and ostentatious.

The ceremony that would take place the next day had the markings of something special. Neither Okib nor Naum could ever remember preparations more elaborate.

A settlement of medium size, K'optela was well ordered and successful. In part, its prosperity was due to Quibián, the local cacique, who administered the village's day to day affairs with a fair and even hand. His people worked industriously in their common fields, nearby Sotuta demanded only reasonable tribute, and mostly life was good. This turn of the ha'ab was different. Each of the preceding years had been a little drier than the one before and this season of drought was the worst in anyone's memory. Because Quibián was a cautious man, K'optela's storage bins were well stocked and, unlike many other communities, no one in the village had yet suffered from want.

The drought, however, persisted, a constant nagging concern that caused Quibián's council to fill endless evenings discussing the state of K'optela's crops, the level of water in its chultunes (cisterns), and the increasing banditry that plagued the surrounding lands. Although no one could agree on the drought's root cause, everyone on the council conceded that the dearth of moisture reflected some displeasure of the gods and that only the intercession of Chaac and the other rain gods could suffice to lift its burden.

It was during a moment of silence in one such discussion that old Boox Soots' (Black Bat), K'optela's respected senior chilán abruptly spoke.

"My friends, we are pious. We make offerings. We observe the rituals. That is no longer enough! In these days of hardship, many voices clamor at the gods pleading for their help, some deserving, some not. If we wish to protect K'optela we must set ourselves apart from those whose sinful deeds have called down our gods' disfavor."

The old priest was a quiet man who rarely spoke up in council and several of the Ah Cuchcab turned in surprise at his brief speech.

"We hear you, Boox Soots'," responded Quibián, "but what do you propose that we do?"

"We must offer the rain gods a banquet!" declared the priest, "a lavish ceremonial feast. One that the gods cannot ignore. A banquet so sumptuous that its petition will rise above the common din, capture the gods' attention, and remind them that the people of K'optela are their faithful servants."

Quibián and the others stared at one another. No one could deny the wisdom of Boox Soots' words. Preparations for the banquet had begun almost immediately, but they were so elaborate that they had taken almost a uinal.

Before the first light of K'inich Ajaw's dawn, Okib and Naum stood at the edge of the village's central plaza, rubbing sleep from their eyes, waiting with keen anticipation. The two chilánob were already at work and the friends were eager not to miss a moment of the day's doings.

"Look," said Okib nudging Naum, "here comes old Soots'."

Days before, a large round sacrificial stone had been wrestled into the middle of the open expanse of packed earth that formed K'optela's heart. Adorned with an elaborate headdress, embellished with the colorful feathers of hummingbirds and macaws, the old priest walked slowly forward and approached the stone. After inspecting it with a critical eye, he mumbled a few words which the young men could not hear. Then, he held up a thick handful of sihom (soap berry) leaves.

With quick deft movements, he swept the leaves across the stone's surface, whisking them back and forth, again and again, until every loose speck of dirt and dust was removed. When he was satisfied that the altar was clean, Soots' motioned for the village's other chilán, Cualli (Good), to advance. As Naum and Okib watched, the younger priest washed and purified the stone with virgin water. Meanwhile Boox Soots' raised his scrawny arms towards the gradually lightening sky and began to chant the names of the many rain gods.

"See us, oh great Chac, supreme god of all storms and rain!"

"See us great Yaluk, who shapes the storms sent by Lord Chac!"

"See us Cakulha, whose jagged bolts light the heavens!"

"See us Coyopa, whose sound and thunder shake the earth!"

"See us oh Ah-Patnar-Unicob, elemental gods of water!"

"See us oh Chicchan, who stand at the four corners of the world!"

"See us great serpent Ix-Tub-Tun, who spits forth the precious stones of rain!"

"See us generous white-haired Yumchakob, brothers of Kukulkán!"

"Your servants in K'optela beseech you, look upon us!"

"Your servants in K'optela prepare for you an offering!"

Sitting at the edge of the plaza, old Hub-tun (Conch Stone), the village's nacon, began to beat on a huge tunkul. With each percussive blow, the great drum's booming echo pulsed and rolled, seeming to lift Boox Soots' supplications and carry them toward the heavens.

Called by the drum, most of K'optela had now gathered in the plaza and Okib and Naum were surrounded by a murmuring crowd of friends and family. Across the way, stood a large group of women, a group that included both boys' mothers.

"Next, it'll be the turkeys," whispered Naum.

While the young men watched, four women stepped forward from the group. As Naum had predicted, each of them carried a struggling turkey.

In preparation for the ceremony the men of the village had set hundreds of snares and caught dozens of the birds. Afterwards, the captured animals had been kept in woven reed cages and fattened on grain.

The women handed the first four of the turkeys to the four men who were elected to serve as chacs. In turn, each turkey was given to the lessor priest, Cualli, who held it out over the altar.

While the bird was suspended, Boox Soots' moved a smoldering censer of copal slowly around the fowl, passing it back and forth, cleansing and purifying the offering with clouds of aromatic smoke. Next, Cualli forced open the turkey's beak and Soots' dribbled b'alche down its throat until the animal could take no more. Once the smoke and alcohol stupefied the bird, it ceased its struggles and the younger priest laid it on the stone. Turning to the crowd, he intoned the name of the great rain god.

"Chaac! Chaac! Chaac!"

The people responded with enthusiastic chants of their own.

"Chaac! Chaac! Chaac!"

Naum and Okib tried to outshout their fellows. The drum beat louder. Soots' drew his sacrificial obsidian blade. The chant reached a peak. He flourished the knife. An instant later, he skillfully severed the bird's head. The people of K'optela cheered and blood, thick and dark, ran down across the stone.

Over and again, in cadence to the somber beat of the tunkul, the ritual repeated itself until all of the captured birds had been sacrificed. Afterwards the turkeys were given back to the women who scalded them, plucked them, cleaned them, and set them to boil.

Now, other drums joined Conch Stone's rhythm, following and playing off his tempo. Swaying in time to the echoing pulse, five brightly dressed warriors of the holcánob gamboled into the plaza teetering dangerously on stilts. Twirling and bouncing they danced their way over to the red-anointed stone, then, encouraged by whoops and praises from the crowd, they swept up the gory turkey heads and spun wildly about dribbling blood upon the earth and calling upon the rain gods to heed their gift. When at last their frenetic dance drew to an exhausted close, the warriors withdrew and the feverish beat of the drums died slowly until only the steady cadence of old Conch Stone's tunkul remained.

The day would call for many rituals, many crescendos of excitement and ecstasy, and these were but the first.

"I could do that," said Okib. "I can walk on stilts! You wait, next time I'll be one of the dancers."

"They're dancers, not wobblers," answered Naum, "better stick to something you're good at."

"And what's that?" demanded Okib.

"Wood gathering, of course!" teased Naum, moving with surprising agility to avoid the kick launched by his friend.

With all of the turkeys sacrificed and the stilt dancers retired, activity in the plaza shifted to a slower pace. The chilánob, assisted by Quibián, the four chacs, and various prominent men of the village set about decorating the blood-stained altar in anticipation of its use as an offering-table.

First, four long flexible branches were placed into holes that had been prepared, one at each of the cardinal directions to symbolize the roots of the sacred world tree. Once the branches were secure, Quibián and two others bent them down and tied them together so that they formed an arched bower above the round sacrificial stone. Next, the chacs wrapped the branches with strips of dyed cloth, red for east, white for north, black for west, and yellow for south and began to decorate the structure with fresh leaves and collected flowers. While they worked, Boox Soots' and Cualli filled small bowls with b'alche and carefully hung one from each branch suspended by a sling of thin leather thongs.

In the days preceding the ceremonial banquet, the women of the village, under the serious and watchful eye of old Soots', had prepared large urns of b'alche and also saca, a slightly bitter mixture of watery corn gruel and ground cacao beans, spiced with ground chili and sweetened with honey. These, they now carried forward and placed beside the bower.

As the urns made their appearance, Okib and Naum turned and stared pointedly at one another. Okib's mother had provided part of the honey for the saca and she was still fuming over the discovery that some thief had been at her hives pilfering honeycomb. When Okib saw her standing nearby, he decided that perhaps it would be better to be elsewhere lest the sight of the urns fan the embers of his mother's banked anger and suspicion.

"Come on," he said prodding Naum, "while the chilánob finish the bower, let's go over and watch the women assemble the cakes."

"Truly?" responded Naum, "My skinny friend would rather watch women prepare food than warriors strut, and priests bless urns of b'alche?"

"It's my mother," answered Okib seriously. "You saw her. She's just over there and she's still mad as a hornet about the honeycomb."

"What honeycomb?" asked Naum innocently.

"You ate just as much as I did..." started out Okib until he saw the wide smile that spread across his friend's face. "Ah chuch (fool)" he sniffed. "Just come along, will you!" Then, he turned and stomped away. Naum followed, laughing.

A short distance from the plaza, several women were hard at work making special cakes for the rain gods' banquet. The cakes were made from sakan (masa/corn dough) formed into flattened circles like tortillas. Each flattened round of raw dough was then spread with a spicy paste of beans and ground squash seeds. Next, the rounds were stacked one on top of another into short towers, each layer representing one of the various rain gods. Finally, the stacked cakes were individually wrapped in aromatic green leaves and tied with pieces of green vine. Naum was pleased to see that there were many more cakes than the gods could be expected to consume.

Nearby, the men of the village had dug a large pit and inside it, using the firewood, Okib, Naum, and others collected, they had kindled a large fire.

"When it burns down to coals," said Naum, "Boox Soots' will bless the fire with a sprinkling of virgin water, that'll raise a big cloud of ash. Then, the leaf bundles will be nestled into the embers and the men will bury the fire with the dirt from the pit."

"Leave it to my large best friend to know all the intimate details of food preparation," chortled Okib.

Later, while the buried cakes were baking, Boox Soots' headed a procession to a nearby cenote. Unlike many such places, a goodly portion of the small sinkhole's limestone roof was still intact. Instead of sitting completely open to the sky, the clear shallow pool sparkled in the shade of a cooling overhang.

Okib and Naum, along with most of the other villagers trailed along as Soots', accompanied by Cualli and the four chacs, all blowing bone whistles and ringing bells made of shell, shepherded a young woman named Iuitl (Feather) to the seep. Although diminutive, the cenote was an important source of K'optela's drinking water. The round pellucid pool was also a fitting place for another offering to the rain gods.

Iuitl, tall and well proportioned, was widely regarded the most beautiful young woman in the village and many were the days when Naum and especially Okib stole longing glances when they believed that she wouldn't see.

Because of her beauty, and because she was unbetrothed and still a virgin, Boox Soots' felt that she would be pleasing to the gods and he had therefore chosen her for the offering at the pool.

To prepare, Iuitl had bathed herself thoroughly. Afterwards, she had rubbed her shoulders, arms, and breasts with a red ointment infused with istahté (liquid amber) until she was strongly perfumed. Days before, two old women using stones and water had filed her teeth. An amber stone had been placed in a piercing through the cartilage of her nose and small circlets of jade dangled from each of her ears. Her long dark hair was arranged in two very fine tresses which were piled upon her head and arranged with delicate bone pins. Her garment, made of the whitest cotton the village could obtain, was a simple sack-like huipil that hung over her shoulders, open at the sides, and fastened at her thighs.

To the young men of K'optela she was a vision of beauty. When she walked past with her head held high Okib thought that surely his chest would burst.

At the lip of the cenote, Boox Soots' helped her down a steep wooden ladder into the limestone pit. When they reached the bottom, the old priest asked Iuitl to kneel at the edge of the waiting pool while Cualli and the chacs also descended. Each of the chacs carried a large basket of flower petals and these they placed at Iuitl's side. Cualli then stepped forward with a gourd and anointed the girl with virgin water. As the sacred liquid dripped from her head and hands, Boox Soots' again began the now familiar chant.

"Chaaac! Chaaac! Chaaac!"

Echoes of his entreaties rose from the cavern's mouth, but as the cenote was small and the sides of its well steep, only those gathered at its immediate edge could see what transpired below. To Okib's frustration, those places were taken by Quibián and other men of importance.

"I wish we could see," muttered Okib, as the crowd around him took up the chant. "I should be a priest. If I was chilán then I'd always be able to see."

"Would that be before or after you become a stilt-dancing warrior?" answered Naum between shouts of the rain god's name.

"I just want to watch Iuitl scatter the flowers," scowled Okib.

"We all want to watch Iuitl," said Naum.

"Hush you two!" snapped an old woman standing behind them. "The gods are listening!"

Down in the well Soots' intoned the names of each of the rain gods and Iuitl solemnly scattered the colorful flower petals across the pool's glittering surface. When at last she climbed back up the ladder, people crowded around and praised her for the grace of her offering. Okib still couldn't get close enough to see.

The culmination of the day's ceremonies came just before dusk. The charred leaf bundles were removed from the buried fire and unwrapped to reveal golden baked rounds. The younger priest, Cualli, placed four loaves of the bread in net bags and tied one at each corner of the bower in the plaza. Next, the chacs arranged other loaves on the altar stone, and a boiled turkey was set on the top of each loaf. The women of the village then added cooked squash, roots, small game, corn, savory herbs, and fruit, until the space around the altar was overflowing with mouth-watering food.

With the banquet laid out, Boox Soots' called for all the boys and young men of the village to gather around and line up. Moving down the line, he asked one small boy and then a second to step forward. Then, to their surprise, he gestured for Naum and Okib to join them. Once the four were selected, the old chilán placed them, one at each corner of the altar.

"Now, you must squat like the small frogs who come with the rain," said Soots', "and when the time is right, you must chant as frogs."

"But how do we do that, grandfather?" asked Naum quietly.

"What is it that frogs sing to greet the rain?" respond the elder.

"Oti, oti, click, click," blurted Papan (Flag) the youngest of group.

"Then that is how you must chant!" declared Soots'.

While the four squatted, the priest sprinkled corn dust around the stone and old Hub-tun with his tunkul drum began to imitate the sound of thunder. Cualli and the chacs each waved smoldering censers and created clouds of smoking copal. Close by, men of the village held hollowed sticks filled with pebbles that when turned produced the sound of falling rain. As the plaza filled with the sounds of hoped-for showers, Boox Soots' waved a bundle of corn silk above the altar and then signaled to his frogs.

"Oti, oti, click, click," they chanted.

The two chilánob added their own voices, "Chaaac! Chaaac! Chaaac!"

With Boox Soot's leading, the sing-song supplication went on and on, weaving together praise for each of the gods and pleading for their intercession. Each word, chanted to the accompanying sounds of thunder, falling rain, and small croaking frogs, was important. Nothing could be rushed.

Long before the prayers ended Naum began to feel tired and hungry. His legs were cramped from squatting and his throat was parched from the clouds of incense and the endless repetition of "oti, oti, click, click."

Wondering how much longer he could hold out, he gazed at the other frogs. The two young boys seemed oblivious to any discomfort and Papan was even hoping about. Naum tried to catch Okib's eye, but his friend had a strange look on his face and seemed to be somewhere else entirely. Just at the point where Naum thought he might have to embarrass himself and stand up, Soots' shouted "Chaaac!" one last time and declared the offering a success.

Afterwards, everyone celebrated by eating the unoffered loaves and turkeys, manioc, chaya, jicama, squash, and, to both Naum's and Okib's delight, combs of Muzencab's honey. At the end of a long day, with their bellies full, the two friends walked back toward their hammocks in the young men's house.

"I understand the firewood collecting," mused Okib, "but why do you think old Soots' chose us to be frogs? That was a job for little kids like Papan, not for men."

"I don't know," answered Naum, "but I'm pretty sure it meant something."

"Okay, something, but what?" quizzed Okib.

"You know, I almost stopped chanting," confessed Naum. "My legs went numb from squatting and my throat was so dry that I think that if I'd tried to croak one more time nothing would have come out."

"I think it was a good thing that you didn't stop," said Okib. "I think Chaac was watching and listening."

Again, Naum saw the strange look on his friend's face.

Naum looked about at the heavens and then chuckled. "What makes you think that, oh chilán?"

"I...I felt something. I just know," snapped Okib.

"So, oh great chilam (one who reads the future)," goaded Naum, "do you prophesize that Lord Chaac is going to strike the sky snakes with his lightning axe and bring us rain?"

"I'm sure of it," said Okib seriously.

Naum glanced at the heavens again, "Look at the sky Okib, it's as clear and dry as it's ever been."

Okib scowled at his friend. Even in the dark, Naum saw the yet darker look that passed across his friend's face.

"Of course it was a very good ceremony, Okib. I'm sure you're right."

Despite himself, Okib smiled. He always liked it when Naum agreed.

Chapter 23

Storm and Flight

The 14th of September, Year of Our Lord 1511

Although Gonzalo strained at the effort and tried to steer his thinking into useful directions, he couldn't hold the course. No matter how hard he tried, his unbidden thoughts slipped slowly into unaccustomed regions of self-pity and despair. His heart felt empty, a cavernous space that echoed with a hollow ring. Trudging under a basket-load of stones, he gazed out at a curved arc of sand and beyond that a glittering expanse of startlingly blue-green sea.

The basket's makeshift straps of cordage chaffed at his shoulders. His body still ached from Sansón's pounding, but despite the purple yellow-tinged bruises that still blotched the injured skin of his face and ribs, much of his old strength had returned. What had not returned was the soldier-of-fortune's bravado and his previous self-assurance. The beating, and the failure of his impetuous escape, stole something from Gonzalo. Something which left a deep hole in his chest, a hole now filled by a profound and abiding melancholy.

In front of him, following in the footsteps of their guard, Mole-face, plodded Hernando weighted down with his own basket of stones. Behind him Gonzalo sensed the shuffling presences of Pedro and Geronimo. The four Spaniards were strung together with a tough woven rope that looped around each man's waist, an onerous precaution that Sansón instituted after Gonzalo's attempt to flee. From time to time, for no apparent reason other than his own perverse satisfaction, Mole-face gave the rope a nasty tug.

Perhaps Nando is right, thought Gonzalo. *Maybe there is no place that we can run to, no watchful God who wants our escape. Curse this land and damn the stupid pride that brought me here, freedom, Spain, just dreams of a foolish, foolish, man.*

Sweat dripped from his brow. Small grains of sand blew along the beach and tickled at his feet.

I'm like this sand. The wind carries it where it will; it has no joy, no hope, the sand simply endures. I wish I was back in my soggy bed aboard the Viñas de la Barca. Better still, I wish I'd never heard of that cabrón Alonso de Ojeda and this accursed adventure.

Round and round went his thoughts. Under nearly perfect skies, the Bay of Turtles, where the castaways first came ashore, stretched before him. Peaceful, rippled by light playful zephyrs, its untroubled waters cast jewel-like reflections of the bright midday sun and lapped quietly against the sandy shore, one gentle lingering kiss after another. Despite his despair, Gonzalo still succumbed to the splendor and tranquility that surrounded him.

How is it possible that Hell contains such stillness and beauty?

Unmarked by the disheartened slave, weeks earlier and a world away, a gentle eddy of blustery air had rolled out of the heights of the Himalayas. Herded by that continent's prevailing winds, it had blown westward.

As the restless eddy moved across the hot dry sands of the Sahara it encountered moist warm coastal air from the south and developed into a dark line of thunderstorms that rumbled across Africa.

Moving steadily westward, the tropical wave passed into the Atlantic. There, fed by the moisture-laden air above the warm equatorial ocean, it grew and intensified. Nudged by the earth's rotation, the unstable air developed a lazy spin and in its new guise the rotating storm crawled slowly through the subtropics.

Buffeted by other westerly winds and perhaps drawn by the prayers, offerings, and blood of the people from The Land of the Turkey and the Deer, it plodded across the ocean, ever growing, ever gathering in strength.

Blood and banquets were offered to Chac and to the benevolent Yumchakob, but, as the venerable Boox Soots' would later explain to Quibián and to his Ah Cuchcab, it was another deity who heeded their supplications.

Twenty days after departing Africa, the growing storm swept past Barbados and came to the attention of the old god.

Hurakán, U Kúx Kaj (Heart of Sky) lived in windy mists above the water and was ancient beyond reason. As one of the thirteen creators, he was present at all three attempts to craft humanity. When the second men proved a failure, it was he who sent floodwaters to destroy them. It was also he who blew his powerful breath across the chaotic waters and repeated the word "Earth" until the sunken land remerged.

Standing in the heavens on his one human leg, the old god smiled and his serpent leg writhed with joy. Hurakán loved wind, and even better, storm, and fire.

Using ocean currents and trade winds as his crook and prod, he shepherded the storm northward. He flirted with the idea of tossing it onto the coast above Darien, but too few men lived in those lands to truly appreciate his power. Instead, Heart of Sky urged his new plaything back to sea, and pushed it toward Hispaniola.

By the time Gonzalo and his three remaining companions sat gratefully down for their meager afternoon meal of uncooked maize, the morning's idyllic calm had fled. Above Xamanzamá, the sky, now an ominous purple-grey, churned and roiled with the undulating shapes of scudding clouds.

The wind picked up and all the trees and bushes stirred restlessly as though quivering in uneasy anticipation. Far out of the four Spaniards' sight, well beyond the horizon, in a world gone black, a vortex of whirling winds howled like shrieking demons and giant cymbals of thunder clashed and echoed with unceasing fury.

Screaming with child-like pleasure the god, Hurakán, gave his toy a final mighty shove. With a St. Vitus-like jerk, the storm changed course one last time and wheeled its considerable power toward the parched Land of the Turkey and the Deer.

The afternoon grew hot and sticky, and a concerned-looking Mole-face herded his charges away from the shore and back toward the village. The wind that blew in from the sea brought with it a sour smell of salt, a cloying unclean breeze that made Gonzalo believe that the very air clung to his skin. Soon, a spitting rain began to fall.

"I think we're in for a real whore of a blow," offered Hernando, raising his voice slightly to be heard above the wind and the rustling of bushes. "Maybe one as bad as when we lost the ship."

"If God wills it," answered Geronimo, crossing himself. "At least if a true storm comes upon us, this time we'll face it with land beneath our feet."

At the sound of their exchange, Mole-face looked back and gave a vicious yank on the rope. Hernando staggered under his load of stones and the balding steward nearly fell.

"Seba'an! (quickly)" hissed the guard.

Within moments the sprinkling rain began to hammer a noisy tattoo upon the dry ground, each large drop throwing up a small explosion of dust. Falling water drenched the castaways and their guard, and the sodden baskets of stones grew ever heavier.

As the group worked their way through Xamanzamá's outlying structures, the day turned dark. People they passed were lighting fires and torches which spat and crackled in the deluge. When, at last, Mole-face allowed the castaways to dump their loads of stone and shoved them roughly through the mat-covered door of their hut, the clatter of the rain had become a low roar that rose and fell as solid sheets of water dropped from the sky.

The thatched roof of their one-room cell kept out most of the squall's fury, but the storm felt as though it was growing in strength, a monster that might never stop. Alone with their thoughts and the howling of the storm, the four huddled together and crowded into the hut's driest corner. No one spoke and their world filled with the resonance of rushing winds and splashing water. A flash of lightning momentarily seeped around the hut's door and lit the space within. Then, as the bolt's crash of thunder faded, Pedro spun up to his knees and faced his companions.

"This is it!" he burst-out.

"This is what?" demanded Hernando.

"The right moment, Nando, it's here!" answered the gangly cabin boy, becoming excited.

"The right moment? Right moment for what?" answered the steward. "What are you chattering about?"

"Escape!" announced Pedro in a firm voice. "God has sent us this storm."

"Oh, sit down," muttered Gonzalo, "There's no God, or if there is, he doesn't care about us."

"You blasphemous fool, Aroça," stammered Geronimo, his face turning beet red. "Once again your words carry your mortal soul toward damnation. God does exist! He cares about us, now more than ever! Young Pedro is right! This tempest is a gift. It's a sign. It's the opportunity we've awaited. We must take it. It's what God wants us to do!"

"Have you gone completely mad?" shouted Hernando. "You saw what happened to Gonzalo! At least he's had some sense beaten into his thick head."

At the steward's words, a damped flame flickered deep in Gonzalo's heart. For a moment the tiny flame only fluttered, then it burst into light.

"Shut up, Nando," he snarled. "All of us are crazy! I don't agree with Pedro and Geronimo that this storm is some miraculous gift from God, but, God or no God, it's an opportunity. My beating changed nothing! Nothing here has changed! Our lives are shit! If you want to stay and wallow in shit like a pig, then stay! I'm going to run again, and this time, live or die, it will be as a free man. One way or another, I'm never coming back!"

As he uttered the words, the weight in his chest lifted and the hollow filled with resolve.

"Me too," declared Pedro, "I'm going too!"

Hernando threw his hands in the air and made a sound of disgust.

"Hernando my friend," reasoned Geronimo, turning in the gloom to face the steward, "despite Gonzalo's blasphemy and his thoughtless refusal to acknowledge Our Lord's truth, God still guides his heart. This storm is a gift from our Lord. It's a precious gift. A gift that we must use to free ourselves! God hears our prayers, but he expects all men to see to their own welfare. I intend to flee along with Aroça and young Urtubia. You cannot remain here alone. If you join us, and if God is willing, we may all escape. If you stay and the rest of us run, you will surely be punished in our stead. We are four and four we must remain!"

Hernando peered into the darkness and one by one studied the serious shadowed faces of his three companions.

"Very well," he sighed, "how do we do it?"

After an extended and sometimes contentious debate, the four Spaniards finally agreed. Without any solid information about the surrounding countryside, they would stick close to the coast. The four also agreed that south, the direction of Gonzalo's previous attempt to flee, was as good as any.

"It's decided then," declared the escudero. "We wait until the storm reaches its peak; then, we go. If any of us get separated from the rest, we make our way to the beach and we go as far as we can by tomorrow night. Then, we hide. If we don't find each other by the morning of the second day, whoever is left goes on alone."

In the dark all four heads nodded. With their choices made, the castaways sat, listened to the growing storm, and waited. Time, which all hoped would be their final hours in captivity, seemed not to move at all. Its passage from one minute to the next was marked solely by the wailing of the wind and the clattering sound of falling rain.

Their wait reached toward an unknown end and their thoughts raced. Worries about the need for caution and restraint mixed silently with untold fears and irrational urges to run screaming out into the night. After months as prisoners, months of hardship and terror, the prospect of fruitful escape twisted away at the castaways' insides. It excited them, terrified them, and filled each of them with a restless anticipation.

Huddled against the wall of their hut, the wait stretched; with each passing moment, their struggles to remain still and calm grew ever more difficult.

Outside the false dark of the storm mixed with the true dark of night. The bitter winds and lashing rains roared. Lightning flashed. Again and again, for half a heartbeat, gaps around the covered door and streaks across the inside walls of the hut blazed blue and white.

Geronimo began to count, "One, two, three, four ..." quietly measuring the lull that preceded each new roll of thunder. With every crash his count grew shorter. At length the booming merged into a nearly continuous cannonade that all but drowned out the howls and shrieks and other sounds of the storm's fury. Then, the walls of the hut began to shake.

"Now," shouted Gonzalo.

"Now?" queried Pedro.

"Now or never," yelled Gonzalo.

He began to tear away thatch at the back of their hut. The four had agreed that it would be a mistake to try to slip out though the door. Once the hole was big enough to crawl through, Geronimo raised his hands in prayer.

"Lord, we beseech your protection. We ask that you watch over us, your only servants in this savage land. We commend our souls into your keeping."

"Amen!" chimed Pedro and Hernando.

Saying nothing Gonzalo wriggled through the muddy hole and out into a world of flashing black skies, bitter winds, and lashing rain.

Rising to a guarded crouch, he backed up against the wall and waited. One by one, Hernando first, then Pedro, and finally Geronimo, the others slithered through the opening. Gonzalo's heart pounded and, despite the drenching downpour, his mouth was bone dry.

Each brilliant glare of lightning followed almost immediately upon the one before it leaving no space for eyes to adapt to the dark. Light blazed with a power that man couldn't equal. Each flash rendered the world into harsh juxtaposed planes, blue and white incandescence contrasted against coal back shadows. The next it descended into a darkness of the deepest stygian abyss lit only by a confusion of ghostly afterimages.

Nearly blind, Gonzalo signaled to the others and crept toward a hut on his right, a direction that he knew would lead them away from the village.

With an eerie and terrifying sense of exhilaration they all leaned into the maelstrom. Wind howled and they staggered through the torrent. Rain stung their exposed skin. Small sticks and flying debris assaulted them at every step. The four hurried as best they could, but their progress was like thick syrup reluctantly oozing across a plate.

As they staggered past the third hut in their path, Gonzalo jerked to a stop. Above the roar of the storm, he'd heard something. He closed his eyes and concentrated on the sound. Pedro grabbed at his arm and Gonzalo motioned him and the others to stay still. Ever so slowly, he edged them toward the wall of the nearby hut where they were less exposed.

The noise came again and Gonzalo stiffened, not trusting himself to breathe. Time seemed to stop. He held his breath. The four crouched frozen, fearing to make the slightest sound or movement.

Suddenly, Hernando, who was pressed against Gonzalo's side, choked out a strangled cry and flailed in the darkness.

Lightning flashed. Pitch black turned to day.

In that split second, momentary vision revealed the hapless steward sprawled on his back in the mud. The shaft of a heavy throwing spear jutted from between his shoulder blades. Its point, black and dripping with gore, jutted from his breast. Hernando's dead eyes stared up into the rain fixed in a look of offended surprise.

Darkness rushed back. Pedro screamed. Geronimo yelled. The image of the steward etched into his mind, Gonzalo searched wildly about in the blackness seeking the source of the attack. His sight was useless as that of a blind man.

Lightning flared again and in its momentary flash, Gonzalo beheld Sansón charging out of the storm. The powerful savage's mouth was drawn wide in a wind-swallowed scream of rage. One hand brandished a dreadful obsidian knife and the other wielded his great stone-headed war club. With his garish tattoos and his skin turned an unhealthy greenish white by the flash, the warrior fit the true image of a demon escaped from Hell.

Gonzalo raised his arms in front of his face to ward off the coming blow and tried to duck out of its way. His last impression as the world again went dark was of Pedro flinging himself into the giant's path.

Gonzalo's leap to the side and saved his skull, but it wasn't quick enough and Sansón's heavy weapon smashed into his shoulder and sent him sprawling.

Immediately, his shoulder throbbed and shock waves of pain rolled through his body. Before he could rise the savage was on top of him.

Choked by the downpour and gasping for breath, Gonzalo grappled in the mud and darkness. Instinctively, he clutched Sansón's thick wrists. He bucked and he twisted. He threw his weight on the warrior's knife hand. The blade nicked across his throat, but slid away.

Gonzalo shook. Sansón was too strong. The struggle was one-sided. Although he strained with all his might, Gonzalo was forced onto his back and pinned. A heartbeat later Sansón's wrists were free. A grip like iron clutched the escudero's throat. Lightning flashed and Gonzalo faced his own death. The warrior's face was stretched and brutal, contorted with anger. His knife was raised for a killing blow.

Gonzalo watched helpless. Lightning flashed again. Then, rising above the shrieking of the storm, he heard a wailing scream.

"God have mercy on me!"

In that instant, a shape loomed behind Sansón. Suddenly, Geronimo was there, his arms upstretched, and between them a great block of stone. The savage's knife began to fall. As utter darkness swallowed the awful vision, a mighty blow shook Gonzalo. Suddenly, he was suffocating, his mouth and nose pressed hard into the flesh of Sansón's chest.

As he struggled, Geronimo grabbed him under his armpits and tugged him from beneath the lifeless corpse. Searing pain wracked Gonzalo's shoulder with each heartbeat, but otherwise, to his vast surprise, he was uninjured. The Franciscan held him, only inches away.

"I killed him," he howled. "I took his life."

"And, you saved me!" shouted Gonzalo. Then, he remembered Hernando. "Where's Pedro?"

"Dead," groaned Geronimo, "dead!"

Unbidden, an image leapt to Gonzalo's mind of the cabin boy trying to block Sansón's attack.

"Nando and Pedro both? It's my fault!"

"Later," yelled Geronimo. "We're both damned. For now, we have to flee."

Then, he seized Gonzalo and shoved him into the darkness. Soon, the two were stumbling forward as though devils snapped at their heels. What followed, was the worst night of both men's lives. The world around them was reduced to brilliant afterimages and darkness so black that it made no difference whether their eyes were open or shut. The rain drummed as if it would never stop. It pounded the ground and bounced back making the earth appear to boil. The very air seemed as though it had turned to water.

The storm raged around them from every point of the compass. It roared. It screamed. It shrieked with glee. Pummeled by wind-born flotsam and jetsam they dragged their bodies through unyielding bracken. Streams of water sluiced around their feet. Thorns, spines, and saw-toothed leaves raked across their legs and tore at their skin and rent their already tattered clothes.

An eternity later, Gonzalo pulled himself over the fat trunk of a downed palm tree. The storm was abating. His shoulder ached, and for the millionth time, he regretted yet again the loss of his shoes.

In the dark and wet, it was nearly impossible to tell, but his right foot throbbed, and he was almost certain that it was cut and bleeding. In all his life, he'd never been so tired. He searched for any strength left in his legs; there wasn't any.

"Geronimo," he shouted, "we have to stop!"

The friar didn't answer, he simply collapsed onto the ground. As a faint brightness seeped into the eastern sky, the two remaining Spaniards clawed their way into a small soggy hollow and halfheartedly pulled fallen palm branches over their exhausted bodies.

When friction with the land at length slowed the ferocious spin of Hurakán's plaything, the old god allowed it. This was proper because it wasn't the creator-god's intent to punish the people of The Land of the Turkey and the Deer, merely to remind them of his nearly boundless power.

Deprived of Hurakán's guiding hand, the tempest quickly weakened and its feral splendor faded. As his own interest waned along with it, the old god wiggled his snake-like leg at one last joyous bolt of lightning, then he turned away and permitted his storm to die.

Sometime later, Gonzalo and Geronimo shook off their blanket of fronds and crawled out from the shallow depression that might just as well have proven their grave. A light drizzle was falling. A brisk wind tugged at them and tussled their hair, but it was no longer the shrieking demon of the night before.

Above them, heavy clouds raced across clearing skies allowing occasional warming rays of sunlight to slant down onto the earth. The two dazed Spaniards looked about themselves in wonder. Although neither Gonzalo nor Geronimo knew it, they had fought their way through the heart of Hurakán's storm.

The worst of the tempest passed directly between Tzamá and Xamanzamá leaving in its wake a kind of terrible devastation. The sparse dry jungle that covered the rocky ground between the two settlements had turned into a muddy snarling morass of soggy roots and vines, wet brush, and fallen trees.

Looking out upon the devastation, Geronimo fell to his knees and clasped his hands in prayer.

"Dear Lord, thank you for our salvation from the fury of the storm and thank you for delivering us from the idolaters who held us against our will."

Gonzalo began to laugh quietly, a humorless noise that verged on hysteria. Abruptly he sat down.

"Geronimo," he groaned, "You call this salvation? Deliverance? Look around! If some god took a hand in last night's doing, it wasn't the one that you're always praying to; that one doesn't exist."

"Damn you, Aroça," cursed the friar. "I killed a man. I put my immortal soul at risk to save your miserable life and the first words out of your ungrateful mouth deny the very existence of our Lord."

"How can they not?" cried Gonzalo. "Pedro and Nando were alive last night and now they're just as dead as Valdivia and the rest. It's our fault! Yours and mine, without our arrogance they'd still be sitting in our hut waiting for Mole-face to bring us our gruel. What sort of a god demands the death of children and old men?"

"When you speak of arrogance, you speak wisely," answered Geronimo. "It's arrogance to believe that Pedro and Hernando's lives were ever in our hands. We are all God's instruments. What we do in life and what becomes of us is his alone to decide."

"Instruments...," sighed Gonzalo.

"Aroça," said the Franciscan, moving closer to stare into Gonzalo's face. "God is ever a mystery. When terrible things happen, it's normal that we grieve, but when we give ourselves over to anger it's only because we're unable to see the higher purpose in Our Lord's works. The mind of man is too small to see the extent of his glory. To accept his will, without explanation, is the true measure of our faith."

Gonzalo stared back at his companion. "Geronimo," he said seriously, "you were magnificent last night, and without you I'd be a dead man. I know that, and I owe you a great and terrible debt. But, please, please, will you just shut up. If there was a plan that required Nando to die choking on his own blood, a plan that demanded Pedro to spill his guts in the mud, it was the plan of a madman. I'm no one's instrument and I tell you this, however few remain to me, I'll bear the burden of Pedro's death for the rest of my days."

The two men glared at each other. Then, they sat in uneasy silence. After a time, Gonzalo got onto his knees and then stood. Geronimo looked up at him and Gonzalo reached down a hand.

"Come on, I doubt that the savages are tailing us, but we can't stay here."

"Where do you think we are?" asked the friar as he took the offered hand and climbed to his feet.

"I've no idea," answered Gonzalo, pointing. "But what little morning sun there is, is over there on our left. If we head in that direction we should still be moving toward the coast and away from the village."

"Yes, you're right," nodded Geronimo, and the two began to pick their way through the mud and brush.

Both men were wet and chilled. Worn down by their harrowing escape and hindered at every step by the storm's confused destruction, they inched along and measured their progress in paces rather than strides. While they struggled forward, first one and then the other would look back over their shoulders, ears strained for sounds of pursuit. As they stumbled along, the sky above their heads brightened and then slowly cleared.

At first as the radiant sun glared down, it warmed the two, and briefly buoyed their spirits. Then, as more and more of the clouds fled, the morning's cool wind and drizzle yielded to a profound stillness. In the stillness, their clothes dried quickly and soon they began to sweat. As the day progressed, the sun overhead grew hotter and hotter, a clawing heat that beat down upon the men until its once welcome radiance turned the air around them into a heavy clinging cloak, sticky and impossible to shed.

Draining heat proved worse than the cold and the damp, and it grew with each passing hour. Frequent stops to rest or to dip water from gently steaming puddles did little to ease the Spaniards' fatigue or to slake their nagging thirst. Hunger gnawed at their stomachs.

Gonzalo's initial hopefulness at the sky's clearing proved short-lived. Under the blanket of oppressive warmth, optimism melted away. It mingled with his salty sweat, then leeched silently from his face and chest. Pushing against dense jumbled brush, scrambling over fallen tree trunks, and wading through muddy pools, every muscle and fiber of his being protested in weariness.

The mood of gloom, that poor dead Hernando's words, of the night before, had goaded into angry resolve, once again insinuated itself into Gonzalo's heart. Self-pity and despair hallmarked his previous melancholy, but now it was the ugly sisters, guilt and shame, that drove his despondency. The deaths of Pedro and Hernando stoked the fires of his guilt.

I urged Pedro on. I said that we should run. I told Nando that the storm was an opportunity. I led them to their deaths. If I'd spoken differently, if I'd acted differently...

A litany of self-blame rattled around inside Gonzalo's head. Deep and abiding shame drove his thoughts, dogged his footsteps, and weighted down his shoulders. Shame, not that he was the one who was alive and free, but shame that he was glad of it.

More friends lost, he thought. *If I could have, I'd have fought like a lion to save them both, but would I happily trade my life for theirs?*

In his heart, Gonzalo knew the answer and it filled him with despair.

I want to live.

As they trudged onward, Gonzalo felt worse with each foot he placed before the other. Geronimo had examined him and felt certain that the blow from Sansón's club hadn't broken anything. Just the same, the injury pained the escudero mightily and Gonzalo's consciousness drifted back and forth between the sweltering airless heat, thoughts of guilt and disgrace, and the suffocating ache in his shoulder.

He walked in a daze, prodded from time to time by Geronimo who somehow managed to keep his wits. Sometimes the two men went for what seemed hours without exchanging a word, each of them alone with his own struggle against fatigue and depression.

In addition to his shoulder, the cut on Gonzalo's right foot pulsated with an aching soreness. He also felt reminders of every thorn and spine that had tried to arrest his blind rush through the storm.

"Carajo!" he cursed feebly. "I feel like I've been flayed."

"I too feel discomfort," sighed Geronimo, "but take solace and set your mind on the passion of our Redeemer, Jesus Christ, and the blood he shed for both you and me. Consider how much greater was the torment that he suffered from the thorns than that suffered by you and I."

Gonzalo wanted to close his ears. He wanted to laugh hysterically. He wanted to berate his pious companion. Fatigue rendered him unable to do anything except trudge silently forward.

Late in the afternoon, he tripped and fell down onto some small palm plants that had been thrown over by the storm. As he levered himself back up, he spied something smooth and whitish.

"Look!" he cried.

Although the plants were knocked flat, clawing fingers soon yielded up several small edible cores like those the two Spaniards knew from far away Andalusia.

"The hearts offer little sustenance," mused the Geronimo as they ate, "but at least they taste a bit like artichoke."

"At least they're something to put into our bellies," answered Gonzalo. "I don't care what they taste like."

Later, the two trudged wearily on, only ending their draining flight long after the sun disappeared into deep blue heavens pinpricked by a thousand stars. Weak and exhausted, they scrambled up into the thick limbs of an enormous tree which the storm had stripped of most its leaves.

Sleep eluded them, or came in short unsatisfying snatches. Often as not, when it did come, it brought with it unseen malice and hidden foes who chased them through their dreams and tormented them as they struggled to cry out or run on useless legs.

Now and then, the inky night erupted with strange howls, a chorus of barking roars that left Gonzalo and Geronimo wide-eyed and shaken. Later, in the bitter grey half-light that arrives just before dawn, they watched a play of fog, shadows, and apparitions in which the shade of a great cat waylaid and killed the wraith of a deer.

When the morning finally came, Gonzalo climbed down from their perch dreading the day. He was unrefreshed by his night in the tree, but his shoulder felt marginally better.

"Are you sure the beast's gone?" asked Geronimo peering down from above.

"You can see, better than I," answered Gonzalo standing with his back against the trunk.

Geronimo shaded his eyes and carefully searched the nearby landscape. From his vantage point, nothing stirred near the base of the tree nor moved in the surrounding brush, and the Franciscan felt embarrassingly relieved.

"Nothing," he said. "Maybe it was only a dream."

"It was no dream," whispered Gonzalo. "Come down."

When Geronimo was standing beside him, Gonzalo started slowly and cautiously in the direction they'd been walking before sunset. A hundred strides away, they came upon the carcass of the deer. Both men looked fearfully about, but all was quiet and nothing moved. The deer had been savaged and most of it eaten, but the great cat had left scraps.

Without a word, Gonzalo and Geronimo fell to their knees, tore at the bloody remains, and stuffed small scraps of raw meat into their hungry mouths.

It's not manna, thought Geronimo, *but it's still a gift from God.*

After leaving the deer, the men pushed on. They didn't really know where they were headed, but with a bit of food in their stomachs, the going was easier. For want of a better plan, they simply continued in the direction that they were headed and tried to put as much distance between themselves and their captivity as possible.

A sameness blanketed the ravaged landscape, and Gonzalo and Geronimo passed through it like sleepwalkers. Despite their injuries and overall poor condition, the somnambulists repeatedly put one foot in front of another and their paces slowly turned into miles. Near sunset, with their bellies again empty and their strength spent, they came upon another large tree.

"It'll be night soon and I'm too tired to go on," sighed Gonzalo. "Let's stop here, at least we can sleep off the ground."

Geronimo agreed, and after resting for a few moments he pulled himself up into the branches to see if the tree offered a refuge for the night. Gonzalo, whose shoulder was paining him, remained seated. Suddenly, above his head the Franciscan gave an uncharacteristic gasp.

"Mother of Our Lord!"

"What is it?" shouted Gonzalo.

"You'd better climb up," croaked Geronimo.

Favoring his shoulder, Gonzalo shinnied his way into the tree. When at last he managed to balance himself upright next to the friar, the sight that greeted his eyes beggared his imagination.

Before him stretched a close-packed legion of thatch and stucco huts. Some of the high houses had been overthrown by the storm, others had been crushed by falling trees. Many evidenced destruction by fire. Overall the scene was one of considerable loss, yet despite the ruin a remarkable sprawl of undamaged huts radiated outward in all directions from a focal point that was even more arresting.

To the west the sun was setting and the sky on that horizon was a tapestry of gold, purple, and distant slate grey clouds edged in crimson. Aglow in that waning light, in the middle of ring upon ring of huts, standing atop a high bluff above the sea, rose a massive stone walled fortress. At its center stood a mighty tapered castle or keep, painted in glowing shades of orange, yellow, and red, and surrounding it a mass of other brightly colored buildings, platforms, and plazas.

Pink and salmon shadows crept across the stone until they reached a beach where the fading light turned the sands themselves to shades of orange and purple. Dozens of sailing canoes, both large and small were drawn up on the sand and everywhere among the huts and inside the walls of the fortress surged a veritable sea of people.

After the mud huts of Darien, Gonzalo was mightily impressed by the dressed stones and stucco walls of Xamanzamá's central plaza, but what now spread before him was an order of magnitude beyond anything that he'd imagined. The garish hues of red, orange, and yellow were the same, but there all similarity ended. This was the seat of a kingdom.

"I don't believe it," choked Gonzalo, "there must be more than two thousand souls in that city. And, look at the fortress!"

"Jesus help us, Aroça," whispered Geronimo, "it's like a dream. This is a land of savages and idolaters yet before us stands a city so grand that Seville would not appear larger or better. What... what shall we do?"

"Our choice is made for us," sighed Gonzalo. "If we go back we die, if we stay here we die, our only path is forward."

Chapter 24

City of the Dawn

The 16th of September, Year of Our Lord 1511

With frayed nerves set a jangle and their emotions awhirl, Gonzalo and Geronimo clambered down from their perch. Geronimo reached the ground first and then waited until Gonzalo finished his descent.

"It'll be dark soon," murmured the friar, glancing upward to the branches they'd just left. "Maybe we're precipitous, Aroça. Perhaps now isn't the time for a rash action. We can rest here. We can wait until morning. Things may look different to us in the light of God's new day."

"I can't wait," groaned Gonzalo. "Four months have passed since we washed onto these hard shores, and not a single new dawn since that accursed day has changed anything. If I don't go now, my courage will fail me."

With that, he turned and shuffled away. Geronimo, crossed himself, mumbled a quick prayer and reluctantly followed.

Resigned to whatever uncertain future waited before them, the two men wearily trudged through a final swath of the storm's debris. Then, like a door swinging open, the confusion of jungle gave way and the imposing citadel again rose unrestricted into their view. In the waning light, its every wall and cornice were aflame.

"My God," breathed Geronimo. "Who'd have imagined that savages could build such a wonder? It's as though we face some idolatrous outpost of ancient Babylon."

"It's a city," shrugged Gonzalo, "just stones and mortar. Savages are yet men, and men build things."

"Our Lord destroyed Sodom and Gomorrah and cast down Babel's tower," responded Geronimo. "How is it that he allows such a work of evil to exist?"

"Once more, I tell you, just stones and mortar," insisted Gonzalo turning to the friar. "We know nothing of this land, but from everything I've seen it's a place where other gods hold sway."

In that instant he felt himself farther from Spain, farther from the world he'd known, than ever before. Geronimo watched in silence as Gonzalo again turned and walked away.

"Truly, Aroça," he sighed after the escudero's retreating back, "I fear for your immortal soul."

Continuing forward, the two castaways trod slowly and quietly. A short time later, as yet unobserved, they drew near to the chaotic outskirts of the sprawling city. When they reached a point where their next steps would carry them into the open and into certain notice, Geronimo halted and held out his arm to stop Gonzalo's advance.

"Wait," he said, "this is the moment, Aroça. If we continue, there's no turning back."

"There's already no turning back," answered Gonzalo quietly.

"But, the risk," urged Geronimo. "We'll be back in the power of the heathens."

Gonzalo stared at his companion. "Don't you understand? There's no succor in this land. We've nothing left, just you and I. No matter what we do, we're likely to die. Our only choice is whether to face death moving forward, or we let it overtake us as we run howling like curs with our tails between our legs."

"Will you at least wait while I petition God's protection and forgiveness?"

"I want your company," confessed Gonzalo. "Say your prayers."

Recognizing that any surprise might prove fatal, Gonzalo and Geronimo approached the walled city slowly and openly. Cautious in word and gesture, they passed through the bastion's surrounding mass of storm-damaged huts without incident. Even so, almost immediately, natives began to follow them at a wary distance. By the time the two Spaniards reached the city's stone rampart, a small whispering throng shadowed their footsteps. Each step forward saw another savage join the followers, and with each newcomer the accompanying murmured din grew ever louder.

With fear in his heart and no real plan in his mind, Gonzalo led Geronimo stumbling along the city wall in search of a gate. The two continued perhaps one hundred uncertain paces along the stonework when, without warning, several natives abruptly pushed forward and blocked their way.

"Turn around," hissed Gonzalo.

Pivoting to retrace their steps, Geronimo immediately discovered that the crowd had closed behind them and that retreat was also an impossibility.

"What now?" murmured the friar.

"How should I know?" breathed Gonzalo. "You're the one who prayed for guidance. I'm just the fool who's cast us into back into the pit."

With their backs pressed against the warm rough stone of the wall, the two regarded the semi-circle of curious enigmatic faces and everywhere around them the muttering natives edged closer.

"We have to do something," gulped Geronimo. "We can't just stand here."

Three hissed whispers later, long before the Spaniards agreed to any action, five stern looking warriors pushed their way through the crowd. Upon sighting them, Geronimo groaned aloud. In the same instant, Gonzalo felt the grand illusion that he controlled his own actions slip away and snuff out like a guttering candle.

Their hands were bound, ropes were again looped about their necks, and in the flicker of an eyelash their hard-won freedom ceased to exist. Captives once again, the Spaniards were yanked forward. The knot of warriors alternately shoving and pulling, separated Gonzalo and Geronimo from the crowd and roughly herded them through an opening in the thick city wall.

On the other side, the sight that met the castaways' eyes threatened to take their breath. Seen from close at hand the city's core was even more astonishing than what they'd beheld from a distance. As was the sprawl outside its walls, the inner confines of the citadel were marked with unmistakable signs of the recent storm and of its fury. Collapsed huts, scattered thatch, and broken household items, littered the ground in all directions. It wasn't the destruction, however, that captured the Spaniards' attention. Aloof from the detritus stood three to four score of undamaged structures, all of them solid, all of them worked from blocks of unyielding stone.

Upon their first glimpse of the wide plaza where Captain Valdivia and their other ill-fated companions met their ends Gonzalo and Geronimo had been fascinated by its smooth fitted pavement and its three brightly stuccoed buildings. To that point, nothing they'd seen in the new world was its equal. The memory of that sight paled in comparison to the spectacle that now spread before them.

Stretching down to the sandy shore, and to the sea itself, stonework occupied much of the open space within the walls. Picked out by slanting rays of the dying sun vivid shades of red, yellow, white, and blue, made each sturdy edifice seem to glow. The chaos, the imposing maze of buildings, platforms, and sloping terraces, the daunting kaleidoscope of brilliant hues, and the novel architecture all battered the castaways' tired senses leaving them astonished and dazed.

Most impressive of all loomed the huge pyramid or keep which clung to the edge of a cliff from where it threw its considerable shadow eastward over the ocean. To Gonzalo, the great stone castillo rivaled the monuments of Spain. Its magnificent balustrades were fashioned into the form of gigantic plumed serpents and its proportions startled and amazed.

Upon reaching a plaza at the base of the structure, their captors threw the Spaniards to their knees. Before them two large fires burnt brightly in anticipation of the coming darkness and around the fires were gathered a group of elaborately attired men, women, and children. With their heads reeling, Gonzalo and Geronimo stared at what could only be an assemblage of local aristocrats.

While Gonzalo and Geronimo gaped about themselves in wide-eyed anxiety, one of their guards also dropped to his knees and addressed one of the nobles. The native to whom he spoke was the most remarkable savage that Gonzalo had yet encountered.

Although not as powerfully build as the huge savage who stood next to him, even by European standards the man was tall. His forehead was elongated and conspicuously sloped. Large plugs of green jade ingeniously worked into the shape of blooming flowers ornamented his pierced ears. Jade bracelets adorned his wrists and small squares of yet more jade formed a breastplate that accented his muscular chest. A bright feather cape rested on his shoulders, shimmering in iridescent shades of red and purple whenever he moved. Long jet black hair twisted about his head forming a sort of crown worked with colorful strips of cloth, seashells, and bits of semi-precious stone.

After listening to the native who had spoken, he looked down at Gonzalo and Geronimo through crossed but penetrating eyes and said something that to their ears sounded both harsh and demanding.

"Geronimo," whispered Gonzalo, "this king decides our fate. Do as I do. Beg for your life!"

Without shame Gonzalo and Geronimo bowed still lower and with downcast eyes pleaded in their unintelligible tongue that the savage lord spare their lives and accept them as his willing slaves.

At first, their worried entreaties were met with a stony silence. Then, the king and the two impressive personages at his side began to chatter among themselves.

"Look at them," insisted White Worm. "Listen to the gibberish they speak. I tell you it's two of them!"

"Bah," grunted Gucumatz, "they speak nonsense. No god would choose such messengers."

"Look at them closely," urged Worm.

"I am looking," answered Gucumatz, "and not even those fools in Xamanzamá could mistake these two for divine creatures from Ka'an or Metnal (heaven or hell)."

"Of course they're not celestial," continued Worm, "I'm not saying that. I'm saying they're two of Ac Yanto's captives!"

Ah Tabai listened to the back and forth between his nacon and his half-brother and moved closer to the two strangers kneeling at his feet. At first, he'd thought the men vagabonds and had been annoyed that the city guard even brought them to his attention.

The men were filthy and they looked half-starved. They were covered with dried mud and bits of twigs and leaves. Their hair was dirty and matted and their bodies were marked by a multitude of small wounds and bruises. But, as he stared, he immediately realized that there was something odd about the two strangers. Their features weren't quite right and their tattered clothing was strikingly unusual. With growing shock and awareness he realized that the two men lacked any tattoos or other bodily ornamentation and that they were plastered with an abnormal amount of hair.

The man on the left was wrapped in some kind of dark cloth robe that hid much of his form. The man to his right, who was closer, wore a covering something like a woman's pic (undershirt) except that it also covered his arms. Instead of a suyen (loincloth) his lower body was wrapped in another cloth that covered his manhood and also much of his legs. The garments were soiled and badly torn and frayed, but Ah Tabai knew that he had never seen their like.

Stepping forward, he reached down, cupped the nearer man's chin and raised his face. Fear shown in the stranger's eyes, but also intelligence and curiosity. Beneath his hand the Lord of Fire could feel the fur on the man's face.

"Gucumatz, my good right hand," suggested Ah Tabai with a grin. "Once again Zac Nok proves that his powers of perception may be better than yours or mine. These pieces of offal are undoubtedly two of Xamanzamá's 'monkey gods.' What's more I'll wager that our friend Ac Yanto has no idea that they're kneeling at our feet."

When the savage king lifted Gonzalo's chin, the escudero felt that his bladder might betray him. Then, inexplicably, the native smiled and spoke to his companions. The three extravagantly attired lords smirked, gestured emphatically, and eventually laughed out loud.

Following their malicious laughter, the huge warrior who stood beside the king rumbled a command and two other warriors rushed forward. To Gonzalo's terror, they pulled him roughly to his feet and dragged him away. A moment later the heavy savage who stood to the king's other side also spoke and two more warriors laid hands on an equally alarmed Geronimo and hauled him away in a different direction.

Instead of the imminent death that both Spaniards feared, what followed were lonely days of captivity and confusion. Although separated, Gonzalo and Geronimo experienced similar internments. Neither had any privileges, and their new masters again expected them to provide manual labor and to obey unquestioningly. The work they were given however was less onerous and taxing.

From time to time, a minder struck one or the other to elicit a quicker response or to drive home a point, but unlike their previous imprisonment, neither Spaniard seemed to be unnecessarily mistreated.

It was a time like no other in Gonzalo's life, every waking moment vacillated between wonder and fear. A world away from Spain, the daily routines of his past existence, and the people he had come to know over the years, it was as if time had become unhinged.

After a few bewildering days he came to realize that he had been given into the household of the largest and most brutal looking of the three laughing native lords. Once again, he was housed in a small hut. This time, however, its other occupants were three scrawny natives who, apparently, were also slaves. When he was not being made to work, Gonzalo was paraded from one place to another as a curiosity.

Chapter 25

A Spy in Tzamá

11 Bak'tun 14 K'atun 11 Tun 8 Uinal 10 K'in

(September 30, 1511)

Ah-cambal bent over and carefully placed a last basket of trade goods into his loaded canoe, then he straightened and faced his brother.

"You know you don't have to do this," said Nachan Can. "We need fresh information, information that we can trust, but it doesn't have to be you that collects it. Let Hoch Can send one of the younger men."

"Te' K'ab' (Tree Branch) says he's willing to go uncle," interjected the young nacon. "He's a good man and very brave."

"Te' K'ab' is a good man and he is brave," answered Ah-cambal soberly, "but he's not one to sit quietly, watch, listen, and remember. We've been through all of this. There's little danger. I'm best suited to this task and once I'm disguised, no one will recognize me."

"How can you be sure?" questioned Itz'at Acan, who was standing at his sajal's side. "Ah Tabai, White Worm, Gucumatz, and others in Tzamá know your face."

"It's not my face they'll see," smiled Ah-cambal, "and I know The Lord of the Fire and his minions. One and all, they're big-headed creatures whose conceit is such that they won't deign to look into the humble face that I plan to offer them."

"Still the risk..." began Nachan Can.

"Brother," interrupted Ah-cambal, "is there anyone else that you better trust to serve as your eyes? Anyone, you trust more to serve as your ears?"

"You know there isn't," sighed Nachan Can.

"Then," said Ah-cambal, "I didn't ask you three to come out here and stand in the sand to try to talk me out of this visit to Tzamá. You're here to help me launch my canoe. Now, before I lose what little tide there is left in this bay, put your shoulders into it."

Four good heaves, with Ah-cambal and his nephew on one side and Nachan Can and his wiry steward on the other, and the craft was away. As the canoe broke loose from the sand, Ah-cambal pulled himself aboard and began to paddle out into the Bay of Chectumal.

Hoch Can stood in the shallows with his father and Acan and waved.

"Ekchuah watch over you, uncle!"

Ichpaatún's exposed location on the edge of the wide and open bay meant that it was often pummeled by autumn tempests, but such wasn't always the case. When Hurakán's storm came raging in from the sea uaclahun k'in (16 days) earlier, it mostly spared Nachan Can's city. Its winds flattened several huts and gusts blew loose thatch from many roofs. Crashing waves washed away drying nets and, to their owner's dismay, several poorly secured canoes. Few food stores were destroyed and, although several people were injured, no one lost their life.

When rumors filtered into the city of the terrible devastation the storm wrought in and about Tzamá and its vassal, Xamanzamá, many in Ichpaatún rejoiced at their own good fortune.

Two days earlier, a runner from White Worm had arrived bearing a message for Dwarf-wind.

"The Lord of Fire expresses his deep sorrow that plans for the union to his beautiful daughter, Mad Seizure Star, must regretfully be postponed."

The subtext was that Tzamá had wounds to lick. Ah-cambal had exulted and gratefully offered a large chunk of smoldering copal to each of the many gods of sky and rain.

Two uinal (40 days) had passed since Ah Tabai's emissaries delivered the lord of Tzamá's wedding offer to Dwarf-wind and Ah-cambal's perfumed younger brother had expended those days in greedy anticipation. To anyone who would listen, he expounded again and again the glories of Tzamá and the wisdom of their Lord of the Fire. This wisdom of course referred to that ruler's choice of Dwarf-wind himself as an appropriate husband for Lady Mad Seizure Star.

In his thoughts, Dwarf-wind had already arrayed himself with newfound power and prestige, and the wealth that he imagined his union was sure to bring. The message announcing the wedding's postponement came like a harsh slap in the face.

"This delay is a disaster," he'd wailed to Nachan Can and Ah-cambal. "What if the Lord of Fire changes his mind? The destruction in Tzamá must be far worse than we ever imagined. We must send, food and tribute. We must show Ah Tabai that the people of Ichpaatún are his loyal allies!"

Dwarf-wind's brothers had both listened in stony silence. While he'd been walking around with a head full of avaricious dreams, Nachan Can and Ah-cambal had wrestled with concern and indecision. They were as convinced of Ah Tabai's enmity as Dwarf-wind was of his goodwill.

If they forced their younger brother to reject the betrothal, they felt certain that the mercurial lord of Tzamá would treat the rejection as an insult and that he would use the slight as a justification to fan the smoldering skirmishes between their two city-states into an open war. If, on the other hand, they allowed the marriage to go forward, Ah Tabai would surely use the union to tighten his grip on Ichpaatún and try to bind the city to his will.

Despite endless discussions about the possible consequences of Dwarf-wind's acceptance of Ah Tabai's betrothal offer, Nachan Can, Ah-cambal, and Itz'at Acan had yet to devise a suitable counter. When Dwarf-wind threw up his hands in grief and agitation at the Lord of Fire's suggested delay, the other three secretly rejoiced.

Ah-cambal had immediately proposed that he journey to Tzamá, gauge the storm's damage, and try to assess their aggressive neighbor's true intent. So it was that riding on a gentle ebb tide, he raised his canoe's modest sail, tacked out of the bay, and began a long northward reach.

Ah-cambal treasured Ichpaatún, its unpretentious temples, its bustling markets, and its gregarious people, but at the rumbling center of his heart, he was also an introspective man equally at home with solitude. Almost immediately, the shoreline receded behind him and the sea opened before him. The only sounds to reach his ears became those of seabirds, wind, and water lapping against the wooden sides of his craft. Ah-cambal relaxed.

According to the sacred Tzolk'in, the day was 13 Ok, and consecrated to "Dog," who guides the night sun through the underworld.

It's a good day to begin a journey, thought Ah-cambal.

Winds remained fair and constant; sailing day and night, with short naps to rest, he made good time. To the boundless ocean deeps, it was as if Hurakán's storm had never been. Ah-cambal's canoe slipped easily through warm transparent waters, tranquil seas where occasional smiling dolphins played before his bow and indifferent turtles swam slowly past, paddling with an assured and languid grace.

Instead of bearing straight for Tzamá, Ah-cambal veered far out to sea. So doing, he avoided its busy nearby port city of Samal, and then bypassed Ah Tabai's citadel entirely. In The City of the Dawn's place, he landed on the holy island dedicated as a sanctuary to Ixchel, goddess of fertility, reason, medicine, happiness and the moon.

People from the mainland made frequent pilgrimages to the island and small feminine figurines left by the faithful as offerings littered its beaches. In later years, Spanish explorers would find the beautiful little statues and call the island Isla Mujeres (Island of Women).

Ixchel's temple sat prominently on the island's southernmost point and at night the light from many torches shown through holes in its walls. Arriving well after dark, Ah-cambal used the flickering lights to guide him to shore.

The next two days he spent busily exchanging goods from Ichpaatún and Lamanai, its neighbor to the south, for salt from the island's small interior lagoons and the other unpretentious products that Ixchel's sanctuary had to offer.

Throughout the city of Ichpaatún Ah-cambal was known as a shrewd trader and a hard bargainer, but on Ixchel's island he allowed himself to be swindled. His goal wasn't to turn a profit, but to replace one set of merchandise with another.

After a slight change of attire, a few easy modifications to the rigging of his canoe, and the completion of his trading, he again embarked. With good weather and another day and night at sea, his canoe scraped up onto the fine sand of Tzamá. When he stepped ashore, the spy from Ichpaatún was gone and in his place stood a crippled merchant from Ixchel's island come to trade salt and humble products of the sea.

Canoes of all sizes and descriptions crowded the shore, and Ah-cambal's modest dugout was but one among many. As he worked to drag it up from the gentle surf, apparently struggling and ineffectual, two lean young warriors approached, and lent their shoulders to his effort. In a moment, the canoe was well above the tide line.

"So, grandfather," demanded one of the warriors with a voice of authority, "what have you brought us to trade?"

"Trifles from Ixchel's sacred isle," mumbled Ah-cambal, with downcast eyes, "trifles and gifts from the sea."

"We'd better inspect these trifles and gifts of yours," grinned the other.

Turning, he pulled the lid from one of Ah-cambal's baskets. Mussels filled the first and both warriors selected several of the best and stuffed them into pouches tied at their waists. The second lid they removed revealed the insides of a deep fat basket sealed with pitch and packed to its rim with salt.

"Grandfather," said the one with the authoritative voice, "you forgot to mention your salt."

"It is good salt," answered Ah-cambal, looking into the man's eyes, "clean, pure, and white. Perhaps you and your friend here would like a small sample for helping me with my canoe."

Both men stared greedily into the basket. Salt was used not only for the conservation of food and for medicine but also as a generally accepted currency for the exchange of goods throughout the length and breadth of The Land of the Turkey and the Deer.

"Thank you for your generous offer, grandfather," said the leader cagily. "I'm afraid however, that you must give us quite a large sample. If you plan to trade this salt here in Tzamá, we must assure ourselves that it's as clean and pure as you say. Sometimes visiting merchants, unscrupulous merchants, claim that their salt is clean, but then try to cheat our people with additions of sand or lime dust. I'm sure that you're not one of those, but just the same, several persons, perhaps even our nacon, will need to inspect your wares and a small sample won't suffice."

"Hmmm, I see your dilemma," answered Ah-cambal. "I of course wish all of the Lord of Fire's people to hold only the greatest confidence in my goods. Here, let me prepare each of you a sample."

So saying, he dug into his goods and pulled out two large clean squares of cotton cloth, items that in and of themselves had trade value. Smoothing out the two cloths, he scooped salt from his basket and began a pile in the center of each square. After a couple of handfuls, he stopped and looked expectantly at the two warriors.

"It's not enough," said the authoritative voice.

"Of course it's not. Of course it's not," groveled Ah-cambal. "Generous samples are what you need."

Scooping up more salt, he doubled the size of the piles. This time when he looked up at the two warriors they both smiled.

"Before I tie these up, my friends," he enquired with a smile of his own, "you can see that I am lame, perhaps you can suggest someone to help me carry the rest of my salt and trifles to the market?"

A short time later, the two samples of salt again doubled in size, and a short time after that the two warriors helped Ah-cambal lug his goods into the market plaza. As the guards tramped away to return to their duties, he unrolled a mat and pensively began to lay out his wares.

Ah-cambal had just been grievously robbed by the two Tzamáns, but inside he smiled. As a spy, he considered the transaction a bargain. To ease his transition into their city he would have happily given the two thieving holcánob his entire basket of salt.

Ah-cambal wasn't a regular, so the space where he was allowed to set out his goods was in a quiet backwater far from the busy market's heavily contested center. Despite the inferior location, two days later he was still in the same spot, seated alertly at the edge of his reed mat. Prime site or neglected corner, no better place existed for a spy than Tzamá's bustling market.

Despite the effects of the storm and the protracted drought which came before it, the Lord of Fire's city still overflowed with astounding wealth. Sooner or later almost anything and everything of value that could be bartered passed through its market, and each time that goods changed hands banter and gossip lubricated the exchange.

An overweight taciturn seller of stingray spines and colorful bird feathers occupied the space on Ah-cambal's left. During his first day at the market, Ah-cambal tried several times to engage the jowl-faced merchant in meaningless chit-chat and draw him out. His best efforts proved futile. The large man acknowledged his presence, and grunted indifferent one-word answers to his questions, but he refused to be guided into anything that approached a true conversation. Ah-cambal couldn't help but notice that the man's market in spines and feathers was as lifeless as his banter.

The stall on Ah-cambal's right was a different story. Shortly after he first arrived and the two opportunistic holcánob took their leave, a spry, wizened, seller of clay pots and jugs had seized the location. That proved to be a far more fertile field. Where the merchant on Ah-cambal's left was sullen and close-lipped, the diminutive pot seller was outgoing and garrulous.

He was an old man, with the openness of an old man who has lived long and cares little what others think. He was also somewhat full of himself. He had a beak of a nose and squinty eyes. His hair was wispy and thin and it left most of his scalp visible. His face was shrewd and cheerful, and he gesticulated energetically with his thick, knurled, clay-stained hands.

He shouted at anyone and everyone who ambled by, teasing, flattering, and praising his wares. Because of his efforts, the potter's business was brisk. Nevertheless, he was only too happy to chatter non-stop at Ah-cambal whenever his flow of potential customers ebbed.

Ah-cambal quickly learned that the potter's name was Luuk' and many more tedious details about the potters' art than he had ever hoped to hear. He also learned details of the recent storm which he considered far more interesting.

Tzamá had indeed suffered greatly. As Ah-cambal had expected, the stone citadel at the city's center saw little destruction, but everywhere about it structures of stick, thatch, and mud had been torn apart, thrown down, or carried away. In spite of the torrential downpour, fire had aggravated the mayhem. Bone dry fronds and reeds, the inside surface of roofs and walls, had collapsed into fireplaces and many close packed huts, large and small, had burned and drowned at the same time. According to Luuk' perhaps uac kal (120) had died, mostly women and children.

"Uac kal is a sad number," said Ah-cambal. "How is it that Tzamá doesn't seem to be in mourning?"

"After the storm," answered Luuk', glancing away at the Temple of Venus atop its pyramid, "The Lord of Fire gathered many before him and told us to grieve quickly, but then to put away our grief and rebuild. He reminded us that we had all prayed for an end to the drought and that Lord Chaac answered our prayers. The Lord of Fire spoke truth. We all begged Lord Chaac for rain, and all gods demand payment. If he, our Lord of Fire, offered his sacred blood to the heavens should any less be expected of the rest of us whose blood means so little? Those who died were honored as sacrifices," said Luuk' proudly. "But," he continued, "if you ask me, they were lucky it was the rain god who took them and not the other one."

"What other one?" asked Ah-cambal, his interested aroused.

"The other god," smiled Luuk' slyly. "When all of Tzamá gathered and the Lord of Fire and Lady Sunstroke gave their blood to the rain god, sacred smoke carried their prayers into the sky. We all saw it rise, but it wasn't Chaac who took their offering, it was the other."

"I still don't understand," responded Ah-cambal. "If Lord Chaac didn't receive the Lord of Fire's offering which god did?"

"The vision snake appeared," said Luuk'. "Lady Sunstroke saw it first, and then many of us. Its scales shown and glistened, but then Lord Gucumatz began to shout, and it changed into something else. His warriors also saw and began to shout. Then, we all saw."

"Saw what?" urged Ah-cambal.

Luuk' looked about as if suddenly unsure of himself and then whispered, "Buluc Chabtan."

Ah-cambal felt all the small hairs at the back of his neck stand up.

Yajawk'ak' has called forth the god of war, he thought. *Such a summoning can only mean one thing.*

If Ah-cambal had stayed seated in the market for a full turn of the ha'ab (365 day year) it is unlikely he would have heard anything that convinced him of Ah Tabai's intentions as thoroughly as Luuk's whispered words.

Gucumatz's patron god, Buluc Chabtan, expects human sacrifice. That vengeful and bloody demon who would only have answered Ah Tabai's petition if he smelled war.

"I think," smirked Luuk', still whispering, "that Tzamá is about to get bigger."

"War, war is always bad for trade," muttered Ah-cambal. "Are you sure?"

"Do I look like I sit on the Lord of Fire's council?" grinned the wrinkled pot seller. "Of course I'm not sure. But, I've got eyes and I've got ears and they both tell me that something is coming."

Ah-cambal was about to speak again when Luuk' jumped to his feet and then knelt. A man of middling height, thick about the waist, and with round shoulders and more chins than he needed, was wading through the market. His clothing spoke of wealth and a small entourage of servants followed in his wake. As he approached, Luuk' raised his arms in supplication.

"Great Lord, it is indeed a fortunate day when one as illustrious as yourself pauses to examine my humble wares."

The man stopped, and looked down at Luuk's pots and bowls. His demeanor was haughty and insolent and he lowered his brows at what he saw.

"Tell me old man," he sneered. "What makes you think I care to inspect your shoddy goods? I have no need of such rubbish."

"If not rubbish, then perhaps salt," chuckled Ah-cambal.

Instantly, the man spun about and a young warrior who accompanied him took a menacing step forward.

"How dare you?" shouted the well-dressed man brandishing a baton he carried. "You will address me as Ahau (Lord)! Do you know who I am?"

"No Lord," pleaded Ah-cambal. "Please forgive me. I am only an ignorant merchant from Ixchel's holy isle. I meant no offense."

The man appeared somewhat mollified by Ah-cambal's grovel and he lowered his baton and puffed out his flabby chest.

"I am Turix, caluac to the household of Nacon Gucumatz, undefeated leader of Tzamá's holcánob, confidant of The White Worm, and the right arm of our Lord of Fire."

Ah-cambal cringed lower as if the names caused him boundless fear.

"I...I should have known," he stammered. "Now that my eyes are open, I can see that greatness surrounds you Lord. I... I meant no harm. Forgive my temerity, I... I only meant to say that all households require salt."

Turix stared down at the fawning merchant. The old man's skin was nut brown. He was covered with tattoos that marked him as a foreigner, but they were smudged, muddled and indistinct, an effect that Ah-cambal had worked carefully to achieve. Turix frowned.

He looks like he might have been warrior once but now he's just a begging old man.

It was also obvious to the caluac that the old man was in some way lame.

"Very well," he grunted. "Show me this salt of yours."

"Thank you great lord," sniveled Ah-cambal, pushing his basket forward and removing its lid. The salt glistened, white and clean, and Turix saw at a glance that it was of good quality.

The caluac considered himself sly, and the negotiation that followed echoed his estimation. Playing on his status, which he assumed intimidated the merchant, he alternately browbeat and cajoled Ah-cambal all the while making one flagrantly unacceptable offer after another.

After a token resistance, Ah-cambal, with a suitable expression of long-suffering reluctance, agreed to accept a tapir hide of inferior quality, a small handful of cacao beans, and two chipped flint knives for his salt. The exchange was another theft, but again the spy didn't care. Ah-cambal believed that he had learned what he came to Tzamá to learn and the near theft of his principle product gave the sham merchant a faultless excuse to leave.

Turix smirked as he waved a slave forward with his end of the bargain.

The man's not only lame, thought the caluac. *He's an idiot. His salt was worth ten times as much.*

As the servant stepped forward, Ah-cambal abruptly became aware of another thrall who stood at the rear of the caluac's group. The man was unique. His skin, although darkened by the sun, was light in color and free of visible tattoos. Instead of a loincloth and mantle, his legs, manhood, and upper body were covered by tattered ragged garments unlike any that Ah-cambal had ever seen.

His skin tone and clothing created a strange impression, but it was the slave's hair that seized the spy's full attention. The man was covered with it. His arms and what could be seen of his chest were carpeted with dark twists. The hair on his head was black, and instead of being straight, it was thick and curled with waves and ringlets. And his face, his face sported hair rivaling that of an animal!

Turix caught Ah-cambal's surprised stare. Then he looked about himself. The potter and the feather seller were also staring as were several other merchants and a few worthy customers.

Ah an audience, thought Turix. A man driven by vanity, he rarely passed up any chance to strut or preen.

"So, old man," he asked, "do you like Nacon Gucumatz' pet monkey god?"

"Lord?" questioned Ah-cambal genuinely confused.

"According to some of the gullible fools who live in Xamanzamá," said Turix loudly, assuring that all about him would hear, "this one is a messenger of the gods Hun Chowen and Hun Batz."

After this pronouncement, the caluac paused for effect until he was sure that all within earshot were hanging on his words. Then, he continued.

"As anyone of even middling intelligence can see, he's no more a god than you or I." Next, he shouted at his charge, "Turn around you!"

Then, he waved his right hand in a circular motion. The slave nodded and slowly turned fully around. To Ah-cambal it was obvious that he was watching a performance that had been given many times before.

"He's just a man," crowed Turix, "but look at him! Have you ever seen such hair? In fairness, it's not hard to imagine where those simpletons from Xamanzamá got their idea. Rumors say, that the... What is it that Ac Yanto styles himself, the eye of something or other? Anyway his nacon captured this one along with several other hairy monkeys all of which he sacrificed to Lord Chaac."

"How then, Great One, is he here with you?" asked Ah-cambal, still perplexed.

Turix laughed from deep in his belly.

"It seems that the lord of Xamanzamá can't keep even a few monkeys caged. This beast and another equally hairy creature appeared at our gates and were taken before our glorious Lord of Fire. They're an amusing curiosity. Foreigners to be sure, but otherwise of little consequence. Since they only speak a few words, the Great Lord in his wisdom gave one to my master, Nacon Gucumatz, to train and the other he presented to Ah K'in Zac Nok."

"I think my own Lord got the better of the pair," whispered the caluac conspiratorially. "This monkey obeys my commands and works hard enough. Except for his hair, he's almost normal. The other one, the one White Worm received, is worthless," he chuckled. "He keeps making little k'atab ché (crosses of wood) then he holds them aloft, waves them about, and shouts as it they have wondrous virtue."

The words left Ah-cambal stunned. "May I speak to this one?" he asked respectfully.

Turix glanced around. His audience was still paying rapt attention.

Time to be magnanimous to the fool, he thought.

"You're welcome to try, old man, but don't expect much. As I told you, he's nearly mute."

Ah-cambal struggled to his feet with feigned fragility and limped over to the man. The stranger was tall and even if he had not been stooping the spy would have needed to look up into his face. He stared for a moment. In addition to being tall the man was lean, almost emaciated. His body looked like one that had been starved, but was now being fed. Although not long, the man's beard was nonetheless thick, dark, and unusual. It was the hair that had first captured Ah-cambal's attention. It was now the man's dark eyes that held it. The eyes were sullen and angry, but they sparkled in a way that spoke of suppressed intelligence rather than smoldering rage. It was a strong handsome face!

Ah-cambal knew that Gucumatz's haughty majordomo might allow him to speak only once, so he settled on one word.

"Tu'ux? (Where?)"

The hairy stranger looked closely at him, his gaze intent and penetrating, as if he could peer into Ah-cambal's heart, then the man slowly turned, raised his right arm, and pointed to the east.

Much later that day, his guise abandoned, Ah-cambal was back at sea. He no longer looked the cripple and his lightened canoe raced southward ahead of a stiff breeze. Before his eyes the water around him sparkled and glowed in response to an exuberant sunset, but it was in his own mind's eye that Ah-cambal dwelt.

Two hundred and sixty sacred tzintè seeds lay scattered in an immutable design, a geometric pattern that foretold of a strange people and a vahom-ché (an uplifted wood) of great power.

K'inich Ajaw was girding for his battle with the lords of night, but the sacred wheel had yet to turn and the day was still 11 Imix, a day dedicated to the great crocodile that rests beneath the world. Riding across the water, Ah-cambal sensed the stirrings of its sinewy reptilian body and once again he experienced the burden of prophecy and the weight of impending change.

Chapter 26

Atonement

11 Bak'tun 14 K'atun 11 Tun 11 Uinal 0 K'in

(November 19, 1511)

Drawn by the shrill whistling of reed flutes, the strident cries of ocarinas, and by a relentless thunder that issued from of a bevy of small drums, people lay down their work. As Ac Yanto intended, the denizens of Tzamá crowded into the open spaces between their huts. They pushed and jostled one another, all of them eager to see his magnificent procession from Xamanzamá as it swept past.

The colorful parade crept slowly and regally through Tzamá's outlying sprawl. Its movement that of a hurrying snail, a pace carefully crafted and maintained, to emphasize and prolong the spectacle of its passing.

Despite their slow progress, the Xamanzamáns eventually arrived before The City of the Dawn's surrounding wall. Under watchful eyes, the noisy embassy passed beneath a silent guard tower, skirted the edge of the high protective wall, and approached the lone passageway that pierced the great fortification and led into the city's heart.

Rat Skull, warriors of his holcánob, and a most regally attired Ac Yanto, attended and fawned over by several of his Ah Cuchcab, strutted at the head of the column. Close on their heels came finely dressed servants bearing burning censers which filled the air with clouds of aromatic incense. Behind these marched Xamanzamá's enthusiastic musicians, followed closely by a mob of weary slaves carrying lavish gifts for the Lord of Fire. Next, walked Ah K'in Cutz with Kish and Thup Paal. The priest and his assistants were trailed by still more servants, who carried baggage. After these came assorted wives arrayed in their best garments, and, finally, another contingent of brightly attired holcánob.

Ac Yanto had personally dictated the order of the march and, of course Cutz's position in the procession was intended as a conscious slight.

This is as it should be, thought The Batab Kinich, *one influential ruler paying a social call on another.*

Ac Yanto had orchestrated every aspect of his long overdue visit to Ah Tabai and he felt certain that he had left nothing to chance.

Shrill conch shell trumpets brayed the Xamanzamáns' approach, and in return more trumpets, unseen atop Tzamá's wall, bellowed in answer to their shrieking blasts. By craning his neck uncomfortably, Ah K'in Cutz could just make out heavily armed Tzamán warriors spilling from the opening which loomed ahead. The warriors filled the space before the aperture, and the Xamanzamán procession, along with its attendant cacophony, shuddered to a nervous halt.

In the awkward silence that ensued, Rat Skull stepped forward, paced a few steps back and forth, and appeared to review the arrayed Tzamán warriors with ill-disguised contempt. Then, he sucked in a large breath. He puffed out his chest.

"I am Ch'o Ho'ol (Rat Skull)," he announced loudly, "Nacon of Xamanzamá. I am here with Ac Yanto, The Batab Kinich. My master has come, at your Lord of Fire's invitation, to pay his respects. Step aside and give us passage!"

For several heartbeats the crowd of Tzamán warriors stood as deaf and as still as the blank stone blocks which towered at their backs. Abruptly, bowing deeply, those directly blocking the opening edged away. Rat Skull glanced toward Ac Yanto, graced his lord with a knowing smile, and then took a single step toward the wall. Instantly, the grin slipped from his face.

Tzamáns again blocked his way, but now the broad shoulders and wide chest of Gucumatz plugged the gap. With chagrin, Rat Skull realized that the warriors had bowed and moved aside only to allow the passage of their own lord and commander.

"And so Ch'o Ho'ol, Nacon of Xamanzamá," said the giant with a voice that was both quiet and deadly, "who are you to demand entrance into the Lord of Fire's sacred city."

Gucumatz was dressed and armed for battle, and Rat Skull, with his confidence momentarily shaken, looked uncertainly to his master. Ac Yanto stepped forward.

"Well met Lord Gucumatz," he said smoothly. "As one renowned warrior to another, it is always an extreme pleasure to share your illustrious company. Thank you for coming in person to greet us. It's most generous. Nacon Ch'o Ho'ol requests entrance into your city at my command. We're here, as he explained, at Yajawk'ak's invitation."

Tzamá's burly nacon said nothing in reply. Instead, he glared intently into Ac Yanto's eyes until finally Xamanzamá's ruler flinched and looked away.

"It wasn't an invitation," growled Gucumatz. "You were summoned!"

"Invitation, summons, just words," retorted Ac Yanto regaining his composure. "The important thing is that your master asked that we come, and now we are here. If you're done posturing, perhaps you should lead us into his presence."

Gucumatz's reply was low, cold, and tinged with open threat.

"The summons was only for you little batab and for your ah k'in, the one called Cutz. My Lord of Fire said nothing about any of these others. You and the priest shall enter. The rest stay here!"

Ac Yanto spluttered. "How dare you treat me as if I'm some beggar at your master's door? I'm Ac Yanto, The Eye of the Sun, and ruler of Xamanzamá!"

"You forget yourself old man," answered Gucumatz, raising his voice so that all within earshot would hear his words. "Xamanzamá is nothing! You rule nothing! You were once strong," he railed, his words dripping with disdain. "You were once nacon here yourself, a man to be feared. But now, you are nothing, a shadow of your former self, the Lord of Fire's tax collector." Then, in a lower voice intended only for Ac Yanto and those close at hand, "Style yourself whatever you wish, old fool, but never forget that you live... or die at Ah Tabai's command."

Gucumatz was Nacon of Tzamá, reputed to be fearless and ruthless in battle, but Rat Skull was also a powerful warrior, a man of great courage and honor and his blood instantly rose at the insult to his master. His flint killing knife leapt from its leather sheath. A slight snarl escaped his drawn lips and he motioned to his holcánob.

"No, Gucumatz," he snarled, "it's you who goes too far!"

At his words, Tzamán warriors on both sides of Gucumatz brandished their spears and flint edged clubs.

"Enough, Rat Skull!" shouted Ac Yanto, hurriedly pushing his muscular nacon back.

The ruler of Xamanzamá had looked deeply into Gucumatz's eyes as Rat Skull spoke, and in their depths he saw clearly, beyond any shadow of a doubt, that if it came to blows, that he, Ac Yanto, would be the first to die.

"Not such a fool after all," hissed Gucumatz, "greater the pity." Then, in an aside to Rat Skull, "Don't be in such a hurry to die, foolish Nacon of Xamanzamá, your time will come soon enough."

"Very well," sighed Ac Yanto as Rat Skull bristled, "Let us bring this foolishness to an end. Ah K'in Cutz and I will accompany you. The others will stay here, but perhaps also a few of my council and of course Lord Ah Tabai's gifts?"

"Bearers will be sent for Ah Tabai's possessions," grunted Gucumatz. "Your Ah Cuchcab remains here," he continued, nodding toward Rat Skull, "with this idiot and his death wish."

Ah Kin Cutz had edged forward and he'd drunk in every word of the exchange. From moment to moment he wavered between his fear that he was also included in Ah Tabai's summons to Ac Yanto, and his tingling delight that Gucumatz was making the fat chic sweat.

"Where is the ah k'in?" demanded Gucumatz.

"I am here Nacon," said Cutz, stepping forward.

The war chief regarded the Xamanzamán priest carefully, and despite himself was favorably impressed with what he saw. Where Ac Yanto looked like a man going to seed, Cutz appeared lean and hungry. And, where the Xamanzamán ruler was dressed in ostentations, almost ridiculous, finery, the priest was attired in plain and sensible traveling clothing, sturdy sandals and a worn, unadorned, mantle.

This is a man to watch, thought Gucumatz, *a man who might be dangerous.*

Motioning Ac Yanto and Cutz to come, he turned about and walked through the entry. The two Xamanzamáns followed, and as they stepped past, the warriors from Tzamá once again closed their ranks and sealed the gap.

Inside the City of Dawn's ceremonial center, Ac Yanto and Ah K'in Cutz walked in guarded silence; behind them trailed a taciturn pair of warriors. Tzamá's equally aloof nacon led them past several small brightly colored temples, alive with frescos, and past several other structures that were easily as grand as Xamanzamá's main plaza.

Ah Tabai felt confident, and he knew with certainty that White Worm heartily agreed. The wide, low, oratory platform was exactly the right place for their overdue meeting with Ac Yanto. The platform's location and its scale would have both been impressive except that they were effortlessly dwarfed by Tzamá's great pyramid towering just to the east. The platform was a spot that emphasized Tzamá's power and its prestige, but it was also a common setting, the use of which declared to one and all that no special significance was placed on the Xamanzamán headman's arrival.

The platform's roof of palm fronds gave way to Hurakán's storm, so a new one had been raised for the occasion. In its shadow, attended by Ah K'in Zac Nok and the rest of Tzamá's court, Ah Tabai reclined on a low stone bench. While the gathering waited, the Lord of Fire's wives and other ah chibal (elite personages) chatted and availed themselves of delicious food that had been laid out among them. Nearby, his son Yajawte' and favorite daughter, Moson-cuc (Whirling Squirrel) squealed with delight and played with the small wheeled figure of a fat grinning pek' (dog). The Lord of Fire and his half-brother sat silent and aloof.

Ac Yanto's delays and his inane excuses vexed Ah Tabai; nevertheless, he looked forward to their encounter with mixed feelings.

Ac Yanto is nothing more than my appointed ruler of a vassal city, he thought. *He serves at my whim, and, curse him, I'll intimidate and insult him for his repeated conceits. Still, he was my father's formidable nacon. He was once a warrior to be reckoned with and feared, and even now he is a man who other men will follow.*

"Do you think that Gucumatz stripped the Xamanzamán of his entourage?" he asked, turning toward the Worm.

"He is Gucumatz," answered Zac Nok with a non-committal expression on his fleshy face.

Ah Tabai tipped his frothy cup of b'alche toward his substantial half-brother and grinned.

Of course, he thought, *it was a foolish question. If I ask something of Gucumatz, he does it.*

Just as the thought faded, the powerful nacon rounded the corner of the nearby stone dance platform and in his wake trailed Ac Yanto and his high priest. Ah Tabai smiled.

Ac Yanto's grown fat.

As a child, at his father's knee, the Lord of Fire often gazed upon Ah Kumix Uinic's young muscled nacon with awe and also a bit of hero worship. Even now, the memory of the man held some strength, but the Ac Yanto of his father's prime was no longer the proud warrior who approached.

Fat, and overly full of himself, reflected Ah Tabai. *It's high time that he remembers the source of his power and who it is that truly rules in Xamanzamá.*

As Gucumatz reached the foot of the platform, Ah Tabai and Zac Nok arose and stepped to the top of its short flight of steps. Gucumatz started up closely trailed by Ac Yanto. Ever cautious, Cutz hung back. The eager ruler of Xamanzamá spread his arms wide in greeting.

"Ah Tabai, my young friend, it has been much, much, too long since we've enjoyed the pleasure of each other's companionship."

Ah Tabai gave a slight signal with his right hand, and Gucumatz whirled about. Throwing all of his considerable strength and weight into his action, he grabbed a startled Ac Yanto by the shoulders and shoved. Caught off balance by the unexpected violence, the Xamanzamán took one flailing step backward off the stair and sprawled heavily and painfully onto the dusty paving stones below.

"On your knees, little batab," bellowed Gucumatz. "How dare you address the Lord of Tzamá as an equal? He is Yajawk'ak! What are you? You are nothing! Perhaps I should give you the beating you so richly deserve?"

Ac Yanto looked wildly about while Ah Tabai's wives and other nobles of Tzamá twittered and snickered. In Xamanzamá, if someone had manhandled the batab in such a manner the offender's future would have been short, extremely short; nevertheless it would have included a long and creatively painful death.

Bile born of anger and fear churned in Ac Yanto's gut. His eyes blazed, but he forced them carefully to the ground. Off to his side, Cutz sank quietly to his knees and then prostrated himself.

Ah K'in Zac Nok stared down from the raised platform to where the ruler of Xamanzamá and his upstart priest lay stretched on the dusty stones below, and a sly expansive grin spread across his corpulent face.

"So Brother," he smirked, turning to Ah Tabai, "is it not as I've said? The outside of an old squash may be hard, but its insides are often soft, or even rotten."

The ruler of Tzamá graced his half-brother with a slight smile of his own.

"As always, Worm, your council proves both sage and true."

The heavy priest bowed his head in acknowledgement of the compliment, and then Ah Tabai turned and faced his war chief.

"Nacon Gucumatz," he chided, while looking down at Ac Yanto with mock sincerity. "Stay your hand. We don't beat a trusted servant who's made a simple mistake, we show him the error of his ways. If he is helped to learn, then he doesn't make the same mistake again. Now, please help our servant to his knees."

"Thank you Great Lord of Fire," mumbled a seething, but intimidated, Ac Yanto, as the burly image of his past self roughly yanked him up from the ground."

"Consider yourself warned," whispered Gucumatz in an evil hiss.

Rising in silence to his own knees, all of his senses alert, Ah K'in Cutz felt both wariness and a crazy elation. The insult and degradation visited upon Ac Yanto was far better than anything that Cutz had hoped for, far better than he had even imagined. The worry that tempered his euphoria was concern for how much of the Lord of Fire's unpredictable wrath might swing in his own direction.

We're wholly in Tzamá's hands, he thought, *but... where there's risk, there's also opportunity.*

Silence stretched, then Zac Nok handed Ah Tabai a ceremonial axe, a heavy instrument, bladed with cunningly worked eccentric flints and adorned with fiery quetzal feathers. For a moment or two, the ruler appeared to silently appreciate the beauty of the weapon's workmanship, then he turned back to the kneeling Xamanzamáns.

"You call yourself the Batab Kinich," he roared, holding the axe aloft, "but who do you serve?"

"You know well, Great Lord," stammered Ac Yanto, "even as I... I faithfully served your father, I serve only you."

"And you priest," demanded Ah Tabai, skewering the kneeling ah k'in with his eyes, "who do you serve?"

"I serve Ac Yanto," answered Cutz, feeling his tongue go dry in his mouth, "but before all others, I serve the Lord of Fire."

"Am I divine?" demanded Ah Tabai.

"You are, Great Lord!" shouted Ac Yanto.

"You are divine!" echoed Cutz, and others, lounging above on the platform, murmured their fervent assent.

"I am told that in Xamanzamá you respect your gods and that when you believe that you've incurred your gods' displeasure that you offer them blood sacrifices to regain their goodwill. Is this not true?"

"It is true, Lord of Fire," answered Cutz and Ac Yanto almost in unison.

"Ah," sighed the lord of Tzamá, who then paused and seemed to consider their answer. "If you sacrifice to your gods, as you should, and I am divine, what blood sacrifice will you offer to me to obviate my displeasure?"

A trap! Thought Cutz.

"It is said by many," continued Ah Tabai, smoothly, "that messengers from the monkey gods, Hun Chowen and Hun Batz, came to Xamanzamá, cast out from the sea, and, that without our counsel, you saw fit to sacrifice these creatures of Metnal to Great Chac. If such a thing indeed occurred, we would find it most disloyal. What do you say to this story?"

Ac Yanto blanched, then without hesitating pointed at Cutz.

"It was the ah k'in's doing Great One! He told us that in the midst of this time of dire hunger and want that the strangers were gifts from the gods. He argued that Lord Chac would look favorably upon their sacrifice and that he would save our crops. My Ah Cuchcab urged that you be informed at once, but Cutz arrogantly declared that there was no reason."

Ah Tabai frowned, "Who is it that rules in my name in Xamanzamá, batab, is it you, or is it your priest?"

"I do Devine One," stuttered Ac Yanto, "but Ah K'in Cutz is intermediary with our sacred gods, and with our deified ancestors. In such matters the council of the ah k'in weighs heavily."

"Yajawk'ak," interrupted White Worm, casting Cutz a predatory glance, "your batab speaks wisely. Even as you often heed my own advice in matters pertaining to the gods, it is appropriate that your servant, Ac Yanto, should also be mindful of his ah k'in."

"I was mindful of his words," sputtered Ac Yanto, feeling surer of himself, "and to my shame, his words proved false. All of this, this unpleasantness, is his fault!"

"Unpleasantness," mused Ah Tabai.

"A misunderstanding, that rests squarely upon Ah K'in Cutz's shoulders, nothing more," babbled Ac Yanto. "My devotion to you, Magnificent Lord, has never been greater!"

"Well, chilán (priest)," observed the Halach Uinic (Great Man) of Tzamá, turning again to Cutz, "it would seem that you owe me an explanation."

Cutz's heart grew hard and roiled with suppressed anger.

Ac Yanto you're a dead man, he thought. *No more fantasies. There are many ways besides battle for an old warrior to die, and you've just forged the weapon of your own demise. And you... High Priest of Tzamá,* his thoughts encompassing Zac Nok, *your day also draws near.*

Then, quieting his rage and choosing his words cautiously, he addressed Ah Tabai.

"Great Lord of Fire," began Cutz, "as always, my other master, Ac Yanto, speaks the truth. Everything my lord said is correct."

Confusion played across Ac Yanto's face and Ah Tabai and White Worm exchanged looks of mild surprise.

"Alas," continued the priest, "wild rumors have led you astray. Several outsiders did wash up onto your beach at the Bay of Turtles, but these were ordinary men, nothing more."

"Go on," urged Ah Tabai.

"I will be the first to agree that their look was most unusual," resumed Cutz. "They arrived dressed in strange clothing, speaking an unknown language, and their faces and bodies were covered with much more hair than is normal. The first persons that encountered the strangers were simple farmers, peasants. Because of the strangers' uncommon appearance, they came running to us with extravagant tales about the arrival of 'monkey gods.' We have no idea what distant land these foreigners called home, but it was certainly not Metnal. They were mere men, hungry destitute men, who couldn't speak our tongue, and who were obviously from some faraway place that poses no threat."

"How is it that you saw fit to sacrifice them without your Lord of Fire's knowledge?" interjected White Worm.

"Distinguished Ah K'in," answered Cutz, "in Xamanzamá we know full well that anything and all that washes up upon our shores belongs to our master in Tzamá, but we also don't trouble our Great Lord of Fire with trivial matters of little or no consequence."

"How so, priest?" asked Ah Tabai.

"Great Lord," said Cutz. "We examined these captives and it was clear that wherever they were from, most likely they were men of minimal status, lowly merchants who'd lost their wares and also their way, or perhaps escaped slaves. Whoever these strangers were, the gods cast them upon your shore. I fasted and prayed, and the answer I found was that they were an offering, and as such an offering should be returned in kind. This vision was the reason I sacrificed to Lord Chac in your name."

"You sacrificed them to the rain god in Yajawk'ak's name?" demanded White Worm.

"Of course," answered Cutz, "they were a gift from the gods, but even though a humble offering they still belonged to our Lord of Fire. To have not offered them in his name would have been disloyal, an affront to his strength and wisdom."

"And," queried Ah Tabai, "what was the result of this supplication made in my own name?"

"Alas, Great One," sighed Cutz, "Lord Chac found the value of our meagre offering wanting."

"Perhaps the fault was yours," snorted Worm derisively.

"Perhaps," answered Cutz humbly, "but I believe the rain god's displeasure was incurred because we didn't sacrifice all of the strangers. Perhaps if we had shed all of their blood the offering might have been accepted."

"But we didn't," exclaimed Ac Yanto, who felt that his damnable priest might be swaying his listeners. "No, no," he gushed, "we only offered those we felt sure were personages without status, creatures unworthy of your notice. There were others who, although unlikely, might have been ah chibal, even one who aped the part of an ah k'in. These we dared not sacrifice. These we held for your pleasure."

"I see no monkey men," said Ah Tabai, making a slow show of looking carefully about. "Where then are these strange captives who await my will?"

"Dead, Yajawk'ak," responded Ac Yanto feeling himself on yet on firmer ground. "We saved five, but one, a furry giant, larger than Lord Gucumatz, died for no apparent reason. The other four were killed in the wondrous life-giving storm that Lord Chac sent in blessed response to your own magnificent blood offering."

"So... all of the strangers are dead?" coughed White Worm.

"As I said," stated Ac Yanto, "all of them are dead."

"Yajawk'ak," growled Gucumatz. "Ac Yanto has been negligent in his answer to your summons, but if all of the so-called monkey men are dead, what is there left for us to discuss?"

"As always, you are practical, my friend," answered Ah Tabai in a comradely manner. "What more? Now that this... what was the word our brother, the Batab Kinich, used?" The ruler of Tzamá appeared lost in thought. "I remember," he continued, "unpleasantness. Now that this unpleasantness is behind us, what more indeed? Please invite our honored guests to join us here on the platform."

Gucumatz beckoned to Ac Yanto and Ah K'in Cutz and the two men rose from their knees and ascended the steps. Ac Yanto wore a smug expression, a countenance that told any who cared to look that he believed that he'd just made the best of a bad situation. Cutz's face was guarded.

Too easy, he thought, *something's still not right here.*

At the top of the steps the two Xamanzamáns found themselves looking across a thatch-shaded plaza covered with a banquet of food and filled with lounging ladies and nobles of Ah Tabai's court. They had stood but a moment when Ac Yanto suddenly gasped for air as though punched in the stomach. Ah K'in Cutz turned abruptly at the sound, and then followed the gaze of the other man's frozen stare.

At the far edge of the platform stood a pudgy prissy man, a man who Cutz recognized as Turix, Gucumatz's majordomo. But, that wasn't where Ac Yanto's fixed-gaze ended. Behind Turix, looking wide-eyed, distrustful, and confused, stood two bearded men, two bearded men that Ac Yanto had just sworn were dead!

The trap is sprung, thought Cutz.

The spell was broken by the Lord of Fire. "Once more I forget," he said loudly, addressing Ac Yanto and Cutz. "There is after all one more thing for us to discuss! We never agreed upon the blood sacrifice that you would offer to appease my displeasure."

"Perhaps a hand," proposed Gucumatz.

"Again, my friend, you go too far," responded Ah Tabai. "These men are my servants. What good is a servant with only one hand?"

"Might they not serve just as well if they offer you but half a hand," suggested White Worm.

"Brother, your council is always wise," answered the Lord of Fire. Then, he turned and handed Gucumatz the ceremonial axe.

Ac Yanto's screams and whimpers still echoed in Cutz's ears as two warriors stretched his own palm onto the gory stump of wood. He looked down at the ground where a bloody chunk of the batab's hand squatted like some small slaughtered beast, its two attached fingers curled forever into an agonized grimace. Then, as Gucumatz again hefted his axe, Cutz raised his face and stared into the nacon's eyes.

The eyes that Gucumatz met glowed bright, not with fear, but with unveiled hate. *I was right,* thought the nacon. *This is a man to watch, a dangerous man!*

Chapter 27

Slaves of Tzamá

The 28th of November, Year of Our Lord 1511

Food and rest did much to restore Gonzalo's perspective, then the passage of days dimmed his first overawed impressions. After a time, he ceased to regard the natives' great city as any true rival to cities of far-off Spain. Later still, as he considered his own situation, he realized that the gaudy fortified town even failed to match his concept of civilized. Overawed or not, the remarkable cluster of structures was a creation far beyond any that Gonzalo ever expected to find in this distant land and it pulsed, almost alive, with mysterious nearly hypnotic currents of drive and energy.

The people seemed the handsomest, and those with most authority and the greatest sense of order that he'd yet encountered. Stucco sculptures, both geometric and figurative, graced walls, cornices, and friezes. At the same time, as if their artists dreaded to be outdone, colorful paintings and glowing murals of flowers, fruits, farming, and other far more fanciful subjects decorated even small and medium structures. Brilliant hues of red, yellow, orange, and black abounded, while intense shades of blue, white, and turquoise vied for attention.

Boats and bounty from the sea packed the city's small sandy beach, and everywhere, in the shadow of the great pyramid and its lessor companions, people moved hither and thither with apparent industry and purpose.

Following a routine that had quickly grown familiar, Gonzalo carried two large empty baskets and walked close behind his current jailer. From repetition, the captive Spaniard knew that their path would presently lead them into the city's expansive open market.

Some days, he was only one of several basket-carrying menials. On other days it was just him and his jailer. Regardless of their number, the routine rarely varied. His keeper would barter for goods; the baskets would fill. Once full, Gonzalo would obediently lug his load back to the enormous multi-room thatch and stone hall that sprawled next to the tiny dirt-floored hut where he was imprisoned.

This afternoon, as on several previous visits, the market yard teemed with activity. A throng of peddlers, both men and women, hovered beside reed mats and blankets, impromptu stores, piled high with goods and foods of every description. Gonzalo recognized much of what was on offer, but just as much left him guessing.

On one mat, a man carefully arranged a veritable mountain of large pebbly green fruit, all of them the size of a child's head. Nearby, a woman offered chunks of fish mixed with what appeared to be chopped onions. On another mat, a serious looking native sat quietly behind a display of clay bowls. Each bowl in his collection boasted a small conical mound of brightly colored powder, each powder a different color. Next to the rainbow of powders spread a display of long yellow fruits that contained a meat-red pulp which tasted like egg yolks. Another space was covered by a shoulder-high dune of very finely crushed shells, and on, and on.

Vendors screeched, hawking their wares, shoppers haggled. A very bad juggler worked the crowd. Dust, flies, and clamor filled the air and everywhere children, turkeys, and small fat dogs roamed dangerously under foot.

The first time Gonzalo's new captors pulled him through the market, its swirling confusion of sights and sounds had set his heart racing and left his brow dripping with sweat. His second foray proved less intense and by his third visit he managed to bring a semblance of order to the tumult.

At the age of eight, hugging his sister Consuela's side and clinging tightly to her hand, he'd walked, wide-eyed, through a bustling Mudéjar bazaar. That fleeting memory transformed the natives' noisy market and suddenly in Gonzalo's mind's eye the chaotic bedlam became a scene which, in the same breath, was both outlandishly foreign yet reassuringly familiar.

As on earlier visits, the baskets filled. When they could hold no more, Gonzalo's keeper signaled that he was done and led their way out of the market. At first he seemed to be retracing their usual steps, but abruptly he turned and headed in a new direction, guiding Gonzalo into a shadowed narrow passage that ran between two unfamiliar stone temples. The shaded way was short and moments later the two stepped back into bright sunlight. Beyond the buildings Gonzalo faced another extensive native dwelling similar to the one next to which he was imprisoned.

Halting, his pudgy round-shouldered keeper pointed to a shadowed spot where an overhang of roof thatch scattered the sun's rays and lessened the afternoon glare. Following his gesture, he frowned at Gonzalo, and waggled his finger again.

"Pa'tal" (wait)," he grunted.

With frequent repetition, and encouraged by occasional applications of a stout reed baton that the keeper routinely carried, "wait" was a command that Gonzalo had quickly come to understand. It was also one that he quickly learned to obey. This time, unlike certain past occasions, he was more than willing to comply. Already ensconced in the slight crack of shade, his tattered friar's robe pulled tightly around his knees, sat a smiling Geronimo.

Their bewildering separation, which began on the evening of the castaways' arrival in the city, had continued. To the Spaniards' profound dismay, other than on the brief, incomprehensible, and terrifying occasion of Ac Yanto's audience with Ah Tabai, the two companions had been kept at a distance. Isolated from one another, and unable to speak together, both men daily feared the worst, and unbidden each man's soul swelled with pleasure to see the other alive and apparently unharmed.

As Gonzalo set down his baskets and sank down beside Geronimo, his keeper nodded satisfaction with his charge's action. Then, he disappeared into the building's darkened interior leaving the two alone.

"Aroça," beamed Geronimo, "although at one time it would have pained me to say so, it does my heart good to see your ugly face."

"Mine too," smiled Gonzalo, "mine too."

"I feared that I might be alone," continued Geronimo with a slight choke in his words. "Thank Our Wondrous Lord! After that bloody business with our tormentors... I can still hear the older idolater scream. With no sight or word of you for nine days, I... I'd begun to imagine... I considered that I might be the only Christian soul left alive in this benighted land."

"Happily, Friar, that's a title you can't lay claim to, at least not yet," quipped Gonzalo. "Still, while you're not the last of us Christians, I'm willing to concede that you're assuredly the most devout."

Geronimo frowned. "As always, Gonzalo, you jest poorly. You don't pray in thanks to our Lord Jesus and the Blessed Virgin for our deliverance and for all that they've given us?"

"I leave such spiritual matters to you," answered Gonzalo. "For my part, I have no idea what we've stumbled into, much less what we've been given."

"Nevertheless, Aroça," responded Geronimo, "God watches over you. How are you being treated?"

Gonzalo sighed. "Better than before. I'm ordered about and I'm forced to work, but at least my beatings are light and my belly isn't empty. What about you?"

"Much the same," answered Geronimo. "The labor doesn't break my back and I feel that we're perchance safer here than we were. Where are they holding you?"

"I'm kept in a small hut and required to share it with three natives."

Geronimo's eyebrows went up, "You're closeted with savages?"

"As far as I can tell," continued Gonzalo, "their plight is no better than our own. All three fawn and grovel to anyone who comes by, and they were terrified when I was first tossed in among them. I'm not sure, but I believe that we're all slaves to that monster who chops hands."

"I shudder when I think of that creature," quavered Geronimo."

"I suspect he ranks as some breed of war chief or general," said Gonzalo. "Whatever position he holds, he's powerful here; everyone bows and scrapes in his presence."

"And, you saw that round-shouldered native who just went inside, he's my principal keeper. I think his true name is Turix, yet he demands that I address him as 'Caluac.' It's a guess, but he seems to be a sort of head factotum for the big savage's household."

"Ah," said Geronimo, "I've wondered why we were separated. Do you remember the night that we arrived, the native who appeared to be their king was attended by your war chief?"

"How could I not remember?" responded Gonzalo.

"Then you'll remember as well," continued Geronimo, "that he was also attended by another, a savage of wide girth and dissipated countenance. I was placed in that one's charge. I think we've been given as a sort of prize to a pair of valued retainers."

"Curiosities more than prizes," replied Gonzalo. "Turix made it clear that I'm not to cut my beard and when I'm not laboring, he parades me about as an oddity. I feel as though I've become an exotic breed of dog who's used and unloved by his master, but trotted out before his guests for whatever spectacle I can provide."

"I'm convinced that my own keeper is another priest of the demon," groaned Geronimo. "Many times he's ordered me dragged before hideous idols, harangued me in his savage tongue, and poked and prodded me for an audience's amusement. Once, he even brought forth an unclean woman who brazenly shed her garments and tried to grasp my manhood while others howled with drunken laughter. Lucifer is abroad in this land!"

Listening to Geronimo describe his temptation, Gonzalo felt a stirring in his loins. He was a young man and he'd not enjoyed a woman since setting sail with Ojeda, ever so long ago.

In Seville, he'd had a lover, a young Jewess whose family concealed their faith, ignored Ferdinand's and Isabella's edict of expulsion, and remained in Spain. The fact that she was a secret Jew hadn't troubled Gonzalo. They hadn't loved one another, but their desire had been fierce.

"Did you lay with her?" asked Gonzalo recalling his remembered passion.

"Of course not," grimaced Geronimo, "but I'm a sinner and the devil persecuted me with foul dreams of her heathen charms. Sometimes I believe that I'm going mad."

"So, if you didn't lay with her," pressed Gonzalo, "what did you do?"

"You know I lost my crucifix," replied Geronimo.

"Yes, I know," answered Gonzalo slowly, "but what's that got to do with the native woman and her charms?"

"I made another cross," beamed the Franciscan as he pulled something from beneath his robe.

Gonzalo looked closely; the object was indeed a cross, a crude object fashioned from two thumb-sized twigs tied together with a thin twine of thatch. Holding it out, Geronimo continued in earnest.

"Aroça, the symbol of Our Lord's sacrifice holds power over the savages. I know it does! I brandished this cross and I cursed the succubus. Then, I fell to my knees in prayer, held it aloft and cursed the rest of the vulgar assembly. My foul keeper appeared troubled by my act and he ordered me led away. There is great goodness in the cross of Our Lord Jesus Christ and I believe that the malice of the evil one is such that he cannot endure seeing it among his minions lest its miraculous virtue undo them."

Gonzalo stared incredulously at his companion. While his own faith in the hand of divine providence had dwindled to nothing in the face of months of unrelenting adversity, the friar's seemed bizarrely to have grown beyond all credible bounds.

Perhaps he is going mad, thought Gonzalo, *certainly we've been through enough to shake one's sanity.*

"Geronimo, I understand that your faith is strong, but we can't afford to antagonize these people. We have no standing among these natives and when they tire of us as novelties our value may end. It might have been better if you'd lain with the wench."

Geronimo graced Gonzalo with a beatific smile. "As I've told you many times before, Aroça, you and I are in God's hands. That you and I have survived when so many other Christians have died can only mean that he intends us to be his instruments. God doesn't want instruments sullied by sins of the flesh, if we're to spread his holy word among these heathen we must remain chaste."

Why, couldn't I have been left with Juan Pintero or even that prig Diego? thought Gonzalo. *Why must I share my lot with this half-lunatic Franciscan who's never cherished my company nor I his?*

Choosing his words carefully, Gonzalo nodded, "Geronimo, in the past you styled me, 'Guerrero,' and I resented you for it. But, truth be told, it's a fitting name. I'm a simple soldier, nothing more. As a simple soldier, I have simple thoughts. I worry about survival. I worry about my next meal. I grieve for our lost companions. I don't ponder the intentions of God or his plans. I brood over what I can see, hear, and touch with my own two hands. I admit without shame that I was the one who brought us both here, but now, I tell you plainly, we can no longer remain.

Instruments of God or not, this place is no less dangerous than the one we fled, and, with each new day, our peril grows."

"Gonzalo, it wasn't you that led us here. It was Our Lord. If in his wisdom he brought us to this heathen city, I think we must stay."

"Do you profess to know the mind of God, Geronimo?" answered Gonzalo softly. "Even if heaven directed our footsteps, who can say that this is our intended destination? When God led Moses and the Israelites through the wilderness they stopped in many places, but their journey didn't end until they reached the Promised Land. If you and I escape again, can you tell me with absolute certainty that is not what God intends for us?"

"There's some truth in what you say," replied Geronimo. "Nevertheless, we are here, the idolaters are here, and I feel called to spread God's light. Besides, if we flee again, where can we go?"

"We've now seen two stone cities where we once believed nothing existed except mud and grass huts. If these two exist, there must be others."

Geronimo frowned.

"Look here," continued Gonzalo, "I don't know when we'll get the opportunity to speak again, will you at least entertain the possibility that we should try to leave?"

"I'll pray for guidance," intoned the Franciscan.

Anxious for a commitment, Gonzalo groaned inwardly at the friar's reply, nonetheless he held his tongue. On one hand, he chafed at Geronimo's tedious and repeated insistence of God's sovereignty and that like marionettes on strings their every action was controlled and preordained. On the other, drawn-out and worn by their experiences, he involuntarily envied the friar a faith which so easily allowed him to smile and abdicate control of his destiny.

After looking cautiously about, Geronimo once again reached inside his robe. This time, the object he withdrew from within it folds was his ragged and soiled breviary. Despite the book's dilapidated condition, it was a minor wonder to Gonzalo that the pious friar had so long managed to hide and retain the small leather-bound volume.

"Aroça," asked Geronimo as he displayed the breviary and then quickly tucked it again out of sight, "do you know what day it is?"

"No," replied Gonzalo, puzzled, "I don't, I've no idea."

"It's a Friday," answered the friar, "and St. Martin's day is already past us. In two more days it'll be a Sunday, the holy day of St. Andrew the Apostle, and the start of Advent. You and I should prepare ourselves for the anniversary of our Lord Jesus Christ's birth and for his second coming. The mystery of that glorious day has every right to the meagre honor of our thankful prayers, fasting, and penance!"

Fasting and penance, thought Gonzalo struggling to keep his mouth shut, *surely, we've suffered ample starvation, pain, and loss to satisfy the needs any reasonable god.*

Later, walking behind Turix, again under the weight of his baskets, the young escudero felt crowded by the bars of an invisible cage. He wanted to snarl and bite.

Chapter 28

Betrothal

11 Bak'tun 14 K'atun 11 Tun 11 Uinal 14 K'in

(December 3, 1511)

Murky puddles from the morning's rain still dotted Ah Muzencab's (bee god's) plaza and cool damp shadows lurked in its corners. In contrast, along the plaza's western edge the radiance of K'inich Ajaw shone warmly on the raised stone patio of Nachan Can's thatched home. The ruler of Ichpaatún perched comfortably next to his venerable uncle, Ah K'in May, on a wooden bench judiciously positioned so that they both enjoyed the heat reflected by the stucco of the structure's front wall.

Nachan Can's two brothers, Dwarf-wind and Ah-cambal, sat cross-legged on mats at his right hand. Also situated at his feet, on another mat to his left, his son, Hoch Can, waited with his back erect and stiff. Close behind these nobles of Ichpaatún hovered Nachan Can's caluac, Itz'at Acan. All six men directed their unwavering attention toward a small, elegantly attired, delegation that waited just below them, at the foot of the patio steps.

Upon a gesture from Acan, one of the group stepped forward, bowed deeply, lowered himself to his knees, and addressed Nachan Can.

"Sajal, I am Ah Mun and I along with my companions are men of substance in Tzamá and members of its council. We've traveled here to bring greetings and salutations from our master, the Lord of Fire to his people of Ichpaatún."

Nachan Can's jaw tightened and twitched slightly at the implied ownership and arrogance implicit in the man's words. This new batch of "ticks" from Tzamá had arrived at his city wall two days earlier loudly requesting an immediate audience with the sajal. At Ah-cambal's suggestion, one heartily endorsed by Hoch Can, Nachan Can had kept them waiting, a small affront intended to convey to Ah Tabai's messengers that urgency in Tzamá and exigency in Ichpaatún were determined by different masters.

"Ah Mun," answered Nachan Can, "you are of course welcome; nevertheless, it surprises us to see you here within the walls of our fair city. One would think, that lodged between the grinding stones of his nearly empty granaries and the fury of Hurakán's storm, Ah Tabai could ill afford to send away any valuable members of his Ah Cuchcab."

Ah-cambal shifted position and turned his head to the side so that he could hide the slight smile called forth by his brother's deliciously droll response. When he turned back, Ah Mun continued.

"It's true," answered the Tzamán gravely, "times are difficult." Then he resumed in a lighter tone. "Nevertheless, our great Lord of Fire never loses sight of which matters are trivial and which are of true importance. We're here to strengthen the ties that bind our two great cities. Yajawk'ak' is deeply regretful that the question of the union between his eldest daughter, Lady Mad Seizure Star, and your honorable brother, Dwarf-wind, has languished so long unattended."

At the mention of his name, Dwarf-wind jumped to his feet. Despite Nachan Can's earlier admonition to hold his tongue during the audience, Dwarf-wind stepped forward with his beady eyes ablaze, spread wide his outstretched hands, and addressed the Tzamáns.

"Illustrious Cousins," he gushed, "I am Ak Uinic Ik, betrothed of Mad Seizure Star and all of Ichpaatún welcomes you here with friendship and open arms."

"Lord Dwarf-wind," replied Ah Mun, again bowing deeply. "We are truly honored to be in your worthy presence. Our Lord of Fire salutes you and bids us tell you that he numbers the days until you are his ja'an (son-in-law)."

Like a bird that fluffs its feathers on a cold day, Dwarf-wind seemed to puff up and increase in size. With an expansive gesture he swept his arm in the direction of his brothers and his nephew.

"Come Ah Mun, join us here in the sun, so that you and our other valued friends may sit comfortably while we hear your communication from our celebrated Lord of Fire."

When he finished gushing, Dwarf-wind turned to Itz'at Acan and in an imperious voice demanded, "Caluac, don't just stand there, bring refreshments for our honored guests!"

After waiting for a nod of approval from his true master, the wiry majordomo disappeared on his errand. Hoch Can was shocked by his uncle's inappropriate actions. Nachan Can seethed and Ah-cambal waited behind an enigmatic smile while Dwarf-wind fawned and ushered the delegation to places of honor.

Almost as quickly as he'd left, Acan returned with two servants, bringing drinking cups, jugs of b'alche, and trays laden with fruit and nuts. Once the Tzamáns were situated and everyone served, Nachan Can again addressed their leader.

"Well, Councilor Ah Mun, now that my 'little' brother has made you comfortable and even more welcome than you already were, perhaps you would be so gracious as to share your 'great' lord-of-Tzamá's message."

"It is our deep pleasure, Sajal," enthused Ah Mun, possibly ignoring, or more likely oblivious to, the subtle mockery entwined in Nachan Can's words. "Yajawk'ak' bids us extend a warm invitation to Lord Dwarf-wind and entreats him to proceed along with Ichpaatún's ah k'in and a suitable party of retainers to the ancient temple of Yum Kax (corn god) at Tixmul. There, Lord Dwarf-wind will be met by Ah K'in Zac Nok and other persons of rank. Our Lord of Fire deeply regrets that he cannot attend this council in person. Nevertheless, it is his sincere wish that the occasion be used to conclude marriage arrangements, settle upon a convenient date and location, and of course agree upon a suitable dowry."

When Ah Mun spoke the village's name, both Nachan Can and Ah-cambal frowned; the locality was an area firmly in their larger neighbor's control. Tixmul was a small farming village that Ah-cambal and Nachan Can knew well. It was situated four to five days steady walk from Ichpaatún and approximately the same distance from Tzamá. The origins of Tixmul were long forgotten in the shrouds of time, but, in addition to its cluster of meagre huts, it was also the site of a decaying stone plaza, two miniature dwarf-built temples from the time of magic, and a low badly weathered pyramid dedicated to the venerable corn god.

Nachan Can was pondering how best to respond, to what amounted to little more than a cleverly worded summons, when Dwarf-wind again rushed into the breach.

Dowries among the people of Ulumil cuz yetel ceh were not large, but the Lord of Fire personified wealth itself. The avarice of Dwarf-wind knew few bounds and Ah Mun's words had instantly fanned the flames of his greed.

"When?" he nearly shouted in his anticipation.

"Why, as soon as you can be ready, Lord," responded the Tzamán. "Of course Ah K'in Zac Nok's party will include Lady Mad Seizure Star so that you may determine for yourself that she is a suitable match."

At this further pronouncement, Dwarf-wind felt himself becoming erect in his eagerness, then, before he could utter another word, his cursed brother Ah-cambal butted in and the moment was gone.

"Tilizcunaben (honorable) Ah Mun," he interjected, "all of Ichpaatún looks forward to the union between my esteemed brother, Dwarf-wind, and your Lord of Fire's beautiful daughter, but as to the meeting with Ah K'in Zac Nok, to prepare for such a gathering would require time."

"Nonsense," growled Dwarf-wind, pouting his fleshy lips, "we can begin preparations for my party's departure immediately!"

From there, the audience devolved into a squabble between brothers with Hoch Can and the Tzamáns watching warily from the side. On the one hand, Ah-cambal and Nachan Can, still uncomfortable with the idea of Ah Tabai sinking his claws further into their affairs, brought up objection after objection in attempts to delay and possibly spoil the whole undertaking. Dwarf-wind, for his part, strove to parry every objection and move himself ever closer toward fulfillment of his avaricious dreams.

Long after fires were lit and K'inich Ajaw descended into Metnal to begin his battle with the lords of night, they finally reached an agreement. Neither Dwarf-wind nor his elder brothers were wholly mollified by their arrangement, but as Dwarf-wind was eager for his marriage to proceed and Nachan Can and Ah-cambal were unprepared for the open war with Tzamá an outright refusal might foment, it was the best the three could achieve.

The marriage council would proceed. Dwarf-wind would be the nominal head of Ichpaatún's embassy, but he would be accompanied and advised by his uncle Ah K'in May. To his slight disgust, Dwarf-wind was also forced to agree to the presence of his nephew, Hoch Can.

As Ichpaatún's nacon, Hoch Can would lead an honorary contingent of his holcánob, ten warriors and no more, a number that Ah Mun quickly agreed would be matched by Tzamá.

To emphasize the peaceful and joyous nature of the meeting Hoch Can's wife, Za'azil, would accompany the party as would several other women and a suitable number of servants.

In exchange for Nachan Can's begrudging agreement to move forward with the meeting, Dwarf-wind begrudgingly conceded to a delay. Old Ah K'in May had argued passionately and at length, and eventually successfully, that it was auspicious to wait until the renewal ceremonies of Oc-na were complete and the great wheel of the sacred Tzolk'in had again returned to Eb', a propitious day for marriages, that embodies destiny and good fortune.

A final sticking point was Nachan Can's intractable insistence that Itz'at Acan, a personage detested by Dwarf-wind, be included in the selected party as another advisor and the sajal's personal observer. After a heated exchange, one that insulted Acan and somewhat surprised Ah Mun and the other Tzamáns with its intensity, Dwarf-wind had acceded to his brother's demand, not so much an acceptance as a disgusted resignation.

When the uneasy accord was at last concluded, Ah Mun vociferously proclaimed his Lord of Fire's keen approval and then immediately presented Dwarf-wind with a number of lavish gifts. The most impressive of these was a magnificent cloak of shimmering crimson feathers which Ah Mun personally draped across the Ichpaatúnian's flaccid shoulders.

Thrilled with the evening's outcome, Dwarf-wind entreated the Tzamán delegation to forego their current lodgings and join him in his own home where he could show them, "the full measure of Ichpaatún's hospitality."

As Hoch Can watched his uncle walk away, side by side with the liars from Tzamá, he felt that his heart might burst.

"Father," he groaned. "This is a travesty, how can you allow such a mockery to go forward. You know as well as I that Ah Tabai offers us paltry favors with his left hand while his right holds the spear that raids our lands and kills our people!"

"Hoch Can," interjected Ah-cambal, laying a hand on his nephew's arm, "your father and I understand your anger, and we equally feel your pain and frustration. Nevertheless, all three of us must face a cruel reality. Although you are brave and our men of Ichpaatún are fierce and strong, we're not strong enough to stand openly against Tzamá. Ah Tabai has too many warriors at his beck and call. His holcánob is simply too powerful. As you say, the betrothal of Dwarf-wind to Lady Mad Seizure Star is a travesty, but it is a travesty that avoids naked conflict and allows us to wage battle in the arenas of diplomacy and trade where the number of our spears counts for less."

"Your uncle speaks truth My Son," added Nachan Can, "also the betrothal encourages harmony here at home. It pains me to say so, but your other uncle, is a weak man with good reasons to be sensitive about his power. He frets about his own insecurity and this marriage is an opportunity for him to demonstrate his strength. Your outrage is just and well placed, but if Ichpaatún is to survive, and if you are to follow me as sajal, we must all tread with the caution of balam (a jaguar). You are my son, heir to Ichpaatún. It is because of your misgivings about this alliance that Ah-cambal and I want you among the delegation.

"Dwarf-wind is the marriage party's titular head, but it is you and Itz'at Acan who watch our true interests. When the time of the meeting arrives, I will sleep well knowing that my son guards our welfare."

Thick hair, long, blue-black, and shiny, framed the contented oval of Óolal's small face. Za'azil smoothed a few unruly strands, gently pulled together a parted section until it was tight, and then wrapped it around a similar bundle that she'd already tamed. She smiled and sang a quiet song as she worked.

"Little maiden, your skirt is pure and white."

"Comb the tangles from your hair and spread joy with your twinkling laugh."

"Let goodness fill your heart for today is the moment of happiness."

"Know that you are beautiful and loved."

Braiding Óolal's hair was a simple task, but one that gave them both lasting pleasure.

The child is a blessing, thought Za'azil, *unimagined and unlooked-for.*

Since that very first day when Óolal arrived, shyly clinging to Ah-cambal's arm, Za'azil felt some deep part of herself blossoming. Óolal brought with her something that Za'azil had missed without even knowing it.

Except for Za'azil's soft singing, the two sat in companionable silence in the common room of their home. Each of them had enjoyed the slowly ebbing warmth of K'inich Ajaw's day. Now, they took pleasure in the reassuring flicker of a small fire that Za'azil had kindled to keep the night's shadows at bay. Za'azil was about to give Óolal's hair a final faultless twist when Hoch Can unexpectedly thrust aside the woven mat covering the room's outer door and strode purposefully inside.

"Za'azil, my beautiful wife," he gushed, spreading his arms expansively, "and Óolal my beautiful adopted daughter."

Both women, young and younger, stared at him in dumb surprise. Normally, Hoch Can barely acknowledged Óolal's presence in his house, much less, praised her, or acknowledged her in any way as his daughter. After a slight pause, Za'azil broke the silence.

"My husband, has something happened?" she asked.

"Am I so transparent?" answered Hoch Can.

"There's an air about you," she murmured.

"You know where I have been and my feelings about the matter."

Za'azil knew full well that Hoch Can had been in conference with his father, his uncles, and emissaries of Tzamá, and that they discussed Dwarf-wind's proposed betrothal to Ah Tabai's daughter. She also knew full well that Hoch Can abhorred the proposed joining with their powerful neighbor to the north.

"Have your father and Ah-cambal come to see the wisdom of your arguments and forced Dwarf-wind to reject Tzamá's offer?"

"No Ch'ujuk Nikte' (Sweet Flower)," he replied. "Sadly, as I expected, my words of opposition fell on nearly deaf ears. Dwarf-wind is still to marry the Tzamán x-pek' (she dog)."

"Then why are you grinning like a fat pisote who just stole an egg and got away with it?" asked Za'azil.

"Before the marriage proceeds," answered Hoch Can, grinning, "there is to be a meeting at the temple of Yum Kax in Tixmul, a negotiation between Dwarf-wind and that fat deceiver, Zac Nok, to settle its details. Besides the over-large ah k'in, the Tzamán party will include Lady Mad Seizure Star and several other notables. Our delegation is to include Ah K'in May and ..."

"But Husband," interrupted Za'azil, "I'm confused. Why does this turn of the wheel bring you pleasure?"

"The Lord of Fire considers himself above such matters," continued Hoch Can, "so he will remain in Tzamá. Not to appear less, Father and Ah-cambal will likewise remain here in Ichpaatún. As Father's heir, I am to go in his stead and stand for our house!

"The occasion is one that I would rather never see come to pass, but the honor afforded me is great. It means that Father and Ah-cambal value my counsel and that they truly see me as a man. With this journey all of Ichpaatún will finally view me as a worthy nacon."

"They already view you as worthy, my beloved" answered Za'azil. "When must you leave for Tixmul?"

"You mean, when must we leave?" laughed Hoch Can. "You are to accompany me! You're the respected wife of the Nacon of Ichpaatún and your status in our party will rival that of Mad Seizure Star in hers!"

Za'azil stood amazed. Hoch Can's father, Nachan Can, had always treated her well, but it was the first time his actions had unequivocally elevated her to an honored place among the city's nobility.

"Husband," she breathed, "this is indeed a reason for gladness."

Before she could continue, Óolal tugged at her hand, "Mother, am I to go too?"

Hoch Can frowned, "Not this time child. This journey is a distinction bestowed upon the Nacon of Ichpaatún and his wife. Perhaps, someday, if you behave yourself, your own time may come."

Chapter 29

Babble

The 5th of December, Year of Our Lord 1511

Once, when Gonzalo was a small boy, he shared an outing in the countryside with his parents, his sister Consuela, and his brother Esteban. His father, a serious man who rarely indulged in such unashamed triviality, suggested the excursion for no other reason than to enjoy the warmth of a beautiful autumn day.

Toward mid-afternoon the family's carriage halted and their footmen spread out a blanket upon which an impromptu meal was then set. While these preparations were being made Esteban, who was ten years older than Gonzalo, suggested that the two of them climb to the open top of a nearby wooded hill to enjoy the view.

Their mother and father both happily consented and, after parental warnings to take care and mind their way, the two set out. Consuela of course wished to go along, but Esteban admonished her to attend to their mother and nonchalantly refused her request.

"This is a man's adventure, brothers only!" he declared.

Gonzalo was ecstatic, he worshiped his older brother, but Esteban customarily rewarded his adoration with an indifference that was at once both bland and cold. Typically distant, and occasionally cruel, his older brother had never before invited Gonzalo to do anything as remotely exciting.

The distance to the hill's top wasn't long, but the path they followed climbed quickly and Gonzalo had difficulty matching Esteban's longer stride. Once, Gonzalo slipped, at which his brother sniggered darkly. Several other times Esteban grumpily chided him for failing to keep up. Gonzalo didn't care, he was on an escapade.

Everything was wonderful. As they reached the summit, he could barely contain his joy. A rabbit raced off at their approach. He could see for miles in every direction. Close by, overhead, two graceful hawks swooped and played delighting in the day.

Gonzalo plopped himself down onto a patch of dry grass and stared off into the distance. Miniature farms and fields spread out before him and ant-like cattle grazed contentedly miles away. He would happily have sat there for hours just gazing, but, after what seemed mere minutes, Esteban abruptly jerked him back to his feet.

"Come on dolt," he barked, "it's time to head back."

"Can't we stay just a bit longer?" pleaded Gonzalo.

"I'm going," groused Esteban. "You can do as you like."

With that, he tramped briskly off down the hill. Anxious not to be left behind, little Gonzalo immediately brushed himself off and trailed after his idolized brother. After they'd walked a fair distance, close growing trees crowded together to hide the sky and deep menacing shadows swallowed much of the light. That was when Gonzalo realized that nothing about him looked even remotely familiar.

"Esteban," he panted, "I don't think this is the way we came."

Instead of an answer, his brother redoubled his pace. Moments later his tall form slipped around a thick trunk and was gone.

"Esteban," shouted Gonzalo, "wait! I can't see you!"

His only answer was wind rustling in the leaves. For a time Gonzalo ran as fast as his short legs could carry him, shouting every few seconds, in a vain attempt to find his elder sibling. Frantic turns, this way and that, revealed no trace of Esteban. Eventually, hopelessly lost, Gonzalo despaired, sank to the ground and gave himself over to tears.

Hours later his father's two footmen stumbled upon him, still whimpering. On returning with them to the carriage, he learned that Esteban had deceitfully accused him of wandering off on his own. When he contested his older brother's words, his angry father accused him of lying and dictated that, when they returned home, Gonzalo receive a swat and go straight to his bed without supper. It was an incident and a lesson that Gonzalo never forgot.

That, thought Gonzalo reliving the day, *is my life. It's a difficult winding path. At times, like when I sailed from Cadiz with Ojeda, I've soared with the hawks and viewed the world from the heights. At other times, like all these that have passed since the Viñas sank, I find myself abandoned and lost in the woods. No matter what comes, I swear, I swear by my sister's memory, I'll regain the heights!*

The tool that Gonzalo had settled upon to again lead him back up that steep hill was language. From the moment that he and his companions first washed ashore at the Bay of Turtles, Gonzalo's heart had told him that Spain was lost. His companions, now long dead, had loudly proclaimed that they would soon be rescued and all return home. Gonzalo never embraced their hope. Try as he might, the only future he was ever able to envision was one that lay in the green laced shadows of the jungle that had stretched around them.

When the castaways confronted Rat Skull and his band on the beach and the Spaniards struggled to communicate even the most basic of ideas, it had come to Gonzalo like a bolt from the heavens.

If any of us are going to survive this antechamber to Hell, we'll need more on our tongues than Castilian!

Almost from that precise instant, he'd wholeheartedly committed himself to learning his captors' speech. Regardless of the rebuffs and the hidings he received at the hands of his previous jailor, Sansón, he'd listened to every word the natives around him spoke. Sometimes their talk sounded like mere gibberish, but other times, on rare occasions, he derived meaning from the babble.

The castaways were treated as chattels and possessions, and objects have no need to speak; nevertheless, Gonzalo pressed every savage he encountered to communicate. Even in that place, which he now knew was called Xamanzamá, where his attempts to converse most often met with stony silence, he'd still managed a word here and a word there, and he had learned.

Each new sound, each new intonation, added pieces to a mysterious puzzle and Gonzalo eagerly placed them together. Even as he enjoyed a natural ability for running, he possessed an inborn gift for languages. The facility often served him well, but it was a talent he usually held private and close, waiting for whatever advantage it might bring.

All those years ago in the monastery, before Gonzalo fled, an old monk had pounded Latin into his skull. He'd shared those lessons with two other boys, also superfluous unwanted sons of lessor gentry, boys with names he no longer remembered. Of the three, he was the only one who'd truly learned. During his years as a courier and as a sword for hire, he'd acquired an enviable working knowledge of French and Italian, and also a passable grasp of the Greek and Germanic tongues. None of those proficiencies helped his present situation, but his natural aptitude still served him.

The hut in which Gonzalo was now kept prisoner offered an unlooked for boon. After his initial shock wore off, being forced to share a small confined space with several scowling natives quickly grew into an incredible stroke of luck, a stroke of luck good or better, than any that he might have expected.

At first, the natives had cringed away from him in fear, but their temerity was short lived. Once the natives realized that he was just a man and a prisoner like themselves, they were eager to learn his story and to share their own. Each exchange was another piece of the puzzle and another step up the hill.

Of the three men with whom Gonzalo was confined, one proved far more useful to the Spaniard's designs than the other two. The man was older, wrinkled, slightly bowlegged and a bit lame, weathered by the sun, lazy, and gregarious. It was this last trait that Gonzalo found expedient.

Near constant frustration of trying to make himself understood often made Gonzalo want to throw up his hands in disgust, but despite weariness and vexation he'd persisted. Little by little his wizened companion's nearly unbroken stream of babble had begun to take on a spotty form and substance.

It was the evening of his second day in the hut that Gonzalo made what he thought was his first breakthrough. He'd pointed to his own chest, said "Gonzalo," and then pointed to the native's bony torso. He repeated the action several times and suddenly the native's eyes seemed to go wide with understanding. The man pointed at Gonzalo, made a garbled attempt at the Spaniard's name and then pointed to his own frame and uttered a name that sounded like, "Uinik."

Gonzalo, elated at his success, excitedly repeated "Uinik" and his own name, accompanied by many smiles and much pointing back and forth. When he tried the same trick with one of the other savages, that native, who'd been watching the exchange closely, pointed to himself and also cheerfully chimed-in, "Uinik!" At this, the third native also proudly drew attention to himself and echoed his two companions.

It was three days later before Gonzalo understood that "uinik" meant "man." It was another day after that before the three natives agreed to accept that he was also "uinik."

That was how Gonzalo's learning progressed. Some days yielded comprehension, others he waded through a murky cloud of swirling confusion. The wrinkly old man, who helped Gonzalo the most, turned out to be named, "Iccauhtli" (younger brother in Nahuatl) and, by signs, he made Gonzalo to understand that he too was from a far distant land. He seemed to delight in teaching his strange bearded companion and, during all their free moments, he pointed to object after object, spoke the thing's name and made Gonzalo repeat it until he was satisfied with his response. Encouraged by Iccauhtli's example, the two other natives also joined in the game and, with three teachers all pointing and chattering, Gonzalo quickly found himself absorbing more in days than he'd previously learned in months.

Sitting in their shadowed hut, Gonzalo made signs and gestures to Iccauhtli by which he hoped to finally learn the name of the strange land into which he'd been marooned. At first Iccauhtli seemed puzzled so Gonzalo haltingly tried words.

"Ba'ax lu'um lelá (What land this)?"

Iccauhtli smiled and said, "Ci uthan (he speaks well), at which the other two natives nodded agreement.

What Gonzalo heard was, "Yucatán."

Chapter 30

A Journey of Many Colors

11 Bak'tun 14 K'atun 11 Tun 13 Uinal 8 K'in

(January 6, 1512)

Someone nudged at Za'azil's shoulder and then prodded it again. In response, she tucked herself into a tighter ball on her sleeping mat and tugged her mantle more closely about herself. To her profound dismay, this action only caused the nudging to grow more insistent.

"Rise and glow hats'uts (beautiful) a glorious new day is already upon us."

Za'azil reluctantly opened one sleepy cyc and blinked myopically at Hoch Can whose smiling face hovered only a hand's length above her own.

In truth, K'inich Ajaw's new day had scarcely begun, its diffuse smoky glow just starting to bleed into aak'ab's (night's) retreating darkness, but already Hoch Can was awake and alert. Leaning closer so that his breath was warm and moist upon her ear, he whispered the words of a poem.

"I will kiss your lips
Between the leaves of the forest.
Shimmering beauty,
You have to hurry."

Then, he gave Za'azil a quick kiss, a final affectionate nudge, and began to shuffle about the betrothal party's camp. Moving phantom-like through thin retreating mists, he gently shook one person, then another, and then another, awakening each in turn from their respective slumber. His actions provoked grumbles and occasional deprecations, but he suffered the protests cheerfully, meanwhile urging everyone to awake, eat, and prepare themselves so that they might quickly resume their journey.

The delegation from Ichpaatún had walked for but a single day, yet their pace had been slow and Hoch Can knew that for them to reach Tixmul by Eb', only four days hence, they needed to travel more quickly.

Za'azil roused herself and, once prepared, watched with a heady combination of love, pride, and ongoing elation as her husband oversaw the breaking of their encampment.

When his uncle, Ah-cambal, had confirmed Hoch Can's words that a delegation from Ichpaatún would go to Tixmul to settle the details of Dwarf-wind's wedding to Mad Seizure Star, and that Hoch Can would serve as the party's true leader, and further that she herself would go along, Za'azil had felt that she might burst with joy.

Leadership of the deputation to Tixmul offered Hoch Can a much needed chance to once again demonstrate his worthiness as nacon. It was a chance to leave behind his troubled memory of the successful, but ill-starred, fight which had cost Teyacapan his life. It was another chance for her husband to prove himself in the eyes of their people, in the eyes of his uncle, Ah-cambal, and most importantly in the loving but judicious eyes of his father.

Better than anyone else, Za'azil understood Hoch Can's desire to stand tall and proud as the capable man she knew him to be. She understood his need to please his father. She understood his pain.

Her joy, however, was not reserved for her husband alone. She too had looked forward to the many opportunities the embassy to Tixmul could present. Not the least of which were the simple pleasures that she imagined must surely flow from novel sights and sounds of the journey itself.

Za'azil led a contented life in Ichpaatún. She cooked and kept Hoch Can's home. She played with Óolal. She browsed through the stalls of the market. She worked at her loom. She skipped through the waters of the bay collecting shells. She laughed and gossiped with her friends. She made secret love to her handsome husband and she prepared devout offerings to the gods. Hers was an agreeable life; nevertheless, it was an agreeable life circumscribed by the city's thick walls and her quick mind often chafed at their constricting boundary.

Before they departed Ichpaatún, Za'azil, Hoch Can, and the other members of Dwarf-wind's wedding party had joined with those who were to remain behind to perform a ceremony of leave-taking and supplication. They offered prayers and smoldering blue-painted cakes of copal to the god, Ekchuah, and petitioned him for a safe and fruitful journey. These long-winded appeals were followed by further devout prayers and bowls of delectable fruit presented to the goddess, Ix Chel, offerings to entreat her favor for Dwarf-wind's coming union.

Since all present agreed that Ah-cambal held a special reverence for Ekchuah, and a special place in the deity's eyes, he took the lead in their observances to the Traveling God. Nachan Can's wife, Ix Chan Ek presided over their devotions to the goddess of fertility and childbirth. To Za'azil, excited and impatient to be away, her relatives' words of pious supplication had droned on and on, and she'd felt as though the simple ceremony might never end.

When Hoch Can or other men went off to trade or to hunt, or when Ah-cambal shouldered his basket and left to scout Ichpaatún's borders, each time they took their leave Za'azil felt a green flutter of envy flicker somewhere in the depths of her chest. What would they see? Who would they chance to meet? What adventures would they encounter? What tales would they tell upon their return? At those times, her role in life felt unexpectedly confining and even unfair. Why was it that she had no excuse to participate in such pleasing escapades?

But now, now her time had arrived! Za'azil was on a journey of her own. With each footstep her secret yearning was at last unfolding about her.

Ah K'in May was the eldest in the wedding party and it was his long but aged legs that had determined the speed of their first day's progress. At the beginning of their long walk, the old priest had been spry and nearly as energetic as Hoch Can himself, but as the day wore on May's stride grew shorter and shorter and his pace slower and slower. On the dawn of their second day, it was concern for his great-uncle's stamina that caused Hoch Can to arouse his group at such an early hour.

If we're to walk slowly, he thought, *then we must make good use of every precious moment of K'inich Ajaw's day.*

As far as Za'azil was concerned, it was fine to walk slowly. Late on the previous day the party had passed through the tiny settlement of Xul-Há, whose name meant "End of the Water," and so they'd come upon the shores of the great inland lagoon.

Za'azil once beheld the lagoon's waters as a child, but her memory paled in comparison to its glorious reality. The lagoon was truly a work of the gods. It stretched as far as her eyes could see and, sparkling in the sun, its sweet placid waters displayed the total breadth of their liquid color running from lightest turquoise to the darkest of midnight blues. It was the same miracle of colors that the gods had bestowed upon the tropical sea except that here, in this special place, their palette was surrounded by land and jungle.

Today, as the delegation walked, the lagoon was ever on their right hand, drifting magically in an out of sight behind curtains of swaying trees. Za'azil found herself enthralled. When she first imagined her trek to Tixmul, this was exactly the picture that she'd painted in her mind.

Hurakán's storm had quenched the land's thirst. In its aftermath, it was as though every vibrant flower, vine, and tree that lined the lagoon tried to outdo its neighbors and individually vie for her attention. In an unseasonable show of exuberance, the previously dry jungle had burst forth, a lavish eruption of life. Everywhere around Za'azil fresh vegetation sprawled lush and green and the exhaled scents of its new found ecstasy filled her nostrils.

Hoch Can walked at the front of the party setting a comfortable pace that he believed would see them to their goal without overtaxing Ah K'in May's ancient body. Depending on the width of their path, Za'azil walked either at his side or just behind. As they traveled, Hoch Can, unassumingly, shared his knowledge of the country through which they passed.

"Look," he'd whisper, "there, do you see it? A tixula in bloom."

When Za'azil's eyes followed the line of his arm, she beheld a cluster of long thick fresh green spires and at the plant's center rose a flowering stalk. From the stalk's top spread a cluster of delicate white blooms tinged with purple, each bloom fringed with six long feathery tails that swayed gently in the breeze.

Hoch Can squeezed her hand, and smiled. "Whenever I see such beauty, it is as though you are in my arms."

Za'azil returned his smile enchanted, and they walked on. As they continued, Hoch Can kept up his whispered commentary, pointing to hidden animals and describing specific plants.

"Do you see that bush, the one with the waxy leaves and the knobby spear-tipped stalk? That's yaxpahalché. It's especially good for curing of sores."

A few of the plants that Hoch Can pointed out were new to her, but most were familiar friends. In truth, unfamiliar or well-known made little difference to Za'azil. What mattered to her most was the soothing sound of her much-loved husband's voice and the quiet joy of their shared experience.

The journey would have been perfect except for the maddening presence of Dwarf-wind. While Za'azil's mind held no doubt that the sole purpose of their journey was to solidify the details of the man's marriage, she would still have been much happier if he'd never come along. Hoch Can's uncle galled. He strutted and preened, demeaned her husband's position, and constantly belittled his actions.

Shortly before midday, as the party approached another small village, and as had occurred the day before when they passed the humble huts of Xul-Há, Dwarf-wind, dressed in the cape of crimson feathers bestowed on him by the Tzamáns, puffed and elbowed his way to the lead.

"I told you before, Nephew," he hissed red-faced as he pushed past Hoch Can. "In deference to your father, I allow you to play at leader. But remember, this is my embassy, my wedding. You are here only to assist with any tedious details of my journey."

In response, Hoch Can stepped smartly to the side and ceremoniously waved Dwarf-wind forward.

"Of course, dear Uncle," he said, "the glory is yours."

The size of the wedding party was not large, twenty-five in all, but as it included Ichpaatún's high priest, the city's nacon, and its ruler's younger brother; it was still a source of great curiosity and interest to the vassal communities through which it passed. As such, the rural people, turned out to watch the passing of their lords.

Each such occurrence was grasped tightly by Dwarf-wind as a chance to enhance his status. He swaggered through the villages and isolated milpas, calling attention to himself, shouting to the people, praising their loyalty, elaborating on the purpose of their journey, and upon his own exalted status.

Za'azil quietly watched while Dwarf-wind made a spectacle of himself and Hoch Can ground his teeth in a futile attempt to tamp down his frustration. Fearing her husband's anger, she struggled to redirect his attention.

"What place is this?"

When her question failed to elicit a response she grabbed Hoch Can's arm and forced him to look into her eyes.

"Look at me; what place is this?"

For a moment Hoch Can just stared and then, as if slowly returning from a distance, he truly saw her. "Siyancaan Bakhalal," he whispered. "They call this place, Siyancaan Bakhalal (birthplace of the reeds)."

Fortunately, the shores of the great lagoon were sparsely settled and while such incidents tried the patience of Za'azil's husband, they were blessedly brief. Toward evening, Hoch Can felt that everyone had marched far enough and he called a halt. Still near the colored waters, the party made camp at the edge of a medium-sized cenote.

As they arranged the details of their stay Za'azil watched her husband's young determined face. It was a strong face. The prominent bridge of his nose gave it the appearance of being slightly curved. Wind and sun had burnished and burnt his cheeks and had left them glowing and slightly ruddy. His lips were full but not thick and his eyes, his eyes were restless but they sparkled and danced with life. Za'azil thought that he resembled a magnificent Kóot (red eagle) and it pained her to see the tense frown the day's frustrations had placed upon his brow.

When their work was complete, and everyone was settled, she took his hand. "Walk with me my love. I wish to watch the lagoon as K'inich Ajaw withdraws his light."

Hoch Can allowed himself to be led and for some way they strolled in comfortable silence. Overhead, a profusion of bromeliads decorated the canopy. Just before they reached the lagoon's edge, a troop of howler monkeys stared down from the trees and roared indignant protest at the humans who dared to trespass upon their domain. As they reached the water, both stopped and stared, spellbound by the dreamlike display of shifting colors.

"Our lives should always be thus," sighed Za'azil.

As she stood there entranced, Hoch Can nuzzled softly against her from behind and the warmth of his body drew her back against his firm chest. As they pressed one against the other, he slipped his gentle hands beneath the folds of her huipil and lifted the weight of her breasts. His hands moved outward, gripping softly, teasing her nipples and pulling them upward. She made a small noise of pleasure and he ran his hands downward, sliding them along her sides, then stroking the tops of her hips. Next, his hands moved slowly behind her, mapping the delicate curve of her spine. She felt his tongue tease the back of her neck. His hands again sought her breasts gently squeezing and pulling at her erect nipples. When Hoch Can's warm breath played across her earlobe, Za'azil moaned and turned to face him. Almost shyly, he lifted the huipil over her head and pushed the pic down from her hips. He stared deeply into her eyes, took the mantle from off his shoulder, and spread it on the leaf covered ground. Her hands sought him as if possessed by a will of their own. Then, sinking to their knees, they collapsed into one another's arms.

Chapter 31

Summons

11 Bak'tun 14 K'atun 11 Tun 13 Uinal 9 K'in

(January 7, 1512)

Sullen and wary, Ah K'in Cutz waited at the edge of a circle of guttering torches. Darkness cloaked his back. Before him, ruddy flames sputtered, restrained the night, and cast their wavering shadows around the small second-story gallery of Tzamá's observatory. At the center of the reddish light, surrounded by a scattering of family and trusted retainers, sat Ah Tabai, White Worm, and Nacon Gucumatz. From beneath lidded eyes Cutz scowled his hatred at the only three men alive whom he detested with greater passion than his worthless cacique, Ac Yanto.

A summons from Ah Tabai had reached Xamanzamá's high priest three days earlier. And, to Cutz's continuing shame, his knees actually went weak when the messenger, one of Gucumatz's hulking lieutenants, smirked at the priest's maimed hand and then snarled, "The Lord of Fire, again, demands your presence minor ah k'in!"

"And, what of the Batab Kinich?" Cutz had dared.

"Just you," was the messenger's curt reply. "Yajawk'ak' orders Ac Yanto to remain here. You and I are to return alone, at once."

Ac Yanto, who upon receiving word of Ah Tabai's messenger, had hurriedly arrived, relaxed visibly at the Tzamán's words. Then he'd sneered at Cutz.

"Well, ah k'in," Ac Yanto had proclaimed in his most officious voice, "if our great Lord of Fire says, 'at once,' then by all means you and this worthy must be on your way as soon as possible."

Cutz glared at his hated ruler. *Die soon,* he'd thought, *but die slowly and scream until your throat is too raw to scream more.*

The image cheered the nervous ah k'in, but it had offered him no withdrawal from his predicament. Ignoring Ah Tabai's previous summons had cost Cutz half a hand. The priest was sly, proud, and stubborn, but he wasn't imprudent enough to defy the Lord of Fire a second time.

The journey from Xamanzamá was hurried and, for the ah k'in, fraught with worry. Even so, his reception in Tzamá, although insulting and cold, fell far short of Cutz's dire imaginings. He was fed a filling, if lackluster, meal and then commanded by a menial to await his Lord of Fire's pleasure. Eventually, in the deepest part of the night Cutz had been roused from an uneasy slumber and ordered to Tzamá's observatory. Once there, he'd stood at the edge of a council while Ah Tabai outlined in tedious detail plans for an overthrow of nearby Ichpaatún.

Cutz hated the Tzamáns, but, when he heard the particulars of their nefarious scheme, despite himself, their shrewdness impressed.

Their plan was simplicity itself. Ah Tabai's daughter, Mad Seizure Star, was to be betrothed to a royal Ichpaatúnian dupe, then, when that city's annoying rulers presented themselves for the couple's nuptials, an invitation that they couldn't ignore, Gucumatz and a particularly vicious group of his holcánob, would slaughter them one and all. After the deaths, Ichpaatún would cease to exist as a southern power and The City of the Dawn would control all trade with Lamanai and the rest of the Petén.

At first, the audacity of the Tzamáns' plan caught Cutz's imagination, but as Ah Tabai droned on, and on, his mind wandered. The observatory, directly in front of Tzamá's great pyramid, served as a platform from which the city's priests traced the movements of K'inich Ajaw and, more importantly, those of his companion, Chak Ek' (Venus deity).

Overhead, Chak Ek' glowed brilliantly. When the god stalked the darkening night sky, he was hailed as Lamat. When he arose shortly before the coming of the dawn, he was worshiped as Ah-Chicum-Ek'. This particular night was not Chak Ek's first appearance in the morning sky as Ah-Chicum-Ek', a day that would have been auspicious for the beginning of a full scale war; nevertheless, the god glowed brightly which Cutz took as an assured sign that the Tzamáns' devices against Ichpaatún were favored.

The flames of the dying torches wavered and with them the thread of his thoughts. Before Cutz's tired eyes, the temple's frescos and niched figurines of Chak Ek' appeared to dance with an impression of life. On a cornice, across from him, a relief of the rain god's face stared at him with a fixed intensity.

"Cutz! Do you listen?" demanded Zac Nok, yanking Cutz away from his reverie of the gods and the heavens and once more into the circle of dying light where Ah Tabai yet pontificated.

"Return of the rains," declared the Lord of Fire, ignoring Zac Nok and Cutz, "has taken the common people's minds from the drought, but, as each of us knows, any harvest is still many uinal (months) away. Too soon, peasant thoughts will return to empty bellies. I've heard it rumored that the drought even caused certain fools to question my divinity!

"The lingering dryness of our god's displeasure is an open wound that leaves us vulnerable, so we must act. We can no longer allow those ta'ob (turds) in Ichpaatún to interfere with our trade to the south. It is no longer enough that they profess alliance. The time for prostrating themselves is past. It's time that Nachan Can and his entire family are swept aside.

"This first meeting is crucial. It prepares our way. Ichpaatún is weak, but they are not without sharp teeth. If each of you play your role, they will die with celebration cups in their hands and there will be no need, no need at all, to face them in open warfare."

"Remember!" interjected Gucumatz. "The boy is mine. For his insult," hissed the nacon, touching his scarred face, "I shall tear the flesh from his bones, piece by piece, and make him scream day and night. When his screams stop, his head will decorate my tzompantli (skull rack) and I'll piss on what's left."

Your scar is a petty trifle, thought Cutz at the outburst. *What of my hand? My hand! If your blemish demands such retribution what greater reckoning must I be due?*

"We all know that Hoch Can is yours," cautioned Zac Nok, "but this first meeting is not the moment for your revenge. No matter how disagreeable, you and I must both hail Dwarf-wind as a future brother, and greet his party from Ichpaatún as our honored friends, all of them. That, includes young Hoch Can!"

"His death comes," growled Gucumatz, "and it will come at my hand."

"True enough, my trusted friend," placated Ah Tabai, "but my brother speaks with reason. For now, you must bank the fires of your vengeance. When the time is right, we will both help you to fan them to flame!"

At that point, to Cutz's surprise, Mad Seizure Star addressed her father in a petulant tone.

"I tell you, I still refuse!"

Ah Tabai, glared flint chips at his elder daughter.

"I am Yajawk'ak'," he barked, "ruler of Tzamá. We have spoken of this and you will do as I tell you to do!"

"I will not!" screamed Mad Seizure Star. "I won't go!"

"Stop this childishness at once," snapped her father.

"It's not childishness," she threw back, "it's an insult. It insults me! It insults you! Father, as you say, you're the Great Lord of Fire. Well, I am your eldest daughter, and I will not be paraded before that worm-fart from Ichpaatún like some polok t'u'ul (fat rabbit) that he haggles over in the market. He reaches far above his station and you ask me to bend down to lick his ass!"

"Enough!" roared Ah Tabai. "He reaches for his death! You know as well as I that this meeting is a sham. Your betrothal is but a thin veil of smoke waiting for the wind to blow it away."

"Exactly," pouted Mad Seizure Star. "If this delegation is nothing but a stupid pretense, why must I degrade myself and our family by treating the Ichpaatúnian fool as a true suitor?"

"We've been over this," sighed Ah Tabai. "Dwarf-wind may be a fool, but Nachan Can and Ah-cambal are not. If we wish to draw cautious enemies into the snare we set, then you too, my daughter, must play your role!"

"Brother," interjected Zac Nok, who along with Gucumatz, had been listening in bemused silence. "Perhaps my obstinate, yet lovely, niece has a point."

"How so, most learned Ah K'in?" demanded Ah Tabai sarcastically, annoyed that White Worm had taken his daughter's side.

He was also again annoyed by his brother's slovenly appearance. White Worm was sucking on the leg bone of a roasted kambul (Blue-billed Curassow) and the juice had dripped down onto his chest.

"Perhaps we are too eager," replied Zac Nok evenly, around the bone. "Nachan Can and Ah-cambal know that we believe ourselves their betters. Allowing Mad Seizure Star's whim is just the sort of arrogance they'll expect."

"Whim? Arrogance? Uncle! Is that what you think of me?" shrilled Co-tancas-ek.

"Calm yourself, hats'uts (beautiful)" put in Gucumatz. "Worm is right! Having you refuse the journey to Tixmul serves us just as well as does your exquisite presence. The scum from Ichpaatún will doubtless rail against your affront, still it's just the sort of conceit they'll expect."

Gucumatz then turned to the Lord of Fire, "The insult will provoke their anger. It will also enflame Dwarf-wind's lust. Mad Seizure Star's insult will be exactly as the ta'ob expect. Great Lord, be assured, its sting will dull their suspicion."

Ah Tabai, still felt irritable, but he immediately appreciated the reasoning of his trusted advisors.

"Very well, sweet Co-tancas-ek," he exclaimed, "your Uncle and Gucumatz have my ear; stay in Tzamá if you must. But, willful child, because of your recalcitrance, like the rest of us, before our embassy departs, you will offer your blood to Buluc Chabtan."

Just to Cutz's left, the first of the torches sputtered and died and, in the absence of its light, Xamanzamá's ah k'in smiled as the dark crept closer.

Chapter 32

Oddities

The 7th of January, Year of Our Lord 1512

While his native companions slumbered, Gonzalo rested quietly against the back wall of their shared hut. Alone with his thoughts in a world of muggy darkness, he waited for the seeping grey light that signals the coming dawn.

Until recently, the castaway would have reckoned such early risings an aberration. Now, with each new daybreak, they were slowly becoming habit. The darkness consoled Gonzalo. Wrapped in its silent shroud, he easily imagined himself alone and once again free. Enfolded in its soothing embrace, his mind wandered unrestricted to familiar people and places, comforting memories that he reluctantly acknowledged were truly gone forever.

Gonzalo knew in his heart that it was the height of stupidity to dwell on all of the things that he had lost. Nevertheless, morning after morning, he arose in the close darkness to sit silent and alone. Despite the inherent folly, the quiet hours encompassed hints of freedom and it was a freedom that the Spaniard sorely missed. The glimpses of it were like crutches that he couldn't bring himself to cast away.

Gonzalo had lingered in silence for some time when, abruptly, the reed mat that covered the hut's door was lifted aside. A yellow-orange light flooded the opening, causing him to squint protectively. Then, carrying a smoldering torch, Turix ducked through the entry.

Gucumatz's pompous majordomo stared at Gonzalo for a moment in slight surprise, then he painfully kicked Iccauhtli with his sandaled foot. Yanked unceremoniously from his slumber the older man grumbled and then clambered stiffly to his feet. Gonzalo also rose.

"Tal beora ppentac'ob (come now slaves), commanded Turix. Then, waving his torch, and ignoring the two men who still snored unperturbed on the dirt floor, he ushered Gonzalo and Iccauhtli from the hut.

Outside the night was tranquil and to the east Gonzalo could just make out the first tenuous peach colored stains of morning.

The new day approached, but it's time had not yet come. Overhead night yet reigned and told a different story. When Gonzalo looked up, he stared into a cobalt basin into which the stars still cast their shimmering pinpricks of silver light.

That Turix should call for him and Iccauhtli at such an hour was highly unusual and Gonzalo felt a twinge of uneasiness. His first instinct was to try to question his keeper, but, by repeated trial, he had learned that such efforts were invitations to ill-use and so he held his tongue.

There was no denying that Gonzalo was a prisoner and that he was also a slave, but, as the novelty of his presence in Tzamá had worn down, his life had settled into a more or less acceptable existence. The punishments that he suffered at the hands of Turix were routine and always meted out to train rather than to injure. As a slave, work filled his days, but usually it was far less onerous than the grueling toil he had been forced to endure during his captivity in Xamanzamá. Some days, he trailed Turix carrying the chief factotum's loads. On other days, he and his hut-mates worked making reed mats until their hands were sore.

On still other days, they scraped fresh hides. At first, he'd scorned that labor, but then Iccauhtli had excitedly demonstrated that they could scrape hides very hard and eat the scrapings. Now, Gonzalo considered the work good fortune.

But I'm not fortunate, he thought, reviewing his condition. *I'm a slave. I mustn't lie to myself. I mustn't surrender myself to apathy.*

Setting a quick pace, Turix steered Gonzalo and Iccauhtli in a familiar direction. Moments after leaving his hut, Gonzalo knew that they were headed toward the expansive house occupied by the fat priest who held Geronimo. After a short walk, they indeed reached the open plaza that fronted the home, and to Gonzalo's surprise they discovered it well-lit and alive with activity.

A large bonfire burned at either end of the plaza and in between the two blazes people milled around piles of bundled goods and portage baskets. Some were slaves, men and a few women, none of whom Gonzalo recognized. Others were men that he recognized by their dress as minor noblemen. Near the foot of the steps that led to the native priest's house hovered a knot of formidable looking warriors outfitted in their fearsome war regalia of feathers, fur, cotton, and leather. Above them, at the stair's top, stood the towering war chief, Gucumatz. Beside that savage, who Gonzalo knew to be his owner, stood other native personages that the Spaniard also recognized. The hulking warrior was flanked by the fat priest, the king of Tzamá, the king's savagely beguiling daughter, and a coterie of the city's notables.

Growling, "pa'tal (wait)", to Gonzalo and Iccauhtli, Turix climbed the stairs to join his master.

Gonzalo looked about himself in confusion and then made an open hands gesture to Iccauhtli to express his bewilderment. His swarthy wizened companion merely smiled and nodded several times. Iccauhtli then scuffled a few paces away, where he leaned down and spoke to another slave who was bent-over securing a bundle.

"Aroça!" At the sound of his name, Gonzalo turned and saw his fellow castaway descending from a darkened corner of the steps.

"Geronimo," smiled Gonzalo, "we both still live."

"Thanks be to God's great mercy, we do!" beamed the Franciscan.

Both men stared. More than a month had drifted pass since they had last seen one another, and again they were both relieved to see the other alive. Gonzalo observed that Geronimo was still dressed in the ever more tattered robe of his order. Now, however, the friar's crude homemade cross hung openly, suspended about his thin neck by a roughly woven grass cord.

For his part, Geronimo remarked that, although thickly bearded, Gonzalo now dressed as a savage. In fact, beyond a pair of reed sandals and a strip of cloth wrapped about his waist and genitals the escudero wore nothing.

"You're practically naked," frowned the friar.

"They took my clothes, this is all that I was given," Then Gonzalo waved his hand toward the bustling plaza.

"Do you know what all this is about?"

"Who can know the reasoning of these idolatrous pagans," responded the friar.

Gonzalo felt puzzled. "Geronimo," he asked, "how is it that you walk free and wear your cross openly?"

"It's Our Lord's doing!" he answered forcefully. "Every sound these savages utter is heathen gibberish and my discourse is equally incomprehensible to them. Yet somehow, through the mercy of Our Holy Father, I believe they've come to realize that I'm a servant of God and that I offer them no harm. I preach salvation to them at every opportunity," he said earnestly. "Although I often fear that my words fall on deaf ears, I truly believe that eventually, with God's help, my prayers will work on their hearts and lead them into Our Lord's grace."

At that point, Iccauhtli shuffled back. Ignoring the tattered friar, who people had told him was ah chuch (crazy), he leaned close to Gonzalo and with words and gestures tried to impart what he had learned. Geronimo watched the exchange with unfeigned interest.

"Aroça, you speak their language!"

"No," denied Gonzalo, "but I'm trying to learn. If I understand correctly, Iccauhtli, here, says that he and I are to undertake a journey, a walk that will last perhaps six days. He also says something about a wedding and that Turix counts it a great honor that we slaves are chosen to serve."

Geronimo's countenance darkened into a frown. He looked askance at the wrinkled native and then back at Gonzalo.

"You are a Spaniard, Aroça! At this time and in this place, our only honor is to serve Our Lord Jesus Christ and the Crowns of Aragorn and Castile. Today, today begins the Octave of the Epiphany, the time when our infant lord was adored by the Magi! Have you prayed Aroça?"

As his captivity stretched, Gonzalo had lost count of the days, and he was taken aback by the pious fervor of Geronimo's question. He supposed that it was either, the year 1511 or 1512, and that it was well past fall, and probably past Christmas, but he was unaware of the day of the week or its place on the calendar.

Why must my only true companion in this benighted place be so besotted with his God?

"No Geronimo," he retorted, "I haven't prayed."

Before the friar could reply, Gonzalo glanced toward the gathering atop the stairs where he was immediately distressed to see to the unclean priest from Xamanzamá, the creature responsible for the death of Captain Valdivia and so many others.

"It's him isn't it," he muttered, "the one who slaughtered our friends."

It wasn't a question. Geronimo, followed Gonzalo's gaze and then made the sign of the cross to ward off evil.

"That creature is a servant of the evil one," he hissed.

At that moment Turix came bustling down from the platform in front of the house. He waved his hands at Geronimo in a manner that communicated both disgust and careless dismissal. Then, shouting something that sounded vulgar and incomprehensible at the friar, he grabbed Gonzalo and Iccauhtli and shoved them toward the center of the plaza where day was slowly taking hold.

Behind them, Gucumatz, the fat Tzamán priest, the half-handed tormentor from Xamanzamá, and several others descended the steps and also walked into the plaza. Gonzalo watched as the fat priest stepped onto a prostrated slave's back and climbed into a sort of litera (sedan chair). Turix then prodded Gonzalo, demanded his attention, and gestured that he and Iccauhtli should both shoulder large bundles that lay at their feet. With reluctant assistance from the flabby Caluac, they lifted the loads and secured carrying straps around their foreheads. At a guttural shout from Gucumatz, porters lifted all the other bundles and four burly slaves hoisted the litera onto their shoulders. The milling crowd then formed itself into a line and began to move.

As Gonzalo shuffled forward, Geronimo again pushed himself near.

"Aroça," he warned, gesturing toward the half-hand from Xamanzamá, "you must watch yourself; wickedness follows that impure priest of the demon."

"We must both watch ourselves," countered Gonzalo.

"True! That's true!" affirmed Geronimo. "We must again commend ourselves to God, while these heathen go about their unholy business." With a smile on his face, the friar then raised his right hand in benediction.

"God bless us both, and take heart! God would not have brought us so far from our homes and preserved us amid so much hardship and danger if we are not tools for his purpose."

Why, must you be so single-minded, thought Gonzalo. *If we are to survive in this land of insanity and not break, we must look to the real world that surrounds us, not the mystical world in your mind.*

"Remember the pain of the saints and the holy martyrs," bellowed Geronimo as Turix roughly shoved him aside. "Suffering will cleanse us, Guerrero, and make us ready for God's work!"

"Keep safe!" shouted Gonzalo.

Then, the procession rounded a corner and the only other Spaniard for more than a thousand leagues was gone. Moments later, following Iccauhtli, Gonzalo ducked under a low corbelled arch, walked through a short narrow passage, and for the first time in months found himself outside the formidable bulwark of Tzamá's walls.

For a second, he paused astounded by the change those months had wrought. When he and Geronimo arrived, it had been through a drought stricken land laid waste by storm. Taller trees still bore testimony to the storm's passage but otherwise an explosion of green life had completely replaced the devastation. For a second he stared wide-eyed at the altered landscape and then someone shoved him from behind and he was walking.

The warriors who led the procession set a quick pace and in short order Gonzalo found that he'd passed through the city's adjacent maze of huts and had entered the surrounding jungle. As the envelope of green pressed in from all sides, his mind turned to flight.

Inside that accursed city, I'm a prisoner without hope, he thought. *All I have to do is drop this bundle and run.* But then, despair once again rose its ugly head. *Where? I know nothing of the land beyond the reach of my arms. If I flee, I'll be caught and killed. And, if I'm not, what awaits but starvation or madness?*

Nearly overwhelmed by his own ruminations, he doggedly shoved aside thoughts of what might be, let his mind go slack, and stoically put one foot in front of another.

The pace of the march set by Gucumatz and his warriors proved fierce. While soldiering about Spain, Gonzalo had endured forced marches and the current journey was every bit as difficult.

At about three leagues south of Tzamá the party wound through a busy vassal city that lacked defensive walls, yet nevertheless boasted a steep walled central pyramid and many buildings of painted stone. Several score of people turned out to meet the procession, but Gucumatz took no notice. Ignoring the beckoning of two important looking personages, he pushed his charges forward and led the way down a narrow but well-worn path quickly leaving the small trade center behind.

After that, the group hurried through an unchanging backdrop of unexpectedly lush jungle interrupted only by the occasional tiny village or isolated farm. All of these were paid no heed. Under the unrelenting pace, the load Gonzalo carried seemed to grow heavier with each league covered. Just the same, he counted himself lucky, as the slaves who carried the fat priest's sedan chair suffered more cruelly. Although they were frequently replaced, Gonzalo witnessed one exhausted drudge collapse by the wayside only to be cursed by the priest and left where he fell.

The pace also punished Iccauhtli who walked with a slight limp in his left leg that Gonzalo knew to be the legacy of a grievous injury suffered long ago. Rest stops were brief and far between.

If anything, the second day of the trek was even more miserable than the first. With The Land of the Turkey and the Deer's drought well past, the morning commenced with a warm viscous rain. The unpleasant soaking was then followed by a damp and heavy clearing. Thick warm air pressed against Gonzalo, and moved soggily in and out of his lungs and the cadence of the sweltering march was made to the sound of a million screeching cicadas.

That night, as on the night before and so many before that, Gonzalo sprawled on the ground and, despite his absolute exhaustion, slept fitfully. Sleeping well surrounded by others is an act of faith and Gonzalo no longer had any.

Sometime before dawn, he awoke to the confusion of a fading dream, a nightmare in which details hovered just beyond his reach: Spain, betrayal, lost love, severed ties. Darkness pressed in on him from all sides and for a time he simply lay still and paid attention to the night.

At first, only the phantom sounds of his dream, the pounding of his own heart, and the soft whisper of his own breathing broke the silence. Then, as he listened, these internal sounds were slowly replaced by quiet stirrings in the surrounding jungle. Gonzalo heard the rustling of a light breeze through leaves, the scrabble of tiny claws on wet wood, and the staccato beat of some winged creature rising from it bushy perch.

Overhead, above the surrounding darkness, he beheld stars spread across the canvas of the night sky. And, what stars they were! The sky was clear above him and there twinkled the constellations of Virgo, Leo, and Libra. Near the darkness of a far off horizon he could see Las Guardas (The Southern Cross), a myriad of tiny points of light cast upon a field of ink. Gonzalo sat up and stared at the heavens. He hugged his arms about his knees and rocked back and forth.

I live, he thought, *but my life isn't my own. I'm worthless, a thing with no future, a piece of chaff blown hither and thither.*

Unbidden, the journey outside Tzamá's walls was once again forcing him to plumb pits of misery and gloom. With all his heart, he wanted to envision his life leading somewhere meaningful, but, with each new day of captivity, time had become almost meaningless and the task grew ever harder and his efforts ever more feeble. He'd been sitting for some time when abruptly he realized that he was no longer alone. Iccauhtli, who'd slept by his side had also risen.

"Gonzalo," he said gazing upward, "The lights that move, they are gods. The ones that remain still, those are fires. In my land our priests say that those flames are tended by the spirits of the Centzonmimixcoa (400 gods of the northern stars) so that it does not become completely dark on earth. Our world is dark, but there is still light."

They're beautiful, thought Gonzalo, *and it's as good an explanation as any.*

Late the next day, the Tzamán delegation halted at a small farming village which consisted of little more than a grouping of modest huts haphazardly thrown up around a large plaza of ancient moss covered stone. Nearby stood a couple of miniature temples that had fallen to ruin and a small also crumbling pyramid. Despite the apparent insignificance of the place Gonzalo quickly realized that it was in fact his party's destination.

Soon after arriving, other slaves approached and relieved him and Iccauhtli of their loads. Shortly thereafter, Turix, of whom they had seen little during the march walked up accompanied by another slave who carried two different bundles. Each of the bundles was wrapped in a woven mat and tied with braided twine. At a signal from the caluac, he handed the larger of the packages to Iccauhtli, the smaller to Gonzalo, and then turned and left. Turix, then uttered some command and Iccauhtli started to unwrap his bundle.

Gonzalo didn't recognize the order, but decided to do likewise. Since Turix didn't interfere, he assumed that he must have chosen correctly. As the contents of the bundle revealed themselves he was astounded to discover the tattered shirt and breeches that he had worn upon entering Tzamá. Even more astonishing, neatly folded underneath these lay the fancy waistcoat that natives had stripped off of poor Captain Valdivia before his murder. To Gonzalo's further surprise, the three garments had all been carefully laundered.

Stunned and perplexed, he looked at Iccauhtli and beheld his weathered companion staring with undisguised elation at a worn yet ornate wooden helmet. Reverently, Iccauhtli set the helmet over his head and, once it was settled, the proud head of an eagle framed his face, its savage beak open in a defiant scream. Besides the helmet, there were what appeared to Gonzalo to be some sort of bracers or arm guards fashioned in the form of wings and several other feathered ornaments.

Turix then indicated that both of them should don the garments. Once they carried out his instruction, he surveyed the result, nodded his approval, and led them toward the plaza.

The Tzamáns arrival at Tixmul had been both unexpected and unheralded. Led by well-armed holcánob, their sudden appearance had immediately triggered a panic among surprised villagers who promptly grabbed up minor children, a few miserable possessions, and fled into the nearby jungle.

After getting their own people settled, Zac Nok and Gucumatz waited in the open plaza and stared out at the nearby curtain of greenery

"This has gone on long enough," growled the nacon. "Call them back."

From where he stood, Gucumatz's sharp eyes could spot several wary faces peering from behind the trees and undergrowth which marked the compound's edge.

"I grow tired of this foolishness. We've preparations to make and we need to put those fools to work."

Zac Nok, acknowledged his companion with a nod, then raised his voice and shouted.

"Good people of Tixmul, have no fear! Your Devine Lord of Fire holds you in high regard. He places trust in you and so has chosen you to play a joyous role in the upcoming nuptials of his most beloved daughter, the Lady Mad Seizure Star. The Lady is promised to Lord Dwarf-wind of Ichpaatún and your own Tixmul has been selected as the site for a feast that will seal their betrothal. A royal feast and celebration in which you are all invited to take part!"

Gucumatz grinned bemused by White Worm's oily words. "Will they come?"

"Of course they'll come," answered the Worm. Then, he continued in the raised voice, "I am Ah K'in Zac Nok and this is Lord Gucumatz, nacon of Tzamá, and we bring you the Lord of Fire's blessing."

Speaking soothingly he cajoled the villagers to return alternating between flattery and hints of reward. And, as his appeal continued, slowly, one by one, with much trepidation people began to emerge from their hiding places.

In a short time a small crowd had gathered in front of the Tzamáns. Zac Nok was about to order warriors to put them all to work when he noticed that the peasants' attention was focused not on himself nor on Gucumatz but rather on some point behind their backs. Swiveling his head, he spotted Turix leading his charges.

"People of Tixmul," he intoned, turning back, "look at the astounding oddities that Great Yajawk'ak' commands. Behold, a servant of the monkey gods Hun Chowen and Hun Batz, and a baczah (prisoner of war) a fierce eagle warrior from lands far away. Do not fear. The power of your Lord of Fire holds these strange creatures in thrall. Come closer. Satisfy your curiosity."

Several villagers approached. Gingerly, they touched Gonzalo and Iccauhtli with their hands. Then, they ran their hands over their own faces and bodies and chattered enthusiastically at their friends.

Gucumatz and Zac Nok watched their excitement in amused silence, then the fat priest turned to his companion.

"You see, I told you that we should bring the monkey man and the old eagle warrior. They'll amaze the k'uruch'ob (cockroaches) from Ichpaatún just as they astound these dolts."

Chapter 33

Tixmul

11 Bak'tun 14 K'atun 11 Tun 13 Uinal 12 K'in

(January 10, 1512)

Yaotl hurried back around a bend in the trail returning from where he scouted ahead of Ichpaatún's procession. Looking neither left nor right, he marched purposefully past Dwarf-wind and stopped before his nacon.

"Hoch Can," he huffed, "We've reached Tixmul; the village is close ahead, it sits just out of earshot."

Hoch Can allowed himself a fleeting moment of relief. He wanted to spare elderly Ah K'in May the likely discomfort of a hurried trek, so he'd set an extremely modest pace for the nuptial group. With the coming of the current day, he'd begun to fear that the speed he'd chosen was too slow. The sacred Tzolk'in had turned; it was 11 Eb'. The day that Ah K'in May had declared most propitious to treat with the Tzamáns was upon them, yet already K'inich Ajaw had soared across much of the sky.

If because of Hoch Can's miscalculation they required still another day to reach their destination, a disastrous possibility that Dwarf-wind had repeatedly voiced, he'd worried that his betrothed uncle would fly into an ungovernable rage. Yaotl's revelation, that Tixmul lay close at hand, put that unpleasant prospect to rest once and for all. Silently, the young nacon closed his eyes and fervently thanked dark Ekchuah for watching over their journey.

"I am leader here!" spluttered Dwarf-wind as he came stomping up. "You will report to me!"

"Lord," replied Yaotl glancing at Hoch Can who nodded, "we approach Tixmul it lays but a short walk ahead."

"Wonderful, wonderful! We must all make ready," gushed Dwarf-wind.

Then, he began to shout commands. For a moment, mild disorder reigned as he directed people here and there, and demanded that this and that be arranged just so. Gradually, as his huffy demands were met, the trifling confusion fell into order.

In keeping with Dwarf-wind's orders, Chiccan, his personal caluac, was designated to lead the procession into the village. Strutting with his head held high, the majordomo was commanded to herald his master's arrival with repeated strident blasts upon a conch horn.

Just behind Chiccan would trail Ihuicatl (Sky) and Xoco (Youngest Sister), two female servants from the prospective groom's household. These retainers were ordered to carry large baskets and cast fresh sihom leaves onto their master's path. Immediately behind the two women, strode Dwarf-wind himself, oiled, perfumed, and pretentiously attired in his Tzamán cape of shimmering crimson feathers. To enhance his status, he required that he be flanked by the venerable Ah K'in May and his young acolyte, Tohil. Tohil, who all considered an accomplished musician, was commanded to play upon his favorite reed flute.

Only a pace behind the two priests strolled Akbit and Bitol, two fussily dressed brothers. Both were merchants, lessor members of Ichpaatún's Ah Cuchcab and sycophantic followers of Dwarf-wind. Next, again according to Dwarf-wind's dictates, followed Yaotl, Chicahua, Te' K'ab', and the six other warriors of Hoch Can's holcánob. Behind the warriors walked three of Dwarf-wind's male servants carrying gifts and supplies.

"It is my wish," Dwarf-wind declared to Hoch Can, "that you and Lady Za'azil walk in safety behind my servants. Of course, Itz'at Acan should walk close behind you where he can protect your backs and attend to your needs."

What dung, thought Hoch Can. *If Ah Tabai's purpose is true, there's no danger to any of us, and Acan serves my father not me.*

Both Hoch Can and Itz'at Acan were well aware that Dwarf-wind insulted them while feigning concern.

He's a pompous ass, reflected Hoch Can, *but he's also my uncle and it is his wedding. Let the a ch'o' (rat) have his day.*

Just as Yaotl had reported, after a short march the procession stepped out of the jungle. Close by in front of them stretched Tixmul's plaza. Hoch Can had scouted the village two years earlier so it startled him to see its old weathered square swept clean and adorned by a pair of large thatched pavilions. Sundry people clustered under the obviously new pavilions and elsewhere many more moved busily about the plaza.

Too many, he worried. *Many more than we agreed should be here.*

As Dwarf-wind's procession drew near, three ostentatiously dressed men walked forward to greet them. Even from his position at the rear of the group Hoch Can easily recognized the fat Tzamán high priest, Zac Nok, and Ah Tabai's previous emissary, Ah Mun. The third man, a stranger, was tall and sinewy with an unfriendly face, stony eyes, and a maimed hand. Upon the three men's approach, Chiccan and Tohil stopped sounding their instruments. For a moment the cacophony yielded to silence and then Zac Nok bowed.

"Lord Dwarf-wind," he enthused, "you are most welcome! This is a joyous occasion. You've already met my honored companion Ah Mun, a member of Our Lord of Fire's council. And this," he said gesturing to the man on his right, "this is Ah K'in Cutz, of Xamanzamá, a most holy man, who brings you the good wishes of his people and of his master the Batab Kinich, Ac Yanto."

Dwarf-wind was about to respond when, Hoch Can dropped Za'azil's hand and pushed his way forward.

"What's the meaning of this!" he demanded, his voice harsh with mistrust. "We both agreed to parties of twenty-five, twenty-five and no more!" Then, turning to Dwarf-wind, "Uncle, this is wrong, we should leave."

Dwarf-wind, glared at his nephew. His meaty lips drew into a tight line and his puffy face suffused to a bright red with anger.

"Shut your stupid suspicious mouth, you young fool!" he choked. "You… you insult our friends!" Then, he turned to the Tzamáns, "Ah K'in Zac Nok, I humbly beg your forgiveness! My nephew is tactless and ill-considered. He's a distrustful child with no more brains than an addled saak' (grasshopper)."

"Uncle," snarled Hoch Can, "you must…" but before he could continue Zac Nok smoothly interrupted.

"Don't trouble yourself, Lord Dwarf-wind, no one here takes offense. We understand. We accept your nephew's concern." Then, looking at Hoch Can, "Your young nacon is correct. This is not as his father and Ah Mun agreed. Nacon Hoch Can, I beg that you understand. When we advised Our Devine Lord of Fire that only twenty-five of us were to journey to Tixmul, he reproached Ah Mun. He rightly pointed out that Lord Dwarf-wind is to be his new son and that as such it was unseemly for us to welcome him with so few.”

“We needed servants to cook and serve,” added Ah Mun waving a hand toward the activity behind him, “musicians, porters, and slaves to build these pavilions. Lord Dwarf-wind deserves a noble reception and twenty simply wouldn’t suffice.”

Dwarf-wind listened to the Tzamáns’ words and immediately puffed up with conceit.

“You see nephew,” he sneered, “all is as it should be. Ah Tabai’s people merely accord me my proper respect.”

While Akbit and Bitol made affirming noises and nodded their heads, Hoch Can seethed.

This is wrong, he thought. *Yet, if I argue more, my words will but fall on ears made deaf by greed and ambition.*

“Very well esteemed Ah K’in,” he begrudged to Zac Nok. “I see that you merely seek to honor my uncle. I apologize for my ungracious outburst.”

Zac Nok and Ah Mun both smiled. The face of the stranger, Cutz, remained a mask.

“It was the surprise of seeing so many, nothing more,” offered Zac Nok. “All is forgotten. Come. After your long journey you must all be hungry and of course thirsty.”

So saying, he took Dwarf-wind’s arm and escorted him toward the thatched pavilions. As everyone followed, Hoch Can drifted back to Za’azil’s side.

“My uncle leads us with his head buried in dark swirling clouds of his own making,” he grumbled.

“Iicham (husband),” she soothed, “listen to me and take no offense at what I must say. You are Nacon and Dwarf-wind’s words, were harsh. They insult you. Nevertheless, his words contain hard grains of truth. You do not trust. We both know this to be true. You do not trust and so you suspect hidden motives.”

“The Tzamáns don’t respect us as equals,” hissed Hoch Can. “They killed, Teyacapan!”

“And you, you also killed,” reminded Za’azil. “Now, Ah Tabai makes us a gesture of peace and offers his daughter to your undeserving uncle. Bank the fires of your misgiving my husband and allow this, whatever this is, to unfold. If we wish to avoid further conflict, this is an opportunity to bury the enmity of our peoples. Peace is elusive but perhaps this is how it will be nurtured."

"Very well hats'uts, I reserve my misgivings," muttered Hoch Can.

He still carried doubts, but, they were supported by nothing more substantial than a sour flutter in his stomach. The veracity of Za'azil's words was undeniable and it made his worries seem somehow grudging, small, and unreasonable.

Under the overhang of the closest pavilion, Zac Nok and Ah Mun ushered the worthies of Ichpaatún's delegation to seats where woven reed mats waited. Zac Nok directed Dwarf-wind to a place of honor next to himself on a slightly raised platform. Once seated, they were joined by the taciturn looking priest from Xamanzamá.

Ah Mun then made a fuss of assisting Ah K'in May, Akbit, and Bitol, leaving Hoch Can, Za'azil, Itz'at Acan, and Tohil to seat themselves. Several other Tzamáns led Ichpaatún's warriors, Dwarf-wind's caluac, Chiccan, and the rest of their party toward the second pavilion where they were either seated or put to work according to their station.

While Dwarf-wind and his flatterers made small talk with Zac Nok, Ah Mun, and Ah K'in Cutz, Hoch Can, Za'azil, and Itz'at Acan gave their attention to the feast that Tzamán servants were laying out before them. Hoch Can in particular tried to focus on the food and by so doing shut out the prattle of Dwarf Wind's crude boasts about his lineage and the distinction of his ancestors.

Normally, as a woman, Za'azil would have taken her meal apart from the men, but Zac Nok had cordially insisted that since everyone was here to discuss nuptial arrangements that it was proper that she remain.

It was plain from the foods spread before Dwarf-wind's entourage that Ah Tabai's people wished to impress. The mats under the pavilion were crowded with savory dishes. There were many bowls of well-seasoned venison and vegetables cooked in thick sauces. Beside these lay wooden and clay trenchers loaded with baked fish and roasted stuffed fowl. Other vessels and baskets contained fruits, cooked tubers, and nuts. And, as though these were meager offerings, piles of cooked maize and jugs of delicious frothy cacao filled the spaces between.

Hoch Can had just reached for tidbit of grilled fish when Za'azil nudged for his attention. "Look!" she whispered.

A short distance away, causing something of a stir, Tzamá's great warrior, Gucumatz, strode resolutely in their direction. He stalked brashly across the stone plaza and his each step seemed an exercise in arrogance. As when Hoch Can last saw him, the renowned nacon was dressed to emphasize his position and prowess. The jawbones of defeated enemies again rattled on his powerful upper arms and his snarling jaguar cape draped across one well-muscled shoulder. Although the rest of his attire tended more to elegance than battle, his heavy stone-headed war club dangled from his large right hand.

"Hoch Can," nodded Acan leaning close, "you struck him and that is something he can never forgive. He'll try to provoke you. Compose yourself and remain calm."

The giant's insolent march ignored Dwarf-wind and those seated next to him and came to a halt directly in front of Hoch Can. Barely a pace away, he planted his sandaled feet well apart, placed his free hand on his hip and stared rudely into Hoch Can's eyes.

To Za'azil the Tzamán seemed possessed by the spirit of some savage predator poised to pounce. Gucumatz made no sound, but under his baleful stare Hoch Can was acutely aware that his own knife was no match for the war club which swayed a mere hand's breadth from his face. The stare also made him yearn for the protection of his heavy cotton cuirass which lay far away and unreachable in Ichpaatún.

Weapons or not, thought Hoch Can, *I too am a warrior and nacon.*

He slowly stood, looked up at the bigger man, and met the insolent stare with a steady gaze of his own.

Gucumatz laughed, an ugly sound. "Greetings Hoch Can. Too many days have passed since you hosted me in Ichpaatún, but now it is you who are our visitor and it is my turn to return your kindness."

"Nacon Gucumatz," warned Zac Nok in a stern yet nervous voice, "Lord Dwarf-wind and his family are our friends and the honored guests of our lord, Yajawk'ak'."

"Of course, of course they are," assured Gucumatz never taking his eyes from Hoch Can, "I merely wish to welcome my special friend. Look," he said turning his face. "What do you think of your handiwork?"

Hoch Can took in the ugly jagged scar that disfigured the Tzamán's otherwise handsome face.

"You attacked my father."

Gucumatz made a dismissive noise.

"Come join us," urged White Worm pointing to a spot next to Dwarf-wind.

"I mean no disrespect to our great Lord of Fire's future son," proclaimed the nacon in a voice dripping with sarcasm, "but, with his blessing, I prefer to remain here where I can converse with a fellow warrior."

"By all means," bleated Dwarf-wind, "my nephew is honored by your presence Great Nacon."

"So," yawned Gucumatz, as he dropped his club and settled his bulk down next to Za'azil, "it appears that your husband and I are equals."

The giant smiled expansively, and reached for a chunk of venison. To Hoch Can the smile appeared nothing more than a disdainful mask that belied the hulk's words.

Here at least, he thought, *is one Tzamán who does not want peace.* With that thought his own mouth tightened into a thin line.

Time moved slowly in Gucumatz's presence. While K'inich Ajaw completed his journey across the sky and friendly laughter issued from around Dwarf-wind and White Worm, Itz'at Acan did his utmost to engage and hold the powerful Tzamán's attention.

To Hoch Can and Za'azil the two men's conversation sounded wooden and uncomfortable, and as a result they sat uneasily. They tried to relax, say little, and pick at the profusion of food, but despite Acan's best efforts Gucumatz's unwelcome attention kept returning to Hoch Can. It was a time filled with dark innuendo and prickly silence.

When dusky shadows began to lengthen, men moved about lighting reed torches and large braziers to push back the gathering darkness. Silent Tzamán servant women moved behind the diners filling cups with chicha and b'alche, and then turned their backs until cups were ready to be refilled. Za'azil and Itz'at Acan drank not at all and Hoch Can, intent on keeping his wits, drank carefully. Gucumatz swallowed from a cup that seemed perpetually empty.

The Tzamán was in the midst of another loud boast when a slight commotion drew Hoch Can's attention to his uncle.

"What do you mean Mad Seizure Star isn't here?" demanded Dwarf-wind in a loud and outraged voice. "I've come all the way from Ichpaatún to inspect my bride!"

"Lord," responded White Worm, quiet and unctuous, "Lady Mad Seizure Star's beauty is well known. She is the daughter of a god made man. Surely you must see that it is not appropriate that she should be examined like a ripe melon in the market, even by a personage as distinguished as yourself."

"But what of our wedding arrangements?" Whined Dwarf-wind in a voice grown suddenly petulant.

"Details and toil," interjected the taciturn priest from Xamanzamá, "time enough for that when K'inich Ajaw brings us his new day."

"Esteemed Ah K'in Cutz is correct," threw in Ah Mun. "Tonight is for feasting. It's a night for entertainment and celebration. You are about to become the beloved son of our Lord of Fire".

Dwarf-wind sat in sullen silence and took a deep draught from his b'alche cup. He'd spent much of the long walk to Tixmul daydreaming of his meeting with Mad Seizure Star. As Zac Nok had correctly stated, the woman's beauty was renowned. In Dwarf-wind's daydreams the two of them had sat together, her hanging on his every word. He'd imagined holding her hand, running his hand over her arm, brushing it against the soft flesh of her bare thigh. In a fantasy of lust he'd imagined himself enjoying her pleasures as a prelude and a seal to their marriage. Now, with Mad Seizure Star absent, none of those reveries would come to pass. Angrily he snapped at a nearby serving woman to refill his cup. After b'alche again reached its rim, he drained it.

When Ah Tabai's emissaries first arrived bearing their offer of his eldest daughter in marriage, Dwarf-wind had leapt to the idea. With nothing beyond blandishments as evidence of Tzamá's goodwill, he'd convinced himself of the truth and sincerity of the Lord of Fire's intentions. He had also deafened himself to any and all other possibilities.

As the b'alche warmed him, he consoled himself that Mad Seizure Star's nonappearance, while annoying, was merely a postponement of greater pleasures and power to come.

I am to be the son of a god!

With his mercurial mood again changed, Dwarf-wind giggled. "I'm sorry, I'm being churlish. It was the disappointment that my betrothed is not here, but you are of course right Ah K'in Zac Nok, Mad Seizure Star must not be inspected. She is the daughter of a god! And, you are also right Ah K'in Cutz, tomorrow is time enough for fine points and tedium. Now, tell me good Ah Mun, what are the entertainments you propose?"

Hoch Can listened to his uncle's servile, self-serving, words and struggled to suppress the disgusted groan they tried to wrench from his throat.

Chapter 34

Entertainments

11 Bak'tun 14 K'atun 11 Tun 13 Uinal 12 K'in

(January 10, 1512)

Amid stillness and bewilderment, Gonzalo's thoughts heaped themselves precariously, one upon another.

What's different about this village? Why return my clothes? What's the meaning of Iccauhtli's costume? Why show us to the villagers? Why confine us?

It was Turix, accompanied by one of Gucumatz's armed warriors, who'd pushed Gonzalo and Iccauhtli into a tiny windowless hut. With no hint of explanation, except a stern admonishment to remain absolutely silent, the warrior had roughly prodded them through the hut's low door. Turix, equally unforthcoming, had then turned on his heel and left without a word.

Inside the hut, in truth more of a storage bin, time stretched and crawled. Mute and uncomfortable, the two men sat and brooded. Their situation mystified and worried Gonzalo. Anxious to seek Iccauhtli's counsel, he whispered. Almost immediately, before any reply from his companion, his quiet murmurs drew harsh and threatening rebukes from outside. Nervous and cautious, Gonzalo then held his tongue.

In the close darkness, the soldier of fortune's mind returned again and again to butchered Valdivia's jacket.

Why give it to me now, to what purpose? It's an ill omen!

As the confinement lengthened, sounds of abandon and revelry outside the hut grew ever louder. In response, Gonzalo's thoughts raced round and round and a budding fear rooted itself in his heart. Suggested by the presence of his unlucky companion's garment a small, yet persistent, dread whispered once, and then again and again.

They slaughtered the captain, now they're coming for me!

Time passed, an indeterminable passage marked only by a mounting fear that thudded deep in Gonzalo's chest. Just when he thought he could endure no longer, Turix returned, and, with gruff commands, he summoned the two captives outside. Gonzalo shivered with trepidation.

And so it ends, he thought.

Resolved to meet fate as bravely as his captain, he ran his fingers through his hair, and straightened Valdivia's waistcoat. Then, all but certain that, at long last, that he was about to succumb to the caprices of his cruel and remorseless misfortune, Gonzalo stepped outside.

He glanced warily about. Daylight had fled, and, as on the previous night, the star filled sky glowed clear and bright. It wasn't the heavens, however, that arrested his attention. Some distance away, the large plaza, that in the warm light of the afternoon had appeared old and nearly deserted, now presented itself as vibrant, alive with both people and spirited activity. Deep purple shadows obscured the remainder of the small village and its surrounding jungle, but within the open space of the plaza a wavering glow of braziers, torches, and numerous low fires held sway.

Two large thatched pavilions had sprouted where earlier none existed and a thick aromatic smoke from dozens of smoldering pots hemmed them in. To Gonzalo, beheld in the flickering light, the smoke rose like so many coiling serpents.

Turix led them nearer, and the ruddy dancing light etched features of the plaza's occupants into elusive planes defined by shadows of orange and red. The level of noise erupting from those assembled, and the obvious merriment of all present, made it clear to Gonzalo that spirits of some type flowed freely.

At the center of the tumult, a circle of energetic revelers swayed and writhed. Accompanied by the dissonance of cane and deer bone whistles, large conch shell trumpets, and shrill reed flutes, two heavily tattooed warriors moved about in the circle's center.

One danced erect holding aloft a handful of reeds. The other cavorted around him, squatting. Both men kept time to the rhythmic stamping of feet arising from the surrounding circle. As Gonzalo watched, the upright dancer, using all of his strength, abruptly hurled one of his reeds at his squatting partner. Moving as fast as a cat, the second warrior caught the missile with a small rod. Cheers burst from the onlookers. People thrashed about. The act repeated.

Despite the many months of novelty and tribulation that he had by this time experienced, the acute turmoil of the plaza, set against its inferno-like background of smoke and wavering flames, threatened to overwhelm Gonzalo's reason. Looking about, he felt as though he'd once again stepped off the world of rationality and into an abyss of insanity.

Perhaps this is Hell, he thought. *Is nothing done in this accursed land without the flames of perdition and the stink of incense?*

With a final shout, the dancers completed their gambol and the circle of revelers broke apart. Immediately, Turix thrust Gonzalo and Iccauhtli forward. Ahead of them, clustered near the second pavilion, congregated a group of people, half of whom the Spaniard was surprised to recognize.

On one side slouched Zac Nok. Beside him, looking lean and grim, stood the unclean priest who'd slain Captain Valdivia and torn out his heart. At the sight of this savage, Gonzalo's fears surged and he trembled as though chilled in the depths of winter.

In front of these two, stood a noble from Ah Tabai's court, a savage whose name Gonzalo had never heard, and also another two men that he'd never before seen. One of the strangers was a soft looking youth. The other a short debauched looking native, who he judged perhaps a decade older than himself. Obviously, someone of importance, this unfamiliar person possessed a puffy porcine face with small close-set eyes, and was dressed in a shimmering cloak of crimson feathers.

Somewhat separated from Zac Nok and his companions stood another group. Of these, Gonzalo recognized only a slightly glassy-eyed Gucumatz. The giant didn't appear overcome by drink, yet it was obvious that he was slightly pigeon-eyed.

For a moment the discreet approach of Turix and his charges went unnoticed because everyone's attention was focused on a loud fat dwarf who Gonzalo had once seen attend Tzamá's Lord of Fire. On that occasion the short-statured native with his protruding belly and prominent navel had dressed as a parody of the great ruler himself. Tonight, the dwarf, who Gonzalo knew to be called Kis Lu'um (Earth Farter) was dressed in a costume that mimicked Zac Nok. Garment for garment, the dwarf aped the high priest, right down to a woven fan which the fat cleric carried. The only exceptions to his clever impersonation were a mask with a long distended nose and a hat that to Gonzalo resembled a tall multilayer cake.

Everyone was busy chuckling at Kis Lu'um's antics, when Zac Nok spotted Turix and an imperious command from the high priest sent the rotund jester scuttling away.

"Now Lord Dwarf-wind," gushed Ah Mun, "something very special!"

"Honored guests," intoned Zac Nok quickly, while casting an annoyed look at his companion, "honorable Ah Mun is correct. Look upon two unique curiosities. Beings who live only to serve our Great Lord of Fire!"

With this introduction, Turix drove his two charges forward. Immediately Gonzalo experienced a rising swell of relief. He hadn't understood many of Zac Nok's words, but he'd grasped enough. His life wasn't about to end.

I'm not to be sacrificed, he thought. *I'm again to act the performing dog.*

"Lord Dwarf-wind," bubbled Zac Nok, then he continued with the words that he'd used to address the lowly peasants of Tixmul. "Behold, a baczah (prisoner of war) from lands far away toward Xaman Ek (north star), a once fierce eagle warrior captured by our own Lord of Fire's glorious father, Ah Kumix Uinic!"

Turix hissed something at Iccauhtli and the old warrior-made-slave began a sort of shambling twirling dance. He waved his wing-like bracers at the gathered onlookers, and endeavored to menace them with repeated thrusts of his beaked wooden helmet.

To Gonzalo's discomfort, his companion's proud movements elicited a scornful round of sniggers, smiles, and boisterous snorts from Zac Nok, the pig-faced stranger, and many, many, others.

Once again, Turix hissed, and this time at his command, Iccauhtli drew himself up and at the top of his lungs howled out a long unused war cry. As the echo of his defiant shout died awkwardly away, the dwarf, Earth Farter, darted suddenly back to the center of attention and squatted before Iccauhtli.

Cocking his head quizzically to one side, and then the other, the masked dwarf gazed up into the beaked maw of the other's helmet. Then, to the delight of the onlookers, he bleated a warbling high-pitched screech of his own. When Iccauhtli appeared befuddled, the runt whirled about, bent over, bared his ass to the old prisoner, broke wind, and then hopped away. As Earth Farter made his hasty exit, howls of raucous laughter exploded from Gucumatz, Ah Mun, and the pig-faced stranger.

Anguish painted Iccauhtli's dark lined face. Gripped with sympathy, Gonzalo started to lay a friendly hand on his hut-mate's shoulder, when, before he could act, the laughing pig-faced lord stepped forward and tugged aggressively at the Spaniard's once again thick beard.

"And what monstrosity do we have here?" demanded Dwarf-wind.

"Who knows," replied Zac Nok slyly, "a messenger from Metnal perhaps? You should ask my guest Ah K'in Cutz; he was among those who captured him."

"Bah!" responded the sardonic Cutz. "Foolish peasants encountered this ugly creature on the Bay of Turtles. Frightened, they came running and spread wild tales that Hun Nal Ye (a sea god) had cast servants of Hun Chowen and Hun Batz up onto the sand."

"Well, he's hairy enough to be a flunky of the monkey gods," quipped Dwarf-wind, "but, no, too tall."

"Still, he undoubtedly has the necessary ch'ik'ob (fleas)," snorted Gucumatz while draining his cup.

"So what is he," sneered Dwarf-wind, "man or beast?"

"A curiosity from a degenerate tribe of idiots," announced Ah K'in Cutz. "He claims to have come from a land beyond the edge of the world. Can you imagine, beyond the edge of the world? He maintains that it's a wondrous realm of countless cities, and boundless magic, but his words drip lies. It's an amusing fantasy nothing more."

"Then he speaks?" asked Za'azil, who'd been watching quietly.

"He pretends to have a tongue, Lady," smiled Ah Mun, who stood nearby. "At first we listened, but then we realized that he happily speaks meaningless gibberish just to amuse. Turix is teaching him to speak as a man."

"So who are you and where are you from?" demanded Dwarf-wind.

Gonzalo, had listened carefully, understood much of the conversation, and his hackles rose at the insults.

You want a dog who barks, he thought. *Well, I may be your prisoner, but I am not your dog.*

Frustrated, he took an aggressive step toward Dwarf-wind causing the shorter man to shy backwards.

"I am not a dog!" he yelled at him in Spanish. "I am Gonzalo Aroça de Palos an escudero in the service of Don Alonso de Ojeda, a subject of the illustrious kings of Castile and Léon! And I come," he shouted pointing to the east, "from a land that isn't populated by stupid bloodthirsty savages like you!"

For a moment, taken aback by his angry and incomprehensible outburst, everyone grew silent, then Turix broke the spell.

"This is a lord of Ichpaatún," he snarled pointing to the pig-faced stranger. "He is to marry Lady Mad Seizure Star and so soon become son to Our Divine Lord of Fire. Bow to him you ungrateful chattering monkey!"

With that, Turix stomped a foot into the back of Gonzalo's left leg, the blow, unexpected and painful, sent him crashing to his knees. This was followed by, a vicious shove that sprawled the escudero face down onto the plaza's dusty paving stones.

"Well Turix," quipped Dwarf-wind, "it seems he still has some learning to do."

Zac Nok smiled broadly. *The cuāuhtli (eagle warrior) and the tuucha (monkey) are every bit as amusing as I hoped, and the fools from Ichpaatún are easily distracted. If the rest of the evening's entertainments go as well, we'll never discuss more serious concerns.*

"Lord Dwarf-wind," he soothed, "this amusement grows tedious and your cup requires filling. Come, let us continue our feast."

So saying, he steered Dwarf-wind, Ah K'in Cutz, and others back toward the pavilion's raised dais. As they walked away, Gonzalo roused himself from the dirt and slowly stood. Turix gave him a sharp cuff on the back of the head.

"Behave!" he cautioned.

Gonzalo thought that perhaps the demonstration was over, but then the people from Gucumatz's party drew close and, one after another, they approached to examine him.

The first was a lean young warrior endowed with a handsome if somewhat hawkish face. The proud looking youth circled Gonzalo several times, but the escudero was keenly aware that the stranger's eyes kept flitting back to Gucumatz. In turn,

Gucumatz's own regard returned again and again to the youth. Gonzalo had no idea what connection existed between the two men, but it was clear that they continually took each other's measure.

His master, Gucumatz, was older, taller, and more powerfully built than the young warrior, but likewise Gonzalo discerned a toughness in the youth.

The second stranger to approach, was the young woman who'd asked if he could speak. Like the young man, she walked silently around him, plucked gently at his garments, and stared into his face. Her eyes were dark, her own face round and plain featured. Around her ankles and from her neck hung delicate strings of polished seeds that made a soft clinking as she moved.

Local royalty, thought Gonzalo, *but less haughty than the women of Tzamá.*

From time to time, as she studied him, she also turned and cast her eyes at the young warrior.

They're lovers. She's well-proportioned and pretty enough, mused Gonzalo, *but far from a beauty.*

Still, for some reason her glances at the young man drove home to Gonzalo his own miserable condition. Unexpectedly, when she stepped back and was replaced by a pair older men, he suffered a nagging twinge of envy and regret.

One of the two elders who succeeded the woman was short and wiry. His companion was the oldest native Gonzalo had yet encountered. The man was so ancient that his body looked like nothing so much as an animated bag of bones, a skeletal frame draped with a thin covering of browned and wrinkled parchment. Flying in the face of his apparent frailty, the shriveled native appeared to possess a spry vitality that belied his appearance. The dark eyes of both men shown bright and intelligent and they scrutinized Gonzalo more closely than any of those who preceded them.

After staring at him and fingering the buttons on Valdivia's waistcoat, the older man looked up into his face and quietly repeated Dwarf-wind's question.

"Where are you from?"

Gonzalo stared back and, detecting no venality in the aged stranger, replied in a civil manner.

"Lak'in (east)."

The old man looked at his companion, nodded as if satisfied, and then the two stepped away.

"Surely, this is the one who Ah-cambal described?" suggested Itz'at Acan in a quiet voice.

"He can be no other," asserted Ah K'in May in the same tone. "I fear his presence. If the tzintè seeds spoke truth to Ah-cambal, then, whoever he is and wherever he is from, he is a harbinger of great calamity and change."

A few paces away, Gucumatz, now swaying visibly, tossed the dregs from his cup at Gonzalo's face.

"Enough of this hairy slave," he grumbled so that all could hear. "I grow bored!" Then, he turned to Hoch Can. "What of you little nacon?" he belched. "Why don't you entertain us? Do you dance? Do you juggle? Perhaps you have a voice. I'm sure that you and Earth Farter together would make an excellent sound!"

While Gucumatz roared with laughter at his own cleverness, Hoch Can took note of Acan's earlier warning, *"He'll try to provoke you."* The older man's advice now rang truer than ever. As a consequence, Hoch Can struggled mightily to check the upsurge of hostility that threatened to cloud his reason.

To those watching, the young warrior's face held few secrets. It was tense and open, an arena where resentment and self-control wrestled for dominance. For a moment it looked as if anger had gotten the upper hand, then, Hoch Can visibly calmed himself.

"It is truly a pity Nacon Gucumatz," he replied smiling sweetly, "but, sadly, I don't sing well. Neither do I dance or juggle. I apologize, but you need to fill your cup and look elsewhere for your further amusement."

"Ah, that is a pity," purred Gucumatz.

With a nasty grin, he then stepped quickly beside Za'azil, who stood nearby. Still grinning, he grabbed her arm and jerked her roughly against his chest. Even as shock registered on her face, he slipped his free hand beneath her mantle and crudely fondled her breasts.

"Don't concern yourself, Hoch Can," he laughed, "I'm sure your wife can amuse us even if you cannot."

In recognition of Gucumatz's deed, the jovial mood of the gathering died as promptly as the flame of a snuffed candle.

"Release her!" shouted Hoch Can, his voice quavering with anger.

In response, Gucumatz, howled with laughter and shoved Za'azil so forcefully that she stumbled and sprawled at his side.

"Well, little nacon," sneered the giant. "Do you have a better amusement, one that might keep me occupied?"

Hoch Can's face drew tight. It clenched like a fist. His features blackened with anger.

I am Nachan Can's son. I am Nacon of Ichpaatún.

Because he was young and brash, and because Za'azil sat squarely at the center of his world, Hoch Can could no more ignore Gucumatz's insult than he could stop K'inich Ajaw in his daily march across the sky.

A scream of animal rage burst from his throat. In a single swift motion he drew his knife and, blind with hate, he hurled himself at the bigger man.

Sober or drunk, Gucumatz was fierce and experienced. He merited his fearsome reputation. In the face of Hoch Can's furious charge the giant didn't as much as flinch. Instead, he coolly reached down and retrieved his seemingly forgotten club. Once in his hand, the stone-headed length of fire-hardened wood swung, almost of its own accord, and hastened to meet his onrushing foe.

Gucumatz's move was economical, lazy, unplanned, almost like swatting a fly. Before anyone could as much as draw breath, the terrifying weapon hammered into Hoch Can's face. Its impact devastated. The crunch it emitted sickened.

Za'azil upstretched her quivering hand as if to ward off the inevitable and screamed. Her scream was terrible, hollow, and to its shuddering reverberations Hoch Can collapsed as though hit by a mountain.

Ignoring her rising wail, Gucumatz stepped into a low crouch. He straddled the fallen youth. Then, powerful muscles bulging, he brought his club down again. In death, Hoch Can's twisted skull pulled the angles of his once handsome face into an eerie and blood splattered grin.

Except for Za'azil's wild cries, stunned silence hushed every voice. Gucumatz stared down at Hoch Can's crumpled corpse. He'd planned the rat-dropping's death. He'd fanaticized about it, over and over, in a thousand different ways, each more lingering and painful than the last.

Entertainments 311

The turd's death was too quick. It came too easily, thought Gucumatz, as he experienced a vague wave of disappointment. *There's no satisfaction in the slaughter of a worthless opponent.*

He'd conceived his revenge. He'd imagined it down to the smallest detail. And now, now his own impulsive rage had cheated him of that satisfaction.

Three times in rapid succession, something slammed into Gucumatz's back. Pain! Agony, instantaneous and excruciating threatened to overpower him! He staggered. His powerful body tightened. It recoiled away from the screaming burn.

With a throaty bellow of mortal distress, expanding into rage, Gucumatz spun about. Before him, not two paces away, stood the gaunt form of Ah K'in May, the ancient priest from Ichpaatún. Time had twisted and misshapen the old man's hands. Nevertheless, in his right fist he clutched a saw-like sacrificial knife.

A heartbeat passed. The two men stood eye to eye. Gucumatz contemplated the cruel blade, a blade wrapped in a dripping sheath of his own blood and gore. With a feral roar, the moment broke. The giant rocked forward, and as he moved, his terrifying club again whistled through the air.

Ah K'in May made no attempt to dodge, no attempt to counter the attack. Instead, he dropped his knife. He mouthed the name of his patron, the great god, Itzamna. Then, he died before he hit the ground.

Gucumatz threw his muscular arms into the air and screamed his triumph. Abruptly, he found himself unable to continue. With a look of surprise, and pain, the guttural shout died in his throat. It withered into a soggy choking cough. The great nacon trembled. The heavy war club slipped from his fingers and he raised his right hand to the wound at his back. He felt strength seep from his body. He locked his legs to bend and retrieve his weapon, but, astonished, found that he could no longer stand.

With a sound like a great tunkul pounding in his head, Gucumatz sat heavily beside the dead priest's frail body. His eyes grew large, but he saw only darkness. Then, with a final wet and gasping cough, his spirit embarked on its journey to Metnal.

Pandemonium rolled across the plaza. Za'azil and several of the Tzamán servant women screamed at the top of their lungs. Dwarf-wind, Ah Mun, Akbit, Bitol, and Turix all yelled incoherently. Servants fled. At the other pavilion, men of both parties shouted, brandished weapons, and charged forward.

Ah K'in Cutz had watched the death of the three men with a curious detachment. Now, as he gazed at the growing turmoil, he felt a wash of the same vague disappointment that Gucumatz had experienced. On the day that his hand had been maimed, and before Cutz lost consciousness to the searing pain, he'd silently pledged vengeance on both the hulking nacon and his collaborator, Zac Nok.

I'm glad that he's dead, he thought. *Gucumatz was a kan it (snake anus), but he should have died screaming.*

The end that he'd imagined for the great warrior would have been much worse. On the other hand, while it wasn't the revenge that Cutz would have chosen, he wasn't one to insult the gods by wasting their gift of opportunity.

With confusion reigning on every side, he looked calmly about and saw that all eyes were fixed on the bodies of Ah K'in May and the two fallen warriors. Nonchalantly, without a second of thought, Cutz turned to his left, drew his own knife, and with a cold and remorseless efficiency slit Zac Nok's plump fleshy throat. The high priest's eyes went wide in terrified shock and his pudgy hands jumped to his neck. Gurgling and desperate, he sank to his knees.

Tohil, the acolyte of slaughtered Ah K'in May, who stood with his back to Zac Nok, turned at the strange sound. Before he could register what was happening, Cutz's knife slid into his heart. As the young man fell, Cutz began to shout and to call attention to himself.

"Help! Assassins!" he shrieked. "Murderers! The deceivers from Ichpaatún have butchered our Lords! Catch them! Kill them! Don't let any escape!"

Gonzalo stood next to Iccauhtli rooted in disbelief. In a single instant, Gucumatz and Zac Nok, two of the natives whom he dreaded most, were gone.

Although shocked by their sudden plunge into violence, Gonzalo had recognized the unresolved animosity between his brutish master and the young stranger. The unexpected murder of Geronimo's fat master by the venomous priest from Xamanzamá fit none of his preconceptions.

They punished him cruelly, but he seemed reconciled, even grateful.

While Gonzalo stared at the dark countenanced savage, the man's cold flint-like eyes suddenly turned and stared back. Death, cold and implacable, lurked in his gaze.

He knows I saw him, thought Gonzalo. Then, in alarm, *he'll kill me if he can. I have to run! I need to run now! But, where?*

As the pandemonium mounted, Gonzalo cast urgently about for a direction in which to flee. All around him bedlam erupted. Warriors and others from the far pavilion had arrived and noisy and fatal fights were breaking out on all sides. Already, another of the strangers lay unmoving in a spreading pool of blood. Everywhere, amid shouts and yells men grappled in deadly combat.

A short distance away, still seated on the ground, Gonzalo spied the young woman who'd sparked his momentary envy. The dead youth lay cradled in her lap and amid cries of anguish she caressed his broken face.

Gonzalo was about to turn his attention back to his own escape, when the native, Ah Mun, stepped stealthily behind her. He wrapped his fist into the young woman's hair and yanked. She screamed and resisted. Ah Mun kicked her savagely, yanked again, and then tried to drag her away. In response to her screams, the short wiry stranger with the intelligent eyes rushed to her aid.

Before he could reach her, and to Gonzalo's utter amazement, Turix dove forward and tackled the man. The pompous caluac was soft and unfit, but he outweighed the older stranger nearly two to one and the men went down in a struggling heap.

Even as they fell, a blood curdling cry, spun Gonzalo around. A few paces away, Iccauhtli stooped to pick up Gucumatz's abandoned club. The loud shout that he earlier uttered at Turix's behest was a pale shadow to the terrifying war-scream that now burst from his throat. It was as though a disguise had fallen from Iccauhtli's lined face.

He was no longer a slave. Untold years of captivity and degradation fueled the frail eagle warrior's rage. Suddenly, brandishing the club, he was again in his prime. As Gonzalo stared, his garrulous hut-mate struck down a younger and much larger Tzamán warrior, screamed a cry of triumph, and ran in quest of another foe.

Gonzalo knew that he needed to flee, but the raw clarity of Iccauhtli's act cut through his thoughts. Galvanized, he saw what he had to do. Possibly for the first time since he crawled onto the warm sand at the Bay of Turtles, he saw true opportunity to direct his own fate, to choose his own end.

Ignoring the hateful stare of the murderous priest from Xamanzamá, he bent down, picked up a heavy wooden serving tray, and scattered its cargo of steamed mussels. He waved the stout slab of wood above his head, summoned his courage, and yelled.

"Spain and King Ferdinand!"

Ah Mun heard him coming, but, because of his struggle with the woman, realization came too late. Gonzalo swung the thick wooden tray like a knacker's mallet and drove it into the side of the Tzamán's head. Ah Mun gasped. He released his hold on the woman's hair. Gonzalo struck him again. Then, as Ah Mun crumpled, Gonzalo rammed a knee into his face and threw the Tzamán to the ground unconscious.

The woman stared up at him and her eyes grew wide with fear. Unsure what else to do, Gonzalo slowly held out his hand. Tentatively, she reached for it. Then, just as their fingers were about to touch, a burly warrior, one of her own people, shoved Gonzalo forcefully aside.

A second warrior of her party reached the first and, as they helped the woman to her feet, Turix's wiry opponent also arrived. Gonzalo cast about for the majordomo. When he spotted him, Turix lay face down in the dirt. The first impression that came to the escudero's mind was the image of a fat drunk who'd passed out and spilled his bottle of sweet red wine. Turix's throat was slit.

A frightened male servant and four more warriors joined the group. Then, at a command from the wiry stranger the eight men began to usher the crying woman away from the plaza. Immediately, the young woman screamed and struggled. For a moment the men appeared to argue with her. Then, abruptly, the larger of the first two warriors stepped back and heaved the broken body of her dead youth over his shoulder. Straightaway the group headed toward the nearby wall of jungle.

Indecision wracked Gonzalo. *I'm free. I can make my own way.* He ran through scenarios in his head, but it was the strident voice of instinct that told him what he must do.

My only option is to follow. They're armed. They have a destination. They know where they are. I have nothing and I know nothing.

His decision made, Gonzalo felt his anxiety slide away. Whether his relief was acceptance, courage, or simple fatigue, he couldn't say. Nevertheless, he turned and sprinted after the natives as they vanished into the brush.

He had just reached the jungle's edge and plunged into its shadow when a familiar cry yanked his attention back to the plaza. In the thick of the fighting, his hut-mate stood like a tree in a tempest, his pilfered club raised to deliver yet another vengeful blow.

"Iccauhtli!" cried Gonzalo.

His shout unheard, he watched in dismay as a cruel Tzamán spear pierced his companion's side. Iccauhtli staggered and his well-worn eagle helmet skewed in Gonzalo's direction. Illuminated by the ruddy glow of a torch, its savage beak framed a ferocious smile. Gonzalo watched the club slip from Iccauhtli's hand. The old man's head flopped back and his body crumpled, slowly, lifelessly, into the glorious warrior's death that he'd chosen.

He was a good man, thought Gonzalo, *another lost friend.*

Turning, he chased after the disappearing natives from Ichpaatún. He fled only a few paces into the darkness when unexpectedly one of the group's unencumbered warriors stood before him solid as a wall. The man stared. A knife rested loosely in the warrior's right hand. His eyes were bright and hard in the darkness.

Gonzalo skidded to a stop. Unsure, he opened his hands, and spread them apart. *If he kills me now, my nightmare stops.*

"I mean no harm," whispered Gonzalo.

The warrior frowned. If he was surprised that he understood Gonzalo's words, the frown didn't show it. His face remained stoic and noncommittal, neither friendly nor overtly hostile. Gonzalo waited silent and motionless. The moment stretched. Abruptly, without a word, the warrior sheathed his knife, turned his back, and hurried away. Gonzalo followed.

Almost immediately his world narrowed to the footfalls of the natives sprinting before him. Except for an occasional glimpse of starlit sky, darkness swallowed the world. He pounded through a shadowy seemingly endless tunnel of bushes, trees, and vines, everything about him more intuited than actually seen.

None of the natives spoke, but all seemed to know exactly where they ran. They simply raced along in silence, each concentrating on the unseen path before them. From time to time, Gonzalo glanced nervously over his shoulder to unsuccessfully search the darkness for signs or sounds of pursuit. Each time, no more sure of his escape than before he looked, he swung his head back and redoubled his efforts.

The race stretched on through a seemingly endless night and it wasn't until dawn's first gray light seeped through the jungle foliage that the small party finally drew to a halt. Gonzalo, his legs almost cramping, threw himself down slightly apart from the others.

A short distance away, the young woman, broken hearted and choked with despair, wept quietly. Tears rolled down her face and she made no attempt to wipe them away.

Now, I'm truly alone, thought Gonzalo. *I'll never see Geronimo or any other Christian ever again. Even Iccauhtli is gone.*

Stripped of his last companions, and along with them the final vestiges of familiarity, Gonzalo felt utterly alone.

It's come to pass, he thought, *I've nothing left.*

Just as when he fled the seminary as a youth, he felt a chapter of his life, written and read, had slammed shut behind him. After a short time, a quiet voice interrupted his gloomy reverie and caused him to look up. The party was again on their feet and the short wiry man, who appeared to be in charge, stood before him. The man nodded, then motioned with his hand to indicate that they were leaving and that Gonzalo should follow.

As the group again hurried away, Gonzalo swiftly stripped off Valdivia's jacket. For a single brief moment he regarded the garment with a mixture of sorrow and disgust, then, decisively, he wadded it into a tight ball and cast it as far as he could into the underbrush.

I'm Gonzalo Aroça, he thought. *I came into the world naked, and naked I'm reborn. Neither God nor man controls my fate. I make my own destiny.*

He turned and jogged after the trotting natives.

Chapter 35

The Lord of Fire

11 Bak'tun 14 K'atun 11 Tun 13 Uinal 16 K'in

(January 14, 1512)

The haab' had turned many times following the death of Ah K'in Cutz's father and, with each turn of its great wheel, the memory of his sire's callous uncaring face had grown less defined. Cutz considered himself a particular man and it unsettled him that he couldn't remember those stony features which once so overshadowed his world.

While memory of his father's visage grew increasingly nebulous, his loathing for the man persisted both crisp and sharp. Among the multitude of people that Cutz despised his long-dead father held a special place.

When, drenched in sweat and wracked with pain, the acerbic old aayin (crocodile) lay in wait for the start of his journey to Metnal, young Cutz had struggled not to crow his mad elation to the sky. With his three elderly uncles and his two insufferable brothers already feasting with the skeletal lord of death, Cutz had confidently assumed that he would sit upon Xamanzamá's throne. His detested father was as good as dead and, as his only remaining son, Cutz was the last of his ruling bloodline.

The unexpected arrival of old Ah Kumix Uinic who'd marched from Tzamá with his swaggering nacon, Ac Yanto, had dashed those expectations as surely as Heart of Sky's storm recently laid waste to Tzamá's huts. For Cutz, those long-ago days were a swift procession of delightful expectations, followed rapidly by sweeping despair. In the end, all that had remained was a gnawing anger and a banked but smoldering bitterness.

Cutz, who'd slit Zac Nok's throat, was an older more devious man, his resentment unquenchable, and his hatreds grown larger-than-life. Day in and day out, memories of his lost birthright, past insults, and suffered degradations rang through every fiber of Ah K'in Cutz's being.

Hatred of enemies, both real and imagined, drove most of his waking thoughts and actions. Unexpectedly, somewhere deep beneath the tumult of his unbroken rage, the events at Tixmul had triggered a feeling long forgotten, a budding anticipation.

If I'd planned it, he thought, *I couldn't have laid a better snare, Zac Nok and Gucumatz both dead! Their deaths were much too easy. Just the same, they now sit at Ah Puch's table to be sickened by his protruding ribs and his skull-like grin. And I, I at last, move forward toward my truest destiny. Ah Tabai is alone. He needs support, new advisors. Ac Yanto is a fool and the Lord of Fire well knows it. He'll turn to me. There's no one else. He has no choice!*

Such were the thoughts of Xamanzamá's high priest as he trotted toward Tzamá. Just ahead of him, a lean young warrior set a brisk and unbroken pace. A few steps behind his back, Dwarf-wind, dressed and sweating profusely beneath his gaudy feathered cloak, regaled Cutz with a steady wheezing and puffing. Behind the exhausted would-be groom the footfalls of a second Tzamán warrior beat another steady tattoo.

"Don't worry Lord Dwarf-wind," Cutz threw back, carefully masking his distain. "Our tiring journey draws to its end. You are soon to be the son of a god. Soon you'll enjoy all of the hospitality that Tzama affords its chosen."

The flattering words tried to stick in Cutz's craw, but they were quickly rewarded by an animated grunt from the sweating Ichpaatúnian.

Now, Cutz grinned, *the fat fool will finish our journey with little further delay.*

Upon the cessation of the bloodletting at Tixmul, Cutz, as senior ah k'in, had promptly asserted his authority. When no one stepped forward to question his commands, he'd swiftly and shrewdly assumed undisputed control over Tzamá's delegation.

Immediately, he'd dispatched a runner to Ah Tabai. This was expected of him and unavoidable, but, to maintain control of what narrative reached the Lord of Fire's royal ears, he chose his messenger carefully. Rather than select one of Gucumatz's seasoned and trusted warriors, he picked a fleet-footed but dull-witted slave from the far pavilion. Cutz chose the slave because he knew virtually nothing of the night's events. He imperiously instructed the slave to hasten back to Tzamá as fast as his strong legs could carry him.

"Once you are there," he directed him, "tell the Lord of the Fire that blood has been spilled. Tell him that the deceivers from

Ichpaatún violated the sanctity of our marriage gathering and that they attacked his emissaries."

The slave trembled. "Great Ah K'in," he quavered, "what more?"

"Nothing," hissed Cutz, "not a word. The night is yet confused. It's too soon to know the full extent of Ichpaatún's treachery. In the morning, the rest of us will follow with clearer details."

The slave had shuffled from foot to foot. Although slow-witted, he was much alarmed at the thought of carrying such an incomplete message to his Lord of Fire.

"But Great Ah K'in…"

Cutz cut him off. "You have your message fool! Run! Your life depends on your speed."

With a lingering look of terror, the man turned and fled into the darkness.

Ah Tabai will learn the fates of Gucumatz and Zac Nok soon enough, Cutz had mused, *but it will be from my own lips and, I will be there to drink in his dismay. It's like a game of Bul (war game of chance) and now the kernels fall in my favor.*

Following the messenger's hasty departure, Cutz had organized the remaining Tzamáns into two groups. The larger, which consisted of most of the warriors, the assorted courtiers, and all of the slaves, he placed under the commanded of Tuunich Lap' (Stone Fist) a hulking man, who had been Gucumatz's key lieutenant. Cutz ordered this group to care for and transport the bodies of their Lord of Fire's slain subjects, including those of Nacon Gucumatz and Ah K'in Zac Nok. He also decreed that Stone Fist's party should take charge of their Lord of Fire's prisoners.

When Itz'at Acan and his companions bolted into the jungle with Za'azil, Te' K'ab', two other steadfast warriors from Ichpaatún, and two of that party's porters had remained to battle the Tzamáns and safeguard their friends' escape. Nachan Can's five retainers struggled boldly, but, badly outnumbered and lightly armed, one by one, they fell to Gucumatz's enraged men.

When the killing finally stopped only six of Ichpaatún's delegation remained: Dwarf-wind, his majordomo, Chiccan, his two female servants, Ihuicatl and Xoco, and the brothers, Akbit and Bitol. It was these, with the exception of Dwarf-wind, that Cutz ordered Stone Fist to bind and conduct to Tzamá.

The second group that Cutz assembled consisted of only himself, Dwarf-wind, and two of Gucumatz's holcánob, warriors of lesser rank. Once Cutz arranged the disposition of the two parties, he announced that his smaller group was leaving for Tzamá immediately and imperiously directed Tuunich Lap' to remain in Tixmul until dawn and then follow as best he could.

It was most unseemly that Yajawk'ak' should linger like a simple commoner in Tzamá's entrance plaza. Nonetheless, regardless of the crudeness of the situation, the ruler's agitation had grown to such an extent that impropriety paled in comparison.

A full day, a long night, and most of another day had come and gone since the exhausted messenger from Tixmul had collapsed into the arms of Tzamá's gate wardens.

Ah Tabai, man and god, kept his true emotions on a short leash. Undisputed leader of Tzamá, he prided himself on his ability to suppress fear, elation, joy, and sorrow; his every ruling act was an exercise in cold calculation. Still, when word arrived that other runners from Tixmul were approaching, he had hurriedly gathered his retainers and rushed to the small entrance plaza fronting the city's main gate.

As he waited, Ah Tabai considered the messenger from Ah Kin Cutz and his thoughts again pulled his handsome face into a worried frown. The man had run himself three breaths short of death and on his arrival he had done little more than gasp incoherent babble about bloodshed and betrayal. Even after he somewhat recovered, the fool was so cowed by his Lord of Fire's presence that through chattering teeth he barely managed to mumble that the emissaries from Ichpaatún were deceivers and that several Tzamáns were dead.

All attempts to elicit further details from the slave had proved futile and Ah Tabai raged at his lack of knowledge. For a brief moment he had even considered putting the messenger to death. Then, he had looked into the man's eyes, seen his pitiful condition, his obvious lack of intelligence, and simply waved him away in disgust.

Standing by the gate arch under K'inich Ajaw's sweltering gaze, Ah Tabai felt his dripping brow might burst from the pressure of unanswered questions.

There's no breeze. What has happened in Tixmul? Why did Xamanzamá's ah kin send the messenger and not Zac Nok or Gucumatz? Have our plans somehow unraveled? Which of our people have died? Can this mean that Nachan Can risks open war?

Ah Tabai had just ordered that benches, shade, and refreshments be brought when a glistening young warrior exploded out of the gate arch. At the unexpected sight of his Lord of Fire, the man stammered, "K'uhul Ahua (Divine Lord)," instantly sank to his knees, and then threw himself full length onto the ground.

As dust settled about his prostrate form, Ah Kin Cutz trotted into the plaza. For a moment he locked eyes with Ah Tabai, neither man's gaze revealing anything to the other. Then, he too stretched himself out onto the warm ground. A moment passed, then a coughing Dwarf-wind appeared with the second warrior nearly pushing him from behind. At the sight of the Lord of Fire, the warrior immediately joined Cutz and his fellow on the ground.

Dwarf-wind remained standing, and the crowd of gathered retainers, all of whom were chatting and laughing before the arrival of the first warrior, lapsed into an uneasy stillness. As Dwarf-wind fastidiously dusted himself off, the Lord of Fire stared in disbelief.

This pek' (dog) from Ichpaatún remains standing. He thinks himself an equal!

Ah Tabai wrestled with an urge to lash out at the arrogant nook'ol (worm). Instead, being Yajawk'ak', he held his anger in check and waited close-mouthed for others from Tixmul to arrive.

His presence offends me, he thought, *yet this creature is nothing but a counter in a game that I myself set in motion.*

In the face of Ah Tabai's silence, Dwarf-wind looked closely at the expectant Tzamáns. The Lord of Fire was seated on an ornate carved bench that two stewards had just set in place. Behind him, four slaves were positioning themselves so that the large woven fans they carried would best shield their lord from the harshest of K'inich Ajaw's baleful stare. Slightly behind Ah Tabai, standing near at hand on his left and on his right, Dwarf-wind recognized the ruler's two wives, Lady Sunstroke and Lady Waterlily Sprout. Next, he noticed the Lord of Fire's drooling idiot son, Yajawte', and, on the ground beside the slack-jawed heir's sandaled feet, his younger sister, Whirling Squirrel playing with a shiny green beetle. As Dwarf-wind's eyes roamed across the other edgy notables and servants crowded into the small plaza they abruptly fell upon the sensuous figure of Ah Tabai's elder daughter, Mad Seizure Star.

At the sight of this beauty, a beauty that Dwarf-wind was convinced would soon ride his engorged cock, a rush of lust and ambition shoved the horrific events at Tixmul toward the recesses of his mind and sidetracked all thought of his present circumstances.

Unfortunate, he thought, *but what truly matters is that I'm to be the wedded son of Yajawk'ak', nearly a god myself. A god, an ah k'in, and a chilam, I will stand head and shoulders above my self-righteous brothers. Ah-cambal and Nachan Can, will kneel at my feet.*

Driven by his fantasy, Dwarf-wind raised his voice so that all present would be sure to hear, and then casually addressed the Lord of Fire.

"Father, if I may make so bold to call you such…"

The words scarcely crossed Dwarf-wind's lips when Ah Tabai bolted violently to his feet. The slaves attempting to shade and fan him staggered back in fright and the crowd gasped. Ignoring a stunned Dwarf-wind as though he did not exist the City of the Dawn's ruler sputtered at the prostrate priest from Xamanzamá

"Get up Cutz! What's the meaning of this? Why are you here instead of Gucumatz or my brother? Where are the others?"

Cutz rose cautiously. "Great Yajawk'ak', although I am unworthy, I am here to serve you as best I can."

"Enough," growled Ah Tabai, "save your fawning ah k'in. Give me the truth of what's occurred at Tixmul. The messenger you sent used his tongue to so little effect that I almost ordered it yanked from his empty head. Where are Nacon Gucumatz and Ah K'in Zac Nok?"

This is the moment, thought Cutz. Then, he looked directly into Ah Tabai's eyes and intoned with all the solemnity that he could muster.

"Dead Lord, both of them are dead."

It was as though a stout wooden cudgel struck the back of Ah Tabai's head.

Dead! This cannot be!

The Lord of Fire's thoughts screamed in opposition, but his ears heard the certainty of Cutz's words and his eyes registered their truth in the priest's emotionless stare. As abruptly as he had stood a moment before, Ah Tabai took a wobbly step backwards and dropped heavily onto his bench. Behind him, amid a multitude of gasps and cries, a crazed keening burst from Mad Seizure Star's throat.

At the same instant, unbidden, a powerful image flooded into Cutz's mind. At its heart, the old god Tláloc, in his feral, goggle-eyed, jaguar incarnation, belly-laughed in benediction.

He gloats, this is his revenge, thought Cutz. *Ah Tabai, Gucumatz, and Zac Nok perverted Chaac's ceremony of sacrifice and offered it to Buluc Chabtan. Gods do not forget or forgive. Even the powerful offend them at their peril.*

"Thank you for this gift Oh Great One," Cutz intoned silently. "As soon as I am able I will give you the offering of blood you so richly deserve."

He knew beyond a doubt that his patron had interceded. The momentous shock and confusion in Ah Tabai's eyes spoke of an angry god's intervention and it was far better than any imagining.

Life is good, thought Cutz.

Ah Tabai had consolidated power over all the canob (people) who call themselves Ekab and he had raised The City of the Dawn to new heights of glory. Gucumatz and Zac Nok were the levers he had used to do the lifting.

Gone, he thought, *my strongest spear broken and my endless fount of cunning run dry.* The ruler of Tzamá glanced at those gathered in the plaza. *Who among these sycophants can hope to take their places?* Ah Tabai felt as though he'd suddenly lost two limbs. *A stool cannot stand with two of its legs broken.* But then, just as swiftly as doubt had clouded his mind, the fog cleared. Ah Tabai rose regally to his feet. *I am yet Yajawk'ak',* he thought, *and any stool that can be broken can be repaired.*

"Cutz," he commanded, "speak! I will know the story behind this calamity!"

"Great Yajawk'ak'," began Cutz, "as you wished, we arrived at Tixmul in advance of Lord Dwarf-wind and his party and we prepared to receive them as befits his anticipated station."

Although Cutz's spoke in a strong voice that carried well, angry muttering from the Tzamáns, topped and surpassed by Mad

Seizure Star's ongoing caterwaul, muddled his words. Ah Tabai glared about, and, clearly annoyed, turned to Lady Sunstroke.

"Take our wailing daughter and await me elsewhere. And you, Kuknab (Waterlily Sprout), take the other children and leave here as well."

"Perhaps," ventured Dwarf-wind, "I should accompany Mad Seizure Star to make sure of her health?"

Ah Tabai gave the lesser lord of Ichpaatún a look that he might have employed if he had unexpectedly been addressed by a large scaly iguana.

"You remain!" He snapped. Then, he faced the crowd. "Leave! All of you, except my holcánob!" The small plaza emptied like a pot whose bottom had shattered and, moments later, only the Lord of Fire, Ah K'in Cutz's party, and three fives of grim-faced warriors remained.

"Continue Cutz," grunted the ruler, "but move quickly to the heart of the matter."

"The guilt lies with Ichpaatún's nacon," resumed Cutz, conveniently ignoring the fact that the whole gathering at Tixmul was intended as prelude to an even greater deceit. "While we feasted Lord Dwarf-wind's imminent nuptial, the poisonous young snake, Hoch Can, goaded Gucumatz and then made an unprovoked assault. His violence must have been planned as others acted in concert. While our Lord Gucumatz's attention focused on Hoch Can, Ichpaatún's ah k'in attacked from behind. Before Gucumatz became aware of his danger, the coward stabbed him three times dealing a mortal blow."

"Can this be true?" Ah Tabai croaked in disbelief. "You tell me that a boy and a feeble old man vanquished Gucumatz, Tzamá's mightiest warrior?"

"Truly," answered Cutz, still unrolling the tale that he had concocted. "It was their duplicitous hands that slew our champion, but they paid. While Gucumatz yet drew breath his war-club ushered them both onto the sacbe (white road) to Metnal."

"Lord," whined Dwarf-wind in obvious agitation, "my nephew was ever an impetuous fool. I tried to leave him in Ichpaatún, but my stubborn brother wouldn't hear of it."

Gucumatz dead, thought Ah Tabai. *Was this deliberate? Did Ah-cambal somehow divine our plans? That cannot be; yet can it be discounted?* Ignoring Dwarf-wind, the Lord of Fire again addressed Cutz.

"What of my brother, Zac Nok?"

"More treachery," intoned the priest. "At the instant when Hoch Can threw himself against Gucumatz, and all eyes focused in their direction, one of Ichpaatún's lesser chilán, an acolyte of Ah K'in May, spun about and suddenly slit Ah K'in Zac Nok's throat. Your brother died instantly."

"Yes! Yes!" blurted Dwarf-wind, "another traitor!"

Ah Tabai regarded the short puffy faced Ichpaatúnian with scarcely disguised hatred, but again queried Ah K'in Cutz.

"And this chilán," he growled. "What became of him?"

It is as if I put the words in his mouth, thought Cutz.

"He died with my knife in his heart. I could do nothing for Ah K'in Zac Nok."

"And, the rest of the party from Ichpaatún, were they slaughtered as they deserved?"

"Alas Lord, we killed some and captured others, but some managed to escape."

"Great Yajawk'ak'," jumped in Dwarf-wind, "those who died and those escaped were traitors, traitors all of them, to both Tzamá and to Ichpaatún. Those of us who remained are your devoted subjects. I have no words to express my shame and sorrow, yet everything that good Ah K'in Cutz has told you is sadly the truth. I saw my nephew's and my uncle's treachery with my own eyes."

Ah Tabai stared at Dwarf-wind for so long that Dwarf-wind became self-conscious of his own appearance. Usually, his long hair was oiled and carefully coiffed and his body perfumed with expensive aromatic unguents. After his tiring journey from Tixmul, his hair was in disarray and his usually crisp garments were dusty and ripe with sweat. Worst of all, his exquisite bird-feather cloak, a gift from the demi-god standing before him was soiled and tattered.

Ah K'in Cutz was right, he thought. *I should never have worn it.*

"Come closer," commanded Ah Tabai.

Feeling uncertain, Dwarf-wind stepped forward. "Lord?"

While not a warrior of Gucumatz's size or prowess, Ah Tabai was still an impressive personage. He stood nearly a head taller than most men and his lean body was one of sinew and muscle.

Looking down into Dwarf-wind's face, he held the smaller man's gaze while clasping his large hands to either side of his head.

"You watched your family's treachery with your own eyes?"

"Yajawk'ak', I would that they were never born!"

"You watched them?" demanded Ah Tabai as he placed his callused thumbs upon the smaller man's eyelids. "With these eyes?"

Ah Tabai pushed in against the closed lids and a whimper escaped Dwarf-wind's lips. In response, the Lord of Fire pressed even harder. Suddenly in excruciating pain, Dwarf-wind began to writhe and struggle. His whimpers turned to screams. He lashed out violently with his arms and legs, but the larger man's hands clamped about his head like two immoveable blocks of stone. The claw-like thumbs drove deep into his eyes. When Dwarf-wind's screams and thrashing finally ceased, blood drenched Ah Tabai fingers.

Chest heaving slightly from his exertion, the Lord of Fire fastidiously wiped first one hand and then the other on the unconscious man's once precious feathered cloak. Then, turning his back, he let Dwarf-wind's ruined body crumple to the ground.

"It is almost certain, Lord," dared Cutz, while suppressing a vicious smile, "that he knew nothing of the planned attack upon Nacon Gucumatz and Ah K'in Zac Nok. Nachan Can's young brother was not a man to be trusted with secrets. Dwarf-wind is a conceited fool."

"Now he'll be a dead fool," barked Ah Tabai. Then, he turned to one of his holcánob and nudged Dwarf-wind with a sandaled foot, "Take this offal, slit its throat, and feed it to the crabs."

"His garments also?" Queried the warrior, greedily eyeing the crimson feathers of the once magnificent cloak.

"Burn them!" Shouted Ah Tabai. "And do it now!"

Reacting to the Lord of Fire's outburst, the warrior, and three of his fellows, grabbed Dwarf-wind's limbs and hurried away from their ruler's wrath. Except for the remaining holcánob, Cutz and Ah Tabai now stood alone in the silent plaza.

"Walk with me," grunted the demi-god.

Ah Tabai waved his anxious warriors away and then he steered Cutz into the heart of his domain. After a short silent walk, the two men stood before the steps of Tzamá's great temple.

"The ill-starred deaths of Gucumatz and my brother vex me deeply," confessed the Lord of Fire, "but my own life goes on. I think; no, I believe, that Hun Ahau (Chak Ek' - the planet Venus) yet favors my endeavors against Ichpaatún. What think you?"

It's now as I knew it would be, thought Cutz, *he seeks advice. Soon, he'll follow my lead.*

"Yajawk'ak'," said the flinty priest, "I am a humble ah k'in and although devoted to our gods, many of their whims yet remain mysterious. The ways of men are transparent. If Nachan Can orchestrated this obscenity against you, he must be punished. His family must be extinguished, his name relegated to oblivion. If he was ignorant of events, he will soon rise against you and so needs face the same destruction. I am sure that Hun Ahau supports you Lord. Don't delay! Call out Tzamá's holcánob, rally your vassal towns, and crush the nest of the vipers that infest Ichpaatún."

He echoes Gucumatz's words which I once deflected, mused Ah Tabai. *But where my nacon's words were the ill-conceived offspring of anger and injured pride, Cutz's advice reeks of logic and purpose.*

"I agree," he answered. "Zac Nok's original plan for Ichpaatún's subjugation was a thing of beauty and simplicity. All that is gone. Now, the way ahead of us is difficult, but it still leads to the destruction of our enemies."

"Us" and "our," he includes me in his circle, reveled Cutz.

"The murders of your brother and Tzamá's great nacon weaken you, lord, but perhaps there is yet opportunity to be seized. Nachan Can will reel from the loss of his son and heir, and Ichpaatún is without its ah k'in. If you can put aside your loss and strike before they can put away theirs..."

"Tzamá is also without our ah k'in," retorted Ah Tabai.

Cutz dropped to his knees. "Halach Uinic, I am but the ah k'in of lowly Xamanzamá, but I seek to serve in your shadow."

Ah Tabai gazed down at Cutz, taking note of his submissive posture and his ruined hand.

This one plots and schemes, he thought. *And, although he has been chastised, his ambition still knows no bounds. He professes loyalty, yet I only trust him at my peril. Still, his mind is sharp and devious, and I must now employ every weapon at my disposal.*

A decision made, he addressed Cutz. "Rise," he commanded, "to be ah k'in of Tzamá and stand in the light of your Lord of Fire is a great honor. It is an honor that you have yet to earn. Our future, however, lies before us in shadow and you will have many opportunities to prove your worth. For now you will remain here at my side and occupy my brother's house. Send my summons to Xamanzamá. Tell Ac Yanto that his Lord of Fire commands his presence. He is to pick up his shield and his spear, gather his warriors from far and wide, and then stand in this spot before Ix Chel again shows us her face (full moon)."

"Ac Yanto is not the formidable warrior he once was," murmured Cutz.

"I am aware of my subjects' limitations," responded Ah Tabai evenly. "Yet, Nachan Can knows that I must retaliate for his family's outrage and his people know that my retaliation will be swift and sure. Our warriors gain courage from Ichpaatún's fear so we must act quickly.

"The Batab Kinich was once my father's nacon and, while not the giant of yore, he still serves my immediate purpose. On the other hand, your own words carry truth. What is the name of the formidable warrior who leads Xamanzamá's holcánob?"

"Ch'o Ho'ol, Lord," answered Cutz.

"Good, include this Rat Skull in my summons."

With that, Ah Tabai turned and walked briskly away.

Cutz watched his retreating back and smiled. It was a wide unfriendly smile that lingered many long minutes.

The sacred wheel had turned and the day was 2 Kib'. Death-birds of night and day were taking wing.

Chapter 36

A Trading Party

11 Bak'tun 14 K'atun 11 Tun 13 Uinal 18 K'in

(January 16, 1512)

For the first time in his mostly uneventful life, Okib felt a strong and unexpected gratitude for the untold bundles of firewood that he and Naum, year after year, had collected, secured, and lugged puffing back to their village. K'inich Ajaw was crawling across the heavens for the eighth time since Okib nodded respectfully to his mother, threw back his shoulders, and, bursting with manly pride, marched resolutely away from K'optela.

As each of those long weary days wound past, the basket of trade goods which hung from his back, suspended by a tumpline around his forehead, had grown heavier. Both he and his friend, Naum, were flushed with excitement when Naum's maternal uncle, Xáak'ab (Long Steps), announced that a trading party would soon depart for Ichpaatún. And, that since they were both beyond their em-ku (coming of age rite), they were to be included. Even though the trade embassy represented the boys' first true activity as grown men, Okib had come to view their inclusion in the expedition as a dubious and excessively sweaty honor.

"Naum! Naum!" he hissed at the boy walking in front of him. "Your uncle means to walk us to death. It's well past lunch time."

Although his stride exhibited a slight unsteadiness, Okib's heavier friend had yet to complain, not even once.

"Why must you always prattle so?" Naum grunted back over his shoulder. "Long Steps knows what he's doing. You and I are both warriors now. He expects the same from us as he expects from the other men. We'll stop when we stop."

A good-natured gibe on the subject of his friend's weight, and Naum's usual predilection for food, formed swiftly in Okib's mind. Just as quickly, the clever words withered in his throat. Long Steps trod purposefully at the head of their party and, directly in front of him, a heavily muscled man had leapt scowling from the jungle. Regaled in the paint and trappings of war, the hostile stranger blocked their path, growled and brandished a fearsome spear.

"Why do you approach Ichpaatún?" bellowed the strange warrior.

At his challenge, the men from K'optela fell tensely silent. Surprised and worried, Okib glanced from side to side. His eyes went wide. Two other well-armed strangers crouched partially concealed in the nearby foliage.

"Naum," he whispered urgently, "there are more of them!"

Before he could utter another word, Long Steps spread wide his arms and stepped casually toward the man who blocked his path.

"Chicahua, he reassured, his voice quiet, solid, and smooth, "you know me well. We've drunk and wagered together many times. I'm Long Steps. What's the meaning of this? As always, the people of K'optela come for friendship and trade."

"I do know you Long Steps, and you and your people are truly welcome," smiled Chicahua relaxing his fierce stance, "but you must know that you come to us at a time of great sorrow and misfortune. The death bat soars aloft in our skies."

As the other men of K'optela waited hesitantly, Long Steps stepped forward and conversed with Chicahua in quiet earnest tones. While Naum's uncle and the stranger spoke, Okib and Naum tried their best to listen, but the two men's words were so quiet that neither youth could overhear. After what felt an unbearable wait, Long Steps turned to his companions.

"Unexpected events overtake us," he announced. "But all is well, and as planned, we continue to Ichpaatún. Chicahua here and his friends will serve as our escort."

At that, Chicahua motioned to the surrounding jungle and the two men Okib had spotted stepped forward. To his immense surprise, four others also stepped out, seeming to materialize from nowhere.

"Naum," he murmured in awe, "they're like k'assi ba'al'ob (ghosts). That's how I'll move when I'm a true warrior."

Naum grinned and stifled a laugh. "I thought you were going to be a stilt-dancing chilam."

The rest of their journey to Ichpaatún passed swiftly and as K'inich Ajaw's last light began to slowly fade toward darkness Okib and Naum approached the city's impressive wall. The stone fortification was low, but it was also a public work beyond anything in either boys' limited experience.

"It's amazing," gasped Okib in a surprised whisper.

"One of many wonders," snorted an older man.

A few paces more and the party stood before a v-shaped arch that would grant them entrance. Long Steps signaled a halt and Chicahua and his fellows continued on into the city. Long Steps turned to address his companions.

"Brothers, as always Ichpaatún welcomes our trade, but, before we enter, you must know that Nachan Can's city is in turmoil. It teeters on the brink of war with its great and powerful neighbor, Tzamá."

Following this pronouncement, questions and mutters swirled forth from the K'optelans.

"Did you hear," gulped Okib, grasping his friend's arm. "Your uncle says that Ichpaatún is at war?"

"That's not what he said," retorted Naum. "He said that Ichpaatún and Tzamá are almost at war. That's not the same thing! I've heard my uncle say, many times, that, Nachan Can is a reasonable leader. He won't jump into a conflict that he can't win. Tzamá is much too powerful."

Ignoring Naum, Okib's excitement carried him forward.

"The people of Ichpaatún are our friends. You and I are warriors. Do you think they'll ask us to fight?"

Naum was saved from making the biting reply that poised on his lips by the appearance of a short, wiry, but well-dressed stranger who walked through Ichpaatún's gate with an obvious air of authority.

"Welcome," he intoned, "some of you know me. I am Itz'at Acan, first servant to Nachan Can, our Lord of Ichpaatún."

Further greetings were exchanged, then, the lean seneschal requested that Long Steps' party sit. Bundles were quickly set aside and everyone settled onto the ground. Without preamble, Acan also seated himself and coolly related the bloody events that unfolded at Tixmul and also Ichpaatún's subsequent fears regarding the turmoil that must surely follow.

"Now friends," he finished, "if you still wish to the trade and enjoy the hospitality of our city, your embassy is most welcome. I must return to my Lord, but if you choose to pass within our walls, Chicahua awaits you inside and he will see to your comfort."

With that, Itz'at Acan rose smoothly, turned, and disappeared into the city.

"All of you heard," intoned Long Steps. "All of you have a voice. Do we stay, renew our friendship with Ichpaatún, and risk much? Or, do we shoulder our bundles and return home?"

To Naum's astonishment, Okib spoke up.

"I... I can't explain why," he stuttered, "but I know that the gods want us to be in this place."

Several older men sniggered derisively at the pronouncement, but then Cualli, who was K'optela's second chilán, waved them into silence.

"Heed his words," the priest cautioned. "The gods often reveal to the young that which is hidden from the rest of us."

This pronouncement elicited a wave of responses and much discussion and in the end a vote was taken. Naum chose to return home. Okib voted to continue. The smaller boy's choice carried and, on Long Steps' command, bundles were once again lifted, adjusted, and the traders proceeded through the gap in Ichpaatún's wall. Just inside, they found their guide, Chicahua.

Compared to its larger rival, Tzamá, Ichpaatún was a modest city. Still, it stood a world apart from K'optela's comfortable sprawl of plastered mud and bunched palm fronds. At its core, Ichpaatún boasted plazas, temples, and unpretentious pyramids of painted stone. As Okib, Naum, and their companions followed in the footsteps of Chicahua, the young men's eyes stretched wide. Every few steps brought them another new vista, each of which made Okib feel that his home was hopelessly provincial.

"Naum," he marveled, gripping his friend's arm and shaking, "This is the center of the world! We live in the middle of nowhere! We're men, we need to stay here. We need to ..."

Well accustomed to his best friend's regular flights of passion, Naum often chose to ignore his enthusiastic pronouncements. Nevertheless, he grudgingly found himself forced to admit that their own village felt humble and worn by comparison. Equally plain to him, however, the brutal events related by Itz'at Acan had cloaked the impressive city in a mantle of worry and grief. While the people who passed by appeared outwardly to be about their normal routines, the community's underlying tone spoke of a place where things were sorely amiss.

The simple joys so evident in K'optela's daily life were missing or subdued. Instead, a deep restlessness and a palpable sorrow pervaded Ichpaatún's very air. Although Okib acted oblivious to its mood, the city made Naum feel dispirited and wary. It was as though something unpleasant and hidden watched from concealment.

After a short march, during which Naum frequently looked over his shoulder, the plazas and monuments of stone gave way to an area of more modest structures. Constructed of poles, stucco, and thatch, these edifices radiated out from Ichpaatún's core. Walking among them, their simplicity and familiarity lifted Naum's spirits. At a wide beaten-earth patio, located between a profusion of residences, kitchens, family shrines, and storage facilities, Chicahua drew to a halt and addressed his charges.

"We lack room to shelter you all as we would wish, but this enclosed space is shielded from the night breezes that blow in off the bay. You may set up camp here, lay out sleeping mats, and set cooking fires as you see fit. Our nights have been mild of late, but I'll send someone to you with sí (firewood)."

Pointing to his right he indicated a large, oval, thatch-roofed building, and continued.

"That is our young men's house. If you can find space, and if any of you so desire, you may shelter there, instead of here in the open. In the morning, I'll return and show you where in our market you can lay out your wares."

With that, Chicahua exchanged a few private words with Long Steps and departed. In the gathering shadows, the party from K'optela set down their bundles and began to arrange themselves for the coming night. As Naum and Okib prepared to unroll their sleeping mats, Naum's uncle approached them.

"Instead of out here," he suggested, "why don't the two of you try to find space inside with Ichpaatún's unmarried men? With luck, you'll meet other young men your own age. Perhaps, if you listen carefully, you may learn further information about the situation here. I believe that we've made the right decision by choosing to stay, but clearly the people of Ichpaatún are anxious. It may be that their condition is more perilous than Itz'at Acan and Chicahua have let on. There may be more of value to us that you can learn of their circumstances."

Surprised and almost shocked by Long Steps' words, Naum and Okib hurriedly agreed, gathered up their things, and walked toward the young men's house. Once they were ostensibly beyond earshot, Okib whispered in an awed tone.

"Did you hear? Your uncle confided in us! He wants us to spy!"

"No one said anything about spying," retorted Naum. "Long Steps just wants us to keep our ears open."

"And, then report back to him!" enthused Okib. "If that isn't spying…"

"Quiet!" cautioned Naum, "someone might hear you."

"So hush-hush eavesdropping?" smiled Okib teasing his friend.

Naum slapped him on the shoulder and pushed his smaller friend toward the entrance to the young men's house. The oval communal building was larger than several regular homes combined. Its solid stucco-plastered walls, decorated with simple geometric designs, rose as high as the top of Okib's head. After that, space was open for an arm's reach to allow fresh air to flow in and out. The roof, supported above the walls on poles, was steeply peaked to shed rain, and its thatch extended on all sides so that even a heavy downpour would not enter into the living space.

At the entrance Okib and Naum ducked under the edge of the roof and stepped through. Just across the threshold, they both stopped. Night gathered outside and within the young men's house shadows were even deeper.

"I can't see," grumbled Okib.

"You're not blind," clucked Naum. "Just wait."

Two small smokeless fires flickered dimly in the middle of the large room, and the friends' eyes slowly adjusted. Much of the floor space was taken up by woven mats and small bundles and piles of possessions, but in contrast there were only a few people. Scattered about, two or three young men sat by themselves. Four more squatted in conversation by one of the fires.

As Naum and Okib stood uncertainly holding their sleeping mats, one of the boys seated by himself stood up and walked over. For a moment, he just looked at them with curiosity, then he spoke.

"K'aam yéetel uts (welcome) you must be two of the traders from K'optela. My name is Tepeu."

"I'm Okib and this is Naum. Naum's uncle, Long Steps, is the leader of our party." announced the shorter K'optelan with pride.

Tepeu stared deep into Okib's face and stammered.

"Hoch Can, our nacon who was murdered by the Tzamáns, was my cousin, and Ah K'in May, who they also killed, was my great grandfather."

For a moment the three young men shared an uncomfortable silence. Okib looked down at his feet.

"We grieve for your loss," solemnly offered Naum. "We can only imagine how it must feel to lose loved ones to such sudden ruthlessness."

"It's difficult," replied Tepeu. "They were good men. I miss them both. Their journeys to the underworld are complete, but later tonight we will petition the gods so that they may be born again and take their place among the lights in the heavens."

"We would like to join you in your petition, if we may?" suggested Naum.

"Of course," answered Tepeu, "everyone is welcome. But, for now let's find a place for you to lay out your mats. Follow me."

Turning, he led them away from the entrance toward a back part of the large room that lay mostly shrouded in darkness. As they approached, a man seated in the shadows with his back to the wall quickly rose to his feet. With a start Naum and Okib both took a worried step back. The man was tall, lean, and his face was so hairy that for a moment they doubted that he was indeed a man. Tepeu looked amused.

"Like you," he smiled, "this is also our guest. But if his tales are to be believed, he comes from a world much farther away."

Chapter 37

Grief and Lamentation

11 Bak'tun 14 K'atun 11 Tun 13 Uinal 18 K'in

(January 16, 1512)

Nachan Can was Hoch Can's father. More importantly, he was the undisputed ruler of Ichpaatún, thus the weighty decision rested solely upon his own tired shoulders. It was he, and he alone, who resolved to inter his cherished son alongside the dusty remains of their family's honored ancestors.

A man's burial inside the confines of his own house was a long-followed custom in their city, but Nachan Can could not put aside that Hoch Can had been his chosen heir. His son, his dead son, had been a fledgling man of substance, a future leader of unrealized potential, a war chief. If Hoch Can's own home was ignored, the obvious choice for the boy's interment lay within Ichpaatún's main temple.

The great temple was dedicated to, and, more significantly, watched over by the benevolent bee god, Ah Muzencab. His pyramid dominated the city's main plaza. It served as a central focus for the polity's busy day to day life. Despite the temple's prominence, Nachan Can favored Ichpaatún's smaller plaza. Its lower truncated pyramid already guarded the tombs of two of his family's storied relations. Appropriately, to the sajal's mind, that minor temple also lay to boox chik'in (black west) and long, long, ago, in the time of mystery, it was consecrated to the aged hunting deity, Sip, Sip with his long deer ears and his hoary antlers.

Nachan Can felt certain that if the longstanding and experienced hunter walked stealthily along at his dead son's side that the old god would surely guide and smooth Hoch Can's journey into the afterlife.

From amid the sheltering columns of one of Ichpaatún's royal residences Za'azil stared out into a torchlight-scattered darkness. Her people packed tightly into the small square. Across its crowded expanse crouched the small pyramid with its newly excavated tomb. The vault lay open. It awaited her beloved.

During the long days leading up to this portentous night, Ichpaatún's common people had held their churning emotions ever at bay. With stoic calm they'd endured the pressure of their combined and pent up grief. In K'inich Ajaw's harsh light, they'd wept together in wounded silence, bemoaning the untimely loss of their brave young Nacon, that of their treasured Ah K'in May, and of Te' K'ab' and, indeed, of all those who never returned from Tixmul. Now, cloaked in a night of near moonless darkness, their strident and mournful cries echoed and re-echoed across the square.

Za'azil crushed her hands against her ears until they hurt. It did little good. The wailing laments seemed to pry her fingers apart and insidiously worm their way past. It was as though, each new cry piled a heavy and jagged stone upon the fragments of her broken heart.

K'inich Ajaw stalks the underworld as Lord Balam, she thought. *He battles with the lords of night. When he prevails, as he assuredly must, he will once again bring forth the glorious day. I care not! My light is extinguished! When the sun god again shows his radiant face, I shall remain staggering in darkness.*

In life, Hoc Can seemed to carry a glowing torch that cast a joyous light into all the darkened corners of Za'azil's existence. Now those shadowed corners would remain forever in gloom. The years ahead seemed to promise her nothing save old age and a crushing loneliness.

The remains of her beloved husband lay before the dark maw of his beckoning tomb, a shrouded outline, a tight wrapping of cotton cloth.

Nothing more! In her heart, she fervently hoped that Hoc Can's soul had flown. *Warriors who die in battle are transported directly to the heavens. Surely, the gods are grateful for his sacrifice, the violence of his death.*

Try as she might, she could not find it in her heart to link the spirit of that motionless white bundle with the warm and vibrant man that she so recently held in her arms.

Where is his light? Where is his laughter?

The scene swam before her eyes. Her stomach growled a protest. Za'azil couldn't remember when last she'd eaten. She'd fasted and watched, as expected, while Ah-cambal, assisted by Itz'at Acan, cleaned and carefully prepared Hoch Can's broken body. She'd watched with flowing tears as they painted him red with cinnabar.

That her husband should not lack in the afterlife, they'd filled his mouth with ground maize and koyem (maize, cacao, and water) and placed at his side large piles of cacao seeds, and stone counters used for money. To these grave offerings Ah-cambal had added whistles carved from rocks into the shapes of gods and animals, small aids to ensure that Hoch Can's wandering spirit remained ever at Sip's side and found the secret way out of Xibalba and into the heavens.

Rings of jade were slipped onto her dead lover's stiffened fingers and bracelets tied around his arms. As befitted the heir to Ichpaatún, before his shroud was wrapped tight, a jade necklace was fastened about his neck and an elaborate mask of red shell fitted loosely over his broken face.

The fact that no such honors could be given to Ah K'in May, a friend and mentor that she also loved deeply, dug deeper into the depths of Za'azil's misery.

A small group of seasoned warriors, heavily armed and led by Chicahua, had returned to Tixmul to search for their priest's body, and also for the other members of Dwarf-wind's ill-fated wedding party. Although anger and worry had hurried their pace, and the men raced without stopping, by the time they arrived, Tixmul stood deserted, and the embassy from Tzama long gone. The remains of several of their friends lay scattered and desecrated, but no sign of their revered ah k'in was found. Disheartened, Chicahua's men had trudged back to Ichpaatún, empty-handed and morose.

Everyone agreed that May's soul undoubtedly entered a place of no pain, a refuge where he found an abundance of food and delicious drink, and a refreshing ceiba tree beneath whose branches and shade he might rest forever in peace. The strength of this belief did little to assuage the people's pain. The manner of his death and the disappearance of his remains twisted like a sharpened stake buried deep into the guts of Ichpaatún.

Za'azil felt yet again that she was about to cry. Then, to her uncomfortable surprise, she discovered that her earlier free-flowing tears were now dry. As she stared out across the plaza, and tried in vain, to make any sense of her tragedy, she saw Ah-cambal stand tall and erect beside Hoch Can's open tomb and its limestone sarcophagus. Two chacs were lowering her husband's body. As she watched, her dead husband's beloved uncle raised his arms and a growing silence spread through the gathered crowd. Someone lightly touched her back and she became aware of Nachan Can and Ix Chan Ek standing at her shoulder.

"Come daughter," said her mother-in-law, "it is time."

Am I still your daughter, wondered Za'azil? *When your son needed a wife, both you and your husband favored another. Has our bond died with Hoch Can? Am I truly still a daughter?*

Ix Chan Ek's stoic face gave no answer. At her side, Nachan Can looked beyond weary and his age sat more heavily upon his shoulders than Za'azil could ever have imagined possible. Ix Chan Ek still looked beautiful, the same, unchanging, but she also reminded Za'azil of an al che (child's doll) whose strings were tied so tightly that its limbs could barely move. Nachan Can nodded once in silence and then beckoned, indicating that he would lead the two women down the residence's stone steps and out across the square.

As they entered the waiting crowd, Za'azil looked about. Here in the square's least favorable viewing position, she realized that she was passing among strangers, perhaps the party of traders rumored to have arrived from K'optela. Among their unfamiliar faces, her eyes fell unexpectedly upon Hoch Can's well-loved cousin, Tepeu. The young man, who faced slightly away, was engaged in an earnest conversation with two strangers of about his own age.

At nearly the same time, Nachan Can spotted the youth, hailed him, and called him over.

"Nephew, come walk beside me. I need your sweet presence to remind me that Ichpaatún's future is not lost."

The sajal's voice was low and grave and Tepeu hurried to obey. As he jostled his way among the crowd, several people shifted. Staring in his direction, Za'azil became aware that she was looking into the bearded face and dark eyes of the tall Tzamán prisoner, the strange man who'd slain her attacker during the betrayal in Tixmul.

Unblinking, the man stared back into her eyes, his gaze unnerved her and rendered her motionless. As she stood frozen, a small self-conscious smile crossed the peculiar man's face and he pressed his right hand to his stomach. Holding his left hand out from his body, he drew back his right leg scraping his foot along the dirt, and bent slightly at the waist. She had no idea what his bizarre contortion signified, but the spell broke. She turned and hastily fled to join Ix Chan Ek and the others.

Nachan Can guided them. The throng parted respectfully, opening before them and then quickly closed in their wake. After a score of paces, with her head awhirl, Za'azil paused and glanced back. The stranger was gone.

You did what you believed right, she thought, but the idea brought no comfort. *Why? To what end? You know nothing of me. You should have let me die.*

When they reached a position directly in front of Hoch Can's sarcophagus, they stopped. On the steps of the pyramid, stood pottery vessels fashioned in the image of Sip. Inside burned cakes of the resin, pom. Each cake was carefully painted blue, the color of sacrifice, and decorated with intricate cross-hatching so that the offerings would curry the old god's favor.

Hoch Can's coffin now sat closed and upon its top the two chacs lit a small fire they had previously prepared. As the dry tinder caught and a dark smoke began to rise, the gathered people of Ichpaatún grew silent. All among them felt certain that the soul of their young lord was leaving his broken body and rising to join those of his ancestors.

Standing next to the tomb, Ah-cambal looked down at Za'azil and met her eyes. Then, seeming to grow in stature, he raised his arms and began to speak. The silence of Ichpaatún's people grew even deeper and his words echoed strongly across the plaza.

"Even as Kíimil soots' (the death bat) snatched the head of Hunahpu (one of the hero twins) to use in a ball court for the sport of the gods, monsters from Tzamá have snatched the lives of Hoch Can and Ah K'in May for their own sport. Tzamá didn't commit this terrible unjustifiable act of treachery for the gratification of any gods. They murdered our young nacon and our high priest for their own base and vicious pleasures!"

These words raised a loud and ongoing rumble of anger from the multitude.

"Hoch Can and Ah K'in May were brave men, good men!" continued Ah-cambal. "Rather than submit to humiliation and dishonor offered by the deceivers from Tzamá, they chose to fight back. They, and many of their companions, choose to die resisting, rather than to live submitting. Those who preserved their lives, and returned to us, fled only from dishonor. A time for our vengeance will soon come!"

Again the crowd roared.

"But now," announced Ah-cambal with a calming and placating gesture, "now it is our time for mourning."

Itz'at Acan, who stood nearby, stepped forward and placed a small ceramic pot and a stone saucer on a corner of Hoch Can's sarcophagus, laying them beside the chacs' smoking fire. Za'azil watched with a combination of anticipation and dread as Ah-cambal drew his knife and raised his voice.

"Hoch Can and Ah K'in May gave their precious blood to defend us. They gave their precious blood to propitiate our gods. Now, we sacrifice our own blood that we may hold at bay spirits who would interfere with their peaceful journey from Xibalba. We shed our own blood so that our loss and pain is made manifest."

Without another sound, Ah-cambal lay his left hand on the saucer and deliberately severed the first joint of his third finger. With not so much as a grimace, he lifted the severed finger bone and carefully placed it in the ceramic pot. The crowd roared. Blood dripping, he beckoned to Nachan Can and the sajal took his place next to the plate and bowl.

Za'azil's empty stomach clenched tighter and tighter, as in turn, Nachan Can, Ix Chan Ek, and Tepeu respectively took up the knife and laid their hands on the plate. With each piercing howl of the crowd, and with each bloody offering added to the pot, she felt her trepidation grow. Then, it was her hand placed on the plate.

"Hoch Can, my beloved, give me strength," she whispered as Ah-cambal laid a supportive hand on her shoulder and handed her the sacrificial blade by this time slippery with her relatives' blood.

Gonzalo had found himself in the midst of the disturbingly crowded square because the boisterous young men who shared the shelter in which he slept forcefully escorted him there. They'd tugged and pushed, indicating with excited words and gestures that something significant was going to occur and that he should be in attendance.

The packed plaza itself had immediately filled him with a deep and unnerving apprehension as its smoky torch-lit setting clawed up painful and unwanted memories. Then, he saw the woman. When she later accepted the knife, Gonzalo had turned away. An excited tumult of strange and savage voices filled his ears and the one-time escudero ducked his head and fled the plaza.

Many leagues away, Gonzalo's last shipwrecked companion clung to the darkest of shadows, hidden in a night already grown dark. Scarce ten days had passed since Gonzalo bade him, "Goodbye," and in that time Geronimo's already crazed world had once again changed almost beyond recognition. Some evil had befallen the proud procession that, by the light of bonfires, had marched resolutely from Tzamá.

Because of his failure to learn his captors' tongue, Geronimo could only imagine what that evil was. He knew that some of the party had returned two days before, and he also knew that Zac Nok, Gucumatz, and Gonzalo were not among them. The house in which he was forced to reside had been turned over to the unclean priest of the demon from Xamanzamá. This personage, aside from a swift kick and a few harsh words, ignored him as though he did not exist. Within its thick walls, the whole of the city of Tzamá seethed and churned.

Amidst calamitous turmoil, and disregarded by most, Geronimo had decided that his best option was to trust in the Lord, stay as unobtrusive as possible, and do his best to stay out of everyone's way.

To that end, he had crept to one of the city's most isolated corners where, at the very top of its sheer twelve-meter cliffs and hidden by darkness, he could pour forth his heart to his Lord and the pounding of the sea might carry away his words.

"Lord, I know that I am under your protection," he intoned. "You have sustained me in this benighted land so that I might bring its idolaters into thy kingdom, but I am weak Lord. I am weak! I cannot help but feel afraid. I am so weak. There is sweetness in thy service, yet I fear that the task thou hast lain on me I cannot carry through. I try Lord. I try, but the demon's sway here is great. I preach your holy word and it falls on deaf ears.

"Like Moses, I ask you Lord, why have you been so hard on your servant? And, why have I not found favor in your sight, that you have placed the weight of all these people on me? I know that it is only a burden in my mind, but I am so tired Lord, so tired. I implore thee, give me grace in thy example that I might find refreshment and rest from my toils and that joy might replace my sadness and fear."

In the silence that followed his appeal, Geronimo suddenly realized that someone approached. Using all the furtiveness that he could muster, he drew himself deeper into shadows and crouched down beside the trunk of a large tree.

Please God, he thought, *shield me from this person's sight.*

The person, a young woman, passed only a foot away from where he squatted. Either she chose to ignore his presence or simply overlooked him in the gloom. To his astonishment, even in the darkness, Geronimo recognized the unclean woman who tried to seduce him for the amusement of Zac Nok, Gucumatz, and their friends.

The woman walked to the very edge of the cliff and began what Geronimo immediately recognized as a lament. She cried out. She tore at her hair. She rent her garments. Then, abruptly silent, she adopted a pose that resembled the Diving God whose image adorned so many of Tzamá's temples.

In that instant, Geronimo knew what the young woman intended. He leapt to his feet.

"No!" He cried. "No! You mustn't!"

Then, he ran forward to prevent her act. The woman turned momentarily in his direction and gave him a curious look of resignation. Then, while he was still a heartbeat away, she calmly flung herself over the precipice.

Horrified, Geronimo cautiously stepped to the edge.

Far below, crushed against the jagged rocks at the cliff's base, and barely visible in the starlight, lay the broken body of Ix Co-tancas-ek (Lady Mad Seizure Star) princess of Tzamá.

Geronimo looked about himself to assure that he was unseen, and then hurried quickly away.

Chapter 38

Signs and Beginnings

11 Bak'tun 14 K'atun 11 Tun 13 Uinal 19 K'in

(January 17, 1512)

When the earliest words of Hoch Can's and Ah K'in May's deaths arrived, they struck like a rain of blows, and, with each and every strike, Ah-cambal felt a joyful piece of himself wither and die. He loved Hoch Can and he loved his aged uncle. His nephew's burial was everything it should have been and Ah K'in May had been near his time. Still, a darkness burrowed deep into the recesses of Ah-cambal's heart where it turned ruthlessly in upon itself.

I should take up my spear, my traveling pouch, he thought, *wander on my own. Perhaps if I listen to the whisperings of the gods, offer them sacrifice and acts of contrition they may lift this burden of sorrow.*

He craved solitude. He needed time to be alone. He needed time to mend. With these thoughts in his head, Ah-cambal's footsteps carried him into the young men's house. Moving more by habit than intent, he gathered together those few possessions that he liked to carry when he wandered. Once those were safely tucked into pouches, he filled his water gourd. Then, speaking to no one, he took his leave.

As he walked past Ichpaatún's outer wall, two of Hoch Can's warriors beckoned and called his name. Ah-cambal ignored them both. Aimlessly, he placed one foot ahead of the other and struck out on a little-used path, with no particular direction in mind. As he walked, the day-to-day sounds of Ichpaatún slowly faded from his ears. Thick brush closed in around him, and K'inich Ajaw crawled across the sky toward boox chik'in (black west).

Ah-cambal's thoughts churned and refused him the peace that he so desperately sought. Suddenly, the world felt like it shifted beneath his feet. He stumbled; caught himself. His stomach churned. A fluttering vibration resonated deep in his gut.

The great wheel, he thought. *The sacred Tzolk'in turns.*

Ah-cambal clutched tight to his spear and leaned upon it for support. A short distance further up his path, an unexpected tableau was unfolding.

A large poisonous snake menaced two small turkeys. One of the turkeys was of common plumage. The coloration of the other while not outlandish, struck Ah-cambal as somehow strange.

They're no match, he thought. *Surely the turkeys will die.*

The oddly colored bird bobbed up and down in front of the viper. It held the snake's attention. The other charged. It pecked violently at the back of the brute's head. The snake whipped around. Its fangs flashed. Just barely quick enough, the turkey leapt back. The snake hissed its anger. While distracted by its companion, the other turkey lunged forward and pressed its own attack.

As Ah-cambal watched transfixed. The scene repeated itself. Again and again, the snake struck at its feathered tormentors. Again and again, its fangs failed to find their mark. Ah-cambal slowly came to the improbable belief that the two small birds were gaining the upper hand.

Abruptly, the hard-pressed snake reached the same conclusion. Ignominiously, it slithered away, hissed a final time, and slunk beneath a large protective rock. The two turkeys, ignored the viper as though it had never existed, trotted away, and disappeared around a bend in the path.

The gods speak in our dreams, but they also speak in signs, reflected Ah-cambal. *I've seen their hand in the scatter of tzintè seeds, the shape of scudding clouds, and in the curl of smoke from an offering plate. I've also heard their voice in the cry of night birds and the drip of water in a cave. This is a message. But, which gods speak to me? What do they wish?*

Standing quietly where he stumbled, Ah-cambal searched for insight.

What is the meaning of the oddly colored bird?

As he pondered, a picture formed in his mind, a picture of the tall bearded stranger that he'd met in Tzamá, the stranger whose eyes spoke of intelligence and anger, the stranger who had unexpectedly returned from Tixmul with Itz'at Acan. In Ah-cambal's mind's eye, a rattlesnake curled opposite the stranger, the sun symbol of Tzamá. Ah-cambal struggled to understand the vision.

Intuition cannot be ignored. The Gods speak through instinct.

Because of Hoch Can's death, Ah-cambal had disregarded the stranger's arrival. He'd allowed Itz'at Acan and others see to the man's disposition.

That was a mistake. Instinct is the voice of the gods and instinct tells me that the cords of prophecy are bound tightly around that one. Whether his arrival bodes well or ill, is in the hands of the gods. They have not revealed their purpose, but they have given me a powerful sign and I've been a fool.

Turning on his heel, Ah-cambal hurried to retrace his steps.

At some distance from the bustle of Ichpaatún, Gonzalo, physically and emotionally hollowed, sat quietly on the shore of The Bay of Chectumal. Since his escape from the Tzamáns a range of powerful emotions had washed over him: panic, loneliness, worry, sorrow, and even a slight hint of happiness. With his knees drawn up close to his chest, he grappled with his internal demons.

The late afternoon was pleasant. The sun warmed, but it didn't scorch, and a fresh breeze floated in off the bay. The water which lapped quietly near his feet was clear, but a darker green than the bay where he and his companions first crawled ashore.

Marooned in starvation on the sandy beaches of this unmapped land, he'd sworn himself to survival. After Valdivia's gory death, he'd renewed his angry vow.

And now? I'm still alive, he thought, *but to what end?*

Little by little, regardless of his unwavering resolve, the melancholy and emptiness that once gripped Gonzalo in Xamanzamá were again taking root. Fueled by the senseless deaths of so many companions, Juan Pintero, Valdivia, Domingo, Pedro, Iccauhtli, and by everything else that he felt that he had lost, his gloom had slowly grown. Sitting by the shore, the void of the sea stretched before him and he felt his insignificance. Self-pity and despair again threatened to defeat and define him.

Almost daily since he'd struggled out of the surf in the Bay of Turtles thoughts of Spain had crawled unbidden into his mind. Despite all his past protestations to the contrary, he knew that, hidden away deep inside, he secretly longed for rescue.

I've lied to myself. Am I to go through life waiting for a deliverance that never comes? These people feed me. They let me come and go as I please. I'm no longer treated as a slave. Maybe I'm not even a prisoner?

The apparent ambiguity worried him. Time passed and a native approached from up the beach. The man walked slowly, hand in hand with a small girl who stopped frequently and pointed to things at their feet. As they neared, Gonzalo looked up. For a moment he gazed at the man's free hand and the cloth bandage that wrapped it. Red soaked through from where a mangled finger hid within and images of the previous night's bloody mourning bubbled to the fore of his mind. After staring for a moment, other images came to his mind, images of a crippled seller of salt and harvests of the sea.

"I've met you," he said.

"And, I you," replied the man, who was not so crippled or anywhere near as old as he had appeared in Tzamá. "May we sit?"

When Gonzalo gave a non-committal wave, the man settled comfortably onto the sand at his side. The girl offered him a friendly smile and crawled into the man's lap. The man then pointed to himself.

"I am Ah-cambal," and tousling the hair of the child, "This is Óolal."

"Look at him, Grandfather" gushed the child. "Why does he have so much hair?"

"You are small because it is in your nature," answered the man. "He has hair because it is in his."

Gonzalo repeated their names, "Ah-cambal and Óolal" and then spoke his own.

Ah-cambal was pleased and repeated, "Gonzalo," several times. "This place is Ichpaatún and my brother, Nachan Can, is sajal here," he continued.

"Lord," mumbled Gonzalo while getting onto his knees and bowing. The girl began to giggle.

"Óolal, stop that," hushed Ah-cambal. "He only shows us the respect that was demanded of him by his Tzamán captors." Then, he turned his attention to Gonzalo. "Not Lord," he said, "just Ah-cambal. Now get off your knees and sit."

Once Gonzalo resettled himself Ah-cambal looked into his eyes; "I was told of your actions at Tixmul. I'm not sure that our people would have escaped if you hadn't rushed to the aid of Óolal's mother, Lady Za'azil. I thank you."

"I'm sorry for your losses," sighed Gonzalo, while watching the child and thinking of the young warrior that Gucumatz had slaughtered, "and I thank you for my freedom."

His speech is awkward but passable, thought Ah-cambal, *not the fool the Tzamáns made him out to be. Intelligent, and I expect he learns quickly.*

"Is anyone hungry?" He asked.

At an enthusiastic acknowledgement from Óolal, Ah-cambal reached into a carried pouch and withdrew a fat packet wrapped in a shiny leaf. Working deftly, he unfolded the leaf to reveal two flattened maize cakes. Both rounds were spread with cooked eggs mixed with something dark as night.

"Náaxché yéetel e'el (eggs with corn smut)," he said with a smile as he broke one of the cakes and handed a piece to the girl.

Next, he passed the unbroken cake to Gonzalo. Not understanding the words or recognizing the food, Gonzalo eyed the dark egg mixture with suspicion until Ah-cambal made signs that he should eat. When he took a small careful bite, he discovered a mild earthy truffle-like flavor that called for another bite, and then another.

Until the two cakes were gone, the three ate in companionable silence. When Óolal licked the last crumbs from her fingers, Ah-cambal again spoke.

"When I saw you in Tzamá, you told me that you came from the east. I know that there are a few islands to the east, but you are not from those. Beyond them, there is only water. Tell me of your home."

Gonzalo had told his story many times since his shipwreck, always to be received as a tall tale, a cause for derision, laughter, and abuse. He was reluctant. He considered the man before him.

This Ah-cambal's interest feels sincere, he decided, and so he began.

"You are right, the lands from which I come are far beyond the islands of which you speak. The canoe in which I reached these shores floundered, but it was seventy footsteps from end to end and twenty from side to side. It took us nearly three uinal (months) to reach these shores."

Ah-cambal wanted to accept what he was hearing, but such a vessel and such a journey were hard to envision. He was no stranger to the sea, but even the largest dugout that he had ever seen was four times smaller.

Could this stranger's land really possess trees so large? Holding his tongue, he indicated that Gonzalo should continue.

Stumbling over his words and at time using signs, the castaway drew a meticulous picture of a world so populated and so astonishing that it beggared Ah-cambal's imagination.

This is true, he thought. *His story is too detailed and too passionate for it to be otherwise. Those who've ignored him are also ignoring the gods.*

"I like him," burst out Óolal. "He tells good stories."

Gonzalo smiled at the child, and then, Ah-cambal asked the question that was foremost on his mind.

"Tell me of the vahom-ché (uplifted wood) of great power."

"I'm not sure of what you speak," answered Gonzalo.

"When I saw you in Tzamá, Turix, the caluac to the household of Gucumatz, spoke of another stranger, a slave who he said made little k'atab ché (crosses of wood) and waved them about shouting that they held a wondrous virtue."

It surprised Gonzalo that this would interest Ah-cambal, but he answered easily.

"Turix spoke of my last surviving companion, Geronimo. In our lands Geronimo was a man who you might call a chilán. A cross of wood is the symbol of his god."

"What is the name of this god," questioned Ah-cambal.

"Jesus," answered Gonzalo.

"Jesus," mused Ah-cambal. "It's a strange name. What does this Jesus god do? Does he teach writing and wisdom like Itzamna, or bring storms and rain like Chaac? Perhaps he keeps bees like Ah-Muzen-Cab or watches over merchants and travelers like Ekchuah?"

"You have many gods," answered Gonzalo, "do you believe in all these gods and also that they guide the affairs of men?"

"Each man guides his own life," said Ah-cambal slowly. "But, the gods are the gods. They reward our devotion; they punish our impiety. Do you pray and make sacrifices to your gods?"

"In my land," responded Gonzalo, "we have but one god."

The revelation shocked Ah-cambal. "And, this one god, this Jesus, he must do everything? Do you pray to this god?"

Gonzalo pondered, his thoughts stretching out before he responded.

"When I was a small boy, my family wished me to be a priest... an ah k'in. We kept shrines in our home and my mother prayed at all hours of the day and often well into the night. She was devoted to prayer. She believed that the fires of an awful place await us all. Daily she entreated Our Lord God, his son Jesus Christ, the Holy Ghost, and the Blessed Virgin for her salvation."

"So this Spain of yours, it does have more than one god after all," interjected Ah-cambal. "You speak of your mother. Do you yourself honor these gods?"

Gonzalo was reluctant to reply, but then he thought, *No, this is a new beginning. It must begin with truth.*

"No, I do not."

"Then, you believe in other gods," queried Ah-cambal.

"No," sighed Gonzalo.

Ah-cambal regarded the hairy foreigner carefully.

"I think you must be very lonely. Without gods, our world is a mystery. Their presence comforts us."

"I think that I am no lonelier than other men," answered the castaway. "I agree, it is difficult to explain our world, and perhaps I suffer for my disbelief, yet I think it is better to see all of our acts as wholly our own."

"The gods set our paths," responded Ah-cambal, "but the ultimate directions that we men choose, those are always our own. I think the gods brought you here and I don't think they're done with you yet."

Why am I opening to this man? Wondered Gonzalo.

"Grandfather," whined Óolal, fidgeting and clearly bored with the direction of their conversation. "Can't he tell another story? I'm getting cold."

Ah-cambal looked up and realized that K'inich Ajaw had begun his descent into Metnal.

"It's too late for another story here on the beach. Perhaps your mother, Za'azil, will let you stay at my home tonight."

Compelled by the sign he'd earlier received, Ah-cambal had quickly decided to eschew the young men's house and occupy his own so that he could keep the hairy stranger close.

"And perhaps, this man, this Gonzalo, will come with us." Then to Gonzalo, "I know that Itz'at Acan has given you a mat in the young men's house, but I would like to offer you the hospitality of my home. Will you accept?"

Gonzalo, who felt uncomfortable among the stares and whispers of so many adolescents, each vying to show their manliness, quickly agreed.

"Then, let us go," grinned Ah-cambal. Scooting Óolal from his lap, he rose to his feet. "When we reach my home we can continue our talk."

Gonzalo and Óolal also stood. Ah-cambal took her hand and the three started back toward Ichpaatún. They had walked only a few paces when Óolal reached up and slipped her other small hand into Gonzalo's.

Perhaps I'm no longer alone, he thought, and the thought both comforted and frightened him.

Chapter 39

The Inferno Opens

11 Bak'tun 14 K'atun 11 Tun 14 Uinal 3 K'in

(January 21, 1512)

Nachan Can didn't regard himself closely attuned to the enigmatic ways of his gods. He made his obeisance and he gave to each of them his genuine respect. When need arose to interpret their wishes or their mercurial moods, deference to the wise council of Ah K'in May, Ah-cambal, and others better able to hear when the deities whisper typically served him well.

At this moment, he needed no one to tell him that the gods watched. The weight of their presence was undeniable, their dark and eager anticipation a thing both pressing and tangible. Deep in the marrow of his bones, Nachan Can had shuddered at the soundless growl and low rumble as the sacred wheel of the Tzolk'in turned. The day it spawned was 9 Ak'bal. Its arrival carried with it a chilling promise of darkness and night.

The runner who knelt before him earlier in the day, arrived exhausted and near to collapse. Upon listening to the man's breathless message, Nachan Can had quickly called together a council of war.

The meeting could not be held in secret, but neither was it the ruler of Ichpaatún's wish that it be held within easy earshot of his entire populace. To that end, he arranged for it to convene in the small walled square adjacent to the city's main gate. This was the same minor plaza where Hoch Can foolishly struck Gucumatz, slashed the nacon's face, earned the powerful warrior's vengeful enmity, and so placed the paths of all into the hands of the gods.

Nachan Can looked at the men gathered around him. It was well past chumul k'in (noon) and long streamers of sun and shadow stretched across the worried faces that crowded the small plaza. Some sat, others stood.

Near his right side, Learned Man Acan leaned against the square's back wall. His trusted caluac exuded confidence, yet Nachan Can could almost feel the tension with which his friend and confidant clutched his thick baton of authority.

On his left, Ah-cambal waited impassive, his strong face betraying not a hint of emotion. Out of place to the ruler's mind, beside his brother stood the tall hirsute stranger who'd assisted Za'azil's escape from Tixmul.

Why does Ah-cambal bring this barbarian to our council?

Nachan Can's gaze lingered over the face of his nephew, Tepeu.

He's still too young, his manhood is untried.

The faces of seasoned warriors who'd stood beside Hoch Can looked to him in anticipation. Yaotl leaned on a spear, his visage lined and solemn. Chicahua stood like a statue, his eyes like chips of flint. Nachan Can even recognized and met the stares of two men who belonged to the trading party from K'optela.

Many, he thought, *yet perhaps not enough. The strong arms of Hoch Can and his fallen brothers, Te' K'ab' and Teyacapan, will be missed in the days that come.*

Nachan Can rose from his seat and the plaza's ebb and flow of restless conversation died. Into the waiting silence he spoke with a quiet strength.

"The days of crying, the days of evil.

"The demon is free, the infernos open.

"There is no goodness, only evil, laments and cries."

Then, raising his voice, he continued. "My son, Hoch Can, your nacon, died at treacherous Tzamán hands! Ah K'in May died at treacherous Tzamán hands! We have been wronged. Our hearts cry out for revenge!"

Angry exclamations of agreement responded to his words and filled the plaza.

"But, our hearts do not cry out alone," shouted Nachan Can. "We are not alone in a belief that we are wronged. Ah Tabai's brother, Zac Nok, and his nacon, Gucumatz, died. The Lord of Fire believes they died at our deceitful hands, as did others."

This assertion was met with grumbles and derision. Nachan Can pressed on.

"We are aggrieved and Ah Tabai is aggrieved. I have sent messages to Tzamá, but they have fallen on deaf ears. Today, word has arrived that Ah Tabai turns out all of his city's holcánob. He has summoned his vassals. Ac Yanto and the warriors of Xamanzamá have rushed to their master's call as have holcánob from lesser villages. Ac Yanto's priest has petitioned Buluc

Chabtan (vengeful god of war and violence). Now, Tzamán drums beat and the Lord of the Fire comes. It is possible, that which approaches could have once been avoided. That time is past. The treachery of Tzamá has stirred the death bat from the depths of its cave. Now, good men will die and for no good reason."

Into the silence that followed these words, Chicahua spoke.

"Sajal, how long?"

"The Lord of Fire will come slowly," answered Nachan Can. "He will want his host fresh and well rested when it reaches our walls."

"If Ac Yanto is once more Tzamá's nacon," interjected Ah-cambal, "the so-called Batab Kinich will move with caution. Although he rules in Xamanzamá it has been a great many turn of the haab' since he led the warriors of old Ah Kumix Uinic. Ac Yanto will think upon his own age, remember the uncertainty of war, and also move slowly. If instead it is the young Xamanzamán, Rat Skull, who leads, he will be eager to prove his prowess, but he also will move slowly and with restraint because he is untried and fears a misstep in the presence of the Lord of Fire."

Chicahua looked unsure, "And, so?"

Nachan Can held up his hand with four fingers extended.

"Four days, more if the gods favor us." Then he looked questioningly at Ah-cambal.

"Four days," responded his brother, "five at most."

Learned Man Acan, was not privilege to the runner's message and was taken aback.

"Sajal," he worried, "it may not be enough time to mount our defense. If Ah Tabai brings all his strength, they will far outnumber us!"

Before Nachan Can could respond, one of the men from K'optela stepped forward.

"Lord Nachan Can, I am Long Steps, although we are only jun k'aal (20), we will stand beside our friends from Ichpaatún to face this Tzamán threat."

"Long Steps, we are most grateful for your offer," nodded Nachan Can, "but you and your people must not. The storm which comes rushing toward us is of our own making. It may well throw us over. You must shoulder your goods and depart for your home and families before you too are engulfed."

"Lord," smiled the merchant warrior, "Great Lord, we are sorry, but we cannot obey you. If Ah Tabai brings ruin to Ichpaatún, how long will it be before he demands that K'optela also bend before him and offer up our own wealth? No Lord, we are sorry, but we must remain at your side."

"Very well," sighed the ruler of Ichpaatún, "it is a decision you may soon regret, but you have our sincere thanks. Very soon every strong arm will be needed and welcome."

"Sajal," burst out Yaotl, who'd slowly been edging his way forward, "even with Long Steps and his friends at our side we will surely be outnumbered three to one! How can we hope to defend our walls?"

"We cannot," admitted Nachan Can, "that is why we must prepare tonight and at the first light of K'inich Ajaw's new day make haste to meet the Lord of Fire and his host before they arrive. If we set forth and can delay the Lord of Fire's arrival, it will give time for the rest of our people to flee. I would not make such a choice, but it is the only way that remains open."

Many people began to speak at once. Some agreed with their ruler's words. Others maintained that they should remain and face the Tzamáns from behind their walls. Some raised their voices. A vocal few shouted that they should simply abandon Ichpaatún and flee.

Nachan Can remained silent and listened patiently as hot debate argued the merits of the different options. In due course discussion led to consensus and it was agreed that going forth to meet the Tzamáns was, as Nachan Can had said, their only true path.

Quickly, talk shifted to where and how they should engage their enemy that they might sell their lives most dearly. Noisy contentious discussion continued for some time when Nachan Can realized that he was being addressed.

"Lord, I would speak."

Looking toward the voice, he was surprised to see the tall foreigner on his knees. *What is this?* He wondered, and looked questioningly at his brother.

"He is called Gonzalo. Hear his words," urged Ah-cambal. "I told you of the prophecy given me by Lord Balam (Jaguar). He said that we stand at the crossing of two paths. He told me that we must choose. One he warned, will lead to oblivion, the other to an uncertain future. I believe that this Gonzalo is tied to that uncertain future."

The gods again, thought Nachan Can wryly and motioned for the foreigner to rise and speak.

Gonzalo looked about himself at the multitude of warriors and savage nobility crowded in the small plaza and suffered a moment of doubt.

Should I continue? These people treat me well, but do I really know them? This is a land of enigma. If I do this I shall no longer stand apart. What shall I become?

Ah-cambal saw concern pass across Gonzalo's face and placed a supporting hand against his back.

"In the land from which I come," began Gonzalo, "I am a warrior. I am not a nacon, and I am not a great warrior, yet I know of many battles and have fought in several."

Nachan Can raised his eyebrows. *His accent is strange and his words stumble, but he speaks well enough that I understand.*

Ah-cambal caught the look and smiled back.

"In some of those battles," continued Gonzalo, "more than 16,000 warriors clashed."

To this assertion several of those gathered in the plaza hooted derision. Some shouted.

"Kali'ikil (lies)!"

Learned Man Acan stepped forward, brandished his baton and waved everyone to silence.

Thinking upon his namesake, the great Spanish commander Gonzalo Fernández de Córdoba, Gonzalo continued. "In some of these battles, great hosts met defeat at the hands of adversaries whose numbers were much less."

With that, he picked up a small piece of charred wood from a brazier and began to sketch on the wall behind him.

"Tzamá is here. Men from Ichpaatún with spears are here. Ah hulob (archers) from Ichpaatún are here. And, if the ground slopes thus."

Everyone leaned forward, trying to see the stranger's drawing. What he suggested looked straightforward, almost obvious.

"This can work," approved Ah-cambal, "I know such a place."

At his brother's pronouncement, Nachan Can thought again of Lord Balam and the jaguar lord's unpredictable ways. A wide smile spread across his narrow face.

Chapter 40

Gods of War

The 24th of January, Year of Our Lord 1512

For the first time in many months, Gonzalo dreamed of Consuela. Unsettled, alert, and alarmed he wandered through ankle-deep pools of blood. He choked on the pungent aroma of incense. Thick overpowering gouts of its smoke swirled, danced, and pulsated, flowing into clouds of effervescent color. In his dream, he no longer remembered his beloved sister's face.

With dawn's arrival, the escudero awoke almost as exhausted as when he'd thrown himself down. His stiff right hip nagged and Gonzalo rubbed it vigorously. Feeling a slight relief, he drew the same hand roughly across his face and tried to scatter the night's lingering cobwebs.

During the seemingly untold nights since gently rolling waves first cast him onto these shores, Gonzalo had grown accustomed to sleeping rough. He'd slept in ways that he would barely have entertained as conceivable when he still lived in Spain. He'd slept uncomfortably, but deeply, on hard reed mats. He'd slept sprawled awkwardly among the branches of thorny trees. Deeply exhausted, he'd slept time and time again upon coarse uneven ground without so much as a blanket. Despite these and a host of other discomforts most mornings he found himself at least moderately refreshed. Last night he'd felt every uneven pebble on which he lay.

Following the council in Ichpaatún's small plaza, Gonzalo had accompanied Ah-cambal, and the one called Learned Man Acan, back to the former's home. Inside the dwelling the two natives carefully set out groups of three polished stones. Upon each of those little stone tripods they'd placed a thin pottery disk to create a series of small altars. Looking at Gonzalo with an intensity he had not previously exhibited and using simple words, Ah-cambal slowly reiterated that, dark billowing clouds of war were fast approaching and that an urgent and growing need existed to petition their gods.

"You told me, that your own land has but four gods, Gonzalo," spoke Ah-cambal. "You also told me that you yourself do not honor those gods. Here in Ichpaatún we have many gods, gods both great and small. I have a strong faith in our gods. Acan, here, also places his trust in them. To both of us it is certain that, Ah Puch, a powerful lord of death, Buluc Chabtan, a bloody lord of conflict, and also a small, but important, constellation of lesser belligerent gods now take extreme interest in our impending affairs. A prudent man petitions his gods in times of great need. Itz'at Acan and I will now make sacrifices to curry our gods' favor."

Gonzalo was unsure how to reply, so he simply nodded. He then watched with growing curiosity as Ah-cambal spread a tanned piece of animal hide onto the floor close by the small altars and scattered the hide with a handful of reddish brown seeds. The seeds meant nothing to Gonzalo, but both Ah-cambal and Itz'at Acan seemed fascinated if not excited.

Reaching behind himself, Ah-cambal brought forth an elaborately decorated clay bowl. To Gonzalo's eyes the dish appeared to hold bits of some dried vegetable.

"The gods know of all our undertakings. They always listen," intoned Ah-cambal proffering the vessel to Acan. "Still, they often hear us more clearly if we choose to take a step closer."

Gonzalo didn't understand what his benefactor meant, but, when Ah-cambal passed him the bowl, just as Itz'at Acan had done, he put several pieces of the dried vegetable into his mouth, chewed, and swallowed. The bits were leathery and had a somewhat musty taste.

Next, the two men picked up small pieces of what appeared to be pounded bark. They slowly tore the bits of bark into smaller pieces, then they carefully lay the scraps upon several of the prepared altars.

Gonzalo, watched mesmerized, and slightly repulsed, as, first Ah-cambal and then Itz'at Acan, used a small sharp blade to slit their own ears and drip thick dark globules of their blood onto the fragments of bark. As each plate was anointed, Ah-cambal looked at Gonzalo, and explained to him which god's favor they sought.

"This is an offering to my patron, Ekchuah, a traveler's god, but who is also a god of war. This blood we offer to Itzamna, the mighty god of learning who invented writing, and is wise in all things." So he continued, describing each of their petitioned gods in turn.

After blood of the two men adorned several of the plates, Itz'at Acan passed the blade to Gonzalo. The Spaniard stared at the tiny blade in his palm.

Not really a knife, he thought, *just a sharp flake of obsidian.*

"You need not offer your own blood," confided Ah-cambal, "but, if you do, I believe many of our gods will look favorably upon your gift."

Gonzalo, once again, felt himself teetering on the edge of a precipice. His belief in his own god was weak to non-existent, but if he made a sacrifice to the gods of idolaters, might he be pushing open the weighty doors of perdition.

I am treated better by these people than by any others in this land. I owe them my life. They seem to treat me as an equal. They seem to trust me. If I do this, it further binds me to them. But, if I do this, do I risk my eternal soul? No! No! Their gods are no more real than my own. Anything I do in this moment serves only my own purpose. No magical beings float above or wait to sit in eternal judgement of my actions.

The blade was so sharp that it passed through the apostate's earlobe with almost no pain. Surveying the small altars, Gonzalo squeezed the injured lobe and let droplets of his blood fall onto two hitherto unanointed plates. Afterwards, Ah-cambal beamed at the Castaway with an excited smile and nudged his lean friend.

"For what soon lies before us, you have chosen well," enthused Itz'at Acan, pointing to a plate with Gonzalo's blood. "Most well! This offering belongs to Ahulane, The Archer. And this," pointing to the other altar, "belongs to Hun Pic Toc, He of the 8,000 spears. Our plan, the one you suggested, depends on the flight of our k'aax jalal'ob (arrows) and upon the strength of our lances. It is a good and great omen that you seek the approval of these two gods."

Ah-cambal used a pair of wooden tongs to remove a coal from a small brazier. He placed the coal onto the altar to Ahulane and Gonzalo stared transfixed as his offering produced a dark smoke that smoldered into a sparkling rainbow of thick eddying color.

In that moment, he sensed a gathered multitude, a strong unshakable feeling of presence, and an expectant sensation of anticipation as though a prodigious breath were drawn in and then held. He watched the smoke rise as a shimmering mist, alive with pulsating and impossible colors, gambol about an opening in the roof and then slowly disappeared.

Although Gonzalo could not have explained why, he was certain beyond doubt that the smoke of his blood sought the Archer god's acceptance.

Three nights and two full days had passed since he sat cross-legged with Ah-cambal and Itz'at Acan, yet echoes of those offerings still willfully wove themselves into the cobwebs of sleep that now left him worn and groggy.

An early dawn peeked through a rapidly thinning mist that struggled uselessly against the day's new light. The morning was damp, its colors muted. All about Gonzalo, amid grunts, grumbles, and low shouts, men of Ichpaatún were rousing from their slumber.

Birds chattered in the trees and Gonzalo half expected to hear the cocks of his own childhood crow their greetings at the limpid dawn. For a time, he sat upright in the cold grey of a world that was neither light nor shadow, inventoried his senses, and quietly listened to the other men stirring themselves.

In his former life, he'd passed many nights encamped with other soldiers of Spain. A familiarity to the morning sounds tugged at his memory, yet it was a familiarity that continually gave way to overriding strangeness. Every single warrior who clustered near him was an aboriginal whose life and gods bore little or no comparison to any of the soldiers of his past.

Nonetheless, in their midst, Gonzalo felt an unexpected exuberance. He felt tense, but also fully committed to a path of action, a path that would either define his life in this extraordinary and distant land or put an end to it.

I am no great capitán, he thought, *no renowned leader of men. My stumbling and perhaps ill-considered words have led me, and all those around me, to this encampment. In this bewildering land there is nothing else I could have said or done. These natives who surround me, I must assume are my friends, for in my heart I know that those who approach are my enemies. Whatever becomes of me, there is nothing else I could have done.*

Adrift in introspection, Gonzalo started when someone slapped a hand onto his shoulder. Turning, he looked up into the earnest face of a diminutive man he'd been introduced to as Ch'o' (mouse).

"Get up, jtáanxel kaajil (stranger)" urged the native. "Ah-cambal and Nachan Can wish your presence. They say, we must not tarry if we are to finish our preparations before the Lord of Fire falls upon us with the strength of Tzamá."

Gonzalo stood and followed Ch'o' as the short twitchy native led him toward where the leaders of Ichpaatún waited.

The previous two days had been whirlwinds of activity, days that had tested Gonzalo's endurance. At dawn on the first, he'd accompanied Ah-cambal from the spacious thatched house in which they'd slept and together they walked to Ichpaatún's main plaza. There, already gathered, milled an imposing host of natives. To the Spaniard's eyes every man appeared savage and warlike. Ah-cambal had gripped Gonzalo's shoulder.

"This is good! This is very good." he'd gushed. "Gathered before us are every man of Ichpaatún's holcánob, also many, many, others, strong and of fighting age. Look! There stands Long Steps and the traders from K'optela. And there! Others from nearby villages who've answered my brother's call. Gonzalo, this is much better than we hoped, the Pech'ob (Ticks) from Tzamá may yet be surprised."

After that, urgent shouts from Itz'at Acan had harangued the multitude into a semblance of order and they quickly began what, in Spain, Gonzalo would have decried as a tedious forced march.

Throughout the morning and well into the afternoon, Nachan Can's, seemingly tireless followers had raced along lush jungle trails. The following day was much the same. When at last Itz'at Acan called a halt, declaring that they had finally reached their destination, Ah-cambal had immediately set everyone to work cutting brush and establishing barricades. The work had continued until well after sunset.

In the new morning's pale light, Ch'o' guided Gonzalo onto a slight rise where Ah-cambal and Nachan Can turned at their approach.

"I am pleased," said the Lord of Ichpaatún, gesturing toward the Spaniard. "You and my brother have done well."

"We have all done what we could," responded Ah-cambal. "Whether we have done well is something the gods have yet to reveal."

For the hundredth time Gonzalo looked with critical eyes at the place that they'd chosen to give battle. Just as on the previous ninety-nine times, he wished for more, but wasn't wholly disappointed with what he saw. All of the land through which he'd passed since being shipwrecked had been unusually flat. Here, at least the terrain offered a suggestion of opportunity.

In the warm wet days that followed the passage of Hurakán's storm, the battered jungle that blanketed The Land of Turkey and Deer had reasserted itself and grown ever more exuberant and impenetrable. Oddly, in front of Gonzalo stretched an expansive area of rocky soil all but bare of vegetation.

According to Ah-cambal, years before farmers discovered the sparsely vegetated spot. Believing themselves gifted with land that would be easy to work, they cleared the ground for planting. Alas their crops grew poorly, or not at all. When discouraged, they abandoned the plot and the jungle didn't see fit to reclaim it. The open space, bathed in sunlight and surrounded by dense walls of green, felt strange and out of place.

To Gonzalo's eyes the clearing looked to be about one hundred and fifty vara (yards) from one end to the other. In shape, the space resembled nothing so much as a crude funnel with an elongated spout, perhaps fifty vara across at its widest and narrowing to a mere seven vara where Gonzalo stood at the spout's mouth. From that point, the ground sloped gently down and away to the rocky field's midpoint. It then slowly rose again to where the funnel's wide end once more melded back into jungle. Neither slope could be deemed a true hill, but neither could the land be called flat.

Gonzalo looked about and scrutinized the edges of the field which were bordered by thick jungle. He was pleased by what eluded his eyes. Although invisible to his gaze, he knew that a day, and part of a night, of energetic work by the men of Ichpaatún had increased the Jungle's impassability. Hidden in the foliage were carefully crafted barricades of thick vines, thorns, and sturdy sharpened branches. A slight smile played across Gonzalo's face.

"Is it as you would have it?" questioned Nachan Can, who'd seen the look cross the strange foreigner's face.

"Lord," answered Gonzalo respectfully, "it is as Ah-cambal says. We have done all that we can. Your gods are strange to me, but Itz'at Acan says that it is they who brought us to this place. Perhaps together that will be enough."

Nachan Can nodded thoughtfully and turned to his caluac.
"So what do we do now Itz'at?"

The wiry seneschal looked at Ah-cambal and Gonzalo, both of whom shrugged.

"Now, Sajal," he replied with his own shrug, "we take our positions and wait."

Chapter 41

Arrows of Ahulane

11 Bak'tun 14 K'atun 11 Tun 14 Uinal 6 K'in

(January 24, 1512)

With his eyes fixed on the narrow path ahead, Ac Yanto surveyed the press of warriors who tramped slowly but steadily before him. Crowded several abreast, the men carried shields, spears, clubs, and other weapons. Their robust forms barely fit between dense walls of encroaching jungle. Without looking back to see them, he felt the weight of the similarly armed multitude that followed.

Three paces ahead strutted Rat Skull dressed and painted for war, his head crowned by the barbarian's metal hat that he now so prized. Somewhere behind, four straining slaves labored under the weight of an ornately decorated palanquin upon which lounged Ah Tabai, the Lord of Fire.

Ac Yanto's chest swelled with pride. Many turn of the ha'ab had passed since he last led Tzamá's holcánob for Ah Kumix Uinic. Now, once again, he was The City of the Dawn's nacon. He was going to war.

Many names will be forgotten, he thought, *but I am the Batab Kinich, and mine will be carved in stone!*

When the Lord of Fire's most recent summons had reached Ac Yanto in Xamanzamá, he'd listened to the Great Man's sweat-drenched messenger with growing concern. Only days before, he gloated gleefully when a trader brought word of Zac Nok's and Gucumatz' untimely deaths. But, as Ah Tabai's exhausted messenger panted out that the Lord of Fire required the batab's presence before the full moon, Ac Yanto had remembered the agony of his last audience and his bowels had clinched.

Rather than again respond to his overlord's demands with delay or excuse, he'd nearly fallen over himself to comply. As ordered, he'd quickly gathered all of Xamanzamá's men of fighting age and fearfully rushed them to Tzamá.

When Ac Yanto's people reached the City of the Dawn's walls, stone-faced sentinels once again bared their way. Ac Yanto didn't recognize the grim warrior who allowed him alone inside; as his fear grew, the man had led him to the disturbingly familiar raised platform. Waiting at the top of its steps sat Ah Tabai chatting with ladies and sycophants of his Ah Cuchcab. What occurred when Ac Yanto once more knelt before the Lord of Fire was unexpected and, at the time thoroughly disorienting.

After a courteous, although perfunctory, greeting The Great Man had smiled and beckoned Ac Yanto to arise and sit on a bench at his side.

"As my vassal you grievously strayed," he said earnestly, "but you have paid for your errors. We will not speak of those things again. You heard of the insult and the loss that I have endured?"

Unsure of what to make of his question, Ac Yanto quietly answered, "Yes Lord."

"In retribution I will make war upon Ichpaatún," continued the Lord of Fire, "and my vengeance will be swift, terrible, and without mercy! Your name and your penchant for violence were once nearly as feared as those of Gucumatz."

Then, he grabbed Ac Yanto's jaw and turned it to stare into the older man's eyes.

"You will be the arm that wields my wrath. You served my father as Nacon; now it is time that you remember who you were. It is time that you truly serve me as well! The skills of war are not forgotten. Your man Rat Skull will be your second and together with many angry gods at our side we shall destroy Nachan Can and put an end to all those who call him sajal! Even now, at my command, Ah Kin Cutz again makes sacrifices to curry favor with Buluc Chabtan and Ah Puch."

As Ac Yanto moved through the jungle, his good hand gripped the club that Gucumatz used to crush Hoch Can's skull. Across his shoulders hung the dead giant's snarling jaguar pelt, placed there by the Lord of Fire himself. Surrounded by all the strength of Tzamá, thoughts which should have focused on the coming assault upon Ichpaatún's low walls, instead revolved tightly around Ac Yanto himself.

I must be cautious, he mused. *This is an opportunity that will not come again. Ah Tabai's fire dims and mine grows brighter. War is dangerous to both men and living gods. Who can say what might befall the Lord of Fire when his enemies are vanquished? I am The Batab Kinich. The victory will be remembered as mine. It is good to rule in Xamanzamá. Ruling in Tzamá will be better.*

The only blemishes on his daydream were annoying and unbidden thoughts of Ah Kin Cutz. When Ac Yanto had learned that he would once again become war leader of Tzamá he was elated, but at the same time he'd been filled with disgust that the insufferable and conniving Cutz had somehow managed to also acquire Ah Tabai's favor.

When I am lord in Tzamá, I'll take the rest of that hunpedzkin's (poisonous lizard) hand and then I'll take his other one as well.

A sly smile was forming on Ac Yanto's face when a commotion interrupted his treasonous thoughts. In the distance ahead, two warriors forced their way against the tide. In a moment they passed Rat Skull, who turned and followed, then they prostrated themselves at Ac Yanto's feet.

"Great Nacon," began one.

The Ac Yanto's smile grew wider. In Xamanzamá he expected and received obeisance, but since again being named Nacon of Tzamá the groveling had grown deeper and more sincere. He reveled in the change.

"Our Lord's enemies are before us," mumbled the warrior."

"What are you saying?" Demanded Ac Yanto angrily, puzzled by the man's words.

"Ichpaatún," gasped the warrior turning pale. "Nachan Can and his warriors block our path not waak jo'o k'aal (600) strides ahead."

Ac Yanto's head spun. *How can this be true? Is Nachan Can such a fool that he would abandon his walls and try to meet us without their protection? There must be some mistake.*

Turning to Rat Skull, who seemed equally surprised by the scout's report, Ac Yanto growled.

"Come, we must make sense of this fool's words."

Shoving the two prostrate figures aside and grunting a command that they take their message on to Ah Tabai, Ac Yanto and his second pushed to the head of their temporarily halted column.

Walking stealthily in advance of all those who waited, they cautiously made their way forward. As the distance stretched and they began to question the veracity of the scouts' message, they suddenly reached a widening in the path. Before them spread a slight declivity, open to the sunlight. At its low point stood warriors from Ichpaatún waiting in three ragged lines. Ac Yanto could scarcely believe his eyes.

"It's true!" he hissed to Rat Skull. "They intend to meet us in the open. The slaughter will be magnificent. We will kill them as they run and songs will be sung about this day."

He's old, thought Rat Skull, *he's right that Nachan Can has made a foolish choice, but this day's victory will be remembered as mine. War is dangerous and who can say what might befall an aging Nacon.*

While Rat Skull buried his thoughts, Ac Yanto hurried them back along the path.

"We must tell the Lord of Fire that our scouts spoke truth! Then, we must make a noise to wake the gods and advance. The mice from Ichpaatún will hear us coming and grovel in their fright!"

Rat Skull grinned showing his teeth. The sacred Tzolk'in had turned and the day was 12 Cimi', a day given over to death.

Ac Yanto's fierce elation spread out around him like a contagion. As soon as Ah Tabai heard his breathless excited description, the Lord of Fire ordered his entire host to press forward. With wild yells, the sound of shrill whistles, the beat of wooden drums, and the blaring of conch trumpets, the warriors of Tzamá hurried to meet their enemy.

Upon reaching the clearing, the men edged into the open, warily eyed their foes, and then fanned out to crowd into the open space just beyond the jungle's verge. Ac Yanto and Rat Skull once again moved to the fore and strutted to the center of their mass of warriors.

"Look," gloated Ac Yanto, "at the mere sight of us they huddle together in fear and already they pull back."

Across the field, Rat Skull saw that Ichpaatún's ragged lines of warriors had indeed drawn together and retreated about waak zapal (30 feet).

Ac Yanto raised his voice so that his own men would be sure to hear and yelled.

"Nachan Can, in your arrogance you have defied Yajawk'ak, your rightful lord, a deity made man! Your followers brutally murdered his faithful servants and by so doing angered the gods! Nachan Can, you claim that you rule your noj kaaj (city), but you are less than a dog at our Lord of Fire's feet.

"Men of Ichpaatún, Nachan Can's conceit and pride have led you to this forsaken place and so condemned you all. If you throw down your weapons and prostrate yourselves before your true master, the Lord of Fire, we will give you all swift and painless deaths. Resist and your ends will be slow and merciless!"

Seated on his palanquin in the midst of his warriors, held well above their heads, Ah Tabai nodded his approval.

Ac Yanto is a brutal buffoon, but he speaks well, better than I expected.

From all around their lord, the men of Tzamá jeered at their adversaries, shouted insults, and loudly beat their weapons together. As their uproar increased in volume, a warrior separated himself from those across the field, walked forward and leaned on his spear. As he waited, apparently at ease, the clamor slowly died. When the din was sufficiently abated, the man shouted.

"Ac Yanto, I know you. You are old and flabby. Your best days are well past! If Ah Tabai has chosen you to carry his misplaced vengeance, he has chosen poorly! We of Ichpaatún are more grievously wronged than your lord imagines himself to be. Ah Tabai's star wanes and will soon fall from the heavens. None of you need die here today. Your hearths await you at home. We do not fear you! We will not submit!"

With that, the man stepped back among his fellows. In the silence that followed Ac Yanto seethed.

I recognize you too, Ah-cambal and I'll personally attend to your agonizing death.

To his right, Rat Skull stood tense and impatient. His large flint axe hung loosely from his white knuckled hand and swung slowly back and forth. Glancing about Ac Yanto beheld the same strained intensity reflected on the faces of his warriors. Behind him, the Lord of Fire stood balanced and erect on his palanquin his own face dark with anger.

"We must make them pay. We must do it now!" hissed Rat Skull.

Ac Yanto looked at his subordinate then stared closely at the men from Ichpaatún. To a man they wore either thick ichcahuipilli (protective shirts of double quilted cotton) or thick breast-plates of cured tapir hide. Each carried a large shield of split and woven reeds covered with hardened deer hide, and their hands gripped flint tipped spears.

They look formidable enough, he mused, *but we outnumber them four to one.*

Discovery of Nachan Can's strength in this place had come as a surprise and a bit of a shock. Such plans for battle as Ac Yanto had bothered to consider all assumed that his men would assault Ichpaatún's walls. Here, there would be no plan, just a maddened charge forward. All about the field men on both side were yelling insults and screaming war cries.

"Nacon," again urged Rat Skull, "we must attack!"

For a moment Ac Yanto felt his spirits rise and his gut sour, the killing was about to begin.

Thirst dried Gonzalo's mouth and a muscle in his left thigh quivered slowly of its own accord. Ignoring both, he glanced up at the sheltering sky. It was beautiful and cloudless, an exquisite blue. His restless gaze swept over the two anxious ranks of Ichpaatún's warriors standing before him. Across the field, his regard again settled onto Tzamá's howling surging horde. He'd recognized the man, cloaked in a snarling jaguar pelt, who'd shouted their challenge. He was their lord, Ac Yanto, who, with his unclean priest, had presided over the sacrifice of Gonzalo's fellow castaways. He'd also recognized the large screaming warrior, Rat Skull, who bore the metal helmet that once belonged to his crew's ill-fated master-at-arms, Diego de Arana. The visibly greater number of the Tzamáns was distressing.

In Spain, Gonzalo had served with a few men who cherished the thrill of battle. He was never one of those. His only aspiration in previous battles was always to stay alive. To that end, he'd killed, and he'd done it more than once. The killing was always joyless and terrible.

Despite being privy to the entirety of Ah-cambal's and Itz'at Acan's careful preparations, the coming battle felt distant and worlds apart from his previous experience. This wasn't some familiar ground in Europe with disciplined troops, signal trumpets, flags, and cannon. The forces arrayed here were people he'd recently thought of as savages, loosely organized, hideously painted for war, and armed with weapons of flint, wood, and stone. The Tzamáns numbers and his own hard-nosed logic told him that winning might be impossible.

Perhaps this is how I will die, he mused. He doubted very much any of them would live out the day.

Breaking into his gloomy reverie, the man to his left nudged him roughly and spoke. It was the diminutive warrior, Ch'o'.

"I am small," he grinned showing his teeth, "but together jtáanxel kaajil (stranger) you and I will kill many! Many!"

Before Gonzalo could respond, a great howl for blood rose up from the Tzamáns.

Ac Yanto waved a great club above his head and screeched a war cry.

"Yajawk'ak! Yajawk'ak! Yajawk'ak! Yajawk'ak! Yajawk'ak!"

Those around him took up the shout, and, suddenly, the entire mass of the Lord of Fire's host, faces disfigured with hate, were surging forward.

As the screaming Tzamáns charged heedlessly across the rocky field, Ichpaatún's line of warriors appeared to falter, and then its center seemed to melt away in fear. Nachan Can's warriors turned. They fled, and their excited enemy surged in pursuit.

"They run! They run!" bellowed Rat Skull, and those around him gleefully took up his roar.

After forty short strides Ah-cambal blew loudly upon a shrill reed whistle and the warriors of Ichpaatún ended their apparent rout. Once more, they turned to face their charging adversaries. The men drew together and formed three tight ranks, their thick reed and hide shields pressed hard one against the other, and their flanks anchored tightly against the encroaching jungle.

Gonzalo smelt the stench of fear-emptied bowels and then their enemy was upon them.

Screams of pain joined the roar of their charge as Tzamáns stumbled and impaled their feet in concealed pits. The cunning ploy, devised by Itz'at Acan, did almost nothing to impede the onrushing throng. Warriors simply stepped over or trod upon their unfortunate fallen comrades. Shoved and driven by those behind, the Tzamáns crashed upon Nachan Can's wall of shields like a vast and mighty wave rolling up onto a shallow beach.

Men on both sides shouted. Men on both sides screamed. In answer, the space between the adversaries filled with spreading confusion and blood. For a moment, a fear rekindled in Gonzalo that the Lord of Fire's strength was unstoppable and that everything he hoped for was about to end.

Tzamáns at the rear heaved forward and thrust those ahead of them tightly against the wall of Ichpaatún's wavering ranks. Heedless of their enemies' shields and waiting spears, the Lord of Fire's men pushed. Among the welter of struggling bodies time slowed and stretched. Individual combats became worlds of their own. Spears darted back and forth like striking serpents. Cruel obsidian and flint blades thrust forward only to be driven back and then thrust forward again.

Carried headlong by his warriors' uncontrolled attack, Ac Yanto was among the first of Tzamá's horde to be bloodied. As he reached Ichpaatún's line of shields an enemy with a paint blackened face leapt out to meet him. The man's eyes blazed and his jagged flint blade raked across Ac Yanto's upper arm. Blood splattered across the Batab Kinich's face and onto his snarling jaguar cape.

Shaken, Ac Yanto staggered back, then years of nearly forgotten experience stayed his shock. Acting on pure instinct, he swung Gucumatz' massive war club and put all of his yet considerable strength into the effort. When the blow struck, his enemy collapsed as surely as if the ground were yanked from beneath his feet. Ac Yanto glanced down at the broken corpse and roared his victory.

Emboldened by their nacon's shouts and further cries of, "Yajawk'ak! Yajawk'ak!" a smattering of Tzamá's stronger warriors struggled in among the men of Ichpaatún. Where they forced their way, the clashes grew more desperate.

Motionless in Ichpaatún's third rank, Gonzalo stared transfixed at the bedlam of enveloping carnage. His mouth, before dry, now felt as though it was filled with dust. The muscle in his thigh refused to lay still. Just before him, a warrior that he didn't know was violently jostled to his right.

Out of nowhere a blood splattered specter lunged into the gap. His face was frenzied and he howled like a fiend. The man swung a vicious obsidian bladed club straight at Gonzalo's head. The one-time escudero ducked. Then, reflexively, he lowered his shield and threw his right shoulder into his attacker.

Unbalanced by Gonzalo's weight, the man tripped heavily across Ch'o's extended leg, and sprawled sideways onto the ground. Laughing with unrestrained glee, the small warrior stamped savagely on the Tzamán's neck and was rewarded by a satisfying crack.

"Many! We will kill many!" he cackled.

Here and there, other Tzamáns fell and the outnumbered warriors of Ichpaatún managed to reclose their ranks. The Lord of Fire's initial blow had nearly overwhelmed them, but the field's slight incline, the spiked pits, and their own desperation all worked to their advantage. A scattering of Nachan Can's own warriors lay dead and his ranks were somewhat thinned, but once again their shields pressed tightly together and they held.

The Tzamáns screeched, stabbed, and hammered ceaselessly, but their riotous advance had ground to a standstill. The narrowness of the ground that Ah-cambal and Itz'at Acan had chosen meant that only a small portion of their enemies' true strength could be brought to bear against Ichpaatún's shields. As the Tzamáns spread out trying to bypass their enemies they quickly discovered that the surrounding jungle had been made impenetrable with waiting barricades of thorns, vines, and wood.

Rat Skull was almost insane with excitement and anger. Caught in the precipitous rush of his own warriors, he found himself bypassed and stuck in the scrum. His enemy stood just before him, but also just out of his reach.

That polok ma'ax (fat monkey), Ac Yanto, has already drawn blood! I'm stuck here among fools and farmers. If I am to win the day, I must lead!

"Out of my way! Out of my way!" he screamed and forcefully tried to shove aside those packed before him.

Near the back of the Tzamán host, Ah Tabai's anger also grew beyond bounds.

Why have my warriors stopped! I am the Lord of Fire! I am a god on earth! Nachan Can's strength before me should be as leaves scattered before a tempest. Ac Yanto and Rat Skull are incompetent bunglers! If Gucumatz still lived, the turds who oppose me would already be dead. I must act!

"Carry me forward!" he shrieked at his bearers. "Let our enemy quake in my presence! Now! Now!" he screamed.

Into the throng lurched his palanquin. The Lord of Fire stood erect, balanced on his conveyance, stretched out his arms and shouted.

"Tremble before me!"

The Tzamáns in his path prostrated themselves and his chair pressed into the gap. At their lord's sudden forced approach, an overawed silence fell among many of his people. Into this slight lessening of the battle's din, Ah-cambal's shrill bone whistle once again sounded, once, twice, three notes, all of them strident and clear. This was a sign that the remainder of Ichpaatún's forces awaited.

After serious discussion Nachan Can had reluctantly agreed to split his outnumbered warriors into four groups. Ah-cambal and the largest group stood the ground in the middle of the field and faced Tzamá's strength. Out of sight, in the undergrowth at the top of the field's slight rise Long Steps waited with the party of traders from K'optela. At Ah-cambal's signal, they rushed forward to reinforce his ranks.

To the left of Ichpaatún's line, spread out, hidden in the jungle behind their barricades, waited more of Nachan Can's warriors. In their fear slickened hands they clutched bows and long throwing spears. These fighters were overseen by Yopat, a taciturn man, an archer of exceptional skill. Across the field also concealed in the jungle waited similarly armed men under the direction of Chicahua.

Despite Yopat's renowned prowess, it was from Chicahua's bow that the first arrow responded to Ah-cambal's whistle. The reed shaft, more than five palms long, was tipped by a wickedly sharpened point of flint. Chicahua was tall and powerful and, as befitted him, his bow was long and heavy. The arrow flew faithfully to his chosen target.

Ac Yanto tried to grunt. It felt as though someone had struck his neck with a heavy mallet. He tried to scream and found that he couldn't. Blood bubbled from his mouth and dribbled thickly down his chin. Stunned, he reached up with his crippled hand only to discover the gore covered flint that had skewered his throat. Gucumatz' war club slipped soundlessly from the nerveless fingers of his other hand. As it fell, Ac Yanto heard the clinking of many tiny laughing bells. The sound promised his end and whispered that his ambitions were nothing but ashes cast upon the wind. Ah Puch grinned, then the skeletal lord of death reached out and enfolded him tightly into his cold and cheerless embrace.

In the time it took Ac Yanto to die the air filled with flying shafts. Death crafted from flint and obsidian poured down upon the tightly packed Tzamáns and the locked shields of Ichpaatún refused to yield.

The Lord of Fire and those about him pressed forward. Crushed in the middle, unable to either advance or retreat, the City of the Dawn's warriors began to die. A steady cascade of arrows, hul che darts, stones, and heavy thrown spears plunged into their crush of warriors. Those at the front of Tzamá's ranks began to push back to escape the rain of death. Meanwhile, those at the back continued to shove their way forward. Watching from on high the gods of destruction and war gloated and clapped their hands in pleasure as the rocky field filled with blood and carnage.

Swaying above the heads of his warriors, Ah Tabai could scarcely accept the truth of his eyes.

My holcánob are being slaughtered. Anger pounded in his blood. *This cannot be! They must overthrow Nachan Can's line! They must do it now!*

He again shrieked commands at all those about him.

"Forward! Forward you cowards! Forward! Are you warriors of Tzamá or not?"

Men surged to obey and Ah Tabai's bearers once again advanced and forced their way deeper into the fray.

At the call from Ah-cambal's shrill whistle, Naum and Okib, and all the others from K'optela, had leapt from their concealment and dashed out to join Ichpaatún's lines of beleaguered warriors. Positioned just behind Gonzalo and Ch'o', Okib waited anxiously griping a short spear, his knuckles white with effort. A short distance away, Naum clutched his bow and a quiver of arrows. From one moment to the next, the boys' emotions swung wildly back and forth between utter terror and frenzied excitement. Naum looked over at his companion.

"I'm afraid," he mouthed.

For once in his life Okib looked back at his hefty friend and couldn't find a glib reply.

At the other end of K'optela's short line, Naum's uncle, Long Steps, laid an arrow to his bow, drew its string as far back as he could, and released the barb high into the air. The field's slight slope allowed him to look over the heads of Ah-cambal's warriors and he'd spied the turmoil surrounding the Tzamán lord's approach. Letting loose his shaft, unaware of the mayhem's cause, he thought only to make it worse.

The untargeted arrow, when it eventually fell, dropped like one of the lightening god, K'awil's, thunderbolts. Directed by the hand of some other fickle god, it buried itself deeply into the chest of one of Ah Tabai's bearers.

The ill-fated porter gasped and struggled to remain upright. He bellowed like a wounded tapir, and then the life rushed out of him. As the man collapsed, Ah Tabai, standing precariously balanced up on his ornate chair, pitched forward. One moment he swayed above the heads of his warriors, the next he was plummeting to the rocky ground. With the breath knocked out of him, he turned his head just in time see his heavy palanquin crash down. Again the gods laughed, and at the sound of their laughter the Lord of Fire's world slipped into darkness.

His three uninjured bearers and a distraught servant rushed to Ah Tabai's aid. Struggling, they managed to lift the heavy chair and drag their lord out from beneath. His fine cloak was in tatters and his magnificent quetzal plumed headdress ruined. A long jagged gash ran from his jawline nearly to the back of his head. Blood covered his face. Ah Tabai's eyes had rolled back, and only a shallow wheezing breath asserted that his unconscious body still clung to its life.

Horrified, the four men lifted their lord, as carefully as they could, and then rushed away from the fighting toward the apparent safety of the jungle.

Many of the throng from The City of the Dawn saw their lord fall or witnessed his limp blood-spattered form as it was carried away. To his subjects, the Lord of Fire was a god made man. That he could suffer such injuries seemed beyond belief. Word of the disaster spread among the Tzamáns like a wildfire through dry grass and pandemonium followed in its wake.

One voice after another cried out, "If this can happen to our lord, the gods have turned against us."

Men threw down their weapons and began to flee. Others still pushed forward and as the two groups thrashed past one another the arrows and spears of Ichpaatún relentlessly continued to fall.

Oblivious to Ah Tabai's fate, Rat Skull finally butted his way to the front of the Tzamáns who still fought.

Now, I make my name remembered!

Before he could act, a hurtling arrow rocked his head and bounced off his stolen metal helm.

The gods are with me! I'm invincible! he thought, and then he howled with delight.

Just before him, a narrow gap opened in Ichpaatún's line and one of Nachan Can's holcánob shifted his shield to close it. Rat Skull realized the move left the man exposed. Reacting instantly, he struck with the speed of a serpent. Swinging his heavy flint bladed axe, he smashed it down onto the warrior's forearm. With the sound of cleaving meat, it chopped its way through both muscle and bone. The man screamed, dropped his shield, and staggered back. Rat Skull followed, delivered a killing blow, and then he was in and among his enemy.

"I'm Ch'o Ho'ol!" "I'm Ch'o Ho'ol," he yelled. "I'm Ch'o Ho'ol and Buluc Chabtan is with me! Buluc Chabtan is with me!"

Again his weapon buried itself into the flesh of Ichpaatún. As he wrenched it free hot blood spurted across his face and onto his chest.

They fall before me like t'u'ul'ob (rabbits), he smirked as he turned to seek another enemy.

Crouching warily before him waited two warriors holding spears. One man was small and the other... Recognition widened Rat Skull's eyes.

"I know you monkey man!" he thundered. "Tun Ch'ajom was my friend. Now, you breathe your last breath!"

In Gonzalo's mind lightening flashed. Hernando and Pedro died in front of him, and the man that he'd called Sansón loomed above.

Rat Skull lunged with his axe raised, but instead of the hairy savage who had washed onto his beach. It was the diminutive warrior from Ichpaatún who countered his attack.

The Tzamán was big and clearly enraged, nonetheless Mouse darted forward. *Many! I will kill many,* he thought as he charged. Confidently, and with the skill of many years, he thrust his spear straight at the larger man's waist.

With an almost unnatural speed, the man twisted. As his lance missed, Mouse stumbled. The Tzamán with the strange helmet again moved with a speed that belied his size and his own weapon came down with a force like a falling tree. When it struck, Ch'o's skull shattered and split. A final forlorn breath escaped his lungs and his strength and life slipped away. As the small warrior sprawled on the ground, Rat Skull turned to leer at Gonzalo.

"You next!" he hissed.

Horrified, Gonzalo moved woodenly. Rat Skull jumped to attack. Roaring, he swung his heavy axe, his great strength made greater still by his rage. Gonzalo threw up his shield.

With a sound of breaking reeds, the wicker and leather deflected the blow, but the powerful assault still knocked him to his knees. His hand went numb and the shield dropped from his grasp.

I'm a dead man, he thought.

Rat Skull laughed, an ugly sound, at once both savage and triumphant.

"Stone Scatterer must have been drunk or a thing like you could never have killed him," he snarled. "You're a pitiful opponent."

Grinning, he again raised his axe for a killing blow. Before he could bring it down, a terrible pain in his leg made him cry out. He spun. Just before him, a skinny young man brandished a spear that dripped blood. Enraged to madness, Rat Skull brought down his own still upraised weapon. The heavy flint blade smashed into the boy's neck. Hot blood gushed and the hapless boy crumpled dead at his feet. Rat Skull gave the body a swift kick with his uninjured leg.

The killing happened so fast that Gonzalo was still struggling to stand. Rat Skull spun back to finish him. The large Tzamán barely finished his turn when Naum's first arrow tore into his back. Okib's sudden death had reached into his friend's gentle soul and turned it to stone. In less than the space of a thought, he'd bent and drawn his bow.

Rat Skull turned once more seeking his new attacker and Naum's second arrow plunged into his chest. Almost immediately, a third arrow sprouted next to it. A coppery taste filled Rat Skull's mouth and bloodstained bubbles slipped past his parted lips. He swayed for a moment.

Gonzalo, forgotten and back on his feet, threw all of his weight behind his short spear and rammed it into the Tzamán's back. The razor edged obsidian blade drove deep, slicing through muscle and bone. A dazed look of pain and surprise crossed the large warrior's face. Buluc Chabtan smiled and accepted him as a suitable offering. Rat Skull's lifeless body crashed to the earth and Diego de Arana's helmet rattled across the stony ground.

At the renowned warrior's fall, a great shout rose up from the throats of Nachan Can's people and abruptly the men of Ichpaatún surged forward. With their nacons dead, their ranks decimated, and their lord gone, the City of the Dawn's remaining warriors lost what little courage they yet retained. Almost as one, they turned, cast away their weapons, and ran.

Close on their heels, trailed the vengeance of Ichpaatún. Across the field and back up into the jungle the Tzamáns fled, but only those who were fleet of foot escaped with their lives.

Watching the tide turn, Gonzalo sank back to the ground and drew his knees up to his chest. Nearby, the young archer who had saved him cradled his fallen friend and moaned softly. Just out of reach, Mouse's shattered form rested face down, in death seemingly smaller still. Where Ichpaatún's lines had held, a dozen more bodies lay scattered. Beyond that, dead and dying Tzamáns carpeted the field. Near the front of their advance their arrow-feathered corpses lay two and three deep. Gonzalo felt his throat grow thick with an uncomfortable mix of pride and grief.

We won! Beyond all hope, we won!

A dusty sandaled foot nudged his leg. Looking up, his eyes met Ah-cambal. Filth covered his friend and blood oozed from a slight wound across his chest; nevertheless, his face glowed.

"This is your doing," he praised. "Ahulane and Hun Pic Toc heard your prayers and they answered you! You are in their favor. When we return to Ichpaatún we must make many offerings of thanks."

Gonzalo buried his face into his hands and wept.

<h1 style="text-align:center">Chapter 42</h1>

<h1 style="text-align:center">Cutz Ahau</h1>

11 Bak'tun 14 K'atun 11 Tun 14 Uinal 11 K'in

(January 29, 1512)

K'inich Ajaw would soon descend into the underworld to renew his endless battle with the lords of night. To the west a sky streaked with bands of red and purple foretold of the coming darkness.

Ah K'in Cutz worried and, with the worry, his annoyance grew. Days had passed without a single message from Ah Tabai or Ac Yanto. That in and of itself troubled him, but the muttered rumors were worse.

Old Kish had arrived from Xamanzamá to help and serve Cutz while he oversaw Tzamá in their Lord of Fire's absence. Two days earlier, the elder chilán, whose sharp ears were always collecting information, had brought Cutz a curious whisper of some calamity. Cutz duly went to work, but without success, to discover the truth of Kish's report. The few Tzamáns he questioned, either knew nothing or were too frightened to speak. Left unsatisfied, Cutz waited.

I've done what I can, he reasoned. *The idle gossip of a witless peasant or two means nothing. If anything of importance occurred at Ichpaatún, I would have received word. Ah Tabai is big-headed. He's conceited. Likely he just wants to bask in the glory of his great victory suddenly revealed.*

The temporary sovereign of Tzamá and his elderly retainer were standing next to a long wall, enjoying heat where the day's warmth still lingered, when the elder chilán pointed to a servant running toward them.

"Great Ah K'in," the man gushed, throwing himself to the ground, "I'm bidden by venerable Imix (Crocodile) to tell you that our divine Lord of Fire returns."

Imix was an ageing warrior charged to keep watch at Tzamá's entrance.

Cutz fumed. *He returns without word? No messages, no runners; he'll expect a lavish reception!*

Ignoring the servant, still prostrated on the ground, he turned to Kish.

"Go quickly, spread the word; the Great Man returns and he'll expect to be met by his adoring subjects. Go now!"

Without further instruction, he rushed off leaving the elder chilán to catch up when done. Cutz hurried, but not so hastily as to appear undignified, and soon stood next to Imix facing the city's main entrance.

"Well?" He demanded.

"Our Lord of Fire is nearly here, Great Ah K'in," mumbled the old warrior. "Two women just told me of his approach."

"Two women?" questioned Cutz. "Where are they?"

"They ran off, Ah K'in," apologized the old warrior.

Cutz regarded the man with disgust.

Nearly here, he doubted. *Either this is foolishness, or something is amiss. Why do we not hear his drums? Where are the sounds of his shell trumpets?*

At that moment, a mass of people shuffled into view. Cutz stared at them stunned. No proud warlike host with their triumphant lord held on high, instead a disorganized throng that consisted of bedraggled servants and slaves, and no more than a score of dejected looking warriors. In their midst, they lugged a crude litter. One of the warriors approached Cutz and knelt. The man was dirty and looked exhausted.

"Honored Ah K'in," he choked. "The gods have forsaken us." Then, he gestured toward the litter. "Yajawk'ak'."

Cutz' mind raced. *That's Ah Tabai on the litter? How can this be?*

Despite his contempt and his doubt concerning the man's divinity, somewhere deep inside Cutz still held the ruler of Tzamá in a modicum awe. The idea that the Lord of Fire could be brought to such a sorry state was difficult to accept.

"Hurry," commanded Cutz, "bring him in and lay him there."

Trailed by the rest of the crowd, the warriors carried the litter through the arched opening in the city's wall. Carefully, they set it down on a long stone bench and stepped away. Cutz hurried forward and gaped.

Ah Tabai looked one stride from death. His once glorious attire was disheveled and covered in filth. His labored breath wheezed sluggishly in and out, and his head had flopped to the side. The

Great Man's jaw hung slack, and open, and a thick rivulet of drool dripped across his chin. Near the litter wafted a stench of urine and loosened bowels.

I never realized, Cutz thought suddenly, *how much he looks like his idiot son, Yajawte'.*

At that moment, Kish arrived trailed by Ah Tabai's two wives and a covey of the ruler's lesser councilors. Immediately the scene devolved into disorder. Lady Sunstroke and Lady Waterlily Sprout wailed, sobbed, and threw themselves onto their husband's litter. His young daughter, Whirling Squirrel, took one look at her lifeless father and let out a high pitched keening scream that went on and on. The councilors all yelled at the same time, each trying to shout louder than those around him.

Ah K'in Cutz ignored them all. Purposely, he turned away from the litter and his eyes sought the warrior who'd spoken to him. Without a word to anyone, he stalked over to the man, took him by the arm, and drew him aside.

"Did you lead this rabble and bring our lord back from Ichpaatún?" he demanded.

"Great Ah K'in, when Gucumatz lived I was his third," trembled the man. "There was no one else."

"No one?" questioned Cutz. "What of Ac Yanto? What of Rat Skull?"

"Dead Ah K'in, all dead."

Cutz could barely believe his ears. "Tell me everything! Start at the beginning. Leave nothing out!"

Slowly and apprehensively the warrior related the myriad details of the disaster that had overtaken the host from Tzamá.

Nachan Can and Ah-cambal were devious and cunning, mused Cutz, *and Ah Tabai and Ac Yanto were fools!*

When Ah Tabai marched off to exact his revenge, Cutz had silently seethed with anger at being left behind. While there was a measure of honor in having the Lord of Fire appoint him to oversee affairs in his absence, he'd felt certain that a much greater glory and renown awaited those who marched toward Ichpaatún. After listening to the calamitous tale, Cutz felt thankful that he hadn't accompanied Ah Tabai to his ignominious fate.

Unbidden, an image of the goggle-eyed and jaguar-fanged god, Tláloc, filled his mind. The god's gaze seemed to bore into his core.

This day isn't a tragedy, he realized. *This is a boon, a boon that I've been given! Dead, they're all dead. Ac Yanto is dead. Rat Skull is dead. Once Ah Tabai is dead, no one will remain to challenge me.*

Returning his attention to the man in front of him, Cutz gazed sternly. "You, who were third to Gucumatz, what are you called?"

"They call me, Cheb', Great Ah K'in, replied the warrior."

"Until his return, the Lord of Fire charged me to rule Tzamá in his stead," declared Cutz. "You've returned his broken body, but his wounded spirit wanders. Until its finds its way back to us, I will continue to rule.

"Cheb', you've done well! You are no longer third to anyone. From this moment on, I name you Nacon of Tzamá. Do you understand?"

"Yes Ahau (Lord)," nodded Cheb', but his face registered only confusion.

"Excellent," responded Cutz. "Nacon, organize your men. Disperse this crowd, then carry our Lord of Fire to his residence where I will attend to his injuries. Old Kish, over there, will help you see to his wives and daughter."

Cheb' continued to look perplexed and uncomfortable; nevertheless began to bark orders. Shortly, Ah Tabai's litter was moving away, and the small plaza emptied. Cutz lingered a moment looking about.

There's an irony here, he thought. *This is the same courtyard where I brought word to Ah Tabai that death had overtaken Zac Nok and Gucumatz. All dead! Cheb' said, and he led because, "There was no one else." When Ah Tabai dies, there will again be no one else. The weaklings of his Ah Cuchcab will turn to me and I alone will rule.*

Cheb' had called him, Ahau (Lord) and he liked the sound of it.

Cutz Ahau!

Grinning to himself, he hurried toward Ah Tabai's dwelling where he planned to make convincing but ineffectual efforts to save the Lord of Fire's life.

Perhaps, like the unfortunate stone mason, Paklah-sus, he'll need his skull opened, he mused.

Ten days later, the Halach Uinic still lingered. A little water had been forced down his throat, but from day to day he lay unconscious and unmoving. Cutz stood alone in the ruler's darkened chamber. It was late at night and a single flickering rushlight gave the room's only illumination. Aromatic smoke rose from two small braziers and sought to mask the cloying smell that surrounded Ah Tabai's pallet.

Cutz stared down in hatred. With each passing day, his impatience had grown.

When he's gone, thought Cutz, *I'll suggest that his wives and his brats offer themselves to Ixtab (Rope Woman). It will be a simple matter to convince them that the goddess will welcome their suicides and lead them to Ah Tabai's side for an eternity without want.*

He pictured himself tightening the noose around drooling Yajawte's neck and it brought an unpleasant smile to his lips.

Abruptly, Cutz realized there was no need to wait. Sinking to his knees, he picked up a thick wad of cloth and pressed it tightly against the Lord of Fire's nose and mouth. For a heartbeat nothing happened, then Ah Tabai's body shook and seemed to struggle. Then, there was nothing.

All of them dead! Cutz reveled.

Carefully, he stood, straightened his attire, and prepared to inform Tzamá that their glorious Lord of Fire had begun his journey to the afterlife.

The sacred Tzolk'in had turned and the day was 13 Ahau, the time of rulers and lords.

Chapter 43

Enmity of the Gods

11 Bak'tun 14 K'atun 11 Tun 16 Uinal 12 K'in

(March 10, 1512)

Thup Paal, Xamanzamá's only remaining chilán, struggled with the passage of days. His heart advised him that time itself should have ground to a halt. Yet, K'inich Ajaw persisted in his eternal journey across the sky and the sacred Tzolk'in' continued to turn. From hard-won knowledge that he gleaned as acolyte to Ah K'in Cutz, Thup Paal knew the true count of the Tzolk'in's days. But the significance of each day felt muddled, their meanings no longer relevant.

The death of the Lord of Fire and the startling slaughter orchestrated by Nachan Can, the sajal of Ichpaatún, had changed everything. Two uinal (months) plus one k'in (day) had passed since the night of Ah Tabai's death. Thup Paal knew that the great wheel rested upon 6 Eb', often a day of small problems. Yet none of the young chilán's problems were small. Loss and uncertainty plagued the inhabitants of Xamanzamá leaving them desolate and bewildered. In their grief and despair they had turned to Thup Paal and expected him to provide both guidance and answers.

K'inich Ajaw's day was mild and Thup Paal sat on a reed mat. He'd carefully placed the mat in front of a large empty dwelling that, until recently, belonged to Ac Yanto. Thup Paal's mercurial uncle, had often held public audiences in the same spot. To Thup Paal's mind, the location seemed appropriate for what was to come.

Ac Yanto's sole remaining councilors, a pair of men too aged and infirm to have joined the expedition to Ichpaatún, had urged Thup Paal to meet with the people and try to assuage their growing unease.

How can I help others, he thought, *when such disquiet fills and troubles my own heart?*

The patio's open side faced Xamanzamá's main plaza, and at the appointed hour people began quietly to arrive. They came in ones and twos, and occasionally a small group of three or four.

Those who arrived first, found places close to Thup Paal. One and all they acknowledged him with bowed heads, and murmured greetings of, "Ah K'in."

The lesser chilán had time and again imagined a day when he would merit that title. To have it arrive carried on the backs of so many dead made it feel undeserved and unearned. With each respectful, "Ah K'in" Thup Paal felt more the imposter.

Unsure of what to say, the young chilán waited. Although the chosen time for the meeting was well past, he still hesitated to speak. All of Xamanzamá's people had come, but the plaza remained nearly empty.

Are we really now so few? he wondered.

Ac Yanto had commanded that all able-bodied men, young or old, join with him to carry the Lord of Fire's vengeance, almost none who answered that call had returned.

If my uncle had not counted me a fool and left me behind, I too would be among the dead.

A woman, flanked by two small children, who Thup Paal knew as Eme, broke the expectant silence.

"Ah K'in, My husband, Ikan, was a good man. Why was he taken from me?"

"I was with Ikan," spoke up Makiq, one of the few men to have returned unscathed. "I saw the arrow take him. Their shafts fell upon us like rain. Men of Ichpaatún set arrows to their bows, but I believe some god or gods directed their flight. How else could so few have overcome so many?"

"Why have the gods turned their faces away from us?" sobbed Sacnite (White Flower), who also lost her husband.

"And what of food?" spoke up Itzel, Makiq's practical wife. "We were hungry before the harvest, but it was a poor harvest and our grain baskets are again nearly empty. With so many of our men gone, how will we work our hun vinic (plots)?"

This drew mutters from the gathered people. Thup Paal slowly stood, trying desperately to think of soothing answers. With the same urgent questions on his own mind, he had spent days and nights, praying. He'd pricked his ears and offered drops of blood and smoldering blue-painted cakes of pom to Itzamna, the mighty god of wisdom and knowledge. He believed, that in response, Itzamna had revealed the conduct and transgressions that inexorably led to this day. As to what to do now, he felt the elder god remained silent. Halfway to his feet, Thup Paal abruptly realized that wasn't the case.

Itzamna told me, but I didn't listen carefully enough to hear. Eb' is a day of small problems, he remembered, *but Eb' is also the best day for new beginnings. Today is an auspicious day to begin a journey!* Then, he knew what he had to say.

"I believe that Sacnite speaks truth, some of our gods have turned away from us. Why? Not because of our own misdeeds, rather because we enabled the misdeeds of others. The Lord of Fire, Ah K'in Zac Nok, and Gucumatz grievously offended our lord Chac. And, Ah Puch take them both, Ac Yanto and Rat Skull ordered us to support their sacrilege. To our shame, we followed them as though tootkook (deaf and dumb).

"We are justly punished. In Tzamá Ah K'in Cutz, even now, declares himself high priest and ruler and further provokes the enmity of the heavens!

"Not all of our gods have turned from us, but these lands are surely cursed by those who have."

This pronouncement elicited quiet gasps and moans from the crowd.

"What must we do, Ah K'in? How do we lift this torment?" shouted Makiq."

Thup Paal raised his hands and his voice, "We must all, every one of us, leave this place and with it, its curse. Great Itzamna has shown this to me."

"But, where would we go?" stammered Eme"

"I don't know," shrugged Thup Paal. "I only know that Itzamna wants each of us to make offerings and this day begin a journey that leads us away from these lands."

"Ah K'in," shouted a man at the edge of the crowd. "Are you certain of this?"

"When one communes with the gods, there is always uncertainty. But of this I am certain," declared Thup Paal. "If we want to regain the goodwill of those who have turned from us, this is a penance we must accept. We must leave!"

Later, after discussion and argument ran their course, there was nothing left to say. All those who'd gathered returned to their homes or their toils and Thup Paal walked back to his own dwelling. At its entrance, Ac Yanto's two aged councilors waited impatiently.

"What have you done?" demanded one.

"We asked you to soothe our people," grumbled the other, "not tell them to flee their homes!"

"I spoke the truth," answered Thup Paal. "I spoke as the Lord Itzamna instructed me."

"Instructed you! You are not a true ah k'in! The gods don't converse with you any more than they talk to a feckless pek' (dog)!"

"All you had to do was try to look ts'o'oka'an (smart) and offer comforting platitudes!"

The old men continued to lecture and berate, growing more agitated with each outburst. Thup Paal smiled pleasantly and remained silent which only served to increase their annoyance. Finally, with their vitriol nearly spent, one of them pointed at him with a crooked finger.

"Ac Yanto was right," he grunted. "You are a fool!"

Disgusted, the two turned and hobbled away.

Thup Paal felt serene and knew in his heart that his actions were guided. After the councilors left, he went into his home and began to sort goods for his own journey. He found a large woven carrying sack and into it he placed a few possessions and such foodstuffs as he deemed sensible. At dusk, he burned cakes of incense to thank Itzamna and to petition Ekchuah, the traveler's god, to watch over him.

Stepping outside, Thup Paal shouldered his bag and made his way to the rooms that still belonged to Ah K'in Cutz. Inside the familiar space, he walked straight to where his supposed mentor kept his three precious hu'unob. He picked up the sacred books, slipped them into his bag, and left without a backward glance.

At the outskirts of Xamanzamá, Thup Paal encountered Itzel, also lugging a sack. Beside her waited Makiq a large carrying basket suspended on his back. The couple shyly greeted the ah k'in, then led by the light of the moon goddess, Ix Chel, the three of them turned away from their pasts and walked into the jungle.

Chapter 44

The Castaway

The 17th of February, Year of Our Lord 1519

In the City of the Dawn three men squatted comfortably on the dusty ground before a dilapidated hut. Above the hovel's only entrance, the clear light of K'inich Ajaw's new day drew attention to a crude and clumsily affixed wooden cross. Nothing of appearance separated the three men one from the other. One was perhaps ungracefully tall, thin, and hairy compared to his fellows, but the skin of all three was burnt a deep nut brown, and burnt again, by the tropical the sun. They wore their thick black hair long and tied it back with random bits of twine. Their feet were unshod and thickly callused; their bodies were naked except for narrow strips of cloth that wrapped around their waists and then hung down in front and back. Nothing significant distinguished any of the men, until one of them spoke.

"We implore thee, Oh Lord, that thou give us grace in thy example, that we may serve thee in all things great and small, and that we may keep thy righteous commandments. We know that the demon is abroad in this land and that he schemes endlessly to lead us into damnation. We give our thanks to thee for thy divine protection."

These pious utterances were delivered in out-of-practice Castilian, and neither of the men squatting next to the talker understood even a single word. The speaker then, invoked the Sign of the Cross and gave his companions an equally incomprehensible benediction.

"May almighty God bless you both, the Father, and the Son, and the Holy Spirit."

Switching to the native tongue, in which he was now more comfortable, he finished, "It is done."

All three men stood up and with many smiles and various partings two of them took leave of their lanky companion. Since the fateful day when Fray Geronimo de Aguilar waded in from the sea and onto the shore of The Land of the Turkey and the Deer, nearly eight long years had slowly come and gone. During that seemingly boundless stretch of time, humble trappings of the life he once knew had slowly eroded away.

The torn and threadbare robe of his religious order had rotted to rags and then the rags rotted to tatters, until, to his shame, Geronimo was as unclothed before God as were the idolatrous natives who surrounded him. And, although he went to great lengths to conceal it, his precious, soiled, and well-worn breviary had simply disappeared. One day it was where he always hid it, the next it was gone. He was certain that it was stolen, but he never managed to discover a culprit.

Without his small liturgy of the hours, he struggled to keep track of the passing days and to remember all the prayers, psalms, and holy services that each day required.

At intervals, the spirit and confidence of the solitary Franciscan wavered and he staggered perilously close to losing all hope. At those times, only an absolute certainty that his burdens were placed upon him by his Lord God inevitably tempered his growing despair.

I give myself over to thy heavenly service and in so doing find thy yoke sweet and light. You've brought me to this land that I might carry your holy word to those who've never had a chance to hear it. Thank you Lord for tasking me to bring the idolaters of this land into your loving fold.

Belief in a godly calling motivated the friar's days and nights and, once he acquired the natives' language, he had worked unstintingly to spread his God's word. To his sorrow, although his captors grudgingly tolerated his zealous mission, his energetic and interminable efforts yielded but trivial fruit.

A few natives, like the two with whom he'd prayed, seemed to view him as a potent spiritual actor, yet still they resisted God's grace. Many others were deeply suspicious of him and deliberately shunned his presence.

Over the years, to any who would listen, he'd tried to explain the mysteries of the creation and the fall, the mysteries of the trinity and the incarnation, and the mysteries of the passion and the resurrection. When he finished one of his homilies, he would then hold up his tiny cross of twigs and tell his listeners that he grieved that they were not in the Lord's grace and explain how the one true God had sent him among them to save their souls.

Some of the idolaters who heard his words laughed out loud at his foolish claims. Others shrugged and stalked off bemused. Still others like the unclean priest of the demon, who now styled himself Lord Cutz, took offence and became angered.

"You, a jk'áat máatan (beggar) dare to profess that our gods are false," the self-proclaimed lord of Tzamá had blustered. "You cry that we don't recognize the oneness of heaven and earth. Our very first ancestors were created by the gods! You insult their teachings! They believed! They taught us to honor the gods! That is why we draw our blood and do penance. That is why we burn copal. You are less than an xnook'ol (worm)! Your stupidity offends me!"

On that occasion Geronimo was beaten with a stick and driven from Cutz' presence. That was many years ago and much had changed. Following the death of the Lord of Fire and the ascendency of Ah K'in Cutz, the great city of Tzamá had withered.

In exchange for their unquestioning loyalty, the people of The Land of the Turkey and the Deer expected their rulers to intercede with the gods on their behalf. This intercession was the key responsibility of divine sovereigns like Ah Tabai, and also spiritual guides like White Worm, and Ah K'in Cutz. That they pray, sacrifice, do penance, and thereby secure the gods' goodwill was their obligation.

The gods' acceptance or rejection of the rulers' devotions determined whether impending weather was mild or harsh, the success or failure of crops, the prevalence of disease or lack thereof, and indeed all important aspects good or evil of their subjects' lives.

Following on the heels of many failed harvests and the extraordinary debacle at Ichpaatún, it had become clear to the people of Tzamá that their rulers had failed them. In so doing, Ah Tabai and the others had betrayed their understood compact.

In search of their gods' lost favor, people slowly left. In ones and twos and sometimes groups they quietly disappeared into the jungle. With each passing year fewer people called the great City of the Dawn home. Its markets grew smaller and smaller, more and more huts stood abandoned, and everywhere signs of neglect grew more and more evident.

Then, a few seasons past, a strange and terrible pox arrived and illness and death had stalked the land. Geronimo took the plague as a sure sign of his God's hand. He remained, if not hale, at least healthy while the unfortunate natives around him perished in droves.

When Geronimo first caught sight of the City of Dawn he'd exclaimed that, "Seville would not appear larger or better." Now, he could not imagine having ever held such an absurd thought.

Despite the city's precipitous downward spiral, Geronimo's own status had remained relatively unchanged. As far as he could discern, he was yet a prisoner, a feckless slave whose ownership had passed to Ah K'in Cutz. Nonetheless, even the least of the natives who remained seemed to hold authority over him. Frequently, he was imperiously ordered to perform some unpleasant task or other, but for the most part the work was rarely onerous.

If and when he remembered, an old man named Kish gave Geronimo scraps of simple food. Kish was forgetful, however, and the castaway often went hungry for days on end. From time to time, Lord Cutz engaged him in long talks. On these occasions the cagey ruler questioned him endlessly about his professed god and the lands from which he claimed to have come. Most days, Geronimo wandered unnoticed and forgotten, left to his own designs.

On several occasions, he tried to walk beyond the city's walls. Each time, he was roughly turned back by stern-faced guards. After his fourth attempt, Cheb', a muscular man, who led those few warriors who yet remained in Tzamá, beat him so severely that he never tried again.

On the afternoon following the simple prayers before his hut, the exile's footsteps carried him down to the City of the Dawn's small sheltered harbor. The once busy cove used to be filled to bursting with heavily laden trade canoes of all sizes, each of them jostling for position. At all hours, its small beach echoed with shouts and cries of the traders. Now, on most days, Geronimo expected to encounter few if any merchants, and perhaps a fishermen or two cleaning their catch or diligently mending their nets.

On days that God so chose, a weary trader, or perhaps an idle fishermen, would sometimes be willing to sit and be entertained by Geronimo's outlandish stories. If not, the cove was still a favorite place for the castaway. The air off the sea typically blew in fresh and clean; the sand was warm. With his eyes half closed the castaway could almost see the coasts of his home waiting just over the horizon.

When Geronimo arrived, the cove, as usual, stood deserted except for a single wretched dugout. Its owner, repacking it with his humble wares, was the beach's only occupant. The Franciscan had just settled himself at ease onto the soft sand, when another much larger and more respectable canoe, energetically paddled by four unfamiliar natives, drove itself forcefully up onto the beach. While three men held their craft and looked cautiously about, the fourth jumped out and hurried straight to Geronimo.

"You Christian?" the man slurred.

The two words were awkward and the accent atrocious, but with shock Geronimo realized the man had just addressed him in Spanish.

"Yes, I'm a Christian," he answered in the same language.

Without another word, the man reach up into hair piled on his head and drew forth something. Extending his hand, he offered the object to Geronimo. It looked to be a small roll of paper, held tightly closed by a red wax seal. Warily, he extended his own hand and took the proffered object. Working carefully, he broke the unfamiliar seal and unrolled the tube. At first he couldn't believe his eyes. The small scroll was covered in writing and the writing was also in Spanish.

"Dear Sirs and Brothers, Here, on the island of Cozumel, I received information that you are detained prisoners by a native chief. I beg of you come to me on the island of Cozumel. To this end I have sent out an armed ship, and ransom-money, should it be required. I have ordered the ship to wait for you off the promontory of Cotoche for six days. I am here with eleven vessels armed with 500 soldiers. Come as swiftly as possible and I will treat you honorably."

The brief message was signed with a flourish by some personage, named Hernando Cortés.

The small but momentous document shook like a leaf in Geronimo's hands.

Can this letter be true? he doubted. Is *God truly about to liberate me from my captivity?*

The native who delivered the note began to speak rapidly in his own tongue urging Geronimo to hurry and join his fellows in their waiting canoe.

"Tal beora (come now)."

The castaway roiled with indecision. *What should I do? What if this is some deceit? Should I go with these men, all of whom are unknown to me? And if this is indeed deliverance, what of Aroça?*

Now and again during the long years of the friar's captivity, some native or other had brought hearsay to Geronimo of his companion's supposed fate. He hadn't seen or spoken to Gonzalo in seven years, but he felt certain that he was still alive and living more than eighty leagues to the south. Rumor claimed that his fellow castaway had somehow played a deciding role in the encounter that led to the Lord of Fire's death.

If other stories were to be believed, Aroça was married, had sired three children, and had allowed his face to be tattooed and his ears pierced. Allegedly, the people of Ichpaatún even favored him as their nacon.

If this message is true, thought Geronimo, *this chance will not come again! I must trust in God and go with these men. But still, what of Aroça?*

Looking about, his eyes fell on the lone trader and his modest canoe. Urging the now impatient messenger to wait, he hurried over to the solitary merchant.

"Where do you go from here?" he panted.

The dark-skinned man looked up in surprise. "I follow the coast," he replied. "Muyil, Chectumal, and if my luck holds Lamanai, many stops along the way."

"Will you carry this for me to Ichpaatún, and give it to their nacon?" pled Geronimo, holding up the roll of paper.

"What is it?" demanded the trader, eyeing the roll with suspicion.

"A harmless offering, nothing more," responded Aguilar. "I can pay you for your trouble."

That said, he reached into a fold of his loin cloth and drew out a small cunningly worked jade bead. Years ago, The Franciscan had stumbled across the bauble laying forgotten in the dirt. It was his most valuable possession.

A fleeting look of greed flickered across the native's face, "I will take it."

Geronimo quickly tore a tiny strip from his girdle and tied it around the message.

"Here," he said, handing the trader the bead and the roll of paper. "May your voyage be profitable and may God watch over you."

With that, he turned away and ran to where the four unfamiliar natives waited. The instant he settled in their canoe, the men pushed off and paddled furiously toward the open sea. Once they cleared the cove's headland, the paddlers changed direction and proceeded up the coast.

Resting infrequently and stopping only for brief periods at night, it took several long days for the canoe to reach the point that Cortés had called Cabo Cotoche. During the journey, the four natives repeatedly reassured Geronimo that the message was legitimate and that a great Spanish ship awaited them. When just after dawn they reached that promontory, nothing was to be seen except rolling swells and empty water.

A furious and somewhat heated discussion ensued. Geronimo, scared and accusatory, demanded to know why there was no ship.

"We are late. It has gone," responded the natives as one. "If you want to find the other Christians, we must cross the strait to Cozumel."

The island, just visible on the horizon, lay nearly twelve leagues away. Steering by sight, adjusting for a strong current, and rowing continuously for nearly eight hours, the four oarsmen covered the distance. In late afternoon, under blue skies, they reached Cozumel's coast and shortly after entered a natural harbor on the island's southern coast. The sight that presented itself threatened to rob Geronimo of his senses.

Eleven formidable Spanish vessels, a veritable armada, lay quietly at anchor. From the masthead of each flew a great white and blue banner displaying an image of the blessed virgin and a holy cross of the deepest red. On land a sprawling encampment with many tents and many more banners bustled with activity.

The moment Geronimo's canoe touched the shore, a dozen foot soldiers came running over. Outfitted in chainmail and leather armor the men carried pikes or swords of fine steel. One held a crossbow. The captain who led them wore a heavy metal breastplate with arm and leg greaves, and bellowed in Spanish as he approached.

"Come no closer! What business have you here?"

The other soldiers also shouted and as one they menaced the natives with their weapons. Faced with such fierce intimidation, Aguilar and his companions squatted on the ground and cowered. The native who'd delivered Cortés' message quickly spoke up in his broken Spanish and pointed.

"He Christian! He Christian!"

"He doesn't look like one," shouted one of the soldiers.

"Is this true?" demanded the captain, turning to Geronimo. "Are you a Christian? Are you Spanish?"

After so long among the natives, the words of his own language sounded strange and his own tongue felt thick when he tried to reply.

"Yes, I was shipwrecked on these lands with Valdivia."

"Come with me," ordered the captain, dragging Geronimo to his feet. Then, he addressed his soldiers. "Guard these others until you hear from me."

Walking quickly, he led Geronimo through the camp until they reached a large tent. Outside, a well-dressed man sat on a three-legged stool staring intently at a makeshift table covered with maps. At the captain's approach, the man stood.

"What is this?" he demanded.

"Your excellency," responded the captain. "This one here says that he is a Christian and a Spaniard."

The man walked around the table to stand before Geronimo.

"I am Hernándo Cortés de Monroy y Pizarro Altamirano and this is my expedition. Who are you?"

"I, I'm Fray Gerónimo de Aguilar. I was born in Écija. I received your message. I have been a prisoner for... I, I."

Unable to go on, Geronimo fell to his knees with tears rolling down his face and loudly gave thanks to God. After a time, when he somewhat composed himself, Cortés took off his own jacket, placed it over the friar's shoulders. Then, he helped the castaway back to his feet.

"Your ordeal has ended," said the conquistador. "You are now among friends. But what of the other Christian? I was told that two of you were held captive."

Fray Geronimo thought for a moment before he spoke.

"His name is Gonzalo, my friend," he responded. "He was an adventurer with Alonso de Ojeda's ill-fated expedition to Darien. I sent him your message Sir, but I do not believe that he will come.

"In his heart, he is a verdadero guerrero (true warrior). It is said that he is much valued by the people here. He has taken a wife, he has children. Except for his determination, I would not be alive. No, he will not come. He's no longer one of us."

Chapter 45

Mestizaje

11 Bak'tun 14 K'atun 18 Tun 17 Uinal 9 K'in

(February 29, 1519)

The late morning, like the one before it, was both warm and mild. Za'azil sat with her legs outstretched and her back comfortably pressed against the smooth trunk of the yaxché that towered over the front of her home. Breezes off the bay scarcely moved the air; the tree's thick canopy scattered K'inich Ajaw's rays, and, chin resting on her chest, she drowsed contentedly.

"Mother! Mother! Wake up you lazy thing," teased Óolal lightly shaking her shoulder.

"I wasn't asleep," countered Za'azil groggily. "I was just resting."

"Mother?" intoned Óolal.

"Well perhaps I drifted a bit," admitted Za'azil looking blearily about.

Her adopted daughter, clearly pregnant, stood just in front of her with her hands positioned firmly on her hips. Several large baskets lay beside her feet and Za'azil's two natural sons fidgeted just behind her legs.

"We need to hurry," urged Óolal. "Yunuen (Half Moon), and the other men, are probably already drawing in their net!"

Za'azil laughed silently as she levered herself up. Yunuen, Óolal's husband, was a sweet boy who loved his young wife to distraction. But, evidence of Óolal's gravid condition aside, he was still a gangly youth even now growing into his manhood.

Laughing, joking, and taking the two little boys in tow, Óolal and Za'azil picked up their baskets and ambled quickly toward the bay.

The Bay of Chectumal is full of life which accounted for Ichpaatún's location close to its shore. The people habitually fished its waters using lines, hooks, and nets. Sometimes they worked alone, sometimes together with others. Today, the small fish were running and nearly everyone was on hand to help.

A long net of cotton twine had been carefully prepared with floats, and then weighted with broken pieces of pottery. While most of the men waited patiently on the shore, three experienced older men, paddling crude reed boats, carried the net well out into the bay. They painstakingly lowered it into the water and then stretched it into a huge horn-shaped curve. Two of them carried its ends back to shore while the third paddled along its perimeter nudging and pulling so that the great net held its shape. Splitting into two groups, the waiting men took up its ends and slowly hauled the heavy net and hopefully its wriggling catch toward the beach.

This was the scene that met Za'azil as she walked out onto the coarse sand.

So much has changed, she mused, *yet so much remains the same.*

Her eyes easily picked out Gonzalo, knee deep in the water, standing a head taller than all the other men. Yunuen, who idolized him, stood close behind, both heaving on the heavy net. Gonzalo looked up, spotted Za'azil, and waved happily.

Shortly following the long-ago defeat of Tzamá, and after many serious discussions, Nachan Can and Ah-cambal had attributed their victory to Gonzalo and proclaimed him Ichpaatún's nacon. They then anointed him during elaborate ceremonies, praised his courage and cunning, and bestowed on him all the privileges and responsibilities that belong to that rank. For three years, he would serve as their war chief and during that time, he would hold no congress with women, be provided with a home, and also with food and drink. Since Hoch Can was the last to hold that position it was his home, the one that he had shared with Za'azil, which they presented to Gonzalo.

The next thing that happened was that, Nachan Can and his wife, Ix Chan Ek, had decided to present Gonzalo with Za'azil.

In Ichpaatún, the marriage of widows took place without festival or ceremony. The man simply went to the woman's house, he was admitted and given food to eat, and with that it was deemed a marriage.

Nachan Can and Ix Chan Ek believed this a shrewd solution of what to do with their widowed daughter-in-law. They had accepted Za'azil into their family because of Hoch Can's love, but, with him dead and interred, her situation had grown awkward.

She was the wife of their son, wife of Ichpaatún's dead nacon, and consequently a person of standing. It would be unseemly to unceremoniously send her back to her humble parents.

On the other hand, she was the daughter of a poor salt trader and held no intrinsic or hereditary status among the city's elite. By wedding her to Gonzalo she ostensibly maintained her position. Also the union would serve to bind the now valued warrior more tightly into their community. When they informed her of their decision, Za'azil screamed.

"No! No! How can you ask me such a thing! He's not one of us. He's a barbarian! We know nothing of him or his people."

"It was his counsel that led us to overthrow Tzamá," responded Nachan Can. "The gods smile upon him. It is just that he is nacon!"

"Yes! Yes!" wailed, Za'azil, but there is nothing just about offering me to him as wife. He's a savage! Hoch Can was your son! This shames his memory!"

"Be silent child," scolded Ix Chan Ek. "Hoch Can knew his duty as should you! We offer you a place of respect. Would you rather spend your days digging salt?"

"This is not your choice," snapped Nachan Can. "I am sajal here. You will do as I say!"

Za'azil collapsed to her knees, then buried her face into her hands and moaned. As she knelt whimpering, Ah-cambal softly placed his hands on her shoulders.

"Za'azil, Daughter, we know that you genuinely loved Hoch Can and that he in his turn truly loved you. We too loved your cherished husband, but regrettably he is dead and he is never coming back. Hoch Can now rests among our illustrious ancestors so we must all look toward the future that yet lies before you. I have come to know this man, this Gonzalo. As you say, he is not of our people, but he is wise and he has a kind heart. I would never agree to this proposal if I did not think it was to your benefit."

Za'azil had then stumbled to her feet and fled. Back in her darkening house, she lit incense and pleaded with the goddess Ixchel.

"Please Grandmother, you never answered my prayers for a child, hear me now. I beg you, soften Nachan Can's heart so that he and Ix Chan Ek don't force this terrible thing upon me."

She repeated her plea over and over with offerings of tears and drops of her blood, but the venerable jaguar goddess remained silent. In that silence, Za'azil's thoughts turned to the ceiba tree and to Ixtab (Rope Woman).

Would not such a death be more honorable than the alternative I'm offered? Ixtab will welcome me and will guide my soul.

In the morning K'inich Ajaw brought back the light and Za'azil did nothing. Desolate, she remained in the house and soon Gonzalo also took up residence. She prepared his meals, cared for his needs, and lived in fear. For his part, he treated her with sympathy and respect. He thanked her for what she did, abided by his promised celibacy, and never tried to lay his hands upon her.

Gonzalo doted on Óolal and the young girl delighted in his company. Za'azil watched as they joyfully bonded and slowly her fear grew less. Over time, proximity and mutual respect matured into something more. When the great wheel of the haab' completed its third turn she invited the barbarian into her bed. He was gentle and attentive and shortly Za'azil bore their first son, whom Gonzalo insisted be given the strange name of Juan. Another turn of the haab' and Ixchel blessed them with their second child, another son that they called, Pedro.

Side by side Gonzalo and Yunuen walked out of the water as the last of the net was hauled up onto the shore. As it emptied, a flashing wave of struggling silver spilled out onto the beach.

"Come!" Yunuen shouted to Óolal smiling. "Bring the baskets!"

On days when the catch was poor, people sometimes squabbled over their share. This day's catch was good and there would be no bickering. Gonzalo wrapped his arms around Za'azil when she walked up. Then, releasing her, he tousled the heads of his two boys. Happily, all of them began to scoop squirming fish into their baskets.

They had scarcely bent to their work, when a strange, deeply weathered, dark-skinned man approached and hailed Gonzalo.

"You, you are nacon here, yes?"

"I am," answered Gonzalo. "Who are you?"

"A modest trader, they call me K'as chuujul (Half Burnt). I have something for you. It is from the crazy one like you who lives in Tzamá."

The man then held out something. Gonzalo accepted it and stared curiously at what lay in his hand. It was a soiled roll of paper tied with a dirty strip of cloth. Untying the cloth he carefully stretched out the paper. It was yellowed and slightly water damaged, but he immediately saw that it was a letter written in Spanish. As he read the blurred but legible lines, his knees suddenly became weak and he sat down heavily onto the wet sand.

Za'azil rushed to his side. "What is it my love? What has this man given you? Are you alright?"

Gonzalo looked up. "It is something I never again thought to see. It is a message in the writing of my own land."

"What does it say?" broke-in Yunuen, clearly excited.

"It's a summons. A great chief of my people accompanied by many of his holcánob waits on Cozumel and bids me hurry to join him there."

Za'azil gasped and Yunuen asked quietly, "What will you do? Will you go?"

Gonzalo shook his head. "Yunuen," he smiled. "Look at Óolal, is she not beautiful? Look at my beautiful sons Juan and Pedro. Look at my beautiful wife, Za'azil. I cherish them. I cherish this place. This message is nothing, a k'aasi ba'al (ghost) from my past. I have no reason to answer its call."

Later, to his sons' delight, Gonzalo folded the paper message into a tiny canoe and set it into the bay's ebbing tide. The current quickly carried it eastward, and Gonzalo stared after the fragile vessel until long after it disappeared among the swells.

Chapter 46

Twilight of the Gods

11 Bak'tun 14 K'atun 19 Tun 0 Uinal 11 K'in

(March 13, 1519)

Cutz Ahau, supreme lord and spiritual leader of Tzamá, glared at his worthless Ah Cuchcab. Most of his so called councilors were elderly, minor nobles of little consequence, men who once groveled at Ah Tabai's feet. A few were greedy merchants who believed they smelled opportunity.

Cheb' is dimwitted, but useful, he thought. *Kish is loyal, but so old it's a wonder that he still shuffles about. And the rest, sycophants, pek' ta' (dog shit), one and all squabbling for scraps. Not ever a single useful idea from among the lot!*

Abruptly Cutz sprang to his feet waving his nearly empty cup of b'alche.

"We're done!" he shouted. "All of you get out. Get out of my sight!"

The councilors scrambled to obey and soon only Kish was left. Cutz started to order the old man to refill his cup, but then thought better of it. The strong drink calmed him, but he decided there was too much to consider and that he would keep his head clear.

Since usurping The City of the Dawn's rule, nothing had gone as Cutz had expected. Tzamá was a flickering shadow of its former self. It began with mutterings that the arrogance of the Lord of Fire and his ill-fated clique, Cutz included, had angered the gods and so lost their favor. Cutz had scoffed and ignored the rumors, but as the mutterings spread people also began to whisper that Tzamá was cursed. Soon thereafter, Cutz received cautious apologetic reports that some of his subjects were fleeing to seek their prosperity elsewhere.

"Let them go!" he'd railed. "What do I care if a few ignorant peasants and their ugly wives and snot-faced children sneak off into the jungle to starve?"

These reports were followed by hearsay of a mass exodus from Xamanzamá. This troubled Cutz as his old home was an important source of both labor and tribute.

Immediately, he had sent Cheb', accompanied by several fearsome warriors, to investigate. When the party returned with a tale that his idiot acolyte, Thup Paal, had indeed urged that Xamanzamá be abandoned and that he had also stolen the óox hu'unob (three books) that Cutz had left in his charge, Tzamá's ruler flew into an uncontrollable rage.

"Hunt him down," he'd ordered. "Bring that turd back to me bound and gagged! How dare he claim that I provoke our gods! How dare he profess to know their will! When I sacrifice him, it will be a poor offering, but it will not be quick and it will not be painless."

Cheb' and men of his holcánob spent a full uinal (month) in a diligent but fruitless search that encountered a few people who had fled from Xamanzamá, but found no trace of Thup Paal.

After that, Cutz began to pay closer attention to the swirl of rumor and gossip. He didn't believe any of it, but he was forced to acknowledge that it was causing problems. As he had once advised Ac Yanto, he turned to spectacle to divert his foolish subjects' attention. He called for lavish ceremonies, publically petitioned the gods, and presided over frequent sacrifices. None of his dramatics made any difference, over the years people continued to drift away, tribute continued to drop, and Tzamá withered. If any doubt lingered among Cutz' remaining subjects that their city was accursed, the deadly pox had swept it away.

Now, all of his meetings with his valueless Ah Cuchcab yielded the same result, nothing. They talked. They argued. They complained. The less craven among them even had the temerity to suggest that Cutz needed to do more to petition the gods.

Cutz, glad to be rid of his miserable so-called councilors, beckoned to Kish.

"Old friend walk with me."

"Of course Lord," answered the old man. "Where do you wish to go?"

"Nowhere, and everywhere," responded the ruler of Tzamá. "There is a deep sickness here that I must find and root out."

Kish had no idea what Cutz Ahau intended, but he nodded and followed along.

Cutz wandered without direction, walking at a shambling pace that his elderly retainer could maintain. Here and there he encountered people, busy about their meagre lives, who paused to bow or prostrate themselves. Elsewhere, he passed the city's once prosperous market and hut after abandoned hut. Even more well-to-do dwellings also lay empty.

Why? he wondered. *I honor gods. I pray. I make offerings. I listen carefully, but they remain silent.*

Cutz held a deep faith in the power of his gods. That they had turned their faces from him seemed impossible, yet steadily his fortunes had declined and all of his sacrifices and pleas had passed away unanswered. Among clouds of fragrant copal and rivulets of blood, even his patron, the goggle-eyed jaguar-god, Tláloc, no longer seemed to listen.

Unexpectedly he found himself standing in front of the hovel once occupied by the barbarian chilán. The crazed one who had called himself Geronimo. The one who incessantly proclaimed the power of his unfamiliar god and the virtue of an uplifted wood of great power.

Like so many others, the strange prisoner had simply disappeared. Cutz stared at the crude wooden cross affixed above the hut's door.

The vahom-ché, he wondered, *is it possible that it does hold an unknown power? The chilán always insisted that the defeat of Yajawk'ak' was due to the presence of the other barbarian called Gonzalo and the intercession of his god. He also claimed that the pox was his god's wrath. I had him beaten for saying that his god, who is three and also one, was powerful and supreme. Perhaps I was wrong, perhaps there was some truth in his words.*

Cutz turned to Kish. "Do you see the vahom-ché above the hut's door? Fetch Cheb' and have him make a larger one. It should be made of strong wood and stand at least the height of two men. Tell him that, when it is complete, he is to erect it on this spot."

"Lord, might I ask why you wish this?" hazarded the old man.

"Our gods are silent to me," answered Cutz. "Perhaps the barbarian's hanging god will answer."

The sacred Tzolk'in turned and the evening was 4 Chuwen, the time when the howler monkey screams at the approaching dark.

Historical Note

Warning Spoilers! This book is a work of fiction and dreams. The personalities, most events, and pretty much 99.9% of everything portrayed within it jumps solely from your author's imagination. Dig deeply enough, however, and way down below my romantic ramblings there lies a thin skeleton of truth.

In the year 1511 a Spanish vessel in route to Cuba did shipwreck on a shoal. The wreck's survivors did eventually wash up onto the shores of what is today the Yucatán Peninsula. Some of them were sacrificed by the local Maya. Of those who remained, only two eventually survived their ordeal. One was a friar, Geronimo de Aguilar from Ecija, the other was a man named Gonzalo. In 1519 Aguilar was rescued on the island of Cozumel by Hernan Cortez on his way to conquer the Aztecs of central Mexico.

Almost all that is known of Gonzalo's and Geronimo's time among the Maya comes from Aguilar's words to Cortez as related by writers such as Friar Diego de Landa and Bernal Díaz del Castillo who wrote their accounts nearly fifty years after the fact. To make Aguilar's story even more problematic, statements attributed to him may simply have been made up. At the time that Landa and Castillo wrote their histories rigorous adherence to fact was considered less important than plausibility. In other words, an attributed conversation didn't necessarily need to be true as long as it plausibly could have occurred.

Over the years volumes have been written about Gonzalo, but in truth all that we really know about him comes from echoes of hearsay. Therefore, it's not surprising that Gonzalo has been described as a Godot-like character whose story is told by others, yet who never speaks to us directly.

He is usually referred to as, Gonzalo Guerrero, but even his name isn't absolutely certain. Most historians agree that his first name was Gonzalo, but at various times the surnames, de Morales, Aroça, Marinero, and Guerrero have all been proposed. Other aspects of his life are similarly vague. He is said to have married a Maya princess, fathered children, tattooed his face, and pierced his ears. He is considered to be the first Spanish conquistador to have gone native and turned his back on his origins. He may have been a sailor (marinero). He may have been a soldier (guerrero). He may have been a war chief among the Maya. He may have renounced his God. He may have died in battle against other Spaniards in 1531. He may have died battling Spaniards in Honduras in 1536. He may have died peacefully. No one really knows. He may have been more than one person.

Whatever the truth of his undoubtedly amazing life, for an author hoping to write an exciting historical novel, Gonzalo was the perfect blank slate.

To read a true contemporary narrative of another Spanish castaway in similar circumstances, I highly recommend the first person account, "La relación de Álvar Nunez Cabeza de Vaca" also called "Naufragios y comentarios." This is available in English.

About Language

Throughout this book, the text is sprinkled with non-English words and names to remind readers that the narrative is unfolding in Maya and Spanish. It may come as a surprise to some that the Maya language is still very much alive. Around thirty Mayan languages are still spoken today by nearly seven million people. About 4 million of these live in Guatemala and around another 2.5 million in Mexico.

Although speakers of the various Mayan languages may share cultural traits between groups, the languages are generally mutually unintelligible. That is, a speaker of one will not be easily understood by speakers of another.

Something that modern Mayan languages do have in common is their writing systems. Where before colonization, written Maya was a logo-syllabic system where one symbol represented one idea or sound, today they all use the Roman alphabet.

In the area of the Yucatán Peninsula, where our story unfolds, approximately 700,000 people still speak Maya. Languages, however, evolve and the Maya spoken there today is not the same as it was in the 1500's. At its heart, Maya is mostly an oral language, and as such standards of spelling are still evolving.

All responsibility for errors in the use of Maya that appear in this book (and I'm sure there are many) rests solely on this author's shoulders. I do not speak nor read Maya and, while I have a working knowledge of Spanish, I cannot truly profess to be fluent. This means that as language source materials I relied on a wide variety of printed and online dictionaries and vocabularies. Some of these went directly from English to Maya. For others I had to go from English to Spanish and then to Maya. Frequently, different sources varied in their translations leaving me to randomly choose between them.

Imagine me as a bumbling tourist in an exotic foreign land. A thin phrasebook is clutched in my sweaty hand and I'm struggling to make myself understood. If you can visualize that image, then you have a reasonably good idea of the level of expertise that I brought to my foray into Maya. To all my readers, I sincerely apologize for any and all egregious mistakes.

For Simplicity all date conversions listed in this novel are between the Maya and the Gregorian calendars. In 1511, Gonzalo and his shipmates would actually have used the Julian calendar.

About the Author

I grew up in Santa Paula, California, "Citrus Capital of the World." After graduating high school, I attended the University of California at Riverside, California State University Humboldt, and Lane Community College in Eugene, Oregon. Over the years, I've worked a variety of different jobs: stock clerk, farm laborer, janitor, pot washer, computer programmer, bicycle mechanic, systems analyst, agricultural inspector, information systems administrator, and probably a couple that I've forgotten. Today, I'm happily married and live and write in Prescott, Arizona.

Please visit my Author's Website at donaldhealey.com for more about God's of Rain and Blood plus FREE extras and information about my other books.

Thank you for being one of my readers!